RUNAWAY FAST

and five other stories
by

DAVID A. ESTES

Publishing Coordinator – Sharon Kizziah-Holmes

Paperback-Press
an imprint of A & S Publishing
A & S Holmes, Inc.

ISBN -13: 978-1-945669-80-4

LOVE ME,
LOVE ME NOT

a novella

PROLOGUE

Soaking wet from the pouring rain, Matt Harper kneels beside the mound of dirt where he buried Cathy three years ago. Cathy was his wife for twenty-one years.

Oblivious of the lightning's flash and the thunder's roar, he places a handful of daisies on the headstone of the only woman he ever loved.

Until now.

In his house is a woman who cooks his meals, cleans his clothes, and sweeps his floors. Acting like a wife. The one he had is gone. The one he wants he cannot have.

Hosmer saves the day

Matt Harper stretched out on the brown leather couch in his farm family room. He struggled with the Royals to escape another massacre by the detested Yankees. A can of cold Bud helped a ham-and-cheese sandwich make its way down, but it did nothing for Kansas City's boys in blue.

He wished for Cathy. He always wished for Cathy. Always had, always would. But Cathy was gone, and wouldn't be back. How she died was Matt's worst nightmare.

A rabid Royals fan, Cathy cheered when they made a good

play and screamed at the television when they did something stupid. At Cathy's funeral, Preacher Oren Watts said he believed she was "up there someplace" watching every pitch, every play, pleading for victory at "The K" for the team she loved.

Matt figured he knew as much about that as Oren did.

Bottom of the ninth, Royals at bat, trailing five to four. With a man on first and two outs, the count on Eric Hosmer was three and two. Eric was 0-for-four at the plate. He hadn't hit a home run in six games. When Hosmer slumped, the Royals slumped.

In the broadcast booth, Ryan Lefebvre strategized along with the gurus in the dugout. "Do you let him hit away" Ryan counseled the experts in the viewing audience, "or do you hope he gets ball four with a .200 hitter in the on-deck circle?"

"Eric can do it!" Matt yelled at the TV. "Let him hit away! He'll knock the cover off that ball."

Ryan agreed. "Let him hit, so we can wrap this thing up and go home."

On the pitcher's mound, Yankees reliever Adam Warren leaned in, eyeballing the sign from Sanchez behind the plate.

Matt waited with the world while Warren, six-one, and 220, casually covered his left knee with his glove, twirling the ball behind his back in his right. Warren was in no hurry to make what he hoped would be strike three to Hosmer, so the Yankees could chalk up another W to take back to Yankee Stadium.

Lefebvre shared his strategy with the folks at home. "If Warren's pitch comes in low and inside, Eric walks to first. If it's low and away to the left-handed hitter, Hosmer swings and misses for strike three. If Warren makes a mistake down the middle, the game could be over, and the Royals go to the showers with a walk-off W against the Bronx Bombers."

Still, Eric hadn't hit anything all day.

Sanchez and Warren met halfway to the mound. They'd throw the best they had at Hosmer and hope it worked. On the other hand, the slumping first baseman was due to break out.

Warren stepped back to the pitcher's mound. Sanchez squatted behind the plate.

Hosmer dug in and waited for the pitch he hoped would be a mistake over the middle of the plate.

Warren nodded approval of Sanchez's signal and started his windup. Sanchez set his glove low and inside, expecting Hosmer to swing and miss. Warren's fastball came in waist high on the outside corner.

Matt saw Eric swing. He saw the ball float into the air, high and long to right.

The phone rang on the table at Matt's elbow. He grabbed it.

"Hi, dad, it's me," came the voice on the phone.

Matt watched the right fielder go back, back, back to the warning track, waiting for the ball to drop into his glove. Matt groaned and tried to concentrate on his daughter's phone call. He jumped off the couch, leaned to the right to help that ball get over the wall and into the right-field seats.

No way was it long enough. Matt moaned.

"Hey, Julie!" he said into the phone. "How's the college kid?"

"Good, dad. Would it be all right if I brought a friend with me to the farm this weekend?"

Matt watched the ball keep going—over the fielder's glove—bounce off the top of the wall—and tumble lazily into the right-field seats.

The umpire signaled, "Home run!"

Lefebvre screamed, "Royals win!"

Matt drew a deep breath at the game-winning Royals finish and went back to the phone.

"Dad?"

"Yeah, hon, I'm here. Hosmer just beat the Yanks with a walk-off homer in the bottom of the ninth."

"Oh. Did you hear what I said?"

"About the weekend? Yeah." He was about to ask whether the friend was a boy or girl since his tolerance for sleep-in boyfriends was at a low ebb.

He started breathing again when Julie said, "Alexis will be with me."

Matt never met Alexis Farrell, but Julie mentioned her often when she talked about school. Alexis was the PE instructor at Missouri State. Julie was her student assistant while pursuing her own Phys Ed degree.

"Absolutely," Matt said. "Bring anybody you want."

Julie brings a friend

Mid-day Saturday Matt parked his red Ford pickup near the tool shed and headed for the kitchen's back door. He jerked his head around with an approving smile. Before he saw it, he heard Julie's Kelly green Celica barreling up the lane toward the house. That kid! He grinned and shook his head. Just like her mother. Cathy never could wait to get home.

He waited by the door.

Julie skidded the Celica to a stop, and squealed, "Hi, dad!" She popped out of the car and gave him a hug as only a daughter can hug.

Alexis came around the front of the car with a big smile. She stuck her hand out and Matt shook it. "I'm Alexis Farrell, Mr. Harper," she said. "I'm happy to finally meet Julie's father. She's told me so much about you, I think I know you already."

"Matt Harper," he said. "I'm glad you could come."

He grabbed their bags and led the way inside.

Julie ushered Alexis upstairs and showed her the room that would be hers for the weekend while Matt distributed their bags.

~~~

Matt watched his daughter bounce down the stairway, as she had since she was three. He was pleased that she still wanted to come home. Julie and Cathy were so close. After her mother was gone he thought Julie might rather be with friends at school. Instead, she seemed anxious to spend weekends with him at the farm.

Julie tightened her arms around his waist. "Do Speedy and the Boys still play at the VFW hall Saturday nights?" she asked.

"The last time I went was with your mother four years ago, but I'm sure they do. Why? Do you want to show Alexis the hot spots?"

Julie flashed a bright smile. "Not without you."

"Me?"

"How about we go tonight and trip the light fantastic?" Julie said.

"Trip the what? You know I never went in much for dancing. I used to hold your mom while she danced. I wouldn't be much fun for you ladies."

"Come on, dad, you need to get out more."

On her way down the stairs, Alexis chimed in. "That's right, Mr. Harper. You know what they say about all work and no play."

"Well—" Matt was not convinced it was a good idea but was pleased that they asked him. "Okay, let's do it," he said.

CHAPTER ONE

Matt goes a-dancing

If Emma Hagley hadn't been there, Saturday night would have been more fun.

Speedy and the Boys were cutting down on a series of country classics Matt had heard for half his life. He danced a couple of times with Julie and walked around with Alexis. She acted like she enjoyed it. Humoring him, he was sure.

Mostly, instead of dancing, he concentrated on Colleen Beaty's homemade vanilla ice cream and chocolate cake. He estimated he'd also consumed about a gallon of Pam Luther's lemonade.

Every time he looked around, Emma was grinning at him from her seat at a picnic table against the west wall. It would be a struggle for her to lift her huge body to move any place else.

Emma never danced. She brought her knitting to the party. Nobody asked what she was knitting, nor why. Her deep-set green eyes and buck-toothed grin made Matt cringe when she used them on him. Half a dozen years older than he, Emma's long, stringy hair flopped around her shoulders. She'd tell you it made her look younger.

Matt wondered why she'd want to look younger, unless it made her less ugly.

Emma got no help from the growth of prickly black

whiskers sticking out from her chin like charred oak sprouts. She kept flashing her toothy grin, and Matt kept trying not to notice. She did that a lot since her husband Reuben died of lung cancer the year before. Reuben inhaled three packs of Chesterfields every day for forty years, so his death came as no surprise. Bart Kinsley, the undertaker, said Reuben's lungs were so charred there was hardly enough of them left to bury. Bart buried them anyway.

Some folks said Emma was glad to save the money Reuben would have wasted on more Chesterfields.

Alone now, her four kids up and gone, Emma had more time to sit around being fat and ugly.

Annoyed by her unsought attention, Matt thought he'd better ease over that way and at least say hello. He nodded. "Evening, Emma."

"Evenin', Matt. I seen you squirin' them young ladies around out there on that dance floor."

"Yeah. I never was much good at that."

"Cathy was."

Matt was surprised Emma mentioned the name of his dead wife. He felt a tinge of resentment. Cathy once commented that Emma didn't go much for keeping a clean house, and doubted her personal habits were better.

"Yes, Cathy was," Matt said. Cathy was good at many things, most of which Emma knew nothing about.

With a nod across the room, Emma said, "Is that Julie's friend from school?"

"Yes. They're down for the weekend."

"She's a mighty pretty woman."

Matt glanced over his shoulder and spotted Alexis dancing with one of the Whitworth boys. Watching them swinging around the dance floor, he suddenly felt all his forty-six years.

"Well, it's nice talking to you," he said to Emma, moving away.

Emma's buck teeth didn't show as she said, "A mighty pretty woman."

Matt would remember that.

CHAPTER TWO

Lexie makes a deal

Preacher Watts's Sunday morning sermon was less than inspirational. Matt dozed through much of it. By the time he and the girls made it back to the farm from the Christian Church, he forgot most of what Watts said.

However, when Julie called "soup's on" he revived in a hurry. Julie seated him at the head of a table loaded with skinless fried chicken, ala Mother Cathy, mashed potatoes and cream gravy, green beans, and corn on the cob. She topped it off with a generous serving of freshly baked pecan pie.

Matt didn't have to wonder how Julie remembered about the pecan pie. She knew it was his favorite that her mother made for him. He ate until he confessed to total misery. He hadn't had such a sumptuous meal for much too long. To the ladies' delight, he groaned, "I may never eat again."

Mid-afternoon Sunday the girls cleared the table, cleaned up the kitchen, and loaded Julie's Celica for the return trip to school.

Alexis waited at the foot of the stair for Julie to come down. To Matt she said, "You have a beautiful home, I've enjoyed being here."

"I'm glad you came."

"Thank you."

"I hope you can come again sometime," Matt said.

"I'd like that," Alexis said. "I grew up on a farm. My father believed a farmer's work is never done."

"He's right about that," Matt said. "I guess that's why the good Lord put us down here, to do the dirty work."

"My father farmed in Illinois. He said he could judge a farmer by the dirt under his nails."

"There's something to that. Is he still farming?"

"My father died of a stroke seven years ago," Alexis said. "My mother died of pneumonia three years later. We were a close family."

Matt offered a solemn nod. "No doubt you know farming is not as much fun as some people think."

"Yes, I did," she said. "I hated it. Hoeing corn rows, slopping hogs, milking cows at five in the morning, slapping me in the face with their frozen tails. I couldn't wait to get away."

"Most people don't care much for a farm unless it belongs to them. And, in busy times like this summer, good help is hard to come by."

Julie was slow putting in an appearance from upstairs. Alexis glanced up there, wondering what was keeping her.

Matt called, "Julie."

"This hair!" Julie cried. "I'll be down in a minute."

"Just like her mother," Matt said with a shrug. "The hair takes priority."

Alexis said, "Julie tells me she'll be touring Europe with friends this summer."

"Yes. Her mother and I always wanted her to do some traveling. To broaden her scope, Cathy said."

"She won't be here to help this summer then."

"No. Julie's a good hand too."

Alexis Farrell was thirty-seven years old. She graduated at the head of her class at Southern Illinois University. Her first position was Physical Education instructor at the local high school.

After six years at Carbondale, she accepted an offer at Missouri State in Springfield. She'd taught there seven years.

Her guileless smile and outgoing manner put Matt at ease.

He discovered early that she could also be perplexing.

"I'll be taking the summer off," Alexis said. "Maybe I could help out, here on the farm."

Matt cast her a searching look. "Can you drive a tractor?" he said with a grin.

"You bet." She didn't bat an eye. "Remember, I grew up on a farm."

"Which you hated, and couldn't wait to get away from."

"You've got me there," she said. "But that was then. I'm older now."

Matt didn't know her well enough to question whether her offer of help was sincere. He needed time to think about that. He wished Julie would come down. Yes, he would need help, but he never thought it would come from a friend of Julie's.

"I plan to spend a week or so in Illinois after school," Alexis said. "Then I'll be free for the summer until I go back in August."

Matt stepped into the kitchen to pour himself a cup of coffee. He thought about the proposal of this handsome young woman. He suspected she wasn't afraid to get a little dirt under her nails.

"Here," she said, taking his cup. "Let me do that." She reached for the Silex pot and poured his cup full. She filled one for herself then joined him in the breakfast booth off the kitchen.

"Cream and sugar?" she said.

"Neither, thanks."

Matt sipped at his coffee. Strange notions raced through his head like wind-blown pages of a book. What would Cathy think of this woman spending the summer working on the farm? What would Julie think? Even though she was Julie's friend, his daughter may not approve of Alexis and her father living in the same house together all summer.

"Farm work doesn't pay much," Matt said, "as you know."

"Yes, I know, but I've got nothing better to do till the fall semester. And, as you said, good help is hard to find this time of year."

Matt needed time to think. He'd like to talk to Julie about it. But, this lady was waiting for an answer. "Well, I guess, if you really want to do this," he said, "we might work out some way for you to put up at Nettie's place. Then you could come over here and work some when you had time. There likely would be some down times because of the weather, or equipment breakdowns, but when we work, we work hard."

"I'll work as much as you want me to."

"That's Nettie Coy I'm talking about," Matt went on. "She's got a big old house over there, living in it by herself since Ben died nine years ago. I have an idea she'd enjoy having your company for the summer."

"Uh-huh."

"Nettie's a good cook. She's won all kinds of prizes at the county fair. She'd feed you well, and take good care of you." He gave his head a thoughtful nod as if maybe it could happen. "I'll mention it to Nettie next time I see her."

"How about I stay here—with you?"

Matt had a time pulling his eyes away from her unblemished face, the deep brown eyes pinning him with a frank stare, her serious mouth. Waiting for his answer. Where was Julie? Why was she taking so long?

"If you're worried about what the neighbors might think," Alexis said, "you can forget it."

Married to Cathy for twenty-one years, Matt was rarely faced with decisions regarding women. Even so, within days following Cathy's funeral, he received invitations to dinner, picnics, and family gatherings, sometimes from women he hardly knew. One or two displayed sincere concern for his loss. Early as it was, others made obvious attempts to engage him in romantic relationships. Bolstered by the need to be alone with recollections of his dead wife, to all of them Matt said no.

That was three years ago.

"They won't have anything to talk about," Alexis said. She wasn't ready for him to know about James Chalmers. Maybe she'd never have to tell him. She was willing to spend the summer as a hired hand on the Harper family farm. And live in his house while she did it. That's all.

CHAPTER THREE

Goodbye, Cathy

In the silent hours making way for sunrise the Sunday Cathy died, Matt Harper's world began to crumble. The night before, he and Cathy joined Julie for dinner at her favorite restaurant in Springfield. They returned to the farm late that night. Matt went straight up to bed and was asleep when his head hit the pillow.

For Cathy, hair and face-fixing was a ritual. She never went to bed, no matter how late the hour, before "getting the gunk off." In the early years of their marriage, she didn't even allow Matt to see her without makeup, and never with rollers in her hair.

Matt didn't know what time Cathy got to bed. Nor did he know what caused him to wake up at four o'clock Sunday morning. Every night of their twenty-one years, Matt laid an arm across Cathy's sleeping body, feeling her closeness, the rhythmic cadence of her breathing. This night, she felt cold to his touch. He pulled the sheet up under her chin. It didn't help.

"Cath." He nudged her shoulder. She didn't move. Again he tried to rouse her. "Cathy!"

Too late for an emergency room miracle. Terror couldn't

come close to describing the agony Matt struggled through. He was hardly able to call 9-1-1. He watched in a nervous frenzy while the Med-Aid people worked over Cathy. Finally, he gave up to reality: Cathy breathed her last.

He recalled Cathy's occasional comments about "shortness of breath," or "a little hurt in my chest." She pooh-poohed Matt's urging that she go for a checkup. Her concern was for her husband's aches and pains, built-in side effects of the work he did on the farm, not for herself.

Never before had either of them suffered an illness more serious than a nosebleed. Cathy was an excellent cook. She prepared healthful, nutritious meals. She couldn't resist the challenge of a recipe for a new dish she thought Matt would like. Aside from her desire to please her husband, she need not have bothered. Matt ate whatever Cathy put on the table. Except for the "woman stuff" for which Cathy went to the doctor once a year, the Harpers needed no doctor, nor medication.

One night at supper, Cathy voiced concern for Matt "should anything happen to me."

He waved it off and reminded her that most women outlive their husbands by a wide margin.

"Nothing's going to happen to you," he said.

"Yeah, but what if it did?"

"I'd be lost without you."

"You wouldn't get married again?"

"Cathy," he assured her, "I can't imagine being married to anybody but you."

She nodded with a satisfied grin and refilled their coffee cups.

Four days later she died of a massive heart attack.

Struggling to maintain a life without Cathy, Matt looked for ways to put himself back together. Without Julie he couldn't have done it. Julie seemed always to be there, doing for him the things her mother did before. Walking with him, working with him, hurting with him. Assuring him her mother's death was not his fault.

He needed Julie's counsel now, letting him know how she felt about the idea of Alexis Farrell's working on the farm all summer, often by her father's side.

When Julie called him two days later, the first thing he said after hello was, "How do you feel about your friend working here on the farm while you're in Europe this summer?"

"You mean Lexie?"

"Yes. Do you see anything wrong with that picture?"

"Lexie is a good worker, dad, no matter what she does. I learned that when I visited her family a couple of summers ago."

"She told me about that."

"She knows her way around a farm, dad, and she'll do whatever you ask her to do."

Julie knew her father was concerned about what her mother would think about him and Lexie sleeping under the same roof. She also knew Lexie experienced some unhappy times in her life that negated any hint of a romantic relationship. But Matt didn't know that, and Julie saw no reason to explain it to her father. If Lexie wanted him to know, she'd tell him.

"Dad."

"Yes?"

"It won't work unless you feel right about it. I know you spend a lot of time trying to figure out what you could have done to save mom. But, it wasn't your fault. The medical people said there was nothing you could have done. It's time you stopped kicking yourself and got on with your life. Mom would want you to do that, and so do I.

"Lexie is a truly sweet lady who grew up on a farm. She'll be a hired hand like any other worker. She won't forget that."

"Thanks, Julie. When is school out?"

"A week from tomorrow."

CHAPTER FOUR

Lexie moves in

Matt picked Lexie up at the Trailways bus station in Bolivar. She didn't own a car. During her tenure at Carbondale High, Lexie accidentally struck a five-year-old girl in a mall parking lot. The child was not seriously injured, but Lexie promised herself she'd never drive again.

It was well past suppertime when they arrived at the farm. Matt hauled her bag into the great room, the hub of activity from which all other areas of the house stemmed.

"Where do you want me, Mr. Harper?" She waited for him to tell her which room would be hers for the summer.

"First off," he said, "Mr. Harper was my father. He died years ago. I'm going to call you Lexie, if you don't mind. My name is Matthew, for my mother's family. Most people call me Matt."

"Okay, Matthew, where do you want me to bunk in?"

"Upstairs there are three bedrooms. I sleep in the one at the end of the hall. The room at the top of the stairs is Julie's. It's nearest to the bathroom. You're welcome to use it if you'd like."

"I'd like."

"Can I help with your things?"

What she brought with her in a small brown leather bag were four pairs of jeans, half a dozen changes of underwear, and a few interchangeable tops that would be simple to launder. Whatever else she might need she could pick up in town.

"No, thank you," she said. "I didn't bring many things."

Matt carried her bag upstairs and set it inside her bedroom door.

"Thank you," she said.

"You're welcome." He flipped on the light. "You may want to sleep in tomorrow morning, but if you like breakfast, it comes pretty early around here."

"I'll be ready."

"Well, goodnight then."

"Goodnight, Matthew."

Even with his bedroom door closed, Matt recognized the familiar sound of running water in the bathtub at the other end of the hall. It didn't take much to remind him of what he lost when he lost Cathy.

"Goodnight, Cathy," he whispered.

~ ~ ~

Matt awoke to the sound of sizzling bacon and frying eggs. It took a moment for him to adjust to the fact he was no longer the sole occupant of his home. Lexie rolled out of bed before he did?

With a smile, he reflected briefly, he couldn't recall any morning when Cathy rose before he did.

After a shower and shave, he arrived at the kitchen door, not surprised to find Lexie working over the stove.

She greeted him with a cheery, "Good morning, master!"

He grinned. "I hope you're not serious about that."

She poured him a cup of coffee. He lifted it in a good morning salute. "Waiting on me was not a part of the deal," he said.

She ignored his mild protest. "I bet you like your eggs over easy."

"I do."

16

"So did my dad."

Lexie placed his breakfast in front of him and poured herself a cup of coffee. She sat across the table and watched him eat.

"No breakfast for you?" he asked.

"Not since I left home when I was eighteen. My dad used to insist that we eat hot oatmeal, bacon and eggs, and biscuits and gravy every morning before we left for school."

"That's a lot of food."

"Dad's philosophy was we might not survive 'til lunch without a big breakfast. He didn't want us to leave home with empty stomachs."

"With meals like that, I'm surprised you're not as big as a cow."

"I was–until I stopped eating breakfast."

"You have brothers or sisters?" Matt asked.

"One brother. He's a cardiologist at Mayo's."

She refilled his cup, glad for the chance to do for him. It was long ago when she had a man to wait on. Matt didn't need to know about the other one. Not yet anyway.

Let's go bale some hay

Matt wouldn't say Lexie looked cute and sweet perched on the seat of the John Deere tractor. But that's how she looked in faded jeans, a yellow cotton top, and white sneakers. He thought she looked more like she was headed for a picnic. Her blond ponytail flopped out from under her Cardinals baseball cap and bounced off her neck. She climbed up into the cab of the tractor as if she'd done it every day of her life.

"Okay, Matthew," Lexie said. With a gloved hand, she shifted gears. "I'll rake 'em and you rack 'em, okay?"

Matt admired her spunk. Julie was right. Lexie knew her way around a farm. She raked the fescue into windrows and Matt followed with the baler. He molded the hay into twelve-hundred pound bales, each wrapped in plastic before it was kicked out the baler's rear end. By the time they finished, the lowering sun cast long shadows across the field dotted with bales of fescue. They reminded Matt of the freckles on Julie's nose.

Matt rode with Lexie on the tractor to the barn lot where he parked his red pickup. He climbed in, and said, "I'm going over west to check on that old black bull. He hasn't been very active lately. You go on up to the house if you want. I won't be long."

Lexie watched him splash the pickup across Waubleau Creek before she strode to the kitchen door.

Matt turned west toward the bass pond. In the shade of a one-hundred-year-old oak, he spotted what looked like a fourteen-hundred-pound lump of coal

Bulls didn't like being hit by pickup trucks. They moved out of the path when they saw one coming. This bull didn't move. Matt skidded the pickup to a stop and leaped out. What he found was not a heap of coal.

"Damn!" He didn't need a vet to tell him somebody planted a bullet between the eyes of his prize Angus bull.

Instinct told him to glance around, though he knew whoever fired the shot wouldn't wait for him to discover the deed.

"Hamp Hargrove," he muttered.

~~~

Matt was still stewing about the bull when he walked into the kitchen. Talking to Lexie about a dead bull wouldn't make pleasant conversation over supper. No need to share the bad news with her anyway. There'd be time enough for that. He washed up, and was instructed by the cook to take his place at the head of the table.

"You're spoiling me rotten," he said as Lexie placed before him a platter of pork chops. "Every time I turn around, you're setting me down to a good hot meal, washing my clothes, keeping the house shaped up like it belonged to you. You don't have to do that, you know."

"If I thought I had to, I wouldn't want to," Lexie said. "Besides, a hard-working man deserves to have things done for him. If Cathy were here, she'd be doing this."

Lexie's casual reference to Cathy was almost like she'd known her. Matt liked that. Lately, he'd caught himself subconsciously placing the two women side by side, comparing one to the other, not in any special order. He guessed it was natural for a man to measure other women by the one he was married to for half his life.

"A mighty pretty woman." Recalling Emma's comment, Matt looked at Lexie across the table and nodded his silent agreement.

Over coffee and pecan pie, Lexie said, "Did you find the black bull?"

"I found him."

"And?"

"Somebody shot him in the head."

"Shot? Who'd do such a thing?"

"I don't know for sure. I think it might have been Hamp Hargrove."

"The man you told me about with no left arm."

"He's been trying to get me to sell the farm to some people who want to build a hog operation around here. May be a coincidence, but my bull is dead."

She cast him a questioning glance.

"I'm not selling," he said.

. With half a smile, she was pleased with his response. She refilled their coffee cups. "What's tomorrow?" she asked.

"Wheat."

~~~

Mail from Europe brought photos and enthusiastic reports of Julie's visits to the Tower of London, the Eiffel Tower in Paris, and the leaning tower of Pisa. About Pisa she scrawled, "I can't believe that sucker didn't crash long ago!" Ecstatic about back-packing Europe, hanging out with old friends and making new ones, exploring "loads of places" Julie never dreamed she'd see. Still, Matt detected an undercurrent of melancholy that told him Julie missed being home for the summer.

"And how are you two making out?" Julie inquired

casually in a note from Munich.

Lexie cleared her throat when she read it out loud, and Matt never looked up from the chess board.

Laying aside Julie's postcard, Lexie said, "It sounds like she's having a blast."

"Julie will find a way to do that."

"Is she like her mother?"

Matt checked her king and claimed victory. "Julie is quieter, believe it or not. Cathy was a bundle of unharnessed energy."

To the ears of Lexie Farrell, Matthew's references to Cathy conveyed a solemn reverence. Reluctant to invade the privacy of Matt's devotion to his dead wife, still, there were times when Lexie felt safe asking questions. So, she asked, "How did you two meet?"

Matt looked out the window, off to the west where his cattle grazed in fertile green fields caressed by the softness of waning summer. He took a moment to think about Lexie's question. With the end of summer, he reflected briefly, Lexie would be gone. He loved that farm. Even in the winter, buried in a foot of snow, scented now with the freshness of new mown hay, the golden heads of milo glistening in the sun, to Matt the land was always beautiful.

Cathy once prophesied, if Matt ever died, it would be on the seat of that old John Deere tractor.

"The first time I saw Cathy," Matt said to Lexie, "it was the first day of our senior year at college. She transferred from Colorado when her folks moved back here. She was the prettiest girl I ever saw."

They dated that year. After graduation, Matt joined the Marines and served a tour in Afghanistan. The day he left to join up, Cathy stood at the back door with his mother, waving a tearful goodbye. Matt's father drove him to the bus station in town.

Cathy was heard to say watching Matt leave for the war was the hardest thing she ever did. While he was gone, she wrote to him every week. A month after Matt returned from the war, he and Cathy were married in the sanctuary of the Bolivar First Christian Church. Julie arrived two years later.

"We knocked around some when we were first married," Matt said. "Different towns, different jobs, none of which I was very good at. Then, one year when we came to the farm for Thanksgiving, my dad said he was ready to give it up. He asked if I wanted it. Cathy and I talked it over. She said yes. We decided to move here.

"My brothers had no interest in the farm and wanted no part of it. Dad and I worked out the details. He and mom moved to Arizona, and Cathy and I brought our daughter home. I guess my heart has always been on this farm."

The emotion Lexie heard in his husky voice shifted her mind into overdrive, creating thoughts she'd never verbalize for fear of offending Matthew. He was still in love with Cathy and left no room for anyone else.

The jangle of the phone cut short their conversation. They looked at each other. Lexie's look said, "Do you want me to answer it?"

"Go ahead," Matt said.

She picked it up and said hello. Matt heard a voice on the other end of the line, but couldn't make out what was being said.

"Thanks, Nettie." Lexie hung up and said, "Nettie Coy. She said there's a pie supper at the school Saturday night. She wondered if we'd be going."

Matt took a moment to answer. So, Nettie had bundled them into a "you" situation between himself and Lexie. And Lexie, without blinking an eye, said "we".

"If Nettie said it," he said, "it's gospel. I never knew her to tell anything but the truth."

"If you want to go, I'll bake a pie. Maybe some of those old hairy-legged boys will bid on it."

"I wouldn't be surprised."

"Is pecan all right with you?"

"I've never had better."

CHAPTER FIVE

The harvest

The drier the heads, the better the harvest. It was mid-morning before the sun absorbed enough overnight dew to allow them to get into the field and combine the golden grain.

While he waited for the sun to do its job, Matt checked out the combine with a walk-around inspection, like an airline pilot making the rounds of the plane's checkpoints before take-off. Matt didn't want to be half finished combining the field and have something break down, especially since he needed to beat the rain he heard forecast.

And that dead bull still plagued his mind. Convinced that Hargrove fired the shot to force his hand on that hog deal, Matt needed to challenge him face-to-face. Still, while he suspected the one-armed giant of the dastardly deed, he couldn't go off half-cocked. Biding his time, he must be certain Hargrove was the guilty party.

Matt completed the inspection, climbed into the cab, and started the motor. From the radio came the soulful voice of some old boy moaning "Whatever Happened to Yesterday?" Matt shook his head sadly and confessed that he didn't know what happened to yesterday. All he knew was, it was still there when he came in for supper last night. He threw a few levers, shifted into gear, and the job was underway.

Mounted on the combine was a 300-bushel grain bin. Once the bin was full, Matt signaled to Lexie, and she moved the truck alongside the combine. A long, giraffe-necked augur sucked the grain from the combine and poured into the truck bed like water from a spigot. When the truck was full, Lexie hauled the wheat to the grain elevator in town where an augur, similar to the one that filled the truck, sucked the grain from the truck into a huge storage tank.

With night and rain moving in, Matt flipped on the headlights and kept going, racing to finish the job before the rain hit. By the time he made the last round, rain began to fall, lightly at first, then heavier. He guided the combine full of grain into the tool shed. He shut off the motor and climbed down, relieved that he beat the downpour to cover.

Matt wondered why it didn't always rain when it was needed, instead of coming all at once when it wasn't. But he figured God knew what he was doing. Matt had little regard for people who tried to control the elements, even the temperature. When God was ready for rain, it rained. Or, if he thought it should be hot, He had a way of making it hot.

Cathy loved the rain. Struck by a surge of loneliness, Matt heard himself saying, "Cathy, where are you?" He felt old dog Sport at his side, bouncing around, licking his hand, sensing Matt needed a friend.

Sport came home with Julie one day when she was out for her walk along the country road. This huge animal popped up out of the ditch—Rottweiler and German mix, the vet said. The dog trotted ahead of Julie as if he knew where she was going and he wanted to lead the way. Sport glanced back now and again to be sure she was still coming. When they got home, Julie fed Sport table scraps. He inhaled them like a carpet sweeper. Matt didn't mind the wet dog smell. He and Sport hit it off right away when he scratched Sport's ears. Sport found a home, and Matt found a new friend—a friend that would one day save his life.

Matt came in the back door and heard the phone ring. He

picked it up and heard the frantic voice of Nettie Coy.

"Matt, can you come?" she said. "I've got a cow down with a new calf and I can't reach the vet!"

"I'll be right there," Matt said then banged the phone down. "Nettie's got a cow in trouble," he said to Lexie. "I've got to go help her. I won't be long."

Nettie Coy was a wiry sixty-three-year old who should have long ago given up farming. She kept hanging on because she knew "Ben would want me to."

She and Ben worked the four-hundred-acre farm for forty-three years. After he died, Nettie sold off all but a quarter section, much of which was pasture land where she ran cattle. She rarely asked help from anybody. Matt often reminded her, "If you ever need help, you know who to call." Nettie did.

Matt admired Nettie's determination. Even so, he knew it was too much responsibility for one little old lady farmer to manage on her own. So, whenever she called, Matt showed up at her place as fast as his truck would get
him there.

Nettie's three kids were up and gone and had families of their own. They showed little interest in the farm where they grew up, except for holiday visits when they brought their kids "home to Grandma's."

Nettie was Nettie. If she ever decided she couldn't do it anymore, maybe she'd start thinking about not doing it anymore. Right now she had a calf to save, and maybe a cow. In striped overalls and a blue cotton shirt, soaking wet, she saw Matt's red pickup speeding up the lane. She waited for him near the barnyard gate, where he skidded to a stop, and Nettie hopped in.

"Over east," she said.

Matt bolted the pickup through the gate and across the pasture. He knew where "over east" was. He'd been there before.

"I tried to get that little rascal out," Nettie said as Matt drove, "but its feet must be twisted in there."

They found the moaning cow beside a ravine. Matt braked to a stop and bounced out of the truck. The cow was collapsed onto one side, her sad eyes pleading for help. Every minute lost brought both calf and cow closer to death. The unborn calf could strangle or suffocate, and the cow might hemorrhage or go into shock with the calf inside her. Either way, one or both could be lost.

Matt knelt beside the cow. "Hold her tight, Nettie."

Nettie wrapped her arms around the cow's head. Matt worked a hand inside the suffering cow. He maneuvered the calf's feet until they pointed to the opening with the calf's head between them.

Matt tugged at the calf's feet. "Come on, calf."

No farmer wanted to lose a calf, but it was worse to lose a good cow. Matt knew unless he got the calf out of there, neither of them might survive. He placed both his feet against the cow's hindquarters and grabbed the calf's feet. He pulled with his hands and pushed with his boots till he felt the calf move.

"It's coming, Nettie! Hang on."

A moment later the calf popped out, slick and scrawny. Matt massaged its sides to be sure it was breathing.

It was.

The cow bawled wild-eyed and made a frantic leap to her feet. She knocked Nettie to the ground getting to her newborn offspring. She took charge and licked her newborn son clean.

Matt helped Nettie to her feet and grabbed her in a relieved hug. They saved both cow and calf.

"You all right, Nettie?" Matt asked.

Nettie was grateful for Matt's help and told him so. "I never would've made it without you."

On the way back to the house she talked, and Matt listened. She had a headful of things she'd been saving up that had nothing to do with the cow nor the calf.

"You're not fooling me one bit, Matt Harper," she said, as though she'd waited for that moment to hit him with what was on her mind.

Matt respected Nettie as a friend and made allowances for her unabashed speaking her piece. After Cathy died, each having lost a mate, they became close. Nettie was protective as a mother hen, standing up for him, defending him against the vultures who made derogatory comments about "that woman in Cathy's house."

Nettie decided it was time she let Matt know what was on her mind.

"I know the feeling," Nettie said, "and I know what I see in her eyes when that girl looks at you. She's moony-eyed over you, Matt, and if you're not stuck on her, you're not half the man I think you are."

Taken aback by her abrupt chastising, Matt knew Nettie meant well. He let her talk.

"I don't care what those gaggle mouths say, you're way too young to shut yourself up in that house for the rest of your life, living on what used to be, or what might have been. I've done that for so long I'm too damned old for anything else. But you're not. Lord knows the wound will never heal, Matt, but it's time to stop the bleeding and get on with your life."

He cast her a solemn nod and braked to a stop at her back door. "I'll think about that."

It was raining harder now. He waited till Nettie opened her kitchen door.

"I know Cathy would want you to do that. Don't push that girl away," Nettie said, waving goodbye. "Make room for her. Let her love you."

Matt smiled as he shifted the Ford into gear. He wasn't so sure about what Cathy would want. Maybe Nettie saw things about Lexie he didn't. Or maybe what she saw didn't look the same to him.

He thought about that driving home.

In his rearview mirror flashed the blinding headlights of a car coming up behind him. He stepped on the gas, trying to put distance between himself and the car's brights, but it kept pace. Matt turned in at his place, and the car followed up the lane to the house.

Matt skidded his truck to a stop, hopped out, and headed for the one behind him.

It was not a car. In the glow of the meter pole light stood a black GMC pickup. Out stepped a big man with no left arm. Hamp Hargrove. With a sneaky grin, he leaned against his left front fender.

"What the hell are you doing, Hamp?" Matt said. He was mad and Hargrove knew it.

Hamp Hargrove was six-feet-six-inches tall, tipping the scales at about three-twenty. In a combine accident years ago, his left arm was twisted off. he Hamp gave up farming and sold out to Dude Martin.

After a shooting incident two years ago, Seth Gibbs buried a box. He said Hamp was in it. Most people believed he was, until Hamp showed up back in town a couple of weeks ago. Hamp's job was what he called "the public relations business" for some outfit in Arkansas. The company wanted to buy up farm property in Polk County to build a hog factory. More enforcer than public relater, Hamp's long suit was intimidation. "No" was an answer Hamp had trouble understanding.

"Heard you got yourself a new hand," Hamp said to Matt. His menacing voice a notch above a whisper.

Matt struggled to keep a rein on his anger. "Yeah?" he said. He glanced at the back door, half expecting Lexie to be standing in it. "How would you know that?"

Hargrove emitted a derisive chuckle. "I wouldn't want you to think I was the only one in the county that didn't know about it."

"Is that what you followed me out here to talk about?"

Matt had another thing or two he'd prefer to discuss—like a dead bull. It would make better conversation, but he wasn't yet sure enough that Hargrove was the guilty party.

"What I come for," Hargrove wheezed, "is to find out if you're ready to go along with the other boys on this hog plant deal."

"You know where I stand on that," Matt let him know. "My place is not for sale."

"Thought you might change your mind, like some of the others."

"What others are you talking about?"

"Well, Dude and Elmo say they're ready. Justice sounds like he's willing to talk, you know."

"Uh-huh. Did John tell you that?"

"Justice? Not first hand, no, but—"

John Justice, a former county commissioner, farmed the three-sixty west of Matt. He and Matt had worked together on some road projects. If John was eager to talk about selling out, he'd be talking about it with Matt. The last Matt knew, John was as cool to the idea as he was.

Matt said, "Who else have you been talking to?"

"Couple of others. They'll go along with what the rest of you decide. Farming ain't as good as it used to be, you know. All 'em regulations, gov'ment telling you what to do, how much corn you can plant, how to slop your hogs."

Matt hadn't heard farming was so bad. He'd had some bad years the same as every other farmer. That was the chance every farmer took. Matt knew from the beginning all the years wouldn't be good. But he had enough good ones to make up for the bad.

Matt wasn't surprised that Dude Martin agreed to "go along" with Hamp's offer. Dude was a good neighbor, but he wasn't too work brittle. If there was a way to get a buck without having to work for it, Dude would hold down a spot at the head of the line.

Successful farming, Matt learned early, depended on who was farming, and some on who was doing the talking.

"That hog deal we'll be talking about at the meeting Thursday night," Matt said.

"Yeah, I heard about that," Hargrove said. "I might just drop by to see how it's going."

Matt couldn't care less whether Hamp showed up. "Why don't you do that?" he said.

The derisive smile on the face of Hampton Hargrove disappeared. "You got a lot o' guts, Matt. I'd hate to see you lose 'em over this deal."

"Uh-huh. How about over a dead bull?"

Hargrove climbed into his GMC and started the motor. With a challenging grin, he said, "You lose a bull, Matt?" He spun out onto the lane, splashing mud and gravel as he sped away.

CHAPTER SIX

How about a pie supper?

In the town of Sunny Vale, there were more dogs than people. It wasn't always true. In years past, Main Street was lined with churches, gas stations, a feed mill, a bank, a dry goods store, and two grocery stores. The town also boasted a high school where there weren't enough students for baseball or football teams, boys and girls played basketball the year around.

One day the trains stopped stopping at Sunny Vale, and Santa Fe ripped up the tracks. They didn't ask anybody if it was all right, nor did they explain why they did it. Sunny Vale began to die, and dwindled to hardly more than a ghost town.

One of the few surviving buildings was the Post Office, standing alone, surrounded by a vacant lot. Locals chided that it should have closed long ago because all it did was eat up taxpayers' money. But "them damn Democrats" kept it open for fear of losing the sixty-seven votes of the patrons it served. The Methodist Church deteriorated to where it was good for nothing except storing hay, and that's what Elmo Whisenant used it for.

The old red brick schoolhouse, whose bell rang for the last

time fifty-two years before, showed remarkable stamina after the kids transferred to the consolidated school district in Blessing. Defying time and hazardous weather, the building was the focal point of community activity, such as class reunions, political gatherings, and square dances. It also was the site of the Saturday night pie supper.

In what was once the school cafeteria, Pastor Oren Watts opened the festivities by invoking the presence of the Almighty, entreating his blessings "upon this gathering, thanking you in advance for the outpouring of goodness from this event, and for the new hymn books for the Baptist church its proceeds will provide."

From all over the county, people came to dance, to visit, and to exchange nuggets of gossip of what happened since last they met.

Much of the talk focused on the lady hired hand who invaded the hallowed confines of the Harper farm. Lexie found a place at a table next to Nettie Coy.

"Brazen heifer!" Cuba Adams scoffed in a huddle of cronies. "How in the name of God can she have the gall to show up here?"

"Like she's trying to fill Cathy's shoes," Hazel Cribbs spat. "As if she ever could."

Leona Foster stuck her oar in the water. "And poor Matt. No telling what she's putting him through."

And so it went.

Ethan Ashley was in charge of the pie auction. Ethan was a skinny young man, a recent graduate of the auctioneer's school in Springfield. He was grateful for the opportunity to practice his chant. He'd later be applauded for the good job he did and would accept the accolades with an awkward grin.

Speedy and the Boys picked and sang for an hour before they placed their guitars, fiddle, bass and steel guitar aside and took a break.

In years past, Speedy Haworth was the mainstay of a forty-two-people country music staff at KWTO Radio in Springfield. His guitar also provided backup for leading country artists such as Red Foley, Porter Wagoner, and Leroy Van Dyke. Highly respected by the Nashville establishment as one of the best pickers in the business, Speedy one day decided it was time to give it up. He still made himself available for dances, family reunions, and other community functions around Polk County.

While the band took a breather, Ethan went about arranging the pie boxes on a picnic table in the middle of the room where he'd auction them off to the highest bidders. Most of the bidders were hungry-eyed young farm stalwarts who spent the day aboard tractors, combines and fertilizer spreaders. They already knew whose boxes they'd bid on—the one brought by the girl with whom they hoped to share it. They eagerly awaited Ethan's chant. When he held up the first box, wrapped in white paper, tied with a yellow ribbon, they knew it was bidding time.

"This here box belongs to Jenny Pugh," Ethan announced. "What am I bid?"

The air filled with the hands of bidders on Jenny's box. Each bid was increased by twenty-five cents, until some lucky bidder claimed his prize for the phenomenal sum of $4.75.

When Ethan finally cleared the table of boxes, Cuba and her crew traded whispered behind-the-hand remarks, speculating that "the woman from Harper's considered herself too good to even bring a box.

Lexie hadn't seen her box since she placed it on the table when she got there. She wondered if it was misplaced. After a dramatic pause that silenced the gathering, Ethan brought from under the table, a bright green box tied with a red ribbon. Because all the others were sold, there was no question to whom this one belonged.

"I kept this box to the last on purpose," Ethan said with a broad grin, "because it belongs to the newest member of our community, Miss Alexis Farrell. If it brings a price half as pretty as the box she brought it in, it'll pay for a lot of hymn books."

A chuckle swept the audience as Ethan held the box aloft. He started the bidding at two dollars. Dude Martin's hand shot up. Ethan plugged for three. Elmo Whisenant raised his hand. Ethan pressed for four, five, six dollars.

Their wives didn't approve of Lexie's moving into the Harper house for the summer, but the men were not deterred from bidding on her box. When the final bid was made, Ethan pounded his gavel. "This here box is gonna be sold to Dude Martin for eleven dollars and fifty cents, the most paid for any box tonight."

Nettie Coy led the cheers, and Cuba Adams turned red.

Some questioning glances were cast Matt's way, surprised that he didn't bid on Lexie's box.

Lexie too was puzzled why he only watched and listened, since it was for him she baked the pie.

Cuba smirked at Agnes Gore, "Why should he pay for something he can get for nothing at home?"

With a long look at Matt, and a reproving scowl from his wife, Dude took Lexie's box from Ethan. He carried it to where Matt sat and held it out to him. "I reckon I'd oughta donate this to the cause," he snickered.

Some joker yelled, "What cause?"

"Cause Matt never bid on it," Dude said. To Matt, he said, "Seeing as how she's your woman and all–"

Expecting a response from Matt, a hush fell over the crowd.

Dude's blurted remarks echoed the thoughts of many, but no one else dared say them out loud.

Matt was a good neighbor who came to the aid of anyone who needed help. Only last week he let Dude use his grain truck when his broke down. And there was no question Cathy was regarded as a fine Christian woman, as good a friend and neighbor as a body could hope for. For Cathy's sake, if not for Matt's, no one said anything that might tarnish their memory of her.

But now, Martin broke the silence. In spite of what they thought of Lexie Farrell, many were uncomfortable because of Dude's thoughtless attempt to make a joke.

Matt felt Lexie's eyes on him. He knew she was wondering, along with the crowd, why he didn't react to Dude's barb. Still, she knew Matt as a peaceable man who spent a lot of time minding his own business. She couldn't have known that his insides smoldered with an urge to bust

Dude in the mouth. He wanted to do it for Lexie, for Dude's insinuation that Lexie was his "woman and all." He struggled to keep from taking a swing at Dude to wipe that silly grin off his face. But, most of all, Matt fought the urge to do it for Cathy, for the unfeeling Dude's remark insulted the memory of his dead wife.

The crowd held its collective breath, waiting. Was Matt gonna kill Dude, or what?

Somehow to the ears of Matt Harper came the whispered voice of Lexie Farrell. "Let it go,

Matt." When he glanced her way, she responded with a faint smile.

"Well, Dude," Matt said with a steady gaze, "you paid for the pie, so I guess you'd better eat it."

Tension melted as a nervous chuckle rippled around the room.

Dude turned away and took Lexie's box with him. Speedy and the Boys cut down on "Rocky Top." Ethan shouted, "Everybody dance!"

~~~

At breakfast the next morning Lexie poured the coffee.

Matt said, "Martin was out of line last night."

"Yes," Lexie said. "I guess it's hard for some people to believe a man and a woman can live in the same house without making something dirty out of it. I never wanted that."

"It's not your fault."

"I should have stayed at Nettie's."

Watching him down the hot coffee, sausage and eggs with hot buttered biscuits, what she said was enough. But what she didn't say was what she wanted Matt to know.

~~~

Matt Harper was born in the upstairs bedroom at the end of the hall where his parents slept for most of their married life. After he and Cathy moved to the farm, it became their room. And that's where she died.

His brothers, Clayton and Pete were born in the same bed. Clayton first, Matt next, Pete a few years later. After high school, Clayton couldn't wait to get away from the "hog shit and frozen cows' tits." He headed for the university at Columbia. Except for infrequent appearances on special occasions, Clayton avoided the home place.

Matt last saw him nine years before when they met for their father's funeral in Sun City.

Pete, six years younger than Matt, shared Clayton's loathing of the farm. After high school, Pete melted into some nether world from which he showed no desire to escape. Every few years Pete came straggling back to Matt's place, wanting to hang out for a while until he "got on his feet" again. Pete squandered his portion of what their father left them, then hit Matt up for "tide me over" money.

One late afternoon Matt was replacing a belt on the combine. He looked up and saw Pete ambling up the lane toward the house. Matt gave his head a shake of disbelief. He couldn't remember the last time Pete showed up, but he remembered telling his younger brother he could do nothing more for him. At that time, Matt figured he'd seen the last of Pete. But there he was, again.

Observing the leisurely approach of the lanky, bearded Pete, Matt leaned against the combine and wiped his hands on a rag from his hip pocket. Strapped to Pete's back was an olive drab knapsack, with a black strap slung around his neck. Suspended from the strap was a black guitar. Pete's pale blue eyes searched Matt's face for some sign of welcome. A half smile played at his thin lips.

"You lost?" Matt said when Pete pulled up.

"Damn near," Pete said in a husky, booze-and-cigarette tainted voice. "I thought maybe you could use a hand."

"I've got a hand."

"I bet he's not as good as me."

Whatever his brother had become since, Matt conceded, growing up on the farm, Pete was a good worker, even while he hated it.

Matt crawled under the combine and waved a hand at his

brother. "Help me get this belt back on."

Pete wriggled out of his pack and did as he was told.

The job done, they crawled out and brushed themselves off. They looked at each other, trying to figure out what to say after so long a time apart.

"The last time you popped up here you'd been fired from another job," Matt said. He wiped his hands then tossed the rag to Pete. "What brings you around this time?"

"Well, you know me, Matt," Pete said, lowering his eyes. "LeAnne and I split."

Matt gave that a solemn nod. He'd heard it before.

"It's over this time," Pete said.

"That's what you said last time."

"She's got another guy."

"For a forty-two-year-old, it took you a hell of a long time to catch on."

"Don't hassle me, Matt. I had enough of that from her."

"Don't hassle you?" Matt was angry and made no attempt to hide it. "Is that what you said–don't hassle you? The only time I ever see you is when you're flat ass broke, looking for someplace to hole up until you decide it's time to move on. And you say don't hassle you!"

"I thought you'd be glad to see me."

"Explain that to me, Pete. About the time I get used to the idea you're gone forever, you come strolling back looking for a handout. We go through the routine of patching things up, then one morning I wake up and find out you've flown the coop. Tell me why you think I'd be glad to see you, Pete."

"Well, I am your brother, you know."

"The only time you remember that is when you need something I've got. Neither you nor Clayton found time to even come to our wedding.

"You didn't even show up for Cathy's funeral. And you think I should be glad to see you?"

Pete took a minute to soak that up. "I just thought you might let me hang out for a while, and maybe earn my keep."

"For how long, Pete? Till your itchy feet tell you it's time to move again?" Matt fixed him with a stare that told Pete he'd be better off someplace else.

"Are you kicking me out?" Pete said with a smirk.

"No, I'm not kicking you out. I'm not letting you in."

Pete grabbed his backpack and guitar and slung them over a shoulder. He stomped away, and said, "I'll see you in hell."

Matt watched him go, wondering if there would ever be a last time for his younger brother to appear—without notice, without an invitation. Without anything.

From the kitchen window, Lexie saw Pete huffing off down the lane, striding briskly out of sight without a backward glance.

"What was that all about?" she said when Matt came through the kitchen door.

"Just some guy I used to know." He washed up and joined her at the table.

Matt liked having Lexie there. Between Pete and Hargrove, he was trying to sort things out. Lexie gave him something else to think about. She'd be gone with the fall semester. He wasn't sure how he felt about that. He tried not to think about it at all. But it was one of those things nagging at his subconscious that had to be thought about.

Supper over, Lexie brought out a three-layer chocolate cake ablaze with candles.

"Happy birthday, Matthew."

"How did you know it was my birthday?"

"Nettie put a bug in my ear. Actually, she wanted to throw a big whing-ding for you, but I didn't think you'd want that."

"You thought right."

"Did I get the candles right? Nettie thought you'd be forty-seven."

He nodded yes.

"Blow them out whenever you're ready," Lexie said, "then we'll slash that sucker up."

Matt took a deep breath, exhaled loudly, and blew out all but one candle.

"I guess I'm not as windy as I thought," he said.

"Oh, that's okay. My grandma used to say if one candle is left burning, it means you'll live to celebrate another birthday.

Do you want to cut it?"

He declined with a smile. "I'm better at eating than cutting."

Between her thumb and forefinger, Lexie snuffed out the remaining candle. She sliced the first piece of cake and placed it on his plate.

"Thank you," he said.

"You're welcome. I have something else for you too."

She went away and came back with a foot-long box wrapped in red paper, tied with a white ribbon. She placed it beside his plate.

He said, "What in the world?"

"Open it and find out."

He removed the wrapper and lifted the lid. Nestled in white tissue was a fillet knife.

"Well, I guess Nettie told you I needed this too."

"Nope. Remember when we went fishing last week, and you had trouble skinning that big ole catfish? That's when I decided you needed a new knife."

"I don't know what I've done to deserve all this." The look in his eyes expressed the gratitude for which he couldn't find words.

"My pleasure," she said.

He tossed her a thoughtful nod. "Lexie, I didn't give you a straight answer a while ago when you asked who that man was."

She waited, detecting the tinge of pain in his eyes.

"That was my brother. My younger brother Pete."

Lexie leaned closer across the table. "Oh. His name is Pete?"

"He was born Peter, but nobody remembers that. If there's a black sheep in the Harper family, I guess you'd have to say Pete is it. He was always a kind of free spirit, never very responsible. Do you want to hear about this?"

If it was important to Matt, it was important to Lexie. If it hurt him, she wanted to share his pain. Anything touching the life of Matt Harper, she wanted to know about.

Her response was simple. "Yes, I too."

"Pete was a good kid and a good worker when he was growing up here on the farm, but much of the time he acted like he was off in some dream world where no one else was welcome. We got along well until he finished high school. He went kind of wild after that, blew two marriages, and now, he says he and his third wife broke up."

Lexie listened, feeling an urge to reach out to Matt, to touch his face, take his hand in hers. To wrap her arms around him, to comfort him. But she dared not. She would wish she had.

"You still like him," she said.

"Yes. Pete reminded me that he's my brother."

"But you sent him away."

"Pete has never quite found his way. He needs to do that. I hope it's not too late. I can't help him. He has to do it himself."

Lexie nodded as if she understood. "I'll pour coffee," she said.

~~~

After Cathy died, Matt converted his home into a shrine to her memory. He covered the walls with her photographs, enlarged to four times their original size. On the center wall of the front entryway, he placed his favorite–a portrait of Cathy in her wedding gown. Matt had it painted by a Kansas City artist for her twenty-fifth birthday. The portrait was splashed with a spotlight twenty-four hours a day. Knick-knacks and trinkets they picked up on trips around the country he displayed prominently on tables and shelves. Anything that belonged to Cathy, he wanted in plain sight. In the front yard, he erected a ten-foot monument of roses, daisies and mums. Cathy's favorites.

Nettie knew what he was going through. She'd been there–what she called her "agony of survival" after Ben died. At sixty-three, Nettie suffered the loneliness of loss long enough to understand what Matt was going through. Matt was doing everything possible to keep Cathy alive. Nettie knew how he was hurting. She also knew there was nothing he could take for it. And it would never go away.

Nettie knew about Lexie too. Everybody did. Some people

thought the worst of Lexie's staying at the Harper farm. "Just them two out there all by themselves in that big ole house all summer long! No telling what all goes on out there!"

"Well, I never!" they jabbered, "Matt Harper stooping to that. And that poor little old Cathy hardly more than breathed her last."

Lexie was the primary topic of conversation at the weekly teas and church circles, blistering the tongues of the community gossips.

"A den of iniquity, that's what it is!"

"Ain't nothing going on out there, but the work of the devil."

At the Christian Women's Fellowship meeting Buhlie Bradshaw demanded, "What are we gonna do about it?"

Nettie Coy had heard all she could stand of their jabbering. In no uncertain terms would she let Buhlie, and everyone else within earshot know what she thought they should do about it.

"I'll tell you what we need to do," Nettie said, glaring at the accusing eyes around the table. "We need to mind our own business, and keep our noses out of other peoples'. That man is only forty-seven years old, his wife has been dead for three years, and it would be truly evil, Buhlie Bradshaw, for you or anybody else to condemn him to spending the rest of his life in that big house all by himself because of what a gaggle of barnyard geese think about what's going on out there."

"That's easy for you to say, Nettie," Buhlie said, mounting a weak defense.

"No, it is not easy for me to say. I've been through what Matt Harper is going through now, and so have you."

"You never moved in with anybody."

"Nobody ever asked me!" Nettie shot back.

A horrified gasp made its way around the circle as hands covered nervous lips, concealing outrage that Nettie Coy would even entertain the possibility of living with a man who was not her husband.

"You of all people, Buhlie," Nettie seethed. "A Sunday School teacher and president of the CWF. You should be ashamed of yourself, gossiping about that man and that woman. We all should be ashamed. What we need is to look for ways to help him get through this, whatever it is, instead of sitting around plotting ways to do him in."

Matt was well aware of the hornet's nest stirred up by Lexie's presence in his house. Even so, he found no need to discuss with anybody his arrangement with Lexie. It was none of their business.

That certain women considered it a sin for "that woman to be living in Cathy's house" didn't escape Matt's notice. Some of them, no doubt, were overcome with an acute case of curiosity about what Julie would think about it. Had she been there to ask, they'd likely call a meeting to vote on who had the courage to broach the subject with Matt's daughter—and they'd be shocked out of their supposed to learn Julie approved what was going on in her father's house.

Matt and Lexie made no attempt to disguise the fact that they were occupying space under the same roof. Together they appeared at the pie supper, were seen shopping in town, even sitting side-by-side in church where Matt used to sit with Cathy, for crying out loud! It was almost more than Buhlie and her cronies could abide without respirators.

Pastor Watts himself evinced some concern that all was not as it should be in the Harper household. Indeed, one recent Sunday after church, Watts called Matt aside.

Matt sensed what the good preacher wanted to talk about. Since there was no doubt Owen was privy to the gossip making the rounds, Matt figured he'd waited as long as propriety permitted to discuss with one of his parishioners what Owen perceived to be a matter of grave concern. With a solemn nod toward where Lexie and Nettie had their heads together, the preacher got right down to it.

"Why, Matt, there's been some talk about what that young lady is doing out at your place."

Matt was ready with the answer he'd devised in case somebody asked him about it. He knew the time had come when somebody did.

"I'm not a bit surprised, preacher." He'd wondered how long it would take Watts to get around to talking about what other people had talked about for weeks. "For a while, I couldn't believe it myself," Matt said. "Julie said Lexie was a good worker, but I never thought she'd be as good a hand as she is."

Watts stared at him as if he hadn't heard what he'd prepared his hearing organs to absorb.

"What she's doing out there," Matt went on, "is a good day's work. I pay her for the time she puts in, and that's all I pay her for." He glanced about, meeting inquiring eyes that quickly looked away. "I'll tell you what, preacher, if something comes up I think these folks need to know about, I'll put it in the paper."

"Well now, Matt, you know I didn't mean any ill. I just thought—"

"I know. You've got all you can handle just keeping these good folks on the straight and narrow. You keep doing that, and I'll keep doing what I think is best. Maybe one day the two of us will meet up Yonder and we can talk about it some more."

Holding aloft his King James Version, Watts said, "I get a lot of help from this."

"Well, I'm sure you do. I bet if you looked far enough in that book you'd find where it says something about the sin of gossip, and poking noses into other people's business."

"You're a good man, Matt Harper."

With a gesture at the pastor's Bible, Matt said, "Tell that to your boss."

Watts stuck out a hand and Matt shook it.

"Lord bless you, Matt."

Matt made a move toward Lexie and Nettie. He was hailed by Stuart Billings. Billings was a couple of years older, and two inches taller than Matt's six-one. A narrow-brimmed straw hat shaded Stuart's broad forehead. Billings was born on the place he farmed west of Harper's. Over the years, he and Matt stood side-by-side on most issues.

"Have you seen Hamp Hargrove?" Billings said.

"Not for a few days. I haven't been looking for him either."

"He's looking for you."

Matt was tempted to tell Stuart about the dead bull

incident but thought better of it. He wanted to be sure how deep the water was before he jumped in.

"He knows where to find me," Matt said. "He's been out there."

"I talked to Dude and Elmo," Billings said, "and a few of the others. They agree it's time we all got together and came to some kind of conclusion on this hog deal."

"Yeah, somebody called me about a meeting on Thursday."

"I didn't know if you'd be able to make it."

"I'll be there," Matt said. "The last time I saw Hamp, he said he'd be there too."

"Yeah, he's been making the rounds again, raising the ante." Billings scratched the back of his neck while he thought about what he was going to say next. "I have an idea Hamp thinks you and I will fall in line once the others make up their minds to go along with his offer."

"Have you talked to Justice?"

"Yeah, John and I sat down over coffee and talked about it. He was pretty non-committal since the place belongs to his mother. Any decision would be up to her."

"Uh-huh. The last I heard she'd die before she'd sell out to Hargrove."

"It sounds to me like you and I are sitting right in the middle of the ground those people want," Billings said. "If we don't go, the deal's off."

"How does that strike you?"

"I don't like being pushed into anything, and I think they're trying to pressure us into bending to whatever they want to get done."

"What are the others saying, Stut?"

"From what they've told me, they're anxious to bring this thing to a head—sell out and get it over with."

"How about you?"

"I'm not selling."

Matt grinned and shook his hand. "I'll see you Thursday night."

CHAPTER SEVEN

What about James?

Lexie was nine years old when she fell in love with her third-grade gym teacher, Miss Foley. From there on, she knew a gym teacher was what she wanted to be. Elementary through college, she concentrated on sports—all of them–soccer, track, basketball, softball–every sport except football, which denied girls' participation. Anyhow, she ruefully conceded, there was no room on the beefy football team for a one-hundred-twelve-pound linebacker.

College was Southern Illinois University. She met and fell in love with James Chandler, an engineering major. Chandler was the man with whom she wanted to spend the rest of her life. "Tall, dark, and handsome" were the criteria for romantic success, and Chandler was all of those. He also was an all-conference tight end on the football team and the high-scoring shooting guard on the basketball team. A prime campus catch and Lexie snagged him.

Lexie made weekend trips home to help her mother and sister Bea prepare for her marriage to Chandler, planned for after Lexie's graduation in June.

In the front yard of the family farm, her father built a honeysuckle-covered walkway. It led to the flower garden, where she would be joined in holy matrimony with the only man she ever loved. Lexie's mother designed flower beds in the form of wedding rings and lined the wedding walk with red geraniums, white roses, and pink mums from the patio to the garden.

According to the society editor of the local paper, the wedding was "a gigantic success. The bride was gorgeous in a heavenly white gown hand-sewn by her mother, adored by more than one hundred guests." Six bridesmaids were girlhood friends. The flower girl was the four-year-old daughter of a lifelong friend Sue Bosworh. Five-year-old Kevin, son of Lexie's older brother Dan, was the ring bearer.

During the ceremony, Kevin stood transfixed beside the bridegroom. Asked later what he was thinking at the time, Kevin's response was, "I was thinking I never want to go through this again."

Feeling "really, really married!" Lexie couldn't have been happier. The following week she accepted the position of gym instructor at the local high school. Chandler transferred to the University at Champaign-Urbana to pursue an advanced degree in engineering. As often as possible, she drove to be with her husband for the weekend. James pleaded his workload didn't allow him time to drive home to Carbondale for the weekend.

Lexie understood.

What she didn't understand was what she found, on James's birthday.

She wanted to surprise him with an unannounced arrival at his apartment. Using her key to let herself in, Lexie tip-toed noiselessly across the living room to the small bedroom where James set up a desk and typewriter for a study.

James was not studying.

Lexie discovered why it was so difficult for him to find time to drive home for a weekend with his bride.

James was in bed. Naked. Locked in the arms of another man.

Shocked beyond reality, Lexie struggled to maintain composure. "James, would you like to tell me what's going on here?"

James bolted upright in bed. "Lexie, I can explain this."

The other man appeared as shocked as she. He pulled the bed covers over his head.

"I'm sure you can," Lexie said, on the edge of hysteria. "Would you mind doing that now? Who is that man? And why is he here?"

In a very tired, defenseless tone of voice, James told her. "Charles Romer. Charles and I—we knew each other before you and I married."

James hated the way he lived before and wanted to be different. He hoped marrying Lexie would help him change. Three weeks later he realized he made a mistake. He wasn't going to change and searched for ways to keep it from her.

Lexie raced from the apartment, groping through a maze of frustration, bewilderment and disappointment in the man she loved and trusted. Why did he not tell me before? Why did he tell her he loved her, while the whole time he was in love with some strange man who could never be a mother? Or a father. Frantic, she wondered which position James assumed in the relationship. Why did he allow her to fall in love with him, and go through the mockery of a marriage when he was already emotionally married to some god damned man!

Her eyes were on fire with tears. She climbed woefully into her car, turned the key, and started driving. Where, she didn't know. Little did it matter. Dodging cars dodging hers, irate drivers honked loudly and long, pummeling her with obscenities as she blindly struggled to find her way out of the city.

Clear of zooming traffic, she skidded to a stop and threw open the car door. Her insides gushed forth, splattering the roadside with the bitter bile of revulsion and disgust. She wondered if she'd ever find her way back to Carbondale.

She did. She stumbled through her apartment door, and collapsed on the bed she shared briefly with the man she believed was the love of her life. All of it. Instead of the joy she anticipated while celebrating his birthday, she spent the weekend in tears. She felt used and violated, betrayed by the man who promised to love her forever and ever.

For hours she showered, scrubbing her body, shampooing her hair as though afraid she'd never again be clean.

By Monday morning she convinced herself she was fortunate to find out about Charles before she and James put in place the life they planned together. She'd heard of women whose lives were shattered, who discovered, after years of marriage, that their husbands were homosexual.

Recalling it now, she loosened the soil around a rose bush once tended by Cathy Harper. With vigorous chops of a garden hoe, Lexie's body shook with still smoldering resentment. The harder she hacked the defenseless dirt the angrier she became for allowing herself to be blinded by the fascination she felt for a man who was never hers. She promised herself she'd never again allow herself to get that close to any man. And she did not.

For fourteen years she did not.

And then there came now.

Lexie's proposal that she stay with Matt instead of Nettie was honest, with no hope nor expectation that doing so might open the door to a romantic relationship. Why should she live with Nettie when the work was on Matthew's farm? To Lexie, working on the farm was a logical alternative to spending the summer in Illinois. Her brother Dan was hundreds of miles away in Minnesota? Add to that the venom that spewed from the lips of Dan's wife Gloria—with whom Lexie rarely found herself on the same wavelength. Gloria never recovered from the embarrassment of Lexie's split with James Chandler, and wouldn't let her forget the "smirch on the family name." She condemned Lexie to wearing black for the rest of her life as a penance, though long ago Lexie gave up moping over James Chandler.

She filed James away under ancient history and wasted no time mourning his passing.

Because of the futility of her marriage, falling in love with Matthew Harper hovered at the bottom of her list of things she'd ever dream of doing. She argued with herself that what slowly evolved from friendship to adoration was not really happening. She struggled to maintain control of her emotions and tried to convince herself that whatever she felt for Matt Harper would pass. Likely with tomorrow's sunrise.

Matthew loved Cathy. He always loved Cathy, and he would always love Cathy. So, back off, lady, Lexie scorned herself. You're thirty-seven years old. You promised yourself you'd never get this close again. Get over it.

Sunrise came and went. Lexie's attraction to Matt didn't.

The days of summer grew longer, and Lexie's time on the farm grew shorter. By the time August rolled around, she'd stayed busy with farm activities with little else to think about. A strange kind of common bond sneaked unobtrusively into her relationship with Matt. As he drew strength from his devotion to Cathy, so Lexie's resistance was bolstered by her determination never to fall in love again.

Home free, she counseled herself. She and Matthew were content doing things for each other.

Matt praised her for what she did for him. With pleasure, she continued to do them, serving fried rabbit and hot potato soup when he came in from the field at supper time. He relished the glow in her eyes when he brought her a handful of wildflowers collected along the fence row. They enjoyed each other's company, neither vulnerable.

Uh-huh. So, why did she lie awake nights, aware of his sleeping down the hall a few steps from her door? Wishing he'd come to her. Through her mind tumbled the probable consequences of her going to him, slipping silently into his bed, pressing her body against his. Once, she threw off the covers, swung her legs over the side of the bed, and strode cautiously down the hall toward where he slept. Halfway to Matt's door, she stopped.

"Would he throw me out?" she quizzed herself. Was it worth the chance—the chance of losing him altogether if he felt her beside him?

Slowly she retreated to her room. The risk was too great. She crawled back in bed and stayed there.

~~~

The weatherman promised the morning rain would

dissipate by noon. Unable to get equipment into the wet field, Matt and Lexie hopped in his truck and headed for town. Matt would swing by Ed Mosley's barber shop for a haircut, while Lexie checked the sale items at Sally's Ladies Stuff.

Matt pulled into a parking spot, and Lexie dashed away through the rain to Sally's.

Matt walked down the Main Street hill a block south to Ed's barber shop. The chair nearest the door was empty. Ed motioned Matt into it, as if he'd expected him to show up.

Lined up against the wall, three young men awaited their turn. Bart Kinsley, the undertaker, parked his bulk in a chair near the door. He hid his puffy face behind the daily paper.

Matt glanced at the young men ahead of him. They said, "Go ahead."

Ed said, "They're waiting for George and Slim."

"They don't trust you to cut their hair?" Matt chided.

Kinsley ducked out from behind the newspaper long enough for a jibe. "They know Ed don't need the money."

That brought chuckles all around.

Kinsley wore a tight gray suit and a red tie. He owned funeral parlors in three nearby towns. Ed's barber shop was his favorite place to hang out and jaw with friends when he wasn't burying somebody.

Ed's response was, "Look who's talking about money."

Mosley was sixty-two, stooped from a lifetime of hovering over hairy heads, his own hair about gone. To Bart, he said, "How much did you loan Uncle Sam this week?"

Matt wanted to know if it was hard for Kinsley to be nice to everybody.

The undertaker said, "How's that, Matt?"

"Well, we're all going to die sometime."

"I can wait," Bart said, his paunch aquiver, laughing at his own joke. "I aim to bury the lot of you, and turn out the lights when I go."

Slim said, "Hey, Matt, I hear you boys are about ready to give up on farming and sell out to them Arkansas pigs."

"Where'd you hear that?"

Slim was true to his name, skinny as the comb he used on

hair, with deep-set dark eyes and heavy eyebrows. "Well, you know Hamp Hargrove."

With little enthusiasm, Matt said, "I know Hamp Hargrove."

"I cut Hamp's hair," Slim said. "The way Hamp tells it, you fellers are ready to fold up and head south."

"That's what I heard, too," George said, snipping away at a head of red hair. George was a little man with a tic to his left eye and a bald head. "Dude Martin was telling me about it. Dude talked like the deal was all cut and dried."

Ed swept the apron from around Matt's neck and flipped the loose hair off it.

Matt stood up, removed a bill from his wallet, and handed it to Ed. "I'll tell you what, fellows," he said. He pressed on his John Deere cap and headed for the door. "Dude may think it's cut, but it's a hell of a long way from dried."

"See you, Matt," Ed said.

The rain slacked off to a drizzle as Matt walked back up the hill to his truck. He spotted Lexie crossing the street carrying a couple of shopping bags. He helped her with the packages, climbed in the truck, and started the motor.

"Did you find some bargains?" he asked her.

"Just a couple of things I need for the start of school."

That was not the first time Matt was reminded of the fall semester that would soon start. Summer was winding down, Julie would be coming home. She and Lexie would be going back for the fall term at MSU.

On the way home, Matt couldn't find much to talk about. Not much, except for Hamp Hargrove, and he didn't think Lexie cared about what he heard at the barber shop.

"Something stuck in your craw?" Lexie said.

She liked him to tell her things, especially what he was thinking when he didn't talk. Lately she'd noticed Matt mostly listened while she talked. Sometimes he appeared to be in deep thought about something else.

"Word in town," he said, "is that we're caving in to that hog outfit. Heading south, is the way they put it."

"Does that include you?"

"I've already told you what I'm going to do, Lexie."

Lexie blinked. Never had he spoken to her so sharply.

For two months they combined wheat and soybeans, mowed, raked and baled fescue, trimmed the Bradford pears lining both sides of the lane, and whatever else needed to be done. They painted the outbuildings and repaired fences. They fished together in the bass pond up north of the barn. They went places together, sat next to each other in church. Feeling safe and comfortable.

When she wasn't needed to lend a hand elsewhere, Lexie tended the flower beds along the front of the house, nurtured the roses, geraniums, and impatiens with the care of a mother for her small child. Over the yard, and up and down the lane, she wheeled the twenty-five horse John Deere riding mower. She kept down the grass and weeds along the right-of-way because Matt said it was a part of the place. All to free him for more pressing jobs on the farm.

Their lives unavoidably intertwined. Over time, Lexie noticed pictures of Cathy no longer graced the walls. Cathy's portrait in the front entrance was no longer flooded with light twenty-four hours a day. Lexie dared not ask why. Nor did she ask now, suspecting her concern for whatever occupied his mind would matter little to him.

She'd learn how wrong she was.

The drizzle hung around until they got back to the farm. Matt let Lexie out at the back door. She hurried into the house, her head covered with a shopping bag.

Matt parked the truck in the garage and dashed through the drizzle to the house. Hardly had he made it inside the door when he was shocked to hear Lexie say, "Do you want me to go?"

He cast her a startled look, swallowed hard. "Go?"

"As in away."

He took a minute to decide what to say. "That might be best."

"That's not what I asked, Matthew. Do you want me to go?"

"It must be about time for school to start."

"In another week."

"Julie will be coming home," he reminded her.

"Do you not want Julie to know?" she asked.

"To know what?"

"That I love you."

Nine

Good memories never die

Loving Cathy was something Matt Harper would forever do. After three years he still missed her every hour of every day. His mind was flooded with memories of their life together. It couldn't have been longer ago than last week when they ran barefoot across the meadow on a rainy afternoon. They romped across the wheat field chasing grasshoppers for fish bait, picked wild blueberries along the fence, tested the ripeness of an ear of corn with its tassel flowing in the wind.

Rushing back, too, came recollections of the magical times when the three of them—Cathy, Matt, and Julie—stood gaping at the vast wonders of the Grand Canyon. They marveled at the time and skill devoted to carving the images of Washington, Jefferson, Roosevelt and Lincoln in Mount Rushmore—questioning why Lincoln was set apart from the others. Feeding bear cubs in the Smoky Mountains, when seven-year-old Julie begged to take one home in the car. "Can we, daddy, can we please?"

Now, in the drizzle beside the headstone marking Cathy's grave, Matt knelt. He placed on it a jar filled with daisies, not as a final tribute, but as a token of all the wonderful years they had together.

"It's time to stop the bleeding," Nettie had said. "Don't push her away. Let her love you." A few at a time he'd removed the pictures, the paintings, whatever reminded him of Cathy. As if he needed reminding. In the process, the hurting, the missing, the loneliness began to subside.

Cathy was gone. After graduation in the spring, Julie, too, would be gone, pursuing her career, making her own life. The chances of her returning home to the farm, except for occasional visits, were remote.

Planting his feet firmly upon the ground he walked and worked every day, Matt had a good life.

He'd make the most of what was left of it. Even so, he

couldn't deny, in recent weeks, he felt—and even before Nettie so succinctly challenged him to "get on with your life"— some strange emotions began stirring inside him, emotions he thought died with Cathy, and never expected to feel again. He tried not thinking about it. He'd deny it if anyone asked, "Hey, Matt, why in hell don't you admit you're in love with that lady?"

Pounding fence posts, or training a chainsaw on a stubborn Osage orange log for fireplace wood, his body renewed the urgency with which he found it difficult to cope. From the well that filled the stock tank, he splashed his head with water, aflame with something he dared not give a name.

Matt was frightened. Not terrified frightened, as the time the grizzly attacked their camp in the Rockies. Frightened that the strength to honor his commitment to Cathy might be slipping away.

Further complicating his dilemma was Lexie's expression of love. Why would she do that? He knew how he felt, and he fought it. He'd have bet the farm Lexie felt nothing more for him than friendship, and respect for the father of her friend.

With Cathy it was easy. Never had he struggled with emotions, so filled were they with love for each other. No barriers to overcome, no holding back. Throwing themselves on a haystack, wrapped in each other\s arms in pure ecstasy. Plunging stark raving naked into the pond north of the barn by the light of a midnight moon. Waking at any hour of the night for love that couldn't wait.

All this and more, so much more, Cathy took with her to the grave.

Even so, pushing the combine for one more round before rain and darkness drove him to the house, Matt reflected on bits of what he loved about Cathy. He now found them drawing him to Lexie Farrell. The way Lexie studied his face, her head cocked to one side, an inquisitive gleam in her eyes. Smiling, with never a frown, even before breakfast. Lexie's character provided no room for pretense.

Matt never had to guess where Lexie stood on an issue. Cathy was Cathy and Lexie was Lexie. More and more Matt awakened in the middle of the night with thoughts of Lexie tugging at his mind. That too was frightening.

"There was nothing you could have done," Julie assured him about her mother's death.

"It's time to stop the bleeding," Nettie admonished. Still, he clung to what Nettie called "what used to be," as if by some miracle his beloved Cathy might be raised from her deadness.

Much of what he loved before, he now saw in a different face. A face unknown to him only two short month ago. A smiling face, disarming in its honesty. No longer was he frightened only, but was now he was angry with himself. He ripped his conscience to shreds for allowing himself to forget—though he'd never forget.

Into the night he peered, as if to penetrate the darkness, somehow to see beyond where his vision took him, knowing there was nothing out there for him to want. As far as the eye could see, all he wanted was already his.

For Matt Harper, though, earth and sky were no longer enough. What he wanted, of which he struggled to deny himself, was inside the walls of his home, brewing his coffee, cooking his meals, innocently tantalizing him with her womanness. And her being there, the pleasure of which he fought to deny because of his commitment to a love long dead.

His mind whirling, he guided the combine into the tool shed, turned off the engine, and opened the door to step down. So doing, his foot caught the edge of the door, and Matt tumbled headlong against a hay rake parked nearby.

Lexie was worried. It was an hour past dark and Matt hadn't come in for supper. Every few minutes she looked out the kitchen window, expecting him to show up, wondering what was keeping him. She leaned into the window for a closer look, and searched the night for some sign that Matt was all right.

What she saw in the glow of the meter pole light was old Sport, bouncing up and down, barking, whining, carrying on as she hadn't seen him behave before.

Lexie's first thought was, "Something's happened to Matthew!"

She ran out the door. Sport couldn't wait for her to fall in behind him and took off for the tool shed. Lexie followed. She found Matt crumpled on the ground, unconscious, a bloody gash on his forehead.

"Matthew!" She dropped to her knees beside his unmoving body. Again she shouted, "Matthew!" He didn't respond. She pounded his chest with her fists, but he didn't move.

Sport was nervous, hopping about, wanting to help.

Lexie ripped off her cotton top and wiped the blood from Matt's face. She kissed his face, hoping he would open his eyes. He didn't. Grabbing both his arms, she tried to move him, but couldn't budge him. She tugged at his feet. It didn't help. She shook him by the shoulders with all her strength, and shouted, "Damn you, Matthew, wake up!"

His right hand moved. He was alive! His right leg moved, his head turned slightly, and his eyes opened.

"Lexie?"

Bawling and laughing with relief, she wrapped his head in her arms, swept his face with her rain-soaked hair, and pressed her face to his.

Old Sport bared his teeth in a big smile, twirled his tail in a windmill motion.

Lexie helped Matt to his feet and into the house.

His injury was not as serious as she feared. She coaxed him into lying down on the living room sofa while she swabbed the blood from his forehead, and patched him up with a gauze bandage.

With the sunrise and a grateful smile, Matt declared himself "almost perfect again."

~~~

Like new babies, new calves often arrived in the dead of night. Early morning found farmers "making the rounds," checking the pasture to find out whether their herds increased while they slept.

Matt moved the pickup slowly, looking for newborn calves, wary of the forecast warning of flash floods.

Weaubleau Creek, running across his farm, was hazardous at times. With heavy rain, it often flowed out of banks.

Lexie was still uneasy about his accident the night before, and made the rounds with him. As they approached the creek, they spotted a spindly-legged new calf near the water's edge. The mother cow stood apart, bawling anxiously. The calf kept wobbling unsteadily toward the rushing waters.

"I was afraid of that," Matt said, braking to a stop. He made a move to rescue the calf.

"I'll get him," Lexie said. She bolted from the truck toward the calf.

Matt yelled, "Lexie, wait!"

She was already half way to where the calf was belly-deep in water. She waded in, grabbed it in her arms, and struggled toward
the bank.

"Let the calf go!" Matt shouted.

But Lexie clung to the squirming, bawling newborn, fighting the current to stay upright while being swept downstream.

From the creek bank, Matt saw the current carrying Lexie dangerously close to the bridge downstream across the creek. He had to get to Lexie before she got to the bridge. The rushing waters could cause her serious injury. He plunged into the water, caught her by the arm, and pulled her to him. Lexie still had an arm wrapped around the calf.

Matt strained against the swirling waters. He finally drew close enough to the bank to grab an overhanging branch. He caught the branch and held on. Finally, he was able to work his way out of the water and onto the bank. Both Lexie and the calf were safe.

Lexie let the calf go. Its wobbly legs carried it to the side of its frantic mother.

Matt swept Lexie into his arms and deposited her in the truck.

"I'm sorry, Matthew," she murmured.

"No need to be sorry. You could've drowned saving that calf."

Lexie was soaked and exhausted. "Thanks for rescuing

me."

"Any time."

~~~

In the beginning, Matt questioned whether Lexie's spending the summer on the farm was a good idea. But, he reasoned, if she found the work more than she bargained for, or if he decided her being there wasn't worth the time it would take to show her what needed to be done, all she had to do was grab her bag and split. He'd wish her well. On the other hand, if Lexie turned out to be a capable hand, as Julie said, she'd be treated as any other hired hand. Their living under the same roof would present no problem. If all worked out as anticipated, he'd assign her certain tasks, pay her a fair wage for what she did, and that would be it.

Lexie was Julie's friend, but he'd relate to her as to any other hand. If he thought of it at all, his devotion to the memory of Cathy was strong enough to insulate himself against violating the life he and Cathy had together.

The possibility that Lexie might be tempted to stray from her role as an employee never crossed his mind.

Nor hers. All summer, Lexie did things about the house, cooking, cleaning, things Matt didn't require of her, because she enjoyed doing for him. She did what Cathy once did, except for sharing his bed.

So attentive and efficient had Lexie been, he found himself wishing summer would not be over.

Wishing she didn't have to go back to school, leaving him to spend another long winter in that big house alone.

"It'll be pretty quiet around here without you," he told her at breakfast.

"That's nice of you to say." After a silent pause, she said, "Matthew."

"Yes?"

With a shake of her head, she lowered her eyes and did not respond.

"I'll see to the cattle," he said.

~~~

Thursday night at seven o'clock, Ethan Ashley pounded his auctioneer's gavel on the table and announced to the gathering in the old school house, "This here meetin' is gonna commence right now."

Ethan was fingered for the job because of his exemplary performance at the pie supper the previous Saturday night. In addition to which, he was the only one who owned a gavel.

The cafeteria was filled with farmers, and townspeople who came to find out how their lives might be affected by the hog plant the Arkansas outfit wanted to build in their community. The non-farmers had heard the horror stories of the unbearable odors with which such an operation would pollute the air. They wanted to be assured their kids would be protected against contamination.

Matt hadn't opened his mouth. He was more interested in what other people had to say. He knew what he was going to do, so whatever happened tonight wouldn't affect his decision one way or the other. He listened to all the arguments, pro and con, including the one by the manager of the proposed plant about all the safety features that would be put in place "to prevent proliferation of noxious fumes" which the residents feared would blanket the community.

Stuart Billings stated what Matt considered the position of the farmers, most of whom grew up on the ground their fathers worked before them. John Justice, long and lean, with deep-set eyes that could stare down an irate bull, said a few words in support of Billings.

"You can cave in if that's what you've got in mind to do," Justice challenged his neighbors, "but I'm not moving."

Questioning glances reflected the skepticism of the farmers. Still, Gib Wheeler and Bo Bradshaw, spoke in favor of voting for the plant. But Gib was old, and Bo came to the meeting because Buhlie told him to. Both were already close to giving up farming anyhow. Dude Martin and Elmo Whisenant were eager to sell for different reasons. Dude was sick of farming because it interfered with his hunting and fishing, and because "there ain't nothin' in it no more." Elmo had plans for moving to Tennessee where one of his daughters lived, and he'd be close to the Grand Ole Opry, where he could go recharge his passion for country music every Friday and Saturday night.

Hamp Hargrove "dropped by," and, like Matt, had yet to say a word. But Hamp kept eyeballing the landowners with an intimidating glare. He tried to convince them that selling out would be better than a busted head, a .410 slug between the eyes of a prize bull, or a stick of dynamite under the hood of their Four-by-Four. Nobody was able to prove it, but everybody knew Hargrove was capable of such incidents.

The evening wore on, milking time came early, and, arriving at no conclusion, the crowd grew restless. Finally, Matt, who listened till his ears hurt, had heard enough. Ethan caught him with a disgusted shake of his head,

"Matt," Ethan said, "you haven't made a peep. Something on your mind?"

Matt wasn't keen on making speeches, but Ethan put him on the spot. He decided maybe he should say something. He stood up, and faced the audience of about fifty people. They fell silent, waiting to hear what he had to say.

Surveying the crowd, Matt's gaze fell on Preacher Watts who opened the meeting with an entreaty, ending with "bless this bunch that their actions may be pleasing to you, amen." Next to Watts sat Billy Coan, perennial mayor of the town of Sunny Vale when it was a town. Past eighty now, Billy did little, except count his money—money that would buy anything short of a cure for the lung cancer eating him alive.

Matt's eyes ambled past Coan to Dude Martin. Dude was busy blowing his nose into his fist and never met Matt's stare.

"When I was a kid growing up on my daddy's farm," Matt began, "I really looked forward to rolling out of bed before daylight in the dead of winter. I'd get out there on a cold morning, about eight below, and pull on those cows' tits. They didn't like it, but they seemed to get some kind of kick out slapping me in the face with their frozen tails. That was always a lot of fun at five o'clock on a freezing morning. And slopping hogs was one of my favorite things, especially when they knocked me down and covered me with mud from one end to the other."

Chuckles made their way around the room, and heads nodded as Matt described his "fun times on the farm."

"In the summertime," Matt went on to knowing smiles and nods of recollection, "when it was so nice and cool in the middle of August, tossing hay bales onto the flatbed, and from the flatbed into the barn loft– Remember how much fun that was?

"You know I'm not telling the truth. You likely didn't enjoy it any more than I did. But we did it because our daddies said so, and we didn't know any different. We thought those city kids with their little red school house lunch buckets were the ones who didn't know what was good.

"I don't know whether my father even liked farming, but I never heard him say he didn't. He busted his backside, scratching a living out of dirt and rocks, the same as yours did. Then one day somebody came along and started talking about conservation and fertilizer, and ways to make dirt better so it would grow more beans and corn. After a while crops started growing as tall and pretty as the okra in my mama's garden. My daddy got to making a decent living, and times got better.

"Every time I walk through those fields out there I see my daddy humping his back, his head bowed low to the ground, his fingers gnarled and crooked from working the land. It took a long time for me to understand he did it–to get it ready for me. I didn't know that then. Mama knew it. She used to try to tell me, but my mind was someplace else, looking to the day when I'd be old enough to walk away from that farm and never look back.

"To me, farming was a passel of chores I cared nothing about. Plowing, planting, chopping wood, weeding the corn rows till my fingers bled. Praying for rain that didn't come when we needed it. Fighting bugs and grasshoppers and blight. Remember that? Farming was a job I did because if I didn't do it my daddy would have whopped my backside.

"Every man in this room is in love with that land–has been all his life. Like me, you probably didn't know it then, but why else would you still be here—doing it? Because deep in your heart you know on the land is where you belong, and you hope and pray, like everybody else, that one day it'll be worth something again.

"Well, maybe our time has come. Old Hamp here is trying to make us believe our farms are worth a lot more as a big time hog factory than for making a living. We've all heard the talk about those people with bushels of money, waiting to dump it all on us so they can move onto the land we've spent our lives working, and start manufacturing baby pigs. Three thousand acres of pigs! I've got about fifty head of Berkshires at my place and that's all the stink I can stand.

"But it's not just the stench I'm talking about. It's the life of this community. This land is our lives, the same as it was our daddies' lives. Like the women you married, what would you do without them? Move into town, park on the front porch, and rock your life away?"

While the majority of the crowd knew Matt was speaking the truth, not all his words met with approval. A good deal of varnish was squirmed off the wooden benches as Matt paused for breath. He circled the room, meeting eye with eye, and was surprised he was so long-winded. But he wasn't through.

"Those people are waving a lot of money under our noses," Matt went on. "And I have to tell you, at first I gave some thought to selling out, letting them move in. But then something happened that made me glad I didn't—when I went to the pasture one day and found that old black bull of mine dead. Somebody planted a bullet between his eyes."

The crowd gasped and looked at each other in disbelief. The only man whose expression didn't change was Hamp Hargrove. He kept his glare stuck on Matt.

"I figured somebody was trying to scare me into selling out," Matt said. "And that's when I got my back up. I have no proof of who shot my prize Angus bull." He matched Hargrove's challenging stare. "But I'm looking at a man I never want to see on my place again."

The crowd stirred, craning necks, following Matt's stare to the face of Hamp Hargrove.

Feeling the heat of an open challenge, Hargrove said, "I never shot nobody's damn bull."

"You told me you did." It was the gravelly voice of Amos Quill from the back of the room. Amos was a skinny sixty-year-old farmer in striped overalls and a plaid shirt. He was a friend of Hargrove's, and some were surprised Amos would expose the big man.

"Shut up, Amos!" Hargrove said.

"No, sir," Quill said. "I done shut up for too long over stuff you done, Hamp. You told me hittin' Matt's bull was the best one-handed shot you ever made with a .410 rifle."

"I'm warning you," Matt said to Hargrove, "you sure as hell better make yourself scarce around the Harper place."

Hargrove bounced to his feet. "Are you threatening me?"

Matt said, "You damn right. I don't want to see you within two miles of my place ever again."

The one-armed giant made an intimidating move toward Matt. Matt took a step to meet him.

Both men stopped in their tracks when they heard Amos yell, "Hold it right there, Hargrove!"

All eyes shifted to where they saw Amos with a twelve-gauge shotgun aimed at Hargrove's belt buckle.

"I figgered you might try something like this," Amos said to Hargrove. "I used to think we was friends, but I ain't no friend to any man who goes around killing other people's bulls. You make another move and I'll fill your belly full o' buckshot."

The crowd held its breath, expecting Hargrove to explode.

"Aaah!" Hargrove scoffed with a derisive wave of his good right hand. As he stormed toward the door, he sneered, "You're nothing but a bunch of milk bellies that'll never amount to a hog fart in a whirlwind."

Amos lowered his twelve-gauge. "I reckon that's it then," he said to Matt.

With a nod at Amos, Matt turned his attention back to the gathering. They wondered what he would do next.

"When I came home from Afghanistan," Matt said, "I couldn't wait to get married. The next thing I knew, I had a family to take care of. My daddy taught me the only thing that never changes is the land.

"When I brought my wife and daughter to the farm, I remembered how hard my dad worked to get it ready for me. What was here then has always been here, and always will be." He paused for a look around, half expecting somebody to challenge his stand. Nobody did. "I've got three-hundred-sixty acres out there I aim to keep working as long as God gives me breath."

Dude shocked the crowd by jumping out of his seat, shouting, "Damn it to hell, ain't nobody takin' my land. I'm stayin'."

A rousing cheer went up. Ethan waited for a five count for somebody else to say something. When nobody did, he pounded his gavel. "This here meetin' is over!"

Within a minute the benches were emptied. The silent meeting hall went back to being what was left of the cafeteria in the old school house.

CHAPTER EIGHT

School bells ring

The first week in August Lexie pondered why Matt didn't asked her to help work cattle, haul a stock trailer loaded with hogs to market, bale the second cutting of fescue–things like she helped him with all summer. At mealtime she tried to make conversation. Matt's mind seemed to be elsewhere. Finally, at breakfast one morning she decided to plunge ahead and broach the subject.

"I haven't seen much of you lately," she said. "You've been getting out early and working late."

"Well, there are lots of things to take care of this time of year."

"Things I can't help you with?"

"They're one-man jobs mostly."

"Uh-huh." Lexie thought he was pretty distant, as if putting her aside. She smiled any way. "I've been thinking. School will be starting in a week or so."

Matt knew it was coming, but he didn't know how to head it off. This was the moment he dreaded, almost hoping it would never come. Knowing it would. It had to. She was telling him she was leaving. He may never see her again.

"The summer seems pretty well wrapped up," Lexie said.

"If you don't need me anymore, there's no use my hanging around."

She paused, waiting for a response that didn't come. "Maybe I should just go ahead and leave now, if that's all right with you."

"That might be best," he said. "I'll be going into town tomorrow morning."

"I'll be ready."

~~~

Including a minimum of conversation, the ride from the farm to the bus station took less than a half hour.

Lexie commented that she enjoyed spending the summer on the farm. Matt said he appreciated her help.

"We need to figure up your time," he said.

"You don't owe me anything," she said. "I had free room and board all summer."

"It wasn't all free. You earned it. You're a good hand, Lexie. I want to pay you for what
you did."

"A good hand," she said. She'd hoped for somewhat more. "I never expected to be paid."

Matt drove in silence, wrestling with the reality that he didn't want her to leave. Her confession of love only complicated matters, especially since the image of Cathy was forever etched on his memory.

Cathy. Hovering in the shadowy corners of his consciousness. Peering down on his every move, his every thought. Was she smiling now, or crying? Had he really said he wouldn't marry again after she was gone? "I can't imagine being married to anyone but you," he told her. Was that a promise, or only a statement of fact? Either way, it was true at the time.

He pulled into a parking spot near the entrance to the Trailways bus station.

"Well, I guess–" he said, lifting her bag onto the sidewalk.

"Matthew."

"Yes?"

With a wistful nod, she put out her hand. "I guess this is it then, huh?"

He clasped her hand in a brief shake. "I don't know how to thank you. All summer long I've–"

"No thanks necessary," she said. "It was a fun time for me."

He peered into her eyes, felt she was sounding the depths of his soul, stripping bare his desire, straining his emotions. Something inside screamed at him, "Tell her what you want her to know!"

"I'll just take your bag," he said.

"Never mind, I can handle it."

Saying goodbye to Matthew Harper was the last thing she wanted. Meaning she never wanted to say goodbye. If she did, she was afraid she'd never see him again.

"Lexie."

"Yes, Matthew?"

"Well, goodbye then. Thanks for everything."

He climbed into the truck, shifted gears, and backed out of the parking spot. As he pulled away, the rear view mirror told him Lexie was still standing there. Holding her bag, watching him drive away.

Lexie wasn't ready to go. What she wanted was for Matt Harper to get out of that red Four-by-Four of his, and come running back and crush her in his arms.

Matt didn't want to go. In the mirror, the look on Lexie's face told him she didn't want him to go. What was he waiting for?

He skidded to a stop, flung open the door, dashed back to where Lexie was waiting, and grabbed her up in his arms.

"Dammit, Lexie, don't you know I've been trying all summer not to fall in love with you?"

"Mmmmnn," she murmured between kisses. "Me too."

THE END

NO VISIBLE MEANS

a short story

CHAPTER ONE

Hello, Tyler Fawcett

He pounded the steering wheel of his ancient blue VW Bug. "Damn! Not again"

Tyler was twenty-two years old. The Bug was old when he bought it, but it served him faithfully for four years. He vowed if it ever quit on him, he'd walk rather than replace it with another model. He scanned the area for some place to find a phone and call for help. About a quarter mile up the blacktop, he spotted a farm house. With an affectionate pat on the hood of the Bug, he started walking.

In a cornfield to his right, Tyler saw a man eyeing him from the seat of a overalls tractor. On the other side of the road, a stand of fescue waved in the breeze. He didn't wave back. What Tyler knew about farming he learned from his friend Carl. Carl earned an Ag degree at Missouri State. Drawing on Carl's wisdom, Tyler thought the fescue looked like it was ready for another cutting, and the corn was ripe for harvest.

On his way down the lane toward the house, looking for a phone, Tyler was greeted by a sleek brown-and-white collie and a black mongrel with wet noses. Their lolling red tongues and bouncing barks told him they were glad to see somebody, even somebody they never saw before.

He heard the tractor engine go silent, and saw the farmer walking his way.

Tyler strolled into the lane past the mailbox with Caleb Lindstrom's name on it. He'd bet everything he had, except the Bug, the man a dozen strides from where he waited was Caleb Lindstrom.

He was. Caleb was a big man. Not tall, but broad shouldered. His striped Big Smith overalls struggled to hide his bloated middle, and his high-topped leather brogans were dry and cracked. Caleb walked with a slight limp to the left side.

Caleb pulled up in front of Tyler and dragged a hand across his sweaty face. "You looking for somebody?" he asked with a gruff voice.

"My car quit on me back there," Tyler said. "I thought you might let me use your phone to call Triple A."

Lindstrom limped in a half circle, silently eyeing Tyler up and down and sideways, as he might check an Angus bull to decide whether it was worth what they tagged it. Caleb's instincts alerted him to be wary of anyone he didn't know. This was a clean cut young man though, except for his holey jeans and dirty sneakers.

Tyler didn't appreciate the farmer's dissecting his body, but he needed his phone.

"Phone's out," Caleb said. "Workin' on the line."

"Thanks any way. I'll just–"

"Say your car broke down?"

"Probably nothing serious. It's happened before. I don't know much about cars. If it started when I turned the key, I never had to."

"Uh-huh," Caleb grunted while he made up his mind what to do about it. "I got a jumper cable." He limped over to a black Chevy pickup, climbed in under the wheel, and started the motor. "Get in. We'll go take a look."

Tyler hopped in, and Caleb hustled the truck down the dirt lane. The dogs kept pace with the truck until it got to the blacktop where they turned back

"That your car there?" Caleb said, when he spotted the VW

parked beside the road.

"Yes, sir. That's it."

Caleb wheeled the truck around and parked it nose-to-tail with the truck motor running. He attached the cable battery-to-battery, and said, "Try it now."

Tyler tried it. The motor coughed a time or two and took hold.

Caleb removed the cable and tossed it in the truck bed. He slammed the truck's hood down, got under the wheel, and started moving out.

"I want to pay you for your help," Tyler said.

"No trouble." Caleb moved the truck onto the blacktop. "Mark it up to help your neighbor."

Tyler closed the lid on the Bug.

Caleb did a fast U-turn, headed back to the VW, and screeched to a stop beside it. "You ain't one of them citified, know-it-all college types are you, boy?" he said.

"I don't know what you mean by citified."

"If you are, you don't know your ass from third base about farming."

Tyler thought that was funny, but he didn't laugh. "You're right," he said. "I don't know much about farming."

"I got crops in the field," Caleb said. "My hired hand up and died on me last week. I could use some help." He looked at Tyler as if he thought he might need a job. "Good help's hard to come by this time o' year."

Tyler got the message. "I don't think so. I've got some stuff I need to be doing."

Caleb shot a stream of tobacco juice and watched it form a crater in the dust. He wasn't through.

"I can show you everything you need to know."

Tyler wasn't impressed. "There must be somebody around who'd–"

"Everybody else is just like me. It's a busy time. Only they got help and I haven't. All you'd have to do is keep your hands busy and your mouth shut, and you could be a heap o' help to me."

"Well, I'll tell you what–if I run into somebody who's hard up for work, I'll send him around."

Caleb spat another stream. "You pressed for time?"

"I guess not."

"Fall in behind me. We'll go have a bite to eat and a can o' beer and give it a talkin'."

Caleb didn't wait for an answer. He put his truck in motion, and checked the rearview to see if the VW was following.

It was.

Maybe it was the crippled Bug that caused Caleb to think Tyler might need a job. Maybe it was the faded, wrinkled jeans with holes in the knees, or the dirty Reeboks with the toes out. Or it could have been his long blond hair that looked like it hadn't been cut since the last eclipse. One thing Caleb knew for sure—the boy needed help with his ailing car.

That's what Caleb saw. What he didn't see was why Tyler Fawcett was putting distance between himself and his father. Caleb would one day learn the answer.

Whatever persuaded Caleb to offer him a job, Tyler figured he was desperate for help, and didn't care where it came from. It might be fun to find out what Caleb had in mind.

CHAPTER TWO

Hello, Norman Rockwell

The Lindstrom farm house could have been lifted from Norman Rockwell's book of creations. It was a two-story frame house wrapped on three sides with a veranda, and two dormers on the front. Tyler got a glimpse of a girl peering out an upstairs window. She ducked out of sight when she saw him looking at her. He wondered why.

Caleb's wife Louise was slender, wrinkled at the mouth, and her dark hair was graying at the temples. With a friendly smile, on the kitchen table Louise placed steak, mashed potatoes with cream gravy, a bowl of green beans and carrots from her garden, and a platter of fluffy fresh-baked rolls.

Tyler couldn't wait to wrap his mouth around some of that food. Never had he seen such food at home. His mother wasn't much of a cook. She spent a lot of time chasing for some charity she volunteered for, and his father practically took up residence at his bank. Mealtime, like conversation, was no big deal in the Fawcett household. When Tyler left home, he thought the neighbors probably missed him more than his parents did.

The Lindstroms had no sons. They had two daughters. The younger one, Caroline, was the one they talked about.

She rarely showed up at mealtime. Tyler guessed she was the one who peeked out the upstairs window.

The other daughter Tyler was yet to meet. Her name was Susan. Tyler didn't know any mention of Susan was against the law in the Lindstrom household. He'd soon get the word on that too.

"If you decide to stay," Louise said over lunch, "you'll run into our daughter Caroline. Our other daughter, Susan, who–"

Caleb gave her a stern look that told Tyler Susan was not to be talked about at the table or any other time.

"Well," Louise forged ahead. "Susan is married and–"

"Louise!" Caleb said.

Louise made a quick exit to the kitchen, and wiped her face with her apron on the way. Tyler thought she looked put out with her husband.

Caleb concentrated on his meat and potatoes.

Tyler settles in

Caleb was right. Tyler didn't know much about farming, and wasn't eager to find out. Tyler decided, however, his to-do list could wait while he got a brief taste of farm life. He had no idea how long it would take. He gave it a week.

At bed time, Louise showed Tyler to an upstairs room. "The bath's at the end of the hall," she announced. "Towels and soap for a shower if you want."

"Thank you."

"Breakfast comes early."

Tyler gets an earful

Tyler discovered the best way to find out about the Lindstrom family was to keep his mouth shut and his ears open.

"Well now, you know we've talked about all this stuff long enough, Louise."

It was Caleb in the kitchen one morning before breakfast.

Tyler listened from upstairs.

Louise answered. "No, we have not talked about it long enough. Liney's eighteen years old. She could just up and take off for Nashville, or any place else she wants to go, without asking anybody. You're the one who's blocking the trail, Caleb. All she wants is for you to tell her it's all right for her to go."

"It ain't all right, Louise. Liney's all we got left," Caleb protested. "Way off down there by herself with a bunch o' strangers. I hear her up there in that room—plunkin' on that guitar, singin' stuff she wrote."

"Stuff she wrote is better than some of the stuff you listen to on the radio. Let her go, Caleb. If you don't, you may regret it the rest of your life. It's what she wants to do. She needs to find out if she can do it."

Tyler listened for a couple of silent minutes.

"I can't let her go, Lou," he heard Caleb say. "I don't want nothin' bad happenin' to her like—"

"If you'd let Susan come home—"

"No! I said no, and 'at's all there is to and about it."

CHAPTER THREE

Tyler meets Liney

The eighth day of his learning mission, Tyler was replacing some damaged boards on the front porch. He wiped his sweaty brow, and went for a drink of water from the pump outside the kitchen door. He emptied the dipper, and hung it on the nail he took it from. He went back to work, and noticed an attractive young girl half a dozen steps away, staring at him.

"I'm Liney," she said. Fluffy red hair swept her shoulders. Her green eyes appeared anxious to get something said. With an uneasy smile, she said, "I wasn't sure you'd want to talk to me."

Tyler nodded. "I'm Tyler."

"Mama told me."

"I think I knew who you were," he said.

"How would you know that?"

"I heard your mom and dad talking."

"About me?" she asked.

"About you. Something about your going to Nashville."

"Oh, yeah, Nashville," she said. "They talk about that a lot."

"You want to go there?"

"Sometime—maybe." She looked away, then back at him. "You got a minute?"

He tossed his hammer on the porch. "Should we be talking?"

"It's all right," she assured him. "They've gone off some place. No telling when they'll be back."

She pinned him with a look that rubbed his mind with questions.

"We're not gonna do anything, are we?" she said.

"No." He was surprised she asked.

"You want to know about Susan?"

"Susan?"

"My sister. Daddy won't let her come home."

"If you want to tell me," Tyler said.

"I do. What happened to Susan is why daddy won't let me drive, have company, or see boys. He says all the boys want is to get in my pants."

Tyler couldn't believe she was so candid. He cast her a sharp look.

"You know what that means, don't you?" she said.

He replied, "I know."

"That's what happened to Susan. She got knocked up. Orval Pitts did it. Daddy's afraid that would happen to me."

"Where's Susan now?"

"Tulsa. Daddy doesn't know I know that. Susan wants to bring her baby home, but he won't let her. She used to write letters asking if she could. I read them on the way back from the mailbox. When I got to the house, daddy grabbed the letters and threw them in the fireplace. But I know where she lives. Someday I'll go there."

"How does your mom feel about the baby?"

"She'd let Susan bring him home in a minute. Daddy wouldn't stand for it, though."

"What about you, Caroline? How do you feel about it?"

"You called me Caroline."

"That's your name, isn't it?"

"Yeah, but nobody remembers it. When I was little I couldn't say Caroline. I called myself Liney."

"I like Caroline better. It's a pretty name."

"You really think so?" she asked with a smile.

"A pretty name for a pretty girl."

"Don't be nice to me."

"You are a pretty girl," he said.

"I hope you don't let my daddy hear you say that."

"Why not?"

"He's afraid I'd get pregnant like Susan. He'd chase you off this place. I'm surprised he let me out of his sight this time with you here."

Caroline heard the truck wheeling down the lane. "Here they come," she said. "I have to go." She took off running, and disappeared through the kitchen door.

The pickup turned into the driveway and parked by the tool shed. Caleb was at the wheel, Louise beside him.

Tyler drew another dipper of water.

A surprise guest

Sometime in the night, Tyler felt somebody snuggling next to him in bed. Caroline? Who else would it be?

"Caroline?" he whispered.

"Hold me, Tyler," she answered with half her voice. "Please, just hold me."

What could he do? He held her.

CHAPTER FOUR

A trip to town

"**L**ots o' folks in town today," Caleb said, heading the pickup toward the Farm Club around the corner.

"More than usual?" Tyler asked.

"Oh, yeah. It's the third."

"Uh-huh." Tyler didn't know what the third was, but he grunted as if everybody was supposed to know. He didn't want Caleb to think he was the only one in the county who didn't.

"Third of the month," Caleb explained. "All the old folks get their Social Security checks in the mail. They want to feel that check in their hands, like they're afraid Uncle Sam'll go broke 'fore they get it cashed. The women look for bargains in the shops, and get their hair fixed. Men pay the monthly bills, and get a shave and haircut."

"Sounds like a busy day."

"Yeah. Most of 'em will be back Wednesday for Seniors Day. Ten percent off at most stores."

"You join the crowd?" Tyler asked.

"It'll be a while yet."

"How long?"

"Oh, right at twelve year," Caleb said. "What are you—

maybe half as old as me?"

"Maybe," Tyler said.

Inside the farm club, John Barlow greeted them from behind the cash register. "Big howdy to you.. He winked at Tyler, and said, "Who's that hillbilly you're draggin' behind?"

"You talkin' to him or me?" Caleb asked.

"You know the answer to that, Caleb," Whit Perkins put in. Whit was about half the size of Caleb, and twice his age. "You're the only hillbilly we've seen around here since Carter left the White House."

"Jimmy wasn't no hillbilly," Henry Poor protested.

"I know it," Perkins conceded. "But he's the closest we come to it."

"Look who's talkin' about hillbillies," Caleb said to Perkins. "Everybody knows your daddy found you in a gunny sack dumped out on the road." That brought a round of guffaws.

"This is my new hand," Caleb announced, nodding at Tyler. "His name's Tyler."

"Is that a first name or last?" John wanted to know.

Caleb nodded at Tyler. "Well, I believe it is, yeah."

"First," Tyler said with a grin. "My name's Tyler Fawcett."

"Pretty fancy moniker for a country boy," Poor put in.

"Yeah," Caleb quipped. "You take what they give you any more. But he's one hell of a farm hand, I'll tell you that right now."

"How long you been farmin'?" Barlow asked Tyler.

"This week and one more'll be two." That brought more laughs, and pats on Tyler's back.

"Why, Caleb," John said, "what do you make of that prisoner who got away?"

"You mean the one they're talkin' about on the radio?"

"He better not show up around here," Whit said. "Old Shorty Long will be on his ass like a dog on a bone."

"That's about half right," Caleb said. "I don't know which half."

"How Shorty ever got to be deputy sheriff I ain't figgered out yet," John said.

"Musta been the only one in the county that wasn't

workn'," was Whit's response.

"How do you want to pay for that load of feed you're hauling out of my store?" Barlow said to Caleb.

"Aw, John, you know Caleb," Perkins put in. "He don't pay for nothin'. Got no money, and his credit wouldn't buy a ticket to a turkey fry."

Henry Poor was a skinny sixty-eight-year-old retiree from the Post Office. Henry kept quiet till his patience wore down to the nub. He was jolted into the gabfest by an uncontrolled urge. "Caleb's credit must be pretty damn good," he chuckled. "About everybody in the county's got some of it."

"Bunch o' crazies in here today, boy," Caleb said to Tyler. "We better be gettin' outa here 'fore some of it rubs off."

On the way back to the farm, Caleb drove and Tyler asked questions.

"You been farming all your life?" Tyler said.

"Yeah, pretty much. It's 'bout all I know how to do," Caleb said. "I helped my daddy till I growed big enough to go to the army. Me and my three brothers."

"Your brothers were in the army?"

"Naw, they just growed and scattered. I was the only one went to the army."

"Where'd you serve?"

"In the army? Afghan."

"That where you got that bum leg?"

Caleb eyed him with a strong stare. "No. I got into it with some old boy 'at ask too damn many questions. Left me with a limp"

Tyler studied his face a moment. He decided Caleb was joshing him, and burst out laughing.

Caleb grinned. "Yeah, it was Afghan," he said. "Them a-rabs could drop a mortar shell in your hip pocket. One of 'em landed about twelve foot from where I was. It blowed a chunk out of my leg. The medics tried to fix it and didn't know how. All I got out of it was what you see when I walk."

"Where are your brothers now?"

Caleb didn't answer right away. He took a deep breath, and spent a moment thinking about it. "Felix, he was the oldest," he said. "He was a high-wire-lineman for the power comp'ny. He died about eight year ago. Come up against a live wire.

"My second brother Chauncey, he was–Chauncey was a gospel preacher. Good a man as you'd ever meet. They was talk about him and some woman that didn't belong to him. Chauncey denied it. They found 'im face down one Sunday mornin' in the church baptistry. Ole Chaunce was dead." Caleb didn.t talk for a while. "The woman, she shot herself the next day."

Caleb said nothing for a mile or two. "It ain't easy talkin' about this, boy. I don't tell it to many folks. I don't know why I'm tellin' you, but– "Bout everybody loved Chauncey. Maybe somebody didn't."

Tyler figured he'd asked enough questions.

Caleb shook his head, like Tyler hadn't heard it all. "My daddy come here seventy-seven year ago. No more'n fifty-sixty people in Red Rock then. Now look at 'em. Must be three-four hunnerd, swarmin' all over the place–like flies on a dead squirrel.

"I was born on 'at farm," Caleb said. "All four of us boys was born right there on 'at place." He watched the road, and concentrated on his driving, thinking about what he wanted to say next. "I went to carpenterin' for a while. Bum leg held me back some. I give it up and come back to the farm. My daddy died after coupla years. I bought the place from mama. Ten months later she died."

"What about the other brother?" Tyler said.

"Marshall? Got a feed store in Stockton."

"You buy feed from him?"

Caleb screwed his mouth up as if Marshall was a distasteful subject he'd rather not talk about, but he did. "Marshall and me–we don't talk much. Marshall don't–we don't see eye-to-eye on some of the stuff I do. Mainly about my kids."

"How's that?"

"He never had any. Marshall–he–he never got married. Had no kids. Tries to tell me how to do with mine."

He turned off the blacktop into the lane toward the house, and changed the subject. "How long you say you been farmin'?" he asked Tyler with a grin.

"Long as I've been here on your place," Tyler answered. "You know how long that is."

"You stay around here long enough, you might find out which end o' the hog to feed."

Tyler figured the talking was over. But one more question kept pushing itself to the front. It had to be asked, so he asked it. "You mind if I ask about Susan?"

"Who?"

"Susan, your daughter."

"I got no daughter named Susan," was Caleb's curt reply.

"Shutting her out of your life won't solve anything," Tyler said.

Caleb squinted at him the way he'd look at the blazing sun. "I mind the day you showed up here," he said. "I told you then, and I'm tellin' you one more time—keep your hands busy and your mouth shut, and you can be a heap o' help to me." He slid out of the truck and limped toward a tractor parked by the tool shed. Over a shoulder, he tossed his parting words. "That's none o' your damn business, boy. Don't ever let me hear you bring it up again."

CHAPTER FIVE

Stand by for news!

Tyler woke up to the staccato voice of Paul Harvey on the radio.

Six mornings a week Caleb took time from the field to come in for breakfast and listen to the penetrating delivery of America's finest. With a hot cup of black coffee, he pulled up a chair beside the radio on the kitchen cabinet, and devoted his attention to the words and wisdom of Paul Harvey.

Louise stayed busy frying sausage and eggs, and baking buttermilk biscuits. She was as devoted to Rush Limbaugh as Caleb was to Paul Harvey. Caleb referred to Limbaugh as 'the fat boy'. Louise called him "the champion of the common man." She bought Rush's books, subscribed to his newsletter, and listened to him at noon five times a week.

Tyler listened from upstairs with little interest until he heard Harvey's signature sign off. "Paul Harvey. Good day!"

The station announcer followed with local news. Tyler heard him say, "...his name is Bruce Gladwyn time... six feet tall... wanted for rape and robbery. Armed and dangerous, Bruce Gladwyn was last seen headed toward the Red Rock community. Do not talk to this man. If you see him, call the sheriff right away...."

When Tyler came down for breakfast, Caleb was gone. "Caleb have breakfast?" he asked Louise.

She poured him a cup of coffee. "Yeah. He shot out of here like a rocket. I don't know what set him off." She placed on the table in front of him a plate of sausage, two fried eggs, and fluffy biscuits right out of the oven.

"You better eat your breakfast before it gets cold," Louise admonished.

Tyler took the last bite, and wiped his mouth with a cloth napkin. "I've got some feed to unload," he said, swallowing the last drop of coffee on his way out. "I'll probably run into him out there."

"If he's not in the field already," Louise said. "I heard him say something about fescue."

Don't move or I'll kill you

Tyler lifted an 80-pound bag of calf supplement off the truck and hauled it into the barn.

"Hold it right there, boy."

Tyler dropped the bag of feed and took a look around. Through a hole in the barn wall he saw a twelve gauge shotgun pointed at

his chest.

"Who's that?" Tyler said. He knew who it was. They said the escapee was headed this way, but that voice belonged to Caleb Lindstrom. "Caleb?"

"I said hold it, boy."

The gun disappeared. Seconds later Caleb kicked open the barn door, holding the gun on Tyler.

The look on his face told Tyler he didn't like what he was looking at.

"You come around here," Caleb said with fire in his eye, "sniffin' and lyin' and carryin' on–"

"What are you talking about?"

"Shut up and listen!" Caleb spat a stream of tobacco juice. "I don't want to kill you, boy, but I will if I have to."

"Now wait a minute, Caleb. What in–"

"They said that feller was headed this a-way. That jailbird that got away. Looks to me like you're the one they was talkin' about."

Caleb was sure he nailed the culprit, and wasn't about to let him get away. He moved close enough to nudge Tyler's belt buckle with the muzzle of the shotgun.

"You been a lot help to me, boy, and I appreciate it. But it 'pears to me you're one o' them lowdown, no-good snuggers I went to war to save you from. Now I'm gonna call the sheriff, like they said to, and let him know I got you. Don't want to, like I told you, but if you move, I'll kill you."

"Caleb!" It was Louise calling on her way to the barn. A moment later she appeared in the barn door. "Caleb, when are you ever gonna fix that– Caleb Lindstrom! What in tarnation are you doing with that gun pointed at Tyler?"

"It's him, Louise. Stand away from him."

Tyler said, "Louise, I–"

"Shut up, boy," Caleb ordered. "They said don't talk to him."

"Him who?" Louise wanted to know.

"That jailbird that got away," Caleb said. "They said he was headed this a-way.

That's him."

"That's Tyler, Caleb, and he's no more a jailbird than I am. Now put that gun down and get back to work."

"Go call the sheriff, Louise," Caleb said. "We gotta let him know."

Louise said, "I'm not going to call any sheriff. Besides that, the phone's still out."

"Take the truck to town," Caleb said. "Tell Shorty to get out here as fast as he can. I can't hold a gun on this jailbird all day."

"I'm not driving to town," Louise declared. "I've got prize beets for the county fair cooking on my stove. If you want somebody to go to town, you go, or send Liney. I'm not going."

"Liney's not sposed to drive and you know it," Caleb protested.

"Liney can drive as well as anybody in this family if you'd

let her, and you know that."

They heard the roar of the truck's motor barreling past. It was Liney at the wheel, pushing that truck for all it was worth. She smiled, waved, and kept moving.

She didn't hear her daddy yell, "Liney, you come back here!"

CHAPTER SIX

Liney's escape

For four years, Liney wished she could escape the farm long enough to head for Tulsa where Susan was. Her mama refused to go tell the sheriff her daddy had that gun pointed at Tyler, and there was nobody else he could send. To herself, Liney shouted, "Now! This is the time!"

Caleb never left the keys in his truck. Never. Except this time, he did. Liney didn't give it a thought. Whatever she did, she did by instinct. Not for a moment did she hesitate. She hopped in that truck, turned that key, and felt the winds of freedom lifting her from the shackles of bondage.

Tulsa! Susan! Here I come.

Her first stop was the sheriff's office above Coolie Bledsoe's drugstore. She knew her daddy had that gun pointed at the wrong man. She just knew Tyler wouldn't do what they said that man did.

She shook Shorty awake and told him, "You better get up and head for the farm and take care of what's going on out there."

Shorty yawned, and rubbed the sleep from his eyes. He never asked what trouble Liney was talking about. "I'll be out there quick as I can," he mumbled, still half asleep.

Liney knew about Shorty Long's lackadaisical bent toward sheriffing–it could be a week from Tuesday before he'd get around to it.

Liney didn't waste time waiting for Shorty to fumble his way out of the doldrums. Once clear of Red Rock, she aimed the nose of her daddy's black truck toward Tulsa, and stepped on the gas.

Susan's letters told Liney where she lived in Tulsa. Maple Street, 2928. With the help of a policeman's directions, she turned right at the next corner, left two blocks over, and there it was. A small house, freshly painted white, in the middle of a neatly kept grass-covered yard.

Liney sat for a moment in the driveway. Apprehensive, she wondered how Susan would receive her. Would she even be glad she came? Her family rejected her, after all. No. Not her family. Her father was the one who turned her away. What if Susan no longer cared whether she came?

Liney had to know. She had to rap on that door–ring that bell. Whatever it took. She had to find out. She took a deep breath, and threw back her head. She hopped out of that truck, marched up to that door and gave it a knuckle-cracking rap.

There was no answer. Almost, Liney turned away. No. No! She came this far. She had to go the rest of the way.

The front door eased open. In it stood her sister Susan.

"What is it you–Liney? Liney!" Half crying, half laughing, Susan couldn't wait to hug her little sister. "Oh, how I have longed for this day," she cried.

"Me too," Liney said, crying happy tears.

"Look at me," Susan said. "Had I known you were coming– Please, come in. Would you like some coffee, ice tea? How about some lemonade?"

Liney said, "No, thank you, sister."

Susan moved some toys off the sofa. "Please sit down, Liney. Tell me, tell me, tell me about the folks. Are they well?"

"Oh, yes, they're well. Daddy works all time in the fields, of course. Mama– You know mama. She always has something cooking."

Susan laughed. "Literally!" she said.

"Right now she's working on a pot full of beets for the county fair." They laughed and cried and hugged some more.

"I can't begin to tell you how I have wanted to come home and bring the boys," Susan said.

"The boys?"

"Yes! We have two now. They're napping. Jake is nearly three, and Jack will be one next month."

"Oh my goodness!" Liney said. "Has it been that long?"

"Yes, it has been that long, and it seems a lot longer. I thought I'd never see you again."

"I know. So did I." Liney took a long look at her sister. "When there's time, I'll tell you how I got here today."

"What do you mean—when there's time?"

"Susan, I—I want you to come home with me."

"Home? Home with you? Liney?" She almost broke down on the words.

"Yes. I have to get back. They don't know I'm here. Probably worried sick about me.

Susan, mama wants you to come. She wants you to come home."

"I—I don't know. Orval and the boys—I had no idea—"

"Is Orval at work?" Liney asked.

"At the tire store, yes."

"Could you call him?" Liney said. "I'll call for you if you want me to."

"Oh, no, I—I'll call him, it's just— And the boys. Dad has never seen them. What about my boys?"

"Once he sees those boys, he'll never let 'em go."

The long wait

"Where do you reckon she is?" Caleb said.

It was well past dark at the farm. They didn't know how long ago Liney left, and they had no idea when she'd be back. All they knew was, it was late, and Liney wasn't home.

Shorty Long finally made it to the farm at mid-afternoon. He asked Caleb, "You mind if I talk to the suspect?"

Caleb's arms were stiff from holding the gun on Tyler. "No, I reckon not," he said, surprised Shorty asked, since that was why the deputy was there.

Tyler was standing in front of Shorty, looking him in the eye. He wondered why Shorty took so long to get there, and what he was going to do since he did.

"Did you do it, boy?" Shorty asked.

Tyler was numb from standing at parade rest for the hours Caleb had the gun on him. His eyes were bleary till he could hardly see. The smartest thing he heard from Shorty Long was, "Mr. Lindstrom, you think it'd be all right if you put that gun down?"

"Well," Caleb said, "ain't you gonna take 'im in or nothin'?"

"I don't think he'll be goin' any place, will you, boy?"

"No, sir, I won't. Could I sit down? I've been standing up all day."

Shorty said, 'Mr. Lindstrom, could you bring Mr.–What's your name, boy?"

"Fawcett, Tyler Fawcett."

"Mr. Lindstrom, would you bring somethin' for Mr.–was it Fawcett?–to set down on?"

Caleb looked puzzled, but the sheriff was in charge. He figured he ought to do what Shorty said. He leaned the twelve gauge against a tree stump, and brought a milk stool for Tyler to sit on.

Tyler said, "Sheriff, what am I doing here anyway?"

"Well–" Shorty shook his head. He really didn't have the answer—"Oh!" He shook his head as though struck by an earth shattering recollection.. "I shoulda thought of this before." He cleared his throat, coughed a time or two. "Well, you know–I–I'm plum sorry. I might oughta told you this while ago, but–you know what? I got a call from the State Patrol just as I was leavin'– Said they caught that old boy. Some place out around Chickasha. Ain't that sumpin'?"

Stunned, Caleb said, "You mean this boy ain't guilty of nothin'?"

"Well, no. Like I told you, they caught that guy out west."

Shorty was relieved of the responsibility of figuring out

what to do with Tyler. He climbed in his old green pickup with the rusty fenders, and took off at high speed. His screaming siren announced to the world that Shorty Long was movin' on!

It wasn't too late for a nap.

Three awe-struck people stared at each other. When they recovered from the shock of Shorty's abrupt departure, Louise said to Caleb, "Well, when are you going to say it?"

"Say what?"

"That you were wrong."

Caleb took a sly look at Tyler. "You mean—?"

"Yes," Louise answered firmly.

Caleb was slow about saying it, but he said it. "I—I reckon I was wrong, boy. I'm plum sorry."

Tyler didn't want to say what he wanted to say. It was over. Let it pass. His response to Caleb's reluctant apology was a silent nod.

Susan comes home

Since noon Caleb and Louise expected Liney to be back at any moment. They didn't know where she went, because she didn't want them to know. Had she told them, the keys wouldn't have been in the truck, and her escape would have been foiled.

"Louise, where you reckon she is?" Caleb said.

"I don't know, Caleb," she replied. She didn't want him to know how concerned she was that Liney was still gone.

"You don't sound too worried about it," He complained

"Liney's a big girl now. She's a good driver," Louise said. "Wherever she is, she'll find her way home."

"What if she had a wreck?" He gave his head a dubious shake. "What if she decided to—"

"To what?"

"She wouldn't just take off to— Some place like—without tellin' us. Would she?"

"You mean some place like Nashville, Caleb?"

"Never know. Bad as she wants to go. Maybe she—" He

checked the front window again. This time he saw car lights beaming up the lane. "Louise, she's here!"

All right," she said. "Let's go sit in the living room, like it's nothing unusual. Just be glad she's back. Don't act like you're worried or—"

They heard a car door slam. And voices. Voices? Whose voices?

A knock at the door. What in the world? Who would be coming at this hour?

The door flew open. Two small boys ran to their grandfather, and climbed onto his lap.

Caleb was beside himself. He had no idea what he was supposed to do.

Liney stepped into the room. "Mom, Dad," she said. "These are your grandsons, Jake and Jack."

"And, ladies and gentlemen," Liney said, "may I present their mother, and our beautiful sister and daughter—Susan!"

Caleb stood up. The boys slid off his lap.

Caroline moved aside, and Susan stepped into the room and grabbed her mother. They hugged, and cried, and laughed.

Susan smiled at her dad, and rushed to him. Caleb turned away without a smile or a word. He hurried out the door into the night.

Tyler observed the scene, but said nothing. When Caleb took off, Tyler followed. "Caleb," he called.

Caleb didn't answer. He disappeared into the darkness.

Tyler sank onto an oak bench. It might be a long night, but Tyler would be waiting. Caleb had to show up sometime.

He did.

The two men met. Tyler moved over to make room for Caleb to sit beside him. Caleb hesitated. Neither spoke for several minutes. It was Tyler who decided somebody should say something. "We need to talk," he said.

Reluctantly, Caleb sat down on the bench beside him.

"I heard some place," Tyler said, "love is stronger than hate. I think you've been living on hate and self-pity long enough, Caleb. You love Susan, and you will love her kids. Give them time to love you. Come out of yourself and let it happen.

"I lived with a man for twenty-two years whose life was dedicated to the bank he built from the ground up. He thought I should love it as much as he did. He wanted me to be a banker. I wanted to be a baseball player. I know my father didn't hate me, but I never heard him say he loved me."

"You love your daughters, Caleb. You don't know how to let it show. When was the last time you took them with you any place—told them you loved them?"

"Well, now I—"

"You need to tell Caroline it's all right for her to go to Nashville."

"No. You're askin' too much. I can't—"

Tyler wasn't a fixture on that farm, so he could say whatever he felt. "You're wrong, Caleb. You're dead wrong. You're robbing Caroline of the one thing she wants in life. Let her find out for herself if she's good or bad with music. That's not for to you to decide."

Caleb studied the toes of his shoes. "Maybe you're right."

"You know I'm right."

Caleb raised his head. "How come you're so damn smart?"

"I had a father who never told me he loved me," Tyler said. "I had a mother who was never home. I had no chance to find out what it was like to love someone, or to be loved by someone.

"I haven't been around here long, but long enough to see the love your family has for you, if you'd let them. Give them room, Caleb. Move over and give them room to love you." He paused, took a deep breath. "And by the way, Caleb, when I leave here—and I will be leaving here—I want Caroline to come with me."

Caleb was shocked. "Liney? You want Liney to—to go with you—when you leave? Where—where? "

"Yes, sir. Wherever she wants to go. I haven't asked her yet, but—"

"No! You'll never take Liney. You won't be takin' her away from me."

"She's eighteen now, Caleb. She can go anywhere, and do whatever she wants."

"She won't go–she won't go with you. Her mama– What about Louise? Her mama would–would– She'd never let her go. Louise never would–"

"Caroline can go without your approval, but she doesn't want it that way."

"Liney. Going away. I–I–I can't– She won't go. I know she won't."

"Caleb, you've been swimming around in a pool of hate and self-pity for so long, you haven't considered the feelings of anybody else, and what they want."

Caleb's head stayed down for a long moment. "You mad at me?" he asked, his voice hardly above a whisper. "Tyler?"

"What?"

"Are you mad at me?"

"Yes," Tyler replied. "I'm mad at you, mad at my parents, mad at myself for being mad at you." He paused for breath. "You're a good man, Caleb. I don't want to see you spend the rest of your life being sorry you didn't put in more time with your kids, finding out what they want, helping them get it done." He placed a hand on the shoulder of the repentant father. "Now would be a good time to start."

Caleb held his head in his hands. He wasn't ready to give up, but he knew Tyler was right. To himself, he wondered why he had to be reminded by this upstart, broken-down-Bug driver of things he forgot. Had he been a more caring father, things would be different. Maybe Susan wouldn't have got in trouble. He'd be closer to her and. And her boys. What about Susan's boys? His grandsons. They were all he had.

It may take some time, but– Louise too. He needed to get closer to Louise.

"All right," he said to Tyler." He swept his brow with a humble hand. "You lead the way."

"No, sir. You go first."

THE END

RUN AWAY FAST

a novel

CHAPTER ONE

Nashville: Late afternoon

Jodi Parker couldn't believe all she had to do to set foot on the street of Nashville was step off that bus. For most of her twenty-three years she dreamed of this day. This moment. This place! She just arrived in the music capital of the world! Happy as Dorothy in the Land of Oz.

"Hep ye with yer bags, missy?"

He was a slender, elderly black man with a broad grin and a taxi driver's boxy hat. He picked up her bags and guitar case and placed them in the back seat of his 1974 Chevy. He climbed in, opened the passenger side door. Jodi slid onto the seat beside him. She was about to get a first-hand look at every country singer's wildest dream–Nashville, Tennessee! Home of the world famous Grand–Ole–Opry.

The driver settled under the wheel, and shifted gears. "Reckon I'd oughta know where we're goin', missy?"

She gave him the address etched on her brain–Cal Slater's publishing company on Sixteenth Avenue South. Like a NASA launching pad, this was to be the beginning of a historic era in the life of Jodi Parker, singer/songwriter whose dream was to set the music mecca on fire with her words and music.

"Slater Publishing Company," she said with pride.

"Yes'm, I know." He eased the cab away from the curb.

And so began Alice's journey through the neon-lit streets of Wonderland. Her eyes agog, Jodi's heart beat so fast she thought it might pop out of her blue denim shirt. Her toes curled with anticipation in her black Justin boots as she tried to convince herself she really was riding around in the same world where great country stars such as Jim Reeves, Red Foley, Patsy Cline, Hank Williams, and Roy Acuff once reigned as the royalty of country music.

She marveled at the sight of Ryman Auditorium, the old church, for more than thirty years the home of the Opry. WSM Radio beamed the famous Nashville sound to every town, city, village, farm, and mansion across the United States, and to countries beyond. What a thrill it was to be *here*–the heartbeat of country music heard around the world!

Baker's Bluff, Kansas, seemed a million miles away. And, she reflected, if it hadn't been for

Lucas Malone, she might still be there.

Escape to freedom

Lucas couldn't wait to get out of Texas. He pushed his red Ford pickup past the rocky red canyons and thirsty brown plains north of Borger. Up across the Oklahoma panhandle he sped, and into southwest Kansas. He had nothing against Texas. He was born there, and grew up, around San Saba. In fact, since George Benton gave him a job at Phillips Petroleum after he got out of Huntsville, Lucas was happy as a sniffing hound at a rabbit hole. But, the past four months he spent nights and weekends on a project for the company and was ready for some R&R.

There was Hugh Landry, too. Hugh was a Baylor buddy who kept bugging him to hustle up to Chicago for a visit with him and his wife. Hugh was married to Jennifer Coan, reason enough for a former star wide receiver for the Baylor Bears to pay old Hugh a visit. Lucas decided now was the right time to hustle off up to Chicago. He'd never been there, but he figured a country boy ought to scope it out at least once before he cooled. He laid a heavy boot on the accelerator, headed north on the endless ribbon of concrete stretching out before him. The murky sky threatened rain. Gray telephone poles, silent as Kawliga guarding the cigar store, marched in single file on both sides of the road.

At Pratt, he grabbed a burger and a Coke at a Burger King and took off up Highway 54 toward Wichita. Wolfing down the sandwich and the Coke as he drove, he came close to running up the tail pipe of a slow-moving black Lincoln. He didn't mind that the Lincoln was in no hurry since nobody was holding a clock on him.

Cruising along, Lucas was shocked to see a fluffy little black and white dog dash onto the road, barking and nipping at the wheels of the Lincoln. A second later the dog tumbled into the roadside ditch.

The Lincoln sped away out of sight.

Lucas skidded his truck onto the shoulder and braked to a stop. He bolted out of the truck and, with a couple of long strides, he knelt on the grass beside the whimpering pup. The dog didn't move, eyes glazed and pleading. After a moment the whimpering stopped. The little dog was dead.

"Freckles!"

From somewhere behind him, Lucas heard the frantic cry. A boy of about seven dropped to his knees beside the lifeless dog. He grabbed his little friend up in his arms. "Freckles!" he cried again. Tears streaked his sunburned cheeks as he stroked the furry, blood-stained head.

"I hope you know I didn't do this," Lucas said.

"He wouldn't listen to me," the lad sobbed. "I told him he was gonna get hurt if he didn't stop chasing cars, but he just wouldn't listen."

Lucas scratched the dog's ears. "I bet old Freckles was some kind of good buddy."

The boy gave him a sorrowful nod.

"What's your name, son?"

"Isaac."

Lucas put out his right hand, and the boy placed his in it.

"My name's Lucas. I'm real sorry about old Freckles. I had a dog like him once, and I know what it's like to lose a friend."

A dejected smile struggled across Isaac's face. "That's okay, Lucas,"

Lucas rumpled the boy's blond hair.

Isaac cradled his little friend in his arms and slumped away toward the farmhouse beside the road.

Lucas climbed into his truck and watched in the rearview mirror until Isaac disappeared around the corner of the farmhouse. Across his mind flashed the image of a young friend who, a year ago, swerved his Jeep to avoid running over a dog that was crossing the street in front of him. The Jeep overcorrected and flipped off the street into a tree. His friend was crushed inside. Four hours later, Lucas held him in his arms when he died.

It was a slow drive along Highway 54. The sadness Lucas felt for the boy was deepened by clouds looking like they could dump a downpour on the dry Kansas prairie at any moment. He barely flipped on his headlights when rain began splattering his windshield. Between swipes of the wipers, he spotted a sign that told him Baker's Bluff was ten miles up the road. Beside the sign sat a girl on a black suitcase, her legs crossed and a thumb in the air.

Her name was Jodi Parker.

Lucas hit the brake and pulled over. All he saw under her pulled-down blue denim hat was her chin. As casually as if she'd bet money he'd stop, he did.

Jodi pushed her hat back and nodded.

Lucas rolled down the passenger side window. "Want a lift?"

"Where to?"

"Baker's Bluff."

She waved him off and peered up through the drizzle. "No thanks. If you've got no better place to go than Baker's Bluff, keep on moving."

Lucas gave his head a shake. He couldn't believe she'd pass up a chance to get out of the rain.

"Okay, lady," he said, shifting into gear. "It's your call."

He hadn't moved forward more than fifty feet when he

heard a shrill whistle behind him. He checked the rearview for a look. Two fingers of her right hand were stuck in the corners of her mouth. With her left hand she was waving him back. He gave it a whatever shrug, threw the truck into reverse, and scooted back to where she was still perched on that suitcase. There she sat in black western boots, blue jeans, open-collared blue cotton shirt and blue denim jacket soaking wet.

"Have they still got a bus station there?" she said.

"Where?"

"Baker's Bluff."

"I don't know. I've never been there."

"You said you were going to Baker's Bluff."

"Yeah. The sign said it's the next town up the road."

She grabbed her bag and hoisted it into the back of the truck beside his, and pulled the tarp up to cover them against the rain.

Lucas pushed the door open and Jodi hopped in. Only then did he see the black guitar case almost as big as the girl. She stood it on the floor between her feet.

"Been waiting long?" Lucas said.

She closed the door. "When you're getting rained on it feels like forever."

Lucas moved the pickup onto the blacktop. "You look like a baby chick that just popped out of the shell."

"I feel like it too."

He drove, and Jodi fussed with her mop of chestnut hair.

"Are you a musician?" he asked.

"Writer. And I sing some."

He wondered, but didn't ask, why she was parked out there on that suitcase in the middle of nowhere on a rainy Friday afternoon. If she wanted him to know why, he figured she'd tell him.

She was older than Lucas first thought. Early twenties, he guessed, using his own twenty-nine as a gauge. She wore no makeup. Her lips slightly parted as if about to say something, exposing even white teeth, a gap between the two front ones on top.

"What do you think?" she said.

"About what?"

"The way you're checking me over, I thought you might be about ready to pin a price tag on me."

"Well, you know, I was just thinking, if a guy had to run across a lady in distress, way out here all by herself in the middle of Kansas on a rainy day, you're the kind of lady I'd like to run into."

She gave him a steady look and said nothing. He couldn't tell whether she liked what she heard, or if she couldn't have cared less one way or the other.

She wrinkled her nose. "What do you haul in this truck?"

"Horse shit."

"Smells like it."

"A friend of mine raises strawberries. He says horse shit is the best fertilizer there is for strawberries. I haul the horse shit, and he gives me the berries. Have you got something against horses?"

"Horse shit," she said. "That doesn't say much for the strawberries,"

Lucas grinned.

"You're not from around here?" Jodi said.

"Nope. Borger, Texas."

Lucas was proud to say he was from Borger. When you're walking around with "ex-con" plastered on your forehead like the scarlet letter, and a man like George Benton offers you the world with no strings attached, you take it and call it good.

"Why are you going to Baker's Bluff?" she said.

"Like I said, it's the next town up the road. I got some time off and decided to head north till I find a reason to stop."

"You sure as hell won't find it in Baker's Bluff."

"Is that so?"

"I'm telling you what God loves. It was the pits when I left there nine years ago after my mama died. I hoped I'd never see it again."

"Do you still have family there?"

"No. Nobody but Tess Harmon, if she's still there. We were best friends in school." She fell silent, as if reflecting on the friendship.

"Are you all right?" Lucas said.

She looked at him with sad eyes. "I just ran away from that son of a bitch my mama was married to."

"Uh-huh."

The search for Jodi

A thick-waisted man with a heavy growth of graying beard leaned on the doorbell of the modest brown bungalow in south Phoenix. His name was John Barquist. In army surplus dungarees, a dingy white T-shirt, and a red Suns ball cap, he was looking for Jodi Parker. Numerous times had he threatened to kill her if she left, and now she had.

Wild eyed, Barquist paced the front stoop, blowing puffs of cigarette smoke. Restless as a desert rattler, he silently demanded that someone open the door. But not just anyone. The door belonged to Gloria Sims, Jodi's best friend. If anybody knew where Jodi was, Gloria would know. He flipped the cigarette butt into a bed of zinnias, and pushed the bell again. Still no answer. In a rage, he pounded the door with a heavy fist. The door eased open. In it stood a blond young woman in a pink chenille bathrobe with the sash drawn tight around her waist.

She was shocked to see John Barquist glaring down at her.

"John!"

"Hello, Gloria."

She knew why he was there. Looking for Jodi. John was the last man on earth Jodi would want to know where she was. Gloria's eyes popped wide, her face contorted, struggling to push the door closed. Barquist threw his bulk against it, forced his way in, and knocked her to the floor.

"Where's Jodi?" he raged.

"I don't know, John."

"The hell you don't!" He grabbed her shoulders, dragged her to her feet, and drew back a fist to strike her again. "Don't you lie to me, Gloria. She's gone, and she took that kid with her some place. You might as well tell me where, or I'll beat it out of you."

Gloria wasn't ready to die, but neither was she about to tell Barquist Jodi was on her way to Nashville—and her baby son was asleep in the next room.

He ripped off Gloria's robe and flung it aside. Leering at her naked body, he threw her onto the couch and piled on top of her. With clumsy hands he grabbed her throat, leaving ugly red marks on her skin.

"No, John, please!"

His fumbling fingers tightened around her neck. "Where's Jodi, Gloria?"

Welcome to Baker's Bluff, Kansas!

The yellow letters on a blue background greeted Lucas at the city limits.

"I need some gas," he said to Jodi on the seat beside him. "I'll see if I can find a gas station."

Jodi shrugged. "Okay."

He eased the truck off the blacktop, across a narrow bridge that warned against loads of more than ten tons, and followed a strip of pot-holed asphalt toward where she told him "downtown" was. Nearing the packing plant, Lucas sniffed at the unmistakable stench of dead cattle and hogs being processed into steaks and chops that would wind up on dinner tables across the country.

"I know," Jodi said. "Anybody who can't get a job any place else goes to work at the packing house. My daddy was one of them. He died there."

She pointed to the Baptist Church. "That's where my mama was married to that bastard John Barquist."

The drive-in movie marquee flashed the double feature of "Lawman" and "Rocky" in huge black letters against a white plastic background. Beyond the drive-in, Lucas spotted a Phillips gas station. "I'll pull in over here and gas up," he said. "You might want to check on the bus. Or we could find some place to have a beer and think about it."

She didn't respond.

"It's up to you," he said. "I don't know what kind of time you've got. I'm in no hurry."

He left her mulling that over, while he poked the nozzle in the gas tank. He filled it up, replaced the nozzle and the gas cap, and went inside to pay.

"That'll be a big old twenty-two-forty," said the buck-toothed redhead behind the counter.

Lucas handed her a twenty and a five.

She counted out his change. "What else can I do you for?"

"You can point me toward a good place to eat."

"Depends on what you call good." She crinkled her freckled nose. "The bar and grill next door is Danny's Excuse. Quiet little place. Good chicken and chops. And if you're a country music fan, you're in luck. They have a live band Friday and Saturday nights."

Lucas pocketed his change, said thanks, and left. He made a couple of ends-around cars with hoses stuck in their tanks, and climbed into his red pickup.

Jodi wasn't there. In the ladies' room, he guessed. But, what the hell? If she came back or if she didn't, why did it matter? She was just a girl bumming a ride to where she could catch a bus to someplace else. Her guitar was still standing in the truck where she left it. She couldn't be far away.

A second later the passenger side door popped open and she climbed in beside him. "Hope I didn't hold you up."

"Nope. Are you hungry?"

She lowered her eyes. "Not really."

Lucas didn't believe her. "Well, I am." He moved the truck out of the bay. "Why don't we just mosey on over here and see if old Danny has anything fit to eat?"

He sneaked the Ford pickup in between a silver Eldorado and a Chevy camper with a "shit happens" sticker on the back window. The rain let up, but left puddles of muddy water scattered about. They jumped over some of them to get past the neon Bud sign in the bar's window. Lucas pushed open the wooden door to the shadowy confines of Danny's Excuse.

CHAPTER TWO

If he could have foreseen what was about to take place in Danny's, Lucas would've looked for some other place to pacify his gurgling stomach that cried out for nourishment.

He suspected the girl hadn't tasted food for a while.

They squeezed past crowded tables to one of the vinyl-covered booths lining the wall. On the wall stood a glass display case with a cash register sitting on it. Inside the case were candy bars, packages of Wrigley's gum, four different brands of cigarettes, and Tic Tac breath mints.

Jumbled in one corner of Danny's was an assortment of guitars, drums, a fiddle, and a bass fiddle that belonged to members of the band the freckle-nosed cashier said would be there because it was Friday.

The band wouldn't start playing till seven o'clock, but from the jukebox near the entrance they heard Marty Robbins's classic "El Paso."

"Out in the west Texas town of El Paso, I fell in love with a Mexican girl––"

"There's old Marty," Jodi said with a smile, sliding into the booth.

"Is he a friend of yours?"

"No, but I love his music. He wrote from the heart. Marty

died a while back, you know."

Lucas nodded. "I heard about that."

She thumbed her hat back off her forehead and leaned across the table, eyes glowing with excitement. "I wrote a song about Marty."

Lucas never knew anyone who wrote a song about anybody. "You wrote a song about Marty Robbins?"

Jodi nodded. "That's why I'm going to Nashville. I sent it to a publisher named Cal Slater. He liked the song, and said with a few changes it could make the charts. He liked my singing too."

Lucas was a country music buff, but what he knew about the publishing business Chet Atkins could wrap in his thumb pick. "Are you going to sing the song?"

"Oh, I'll do the demo," she said. "That's short for demonstration."

Lucas nodded as if he never heard of it before. "Well, I guess I'd better start listening for your records on the radio."

A dumpy little waitress with streaks of gray in tired brown hair appeared beside their booth. She'd been there since breakfast. Her attempt at a smile didn't quite come off. She wiped a hand on the front of her soiled white uniform. She removed a stub of pencil from over her right ear. An order pad was poised in her left hand. "What'll it be, folks?"

Lucas asked for a menu.

"No menus," said the waitress. She glanced over a shoulder at the chalkboard on the wall behind the cash register, and rattled off the specials of the day. "Chops and dressing three ninety five. Fried chicken comes with cottage fries or mashed and gravy—choice of white or brown. Green beans and corn same price. Choice of dressing on your salad."

Lucas settled on the fried chicken with mashed and white.

Jodi took her time.

The waitress excused herself. "Be right back."

"I'm really not hungry," Jodi said.

"You have to eat sometime," Lucas said. "Nashville is a long way down the road."

"Well, maybe some chops and dressing would be good."

The waitress came back with water and silver. Jodi asked her about a bus schedule.

"Where to?"

"Kansas City."

The waitress checked the Lite Beer clock behind the counter. "You just missed it, hon.

The last bus to KC left ten minutes ago."

With a quick uncertain smile, Jodi said thanks.

The waitress took their orders and left.

Jodi slid her eyes up even with Lucas's. She looked away, and studied her hands folded in

her lap.

Lucas waited. He could almost hear the wheels turning in her head, struggling with something.

"What's your name, cowboy?" she said.

"Lucas Malone."

"Well, Lucas Malone, I want to thank you for hauling me into town." She pulled her hat down

over her eyes, and made a move to leave. "If I ever get to Borger, Texas, maybe I can pay you back somehow."

She got up and stuck out a hand in a departing gesture, and Lucas took it.

"What's your name?" he said.

"My name is Jodi with an 'i'. Jodi Parker."

The waitress brought their food and turned away.

"What about the chops and dressing?" Lucas said.

"You eat them."

"Jodi."

She stopped and stared at him. His eyes told her he wanted her want her to leave. Why? She gave him no reason to care if she stayed or left.

"You want some coffee or tea or anything?" he said. "How about a beer?"

She made a slow slide back into the booth. "Okay. Coffee would be good."

Lucas gave the waitress the high sign, and she brought two cups of coffee. No sugar, no cream, thank you.

Over the rim of her cup, Jodi's eyes bored into Lucas's face with silent signals he wasted no time trying to decipher. Even so, he had a strong feeling her chestnut head was full of stuff that needed to come out.

She touched a paper napkin to her coffee moist lips and leaned across the table. "Even if there was a bus out of here tonight," she said in a low voice, "I couldn't be on it. I couldn't buy a rasslin' jacket for a flea."

If she thought her revelation would send shock waves through Lucas's system, it didn't work. He suspected she was flat on her luck when he spotted her parked on that suitcase out there in the rain.

She took a deep breath, and tossed the napkin aside. "My mama used to say the best way to lick a problem is to face it head-on." She looked him squarely in the eyes. "My money and my bus ticket ran out in Amarillo."

Lucas's reputation as a character analyst was notoriously suspect. He he'd run into enough phonies to flood the Astrodome. He could fill a book with examples of what not to do, and whom not to trust, accumulated in his career as a victim of sob stories.

As a kid growing up, Lucas's boozing father complained of the yard full of cats dumped along the road and left to starve had they not rubbed against Lucas's ankles. Stray dogs popped up out of roadside ditches when he happened by. They gobbled up table scraps at the Malones' back door. Hand-outs to school friends who never paid him back often left Lucas scrounging for lunch money.

Even so, he was convinced that here sat a sincere young lady, peering into his eyes as if looking for a lost contact, a lady who survived rough times and needed help. He had a few bucks laid away he wasn't using. If she ever stopped talking long enough, he seriously considered offering some of them to Jodi Parker.

"I've got this friend in Kansas City," she was saying. "Chase Witherspoon is his name. He said he could get me a job singing with a band until I saved enough money to get me by for a while in Nashville." Her eyes glistened with the excitement of her plan. "Lucas, this is the best chance I'm ever gonna have to be somebody, and do something I've always wanted to do. My mama used to say most people wait a lifetime for one big chance, then when it comes they don't know what to do with it. I know what to do about it. I've got to make that demo of my Marty song even if it's no good."

Lucas pondered what was driving her. He hadn't heard her sing, so he could only guess what kind of voice she had. But she sounded like her determination was as strong as the guys who scaled the mountain because it was there. What she needed was a track to run her train on. Maybe he could come up with a few cross ties to help her along the way.

"I've got to give it a shot, Lucas," she said. "Know what I mean?"

He knew what she meant. All his life he'd fought pressure to accomplish something his alcoholic father would feel good about. Instead, Mick Malone, in a drunken stupor, often jeered Lucas. "You'll never amount to a lightning bug in a bonfire."

Mick stopped saying it one Saturday night when he stumbled out to the alley back of Jimmy's Jigger and blew a hole in his head with a .38 special.

To Jodi, Lucas said, "You better eat that stuff before it gets cold."

"Eat?" she shrieked. People turned to stare. In a low voice, she said, "Didn't you hear what I said? I don't even have money to pay for this meal."

"Don't worry about it. I read some place if you see ten troubles coming down the road, nine of them will fall in the ditch before they get to you."

"What the hell does that mean?"

"What that means is—if you don't eat your chops and dressing it'll get cold. And nobody—I mean nobody—likes cold chops and dressing. I've seen hound dogs that hadn't eaten for weeks turn up their noses and walk away from cold chops and dressing."

She couldn't hold it back. She had to laugh. "You're funny, Lucas."

He sipped at his coffee and watched her scoop the food in like one of those hungry hounds.

"You know, Jodi, I don't know how you'd feel about it, but I've got a little money I don't know what to do with right now."

There came those eyes again, boring into his. "I'm glad for you."

"I wouldn't be surprised if I could come up with some of it to help out a little—"

"When I get to Kansas City, I'll—"

"—till you get on your feet."

"What do you think I am?" she bristled. "Some kind of slut with no self-respect and no pride?"

"No. I think you're a very nice lady who is hungry, broke, and doesn't know where she's going to sleep tonight."

She let that soak in. "I can't take money from you."

"Uh-huh. I guess you'll be calling old Cal Slater to telling him you've changed your mind about being a country star because you can't take money from some old boy you never saw before."

"What I'm going to do," she said, eyes aflame, "is none of your damn business! Who the hell do you think you are— coming down on me?"

He watched the redness of pride and frustration work its way into her cheeks.

Lucas slid out of the booth. "All right," It was his turn to put a cap on the conversation. "I was out of line. I guess there's nothing I can do for you."

Jodi caught his hand.

"Don't go," she said. "Please." She drew him down onto the seat beside her. "It's just that—I appreciate your offer, Lucas, but I can't take your money."

"Like you said, it's a chance of a lifetime. I'd hate to see you miss it. Money is money, Jodi, no matter where it comes from. It's all the same color, and it buys the same stuff. Pride is a wonderful thing till it gets in the way of doing what's right."

"You just don't get it, do you, Lucas? I can't take money from you, and that's all there is to it."

He spread his hands in a gesture of surrender. "Okay, you win. But don't worry about paying for the food. It's not uncommon in these parts for a guy to buy a lady's supper while she makes up her mind what she's gonna do with the rest of her life."

A small smile forced itself onto her lips. Her mind was still not at ease, and she had more problems than answers. But no matter what happened from now on, anything would be better than what she was running away from.

CHAPTER THREE

Jodi's escape from terror

Barquist passed out on top of her. Jodi tried to wriggle out from under his massive bulk. She was afraid it would wake him. On the lamp table beside the bed she spotted the scissors she used for mending. Many times she'd wished for the courage to use them on him, slashing his flabby body to ribbons. She didn't do it because he woke up from his drunken stupor. Was this the time? Maybe now she could do it. Totally out of it, he probably wouldn't even know she stabbed him in the back, twisted the scissors till she knew he was dead, and couldn't hurt her any more. He wouldn't see her pleasure of watching him die, and her relief of being rid of the monster.

Jodi stretched her arm until it ached, but the scissors stayed just beyond her fingertips.

Across her mind flashed a recurring dream when she was a young girl. In the dream she flipped and flopped like a frisky bass on a cool morning, unaware that she was drifting downstream until the roar of the rapids warned her she was dangerously close to being swept against the jagged rocks below. She struggled to grab an overhanging branch, but the current grew stronger, and no matter how she tried, the branch hung just beyond her reach. Panic stricken, she woke up in a cold sweat, relieved that once again she survived the horrible dream.

John Barquist was no dream. With her eyes, Jodi willed that the scissors would somehow move within reach so she could rid herself of this evil man her dying mother made her promise to take care of.

After what seemed an eternity, the alcohol-saturated Barquist had rolled off her and onto the bed. Jodi bounced up, grabbed the scissors, and, with no thought for the consequences, clutched them in both hands, poised above her head to plunge them into his flaccid belly.

Something told her not to do it. Suddenly, getting out of there safely with her baby Jason was more important than seeing John Barquist dead.

She grabbed up her napping baby and ran out of the house as fast as she could, fearing that, even drunk as a skunk and passed out on the bed, Barquist might be following. Running faster and farther than she knew she could, heart pounding, lungs ready to burst, Jodi prayed for the strength to make it to Gloria's house before Barquist woke up and discovered she was gone.

She did. She shoved the door open, and collapsed in the arms of her friend Gloria, escaping the monster.

Looking back on the horrid experience, she couldn't shake the fear that sometime, somewhere. John Barquist would again raise his ugly head.

Danny's Excuse

The country band at Danny's swung into "Faded Love," trying hard to sound like Bob Wills and his Texas Playboys. They didn't. There weren't enough fiddles in the band, but they accepted with salutes, bows, and waves the patrons' applause for the effort.

A skinny guitar player with a graying beard and a snake tattoo on his right arm stepped to the microphone. A red and white polka dot bandanna was folded around his head, and a gray-streaked pony tail bounced off his back as he began to sing, "I Won't Go Hunting with you, Jake, but I'll Go Chasing Women."

Cigarette smoke hovered like fog on an early morning river, as Friday night fun seekers in cowboy boots and colorful western garb do-si-doed onto the stamp-sized dance floor.

Jodi came back from the ladies' room and announced to Lucas she'd like to dance.

He begged off, pleading "not big on dancing." He yielded when she grabbed his hand and led him away.

Lucas held her while she danced. He liked the way she snuggled close to him with her head on his chest, like one of those long ago stray kittens that brushed his leg looking for a friend. He caught himself hoping the bus wouldn't show up tomorrow morning. Even if it did, he knew Jodi had no money for a ticket, and she made it clear that she wanted none of his. And what about "that son of a bitch" her mama was married to? Who was he? Where was he? And why did she run away from him?

Why did he care? Well, because. She was a nice girl who hitched her wagon to a star named Cal Slater. By the time she got to Nashville, the star may have fizzled and burned itself out. What would become of her then?

From somewhere inside, he heard a small voice whisper, *"You can't leave this kid out here in the middle of nowhere all by herself."*

Then there was that other voice, the tantalizing one that thought it knew everything about him. It pulled at him from another direction.

"Wait a minute," said the voice. *"Old Hugh's been bugging you to come see him and Jenny for almost ever. And you've never even seen their baby daughter."*

"Well, yeah, but I didn't let them know I was coming. Nobody's holding a gun to my head to get me up there. I thought it'd be a nice surprise."

So, Lucas counseled himself, *why don't we just play this thing by ear and see what happens? You've got no place you have to be, and nothing to do when you get there.*

He felt Jodi's hand on the back of his head as they danced.

"Hold me, Lucas," she whispered. It sounded like nothing else would ease her mind.

Lucas had already thought of that. Had she waited half a second longer she wouldn't have had to ask. He felt her press her body close to his. She closed her eyes while the band played "The Tennessee Waltz". He sensed this little girl not only had problems, she also was afraid. He wondered why, and of what. That bastard Barquist? He wished he could hold her forever, protecting her from fire-breathing dragons and monsters of the night.

"You don't have a wife, Lucas." It was not a question.

"No."

"Girl friend?" Jodi said.

"Well–uh–" He was in jail for three years, and his job kept him busy since he got out.

She didn't wait for his answer. "I almost got married once," she said.

"Is that so?"

"Do you want to hear about it?"

"If you want to tell me."

"I do."

The band finished the waltz to a splattering of applause, and Jodi led Lucas back to their booth.

"His name was Ollie McCracken," she said. She leaned across the table, eyes boring into his. "Ollie was a nice boy, but that idiot my mama was married to after my daddy died, beat Ollie up a couple of times. Ollie never came back. I started finding ways to sneak out and be with him. I never really loved Ollie, but he was good to me, and I thought he was the only way I was ever going to get away from John Barquist.

"We knew John would flip out if we told him what we were going to do. Ollie and I made it up to meet at Turner's Market on a Saturday afternoon when I did the shopping– the only time John ever let me out of his sight. We were going to Wichita and get married. Ollie already bought the license."

She looked at Lucas like she wasn't sure she wanted him

to hear what came next, but she plunged ahead anyway. "When I told Ollie I was pregnant, he turned white as a sheet. He said he didn't want to get married just because of that. I told him it didn't matter, but he took off, and I never saw him again." She leaned across the table, eyes boring into Lucas's. "My Jason will be a year old in May. He's staying with my friend Gloria in Phoenix till I get some place where I can have him with me."

Lucas tried to think of something intelligent to say. He couldn't come up with anything except, "I bet there was hell to pay when John found out about that."

She swept her eyes with the back of her hand. "That was the one time he ever let up on me. He made out like it was his baby!" She made a steeple with her hands and covered her mouth. "It's not a very pretty story, is it?"

"That's okay," Lucas said.

Across the room, he saw a skinny, hawk-nosed young man with a wide grin weaving his way around the tables, heading for their booth.

The man stared at her. "Jodi?"

She looked up and saw Freddie Butts staring her in the eyes.

CHAPTER FOUR

Henry hits the trail

Three months ago Henry Bellows's wife Lola died of cancer. His only son, Charles, lived with his family in St. Louis. Henry hadn't been in their home for more than a year before Lola got sick. Left alone after forty-two years of marriage, Henry decided this would be the perfect time to make the trip east.

He'd chop it up into a leisurely drive, and enjoy going back to some of the places along the way he and Lola visited together.

Friday afternoon, Billy Box, the mechanic who had cared for Henry's cars for years, pronounced his 1980 Olds sound and road worthy. The following Monday morning Henry set out from Mesa, Arizona, for St. Louis, Missouri. His plan was to stop in Albuquerque the first night. The second day he'd wave at Amarillo on the way to Oklahoma City. Kansas City would be his the third day, and arrive in St. Louis on day four.

"That's a long hard trip for some old codger to drive all alone, dad," Charles joshed on the phone while the trip was still in the talking stage.

Henry chuckled at that. After he sold his accounting firm

four years ago, he and Lola vacationed all over the country without incident. He had no reason to believe this time would be different.

Denied the capability of divining the future, however, he could not have imagined what awaited him on the road ahead.

CHAPTER FIVE

Trouble at Danny's

Like most of the men in Danny's Excuse, the young man grinning down at Jodi was dressed in faded jeans, scuffed up western boots, and a straw western hat. The grin on his face never changed while he waited for Jodi to respond to his greeting.

"Yes?" she said. She was annoyed that Freddie interrupted her conversation with Lucas.

"I've been sittin' over there at that table watchin' you," Freddie said. "I said to my friends, I know that girl. I kept lookin' and lookin' and–I just knew you had to be Jodi Parker."

Her glance at Lucas told him she had no idea who she was talking to.

"Freddie Butts," the man said. "We were in third grade together."

"Oh, Freddy, yes," she said. "This is–"

Lucas stuck out a hand. "Lucas Malone."

Freddie gave the hand a limp shake. "Would you mind if I asked Jodi to dance?"

Lucas couldn't tell whether Jodi's look at him was pleading for help or seeking his approval.

With a wave of his hand, he said, "Go. Dance."

Jodi scrunched her mouth like she wasn't sure that was the answer she hoped for. She stood up and let skinny Freddie lead her to the dance floor.

Lucas gave the waitress the high sign and she brought him a beer.

The guitar player with the polka dot headband was singing "Today I started loving you again, and I'm right back where I've really always been—"

When the song was over, Freddie ushered Jodi back to the booth where Lucas sipped at his beer.

Freddie said, "Lucas, we'd sure like to have you and Jodi come over and join us at that table over there."

Lucas looked over the heads of the people between the booth and the table where Freddie's glance took him. Seated at a round table were two young women and two men, all about Jodi's age. One of the men had shaggy red hair and a beard. The other one was dark-haired with a big smile. The women were sitting with their backs to him, so he couldn't see what they looked like.

"I don't know, Freddie," Lucas said. It was Jodi's company Freddie wanted, not his.

"Jodi said to ask you," Freddie said, still grinning. "Friends over there. Haven't seen her for a long time."

Lucas nodded at Jodi.

With a grimace, Jodi followed Freddie to the table he came from and introduced her to his friends. She was pleased that one of them was her school-days friend Tess Harmon. She and Tess hugged, and agreed that "we need to get together."

Jodi left Freddie and went back to her booth. Lucas was sipping at his beer. "He wants me to go with him," Jodi said.

"Who?" Lucas said.

"Freddie."

"Do you want to go?"

"It's a time killer for me, Lucas."

It felt funny, as if she'd attached herself to Lucas and was waiting for him to make the decision whether she should go or stay. "Do you want me to wait for you, or what?"

"Yes," she said with a smile, glad he wanted to wait. "It can't take long. I don't have anything to say to him."

"Okay."

"Are you sure you don't mind?"

He managed a noncommittal shrug. "He's a friend from school."

Freddie swung by the booth, and Jodi left with him. She glanced over her shoulder with a disappointed expression, hoping Lucas would call her back.

"Now you've done it!"

Lucas didn't have to look for a body to go with the voice. He knew it was that old accusing snarl from somewhere inside that got some kind of hoot from chastising him. Some people would call it conscience. Lucas called it a pain in the ass—a self-appointed guardian that assumed the responsibility of saving Lucas from himself.

"You've let this kid get to you, haven't you?" came the faceless sneer. *"You met her— What? Three hours ago? I've known you to say no to girls you've known all night. You're already stumbling around over this one like a hot breathing teenager."*

"She's different," Lucas muttered defensively.

"Sure, she is. So was that scuba diver from Houston who couldn't find the Gulf without a road map. The only difference is how they go about getting their hooks in you."

"This one is in trouble and needs help."

"Tell her to write Ann Landers. What have you got, Lucas, a direct line to Dallas First National that you can go around tossing money at every ass-wiggling female—like you own Wal-Mart?"

"You don 't know what you're talking about," Lucas protested.

"I know you, Lucas Malone. Before this is over you'll lose your shirt, and God only knows what
else. Mark my word—.mark my—mark—"

The voice faded like a dying echo. Lucas was glad it was

gone. Here he was, with a good job,

a few bucks in the bank, no responsibility to anyone but himself, and time off to do as he pleased. He was in no mood for a guilt trip. If he decided to help some little girl who couldn't help herself, it was nobody else's business.

Lucas signaled the waitress for another beer, and wished Jodi hadn't gone away.The can of Bud was half way to his mouth when he felt a hand on his shoulder. Two big men were looking down at him, two guns mounted on hips, and two brass badges pinned to wilted khaki shirts above the pockets on the left side.

"Delbert Dobbs," came the gravelly voice of the man with his hand on his shoulder. "Sheriff, Kingman County." He nodded toward his flabby, barrel chested partner. "This here is Deputy Leon Haskins."

Lucas said, "Have a seat. Buy you a beer?"

"Are you Lucas Malone?" Dobbs said. "Yes, sir. Can I buy you a beer?"

Haskins was a red-faced walrus with sideburns that ski sloped to his chin. With his right hand he pounded a heavy flashlight in his left palm. He looked at Lucas as if he couldn't wait to use it on him.

"We ain't here on no social call," Leon wheezed.

The sheriff said, "I think you'd better come with us, Mr. Malone."

"Okay," Lucas said with a grin. "Can I finish my beer first?"

"You ain't makin' things no easier for yourself, boy," Haskins sneered, poking Lucas in the chest with the flashlight.

Lucas's face flushed red with anger. He popped out of his seat to go after the burly deputy, but Dobbs held him back.

"Now hold on there, Leon," Dobbs said. "The man has a right to know what this is all about."

Dobbs sat down across from Lucas.

Lucas glared at the hot-headed deputy who remained standing, itching to get another crack at him with the flashlight.

To Lucas, Dobbs said, "A couple of hours ago we got word

a man was shot in a gas station holdup at Emporia. Witnesses say the robber got away in a red pickup with white stripes like yours, headed this way. Leon here spotted your truck with out-of-state plates, and we checked with Texas. With your record, we figured we'd better pay you a call." Dobbs got to his feet. "Now, Mr. Malone, would you like to come with us?"

"Well, sheriff, I'd be glad to come with you if it'd do any good, but I never heard of

Emporia, Kansas. Besides, what I did was years ago and I paid for it with three years in Huntsville."

"That's why we're lookin' at you, smart boy," Haskins said, pounding his palm with the two-foot flashlight.

Haskins wasn't easy to ignore, but Lucas tried. To Dobbs, he said, "There must be dozens of red pickups with white stripes in this part of the country."

"And we're gonna check 'em all, asshole," Haskins snarled, "startin' with you."

With ham like hands, Haskins made a grab for Lucas's throat. Lucas bounced to his feet and jammed an elbow in the fat uniform's mouth. Leon fell backward against a table. With amazing agility for a three-hundred pounder, he recovered and stumbled toward Lucas, wielding the flashlight.

"Leon!" Dobbs hollered. "Hold it right there, Leon. I'll handle this."

Leon looked hurt at the sheriff, and mad at Lucas, but he stopped, with the flashlight poised to strike above his head.

People from other tables crowded around to see what was going on. The band lit down on "You Are My Sunshine."

"Now, Mr. Malone," the sheriff said with strained patience, "let me explain something to you. Because your truck matches the one used in the holdup, and because you served time in Texas, and because you resisted when we asked you to come with us, I could lock you up in my jail for a while and forget you were there."

"I've never been to Emporia. I don't even know where it is," Lucas said. "I can tell you where I was all day."

"Well, if it wasn't in Emporia, then you've got nothing to

worry about. So, I'm asking you one more time—do you want to come with us?"

Lucas hesitated, and the bull couldn't resist the red flag. Leon slammed Lucas across the shoulders with the flashlight. Lucas felt a sharp pain shoot down his left side. He dropped to the floor, more mad than hurt.

Dobbs yelled at Haskins to "hold it," but Leon either didn't hear well or didn't mind well. He flung aside the table where Lucas sought cover from another blow with the flashlight. Leon came after him with fire in his eyes, spinning the flashlight like a windmill.

Lucas grabbed Leon's wrist and twisted the flashlight out of his hand. Haskins kicked at him, and Lucas locked both hands around his ankle. The deputy buckled and fell backward, sprawled on the floor. Lucas scrambled to his feet, but Leon clamped a claw around his left foot and pulled him down.

Leon rolled on top of him and pounded his chest with his fists. Lucas was able to get the heel of his palm against the deputy's nose, like he'd seen John Wayne do in barroom brawls. He pushed it upward with all the strength he had left. Leon fell spread-eagled on his back.

The circle of thrill seekers gave way, and Lucas scrambled to his feet. He lost his balance and slipped to the floor. His legs were limp as wet noodles, and he knew he wasn't going to win a wrestling match with this walrus. He tried crawling away to safety, but the roaring bull stumbled back for another round.

Somewhere in the back of his aching head Lucas heard a telephone ring. Somebody yelled, "Sheriff, it's for you."

Dobbs shouted at Leon to "hold it." A waitress handed him the phone, and into it the sheriff said, "Dobbs." He listened for a silent moment while the anxious crowd watched and waited. They wondered if the phone call meant the excitement was over, or if he was going to haul Lucas off to jail. Lucas and Leon glared at each other. Dobbs tossed Lucas a glance that told him nothing. He handed the phone back to the waitress who brought it to him.

"Highway patrol got a man," Dobbs said on his way out.

"They say he done it. Let's go, Leon." Over his shoulder, he tossed, "Sorry, Malone."

They left, and the spectators grumbled back to their beer and country music.

Lucas tried to get up but his feet felt bolted to the floor. He grabbed a chair and pulled himself up. It was a painful drag to the men's room. He splashed his face with a double handful of cold water to rinse the blood from cuts and bruises, and patted them dry with paper towels. The image of his face in the cracked mirror above the lavatory told him he looked as bad as he felt. It would be some while before his body could move without hurting.

He felt no malice toward the sheriff. He was just doing his job. Somewhere along the way Dobbs chose between becoming a law man and working at the packinghouse. However, Lucas promised himself, if he ever came face-to-face with that fat deputy again, he'd settle the score.

Emerging from the men's room, Lucas headed back to the booth. The band romped through "Rocky Top" and dancers filled the floor. Friday night at Danny's Excuse returned to normal. Quiet little place.

"Need some help?"

He searched the shadows with half closed eyes for someone who went with the voice. He finally focused on a heavy-set woman in a white smock. She was holding a first-aid kit, and looked like Lucas's idea of a nurse. He didn't care who she was, nor where she came from. He was ready for whatever help she had in mind.

"Why don't you just have a seat over here?" the woman said, motioning him to a chair. "We'll take a look and see what it'll take to put you back together."

Lucas did as he was told, and the woman went to work on him. She dabbed at his face with cotton swabs from the first-aid kit, and bathed his bruises with warm water.

"Best not to cover the sore spots," she said with a soothing voice. "They'll heal better if they get fresh air."

Her advice was little comfort at the time, but Lucas was willing to do whatever she said if it relieved the pain.

"They roughed you up pretty good," she said. This was not

the first time she'd patched up a patron at Danny's.

"You follow them around, do you?" Lucas asked. "Cleaning up their messes?"

The woman chuckled. "That Leon is such a hothead. I'm surprised the sheriff keeps him on. Been there longer than the sheriff though."

"You know him?"

"The sheriff?"

"The other one. Leon."

"I'm his wife."

"...then one night a young cowboy came in, wild as the west Texas wind ..." Marty Robbins took over from the jukebox while the band took a break.

After bouncing around over half of Danny's Excuse, Lucas had little time to think about Jodi. Now he wondered where she was, and whether she'd be back. If so, when? Why did he care? She was out with an old school friend, and owed him no explanation.

Even so, he wondered what she was doing with Freddie that took so long? She said she had nothing to say to him, but she was taking a long time to say it. Would she be back? If so, when? A couple of months ago a friend of his went to the kitchen for a beer and kept going out the back door. He left his brand new wife wondering what happened to him. Lucas hadn't seen him since. Neither had his wife.

It could happen.

"Lucas?"

He peered into the shadows and saw a slender young woman with dark hair that brushed her shoulders. She looked worried.

"I'm Tess Harmon, a friend of Jodi's. We were in school together."

Lucas remembered her from Freddie's round table.

"What happened, Lucas?" she said.

"It's okay, Tess," he said as the woman kept working on his face. "Nothing serious."

"He'll be fine," said the woman who admitted she was Leon's wife.

"Who is she?" Tess said to Lucas.

Mrs. Haskins answered for him. "I work here," she said. "There was a little trouble. It's all over now." She picked up her first-aid kit and the dirty swabs and moved away, "Remember—no bandages."

"Right. Thanks," Lucas said.

"Are you all right?" Tess said.

"I'm fine. Is Jodi with you?"

"We talked earlier, but I saw her leave with Freddie. Are you sure you're all right?"

"I'm okay, thanks."

She tossed him a small smile, and glanced around as if expecting someone. "Do you want to get out of here, Lucas? We can go to my place where you could take it easy for a while."

He was only half surprised by the invitation. The other half wondered how "best friends" she and Jodi were in their years in school.

"I'm sure Jodi wouldn't mind," Tess said.

Uh-huh. Lucas wasn't so sure. But why did it matter? He and Jodi met, he hauled her out of the rain and bought her supper. Now she was gone off with some other guy. No strings. Here was this lifelong friend of Jodi's inviting him to her place where he could "relax for a while." He questioned the integrity of Tess Harmon. What was she after with her offer of a place for him to "relax" and lick his wounds? A gorgeous lady like her doesn't just march up to a total stranger and invite him to share her apartment. And maybe her bed.

There was a time when he'd have jumped at the opportunity to pal around with a woman as attractive as Tess Harmon. Why was he hesitating now? Because of Jodi? Had that sneering voice been right—he had let Jodi get to him? Still, there was no way to guess when she'd be back—or if she'd be back.

He promised to wait for Jodi, but he had nothing better to do at the time. Why not accept Miss Harmon's invitation to troop off to her place? Who knew how long he might have to wait for Jodi to show up again at Danny's Excuse? Beer was a lonely companion. Maybe a change of scenery *would* be good. He'd come back to check on Jodi afterward. Only because he promised? He didn't know.

With some effort he lifted his pain wracked body, maneuvered it out the door with Tess Harmon's arm across his shoulders, and navigated the rain-puddled parking lot to her green Camaro. She slid into the driver's seat, flipped on the ignition, and sloshed away from Danny's excuse, She splattered muddy water like his hundred-thirty-pound black lab in a fish pond.

The last thing Lucas remembered before he passed out was Tess helping him through the door to her apartment, and onto her bed.

Knuckling the sleep from his eyes, he tried to focus on the strange surroundings. His glance wandered from a wooden chest of drawers against one wall to green-curtained windows, a walnut

vanity, to a portable TV on a small table in the corner. He also found himself flattened out on a bed he never slept in before. His sleep-fogged eyes wondered where he was, and how he got there.

A willowy, dark-haired lady in a shimmering pink robe leaned over him, She held out to him a cup of steaming black coffee. He accepted. After a couple of sips he remembered where he was, and how he got there.

The robe covered all Tess's luscious hills and valleys, except for the tantalizing suntanned mounds filling the V on the front of her robe.

Lucas tore his eyes away from Tess and worked his way into a sitting position on the bed. Tess sat on the side of the bed and watched him sip—offering an answer to the question she read in his look.

"No, we didn't do anything dumb," she said, as though wishing they had. "How would you feel about it if we had?"

"Not a good idea."

"For whom?"

"Either of us. Especially you."

"What about you?"

"I'm not her best friend."

She took a moment to let that soak in. "Am I her best

friend?"

His answer was half a smile and a silent sip at his cup.

Tess bounced to her feet and flung the robe aside. She exposed an assortment of tempting curves as she stepped into a black lace bikini.

"I tried," she said, "but you kept pushing me away." She wriggled into faded jean cut-offs and a

white tank top. "Was that because of Jodi?"

"I was out of it, Tess."

"I know. Does that mean if you hadn't been out of it—" She didn't finish the question, and he didn't answer.

Lucas glanced at the clock on the bedside table and couldn't believe it was six-thirty. "Is that AM or PM?" he said.

"AM."

"How far is it to Danny's?"

"Five minutes."

"Will you take me there?"

"Of course."

He grabbed his pants off the foot of the bed and pulled them on, ignoring the pain.

"I told Jodi I'd wait for her there last night." He yanked on his boots, snatched his hat off the chair, and headed for the door. Tess followed him to the car

They rode in silence until Tess offered him an odd smile, and said, "You don't like me much, do you?"

"I think you're a very nice lady."

"I would rather you liked me." She pulled in and stopped beside his red pickup parked in front of Danny's.

"Are you going to tell Jodi?" she said.

"What's to tell?"

"She may take it wrong."

"Does it matter?"

"Yes."

"Why?"

"Like you said, I'm her best friend."

He believed her and got out of the car. "Thanks for letting me impose on you."

"My pleasure," she said with a wan smile. As if it was

important to her, she said again, "Are you going to tell Jodi?"

"She'll want to know where I was (*..if she's still here..*)."

Tess cocked her head at a curious angle. "Are you in love with Jodi?"

"We only met yesterday."

She nodded as if surprised, but flashed a loser's smile. "The really sad part is you'll never know how good I am in bed."

She shifted into gear and stepped on the gas. The Camaro leaped forward and careened out of the parking lot. Lucas jumped aside to avoid being splashed with muddy water. In her rear view mirror, Tess smiled at Lucas's two-finger farewell as she spun the Camaro out of sight.

Danny's Excuse was locked up tighter than Jack Benny's fist. Lucas spotted the bus station on the way from Tess's. He headed for it. He nosed the truck into the curb of an all-night convenience store and parked under its neon "Bus Station" sign.

Through the glass door he saw Jodi curled up in one of those chrome, plastic-covered chairs in which it was impossible to get comfortable. He pushed the door open, wondering how long she'd been waiting for him.

Except for the bald, bleary-eyed man behind the counter, Jodi was the only person in the place. Lucas sat down on the chair next to her.

"I hoped I'd find you here," he said in a low voice. He noticed the bald one was straining to hear what he said to Jodi.

Jodi pouted, avoiding Lucas's eyes. "You said you'd wait for me."

"I meant to, but things sort of got out of hand and I–"

"Don't worry about it. When you weren't at Danny's when I got back, I asked Freddie to drop me here. I've been here all night."

She turned her head and got a look at his face. "Lucas!" she screamed, "What happened to you?"

"I'll tell you about it sometime."

"You look awful."

"I'm okay."

"If you could see your face, you wouldn't think you're okay."

He'd seen his face, and he didn't like it either.

Jodi bounced to her feet and grabbed him by an arm. To the clerk, she said, "Is there some place close where I can put him down?"

"Down a block and across the street," the man said. "Elkhorn Mo-tel."

Jodi wrapped an arm around Lucas's waist and steered him to the door. "Hang on, Lucas. Slow and easy now."

"Is he drunk or what?" the clerk said.

"You blind bastard!" Jodi spat. "Can't you see he's hurt?"

"What about the bus?"

"You take it," she snapped. She hiked up her jeans and pulled down her hat. She was determined to get Lucas out the door and into his truck.

Room 27 at the Elkhorn Motel didn't amount to much, but it had a good bed, and the sheets were clean. Jodi made sure of that before she put Lucas in it. From her mother she learned never to sleep between dirty sheets because all sorts of bad stuff could be wrapped up in them. Sleeping in a bed with dirty sheets was almost as bad as being caught dead with dirty underpants, which she promised her mother she would never be.

She fussed over Lucas, stripped off his boots and clothes, and tucked him in bed. He nodded twice, tried a third time, but fell asleep from the effort. When he woke up a couple of hours later Jodi was in bed beside him, leaning on an elbow, watching him come to life.

"So, there you are," she said.

He squinted, adjusting to the daylight he hadn't seen for a while. "Who are you?" he said.

"Dolly Parton," she said with a grin. "Who did you think it was?"

He stretched his weary bones. "That was some kind of night."

"Do you want to tell me about it?"

He told her. All of it. About he Seven-Eleven holdup, and the time he served in Huntsville. About Sheriff Dobbs and

Deputy Haskins, and why they thought he was involved in the Emporia gas station holdup.

"Fat son of a bitch!" she snarled in response to the Haskins affair. "He needs a good killing."

"Would you like to take care of that for me?"

"I might, if I ever see him."

Lucas cast her an appreciative smile and took her hand.

"Can I tell you something?" she said.

Lucas knew whether his answer was yea or nay, she was going to tell him anyway.

"You're the first man I ever wanted to touch me," Jodi said. "Call it fate, luck, coincidence, or whatever tag you'd like to put on it. I passed up a couple of offers for rides out there on that road before you came along." She waited for some response. What she got was a solemn look. "It was like I was waiting for you, Lucas."

Given the go-to-hell attitude she showed him when he asked if she wanted to get in out of the rain, Lucas displayed mild surprise. "You waited for me?"

"I know it sounds crazy, but I'm a pretty good judge of character, and I could tell those characters had nothing in mind, except getting in my pants."

"So? What made you think I didn't want to get in your pants?"

"You didn't come on to me that way. And you're easy to talk to, Lucas. I feel like I could tell you anything and you'd listen, and try to understand. Know what I mean, Lucas?"

"I'm working on it."

"I've told you things I never told anyone else. Maybe it's because you're different."

"Different? Where I come from different means loony."

"Sometimes what a girl needs is someone to just listen, and you listen."

He flashed her a modest smile.

"You do, Lucas. And most men would have tried to get me in bed a long time ago, but not you. You pick me up out of the rain on some God-forsaken highway in the middle of Kansas, haul me into town and buy my supper, get yourself half killed, and you haven't laid a hand on me. What kind of man are you anyway?" Without further conversation—and with no warning—she flipped over on her back, stuck her feet in the air, and ripped off her clean underpants.

"Hold it!" Lucas said. "What would your mama think?"

She giggled. "Mama ain't here."

CHAPTER SIX

Speak of the devil

Somewhere west of Oklahoma City rain pelted the body of the wheezing 1969 Plymouth John Barquist coaxed along I-40. The farther he drove, the harder it rained. The frenzied wipers hardly kept a spot clear enough for him to see out. He squint through the cracked windshield, hunkered over the wheel, both hands gripping the plastic cover as if he was afraid it might get away. Between swipes of the groaning wipers, he damned the rain, loudly invoking the power of the Almighty to help him do it.

Barquist had no idea how far he'd come, nor how far he had to go to catch up to Jodi. But, in a blind, bull-headed rage, he was dead set on getting it done. Gloria had gasped "Nashville" before he rolled off her and allowed her to breathe. He knew Jodi's dream was to sing her songs on the stage of the Grand Ole Opry. How far it was, or how long it would take to get there didn't matter. His mission was to find her. He'd show her, he would.

Barquist's plan was to leave Phoenix as soon as he got what he wanted out of Gloria, but his car broke down. It took three days to get it out of the repair shop. Keeping his car in dependable running condition was not high on his list of priorities. As long as the motor started when he turned the key, and the wheels kept rolling, what else could a man ask? More important was how far up the road Jodi was, and whether his ancient Plymouth would hold up long enough for him to get there.

That air-headed Gloria! He couldn't believe half of what she said. She'd lie her head off to keep him away from Jodi. And him Jodi's step-daddy too! But when Gloria said "Nashville," he believed her. All Jodi ever thought about was music. Fiddling around on that guitar of hers, putting words on paper, singing along with them pickers and grinners on the Grand Ole Opry! Like she was some kind of big country music muckety muck. He knew where to look for her. Nashville, Tennessee!

CHAPTER SEVEN

Sunrise in Baker's Bluff

Jodi squeezed her eyes open and snuggled close to Lucas. Sometime in the night the rain stopped, and the early morning sunlight sifted through the window.

Lucas made a move to get out of bed. Jodi tightened an arm around him. "Where you going?"

"I thought you were still sleeping."

"I am." She smiled, eyes still closed. "And I hope I never wake up." She opened one eye, like a sleeping cat, and squinted into his face, trying to read his thoughts. "You know what I think, Lucas?'

"Tell me."

"I think I've reached a time in my life when I need someone to take care of me."

Lucas waited, expecting more, but it didn't come. Instead, she switched the subject. "If you had enough money to be any place in the world where you want to be right now?"

He screwed up his mouth and shook his head as if working on a difficult decision. She waited wide-eyed, as though she already knew the answer.

"Well," Lucas said, "I can't think of any place I'd rather be than right here."

She gave him a sharp look. "That's what he said."

"Who?"

"Freddie."

Maybe it was the pang of jealousy that struck like a bolt of lightning at mention of Freddie's name. Maybe it was lurking in the back of his mind all along. Maybe that caustic voice pegged him right. Maybe he did let this kid get to him.

She placed a hand on his arm. "I told him I was your girl."

"Are you?"

"If you want me to be."

"I do."

She threw her arms around his neck and hugged him close.

If a bus left Baker's Bluff that Saturday morning Lucas didn't know it. He was sure Jodi forgot about it too. The subject never came up between them. Lucas eased the pickup into a parking space at the diner down the street from the motel.

They slid into a booth facing each other. They were greeted by a teenaged waitress wearing black horn-rimmed glasses and chomping on a mouth full of gum. "Y'all gonna be wantin' breakfast or lunch?"

Lucas looked at Jodi. She said it was too early for lunch. Lucas ordered two eggs, crisp fried bacon, toast, and black coffee.

"How'd you like them eggs cooked?" the waitress said.

Lucas resisted the temptation to say, "Gee, that would be swell." Instead, he said, "You can play around with the yellow, but the white stuff has to be done."

"Over easy," the waitress murmured, making a note on her order pad.

Jodi ordered a cinnamon roll and black coffee.

The waitress scribbled on her pad, lips moving as she wrote.

Lucas said to Jodi, "You're eating pretty light."

"A kid from the poor side of town has to squeeze pennies."

"It's not your pennies you're squeezing."

"Same thing." She fell silent.

Lucas wondered what was rolling around in that chestnut

head of hers.

When she broke the silence, she said, "My mama used to say I had more guts than the packing house."

"How's that?"

"When I was little, I wasn't afraid of anything or anybody. I was always the first one on stage at church or school when they asked if anybody wanted to do something. I'd get up there, and I'd dance around and sing, and make funny faces. The best part was, when I did it everybody stood up and clapped their hands and smiled as if they were looking at Shirley Temple."

"You were that good?"

"I thought I was. And for a little while I guess they thought so too. But, it's hard sitting here, ordering breakfast, and me with nothing to pay with. It scares me to think what might have happened to me if you hadn't come along when you did."

"Nothing would stop you, Jodi. You're a tough lady. You'd find a way to get to where you want to be. You'd make it somehow."

The waitress brought their breakfast. After she turned away, Lucas said, "There's something I've been wanting to ask you."

"What's that?"

"How the hell did you manage to get yourself stranded out there in the rain ten miles from Baker's Bluff, Kansas?"

She gave him a sideways look. "How long you been waiting to ask me that?"

"Ever since you told me to keep moving if I had no better place to go than Baker's Bluff."

She giggled.

"There you were," Lucas went on, "perched on that suitcase with your thumb in the air like you were ready to take on the world if it didn't go the way you wanted. What I can't figure out is why my truck was the one you hopped into."

"There's not much to it," she said. "Like I told you, my money and my bus ticket ran out in Amarillo. Before I got out of the bus station, lugging that suitcase and guitar, some guy asked me if I'd like a ride in his Cadillac. I said where to, and he said wherever I was going, and I said I wasn't going any place with him. So, I scrounged around in my purse and came up with enough change for a city bus ride to the edge of town. I started walking. In a few minutes along came this little old couple on their way to Perryton. They asked if I wanted a ride that far. Well, I never heard of Perryton, but I figured it must be farther up the road than where I was already. I said yes, thank you very much. I dumped my suitcase and guitar in the back seat and hopped in there.

"They just got back from a Caribbean cruise to celebrate his retirement from the Post Office. They talked a lot about their kids and grandkids. Somewhere along the way they stopped at a Burger King for lunch and insisted on buying mine. I didn't argue because I was starving. The way I pigged out, they must have thought I'd never seen food.

"When we got to Perryton, I asked if they'd let me off at the bus station, like I was going to catch a bus. I didn't want them to know how bad off I was, so they did. I said thank you very much, and waited for them to drive away. When they were out of sight, I started walking again.

"After a while this guy came along in a big black car. He said he was going to Liberal, Kansas, and was I going that far. I pegged him as harmless. I threw my stuff in the back seat and climbed in the front with him. We buzzed along for a while, made idle chit-chat, then out of the blue he says to me, I don't think I'll stop at Liberal, but will go on to Wichita. He said there were some clients in Wichita he needed to call on—some kind of insurance business.

"Well, I'm thinking how lucky can I get with a ride all the way to Wichita. Everything went fine until this little black and white dog dashed out onto the road and started barking its head off, nipping at the car's wheels. The car hit it."

Lucas's ears perked up.

"I never saw a man come unglued so fast in all my born days," Jodi went on. "He never even touched the brake, but floor-boarded it and got out of there. Then what does he do but dump me out down the road, saying he didn't need to go to Wichita after all. Then he took off like a bat out of you know where, and that's when I parked myself on my suitcase. I waited for you to come along and pick me up."

"You waited for me?"

"I must have. I didn't move an inch till you showed up."

"Was that this side of Pratt?" Lucas said.

"It could have been. I wasn't sure where it was."

"I saw him hit that dog."

"You saw him hit it?"

"I saw the Lincoln hit the dog. It belonged to a boy named Isaac. The dog died."

"Oh! That idiot!"

The waitress brought the check. "Y'all can pay me any time you're ready."

Lucas looked at the check, and handed her a bill to cover it. "No change," he said.

She thanked him and went away.

"Lucas," Jodi said with a serious look, "how far am I gonna be going with you?"

"Well." In view of recent developments between them, the question caught him off guard. "Actually, I'm on my way to Chicago to see an old friend."

"What kind of friend?"

"A college buddy. He was quarterback of the football team when I was at Baylor."

"A man friend."

He nodded, and she seemed satisfied it was not a girl type friend he was going to visit.

"I can't get to Chicago from here," he said, "without busting right past Kansas City on the way. Is that where you want to go?"

"Well, yes, I think so. I'll get in touch with my friend Case Witherspoon and work it out from there."

"You're sure of that? Heis going to help you get to Nashville?"

"Yes. Oh, yes I'm sure."

"I mean, given a choice between Chicago and Nashville there would be no contest."

"No contest, no."

"Good." He nodded. "I hope you'll do what's best for you."

"Then it's okay if I ride along with you to Kansas City?"

Was this the same girl who last night said she was his girl if he wanted her to be? Why did she ask that question now?

"Yes, it's okay," he said.

She nodded, pleased with his answer. "There's something I want to do before we leave Baker's Bluff," she said.

"Okay. What's that?""

"I want to drive past the old house where we lived when I was growing up here. It's just a few blocks."

Lucas drove, and followed her directions.

"Turn here," she said. "It's the third house on the left."

In the middle of a grassless yard, surrounded by a shoddy picket fence, stood a paint-faded two-story clapboard house. The glass in the upstairs windows was shattered, replaced by cardboard. A couple of skinny hound dogs with their tails in the air sniffed at the dirt-bare yard. Under one end of the rickety wooden porch lay a black and white collie with half a dozen puppies nudging her nipples. A barefoot toddler in a drooping diaper grinned at them beside the wire gate that opened onto a crumbling sidewalk.

"Lordy!" Jodi said. "My daddy used to take such good care of this place!" She nodded toward the first floor window. "That's where it happened." Her words were tinged with the painful memory. "Right there in the front room of that old house." She stared at the window for a silent moment. "Let's go, Lucas. I've seen enough."

Lucas knew sooner or later there'd be more. And, sooner than later, somewhere along the way Tess Harmon would become the topic of conversation. Jodi would want to know what happened last night at Danny's Excuse, and what he did after his battle with Leon Haskins. There was nothing to tell, but, as Tess said, whatever he told, Jodi might take it wrong. Still—

"I'm sorry I wasn't there last night when the ruckus broke out," Jodi said.

"There was nothing you could have done."

"I should have been there with you any way. Going off and leaving you like that. Freddie was a total bore. I thought he'd never get through talking about his cows and pigs. Twice he asked me if I'd like to get married. I thought, yeah I wouldn't mind, but not to you."

Lucas cleared his throat, deciding to take the plunge. "Your friend Tess came by after it was all over last night."

"Who? Tess? You mean Tess Harmon? How did you know who she was?"

"Well, you know. Freddie introduced us at that table."

"Oh, yeah."

"After Leon and the sheriff took off, she came over and asked if I was okay."

"What was she doing there?"

"She saw I was hurt, and thought I might like to go someplace where I could relax for a while."

"And?"

"She drove me to her place."

"She– You–" She struggled with that. "Tess took you to her place?"

"Jodi, I–"

"Wait. Let me think about that."

"There's nothing to think about. I was out of it, and she–"

"Yes, there is. Please. Let me think about it."

For what seemed to Lucas half an eternity, she spoke not a word. Finally, she said, "Did you go to bed with her?"

"You mean–"

"Yes. Tess. Did you go to bed with her?"

"No. Like I said, I was out of it. The last thing I remember was Tess helping me through the door to her apartment."

She arched her eyebrows. "What was the next thing you remember?"

Lucas shook his head. If this was an interrogation, he'd be better off with Leon.

"I need to know, Lucas."

"When I woke up, Tess was handing me a cup of coffee."

"Was she dressed? I mean–"

"Come on, Jodi. I didn't lay a hand on her, okay?"

In a tiny voice, Jodi said, "Tess was my best friend."

"She still is." With a grin, he said, "Except for me."

"Do you mean that?"

"Which part?"

Jodi gave him a playful jab in the ribs. Lucas stepped on the gas.

CHAPTER EIGHT

Here comes the monster

John Barquist never saw Tennessee. He wasn't sure where Nashville was, but he was hell bent on finding it. It wouldn't be a happy time for Jodi when he did. What the hell did she think she was going to do in Nashville? She had no money, and no way to get around. Lugging that kid of hers half way across the country, probably hitching a ride with anyone on wheels. Dumb kid. Run out on him, would she? Didn't believe ole John would do what he said, eh?

Well, Gloria sure as hell had reason to believe him. She got a taste of what it was like to cross John Barquist. Should have gone ahead and choked the hell out of her. She'd keep her mouth shut though. She was too scared of what would happen to Jodi if she didn't. He sniggered at the thought. What Gloria didn't know was whatever he planned for Jodi was going to happen anyway.

The flump-flump-flump of the left front tire jerked the Plymouth across the median and into the on-coming lane. He fought to get it back into the right lane without a head-on collision. He finally wrestled it onto the shoulder where it hobbled to a stop and died.

"Son of a bitch!" John roared.

He rumbled around to the trunk and popped the lid in search of the spare. There was none.

"Son of a bitch!"

Steaming like a locomotive on an uphill grade, he slammed the lid down. Beside himself with anger and frustration, he stuck out a thumb. Traffic whizzed by, splashing him with muddy water. Soaked head to toe from the rain, he attacked the flat tire with furious kicks of his army surplus field boot. Infuriated that the tire was still flat, he turned up the collar of his dungaree blouse against the rain, and took off on foot. In which direction he didn't know. Nor could he have guessed what awaited him up the road.

CHAPTER NINE

So, we meet again

Barreling along Highway 54 north of Baker's Bluff, Lucas and Jodi spotted a patrol car parked on the westbound shoulder.

"Reckon that's old Leon?" Jodi said.

"I wouldn't be surprised." Lucas pulled onto the shoulder, and stopped opposite the red-faced deputy. "Yep, that's old Leon all right."

When the fat lawman saw Lucas staring at him with a vengeful grin, he peered about nervously. He got busy talking on the radio. He burned rubber heading west, as though he received an urgent call.

Lucas gave his head a derisive shake and steered the pickup in the opposite direction.

"Fat son of a bitch!" Jodi snarled.

"He'll get his one day. He'll crawl the hump of the wrong guy, and old Leon will wind up a greasy spot on Main Street in downtown Baker's Bluff."

Jodi giggled.

"What?" Lucas said.

"I was just trying to picture Mrs. Leon crawling in bed with that fat ass every night."

They shared a laugh about that. They raced past ranches, cattle feeder lots, farms and small towns on their way to Kansas City.

"What did you do with the money?" Jodi said.

"What money?"

"The money you got in the Seven-Eleven holdup."

Lucas knew she didn't care what he did before—least of all what he did with the money. Right now was more important. She just thought the money was something to talk about while they weren't talking about anything else. Her question deserved an answer. He didn't think the time was right to go into the details of how it felt to sacrifice three years of his life for some stupid stunt he pulled.

He told her any way. "There was no money."

"You served all that time for nothing?"

"Well, you might say that. We didn't do it for the money. We had too much beer. We just looked for something we never did before. Actually, I served all that time because I went along with a couple of soused friends. I haven't thought about it for a long time."

"Why did you do it?"

"You mean the holdup?"

"Yes."

"It wasn't really a robbery. We had no guns. Just handkerchiefs over our faces. Of course, the old guy behind the counter didn't know that. The three of us were sitting around a table at this bar, celebrating our win over Texas. Somebody said let's go hit a Seven-Eleven. We had too much booze and not enough sense, so we went and hit a Seven-Eleven. We didn't even get out of the parking lot before they nabbed us. We got three years apiece. I spent mine in Huntsville. I haven't seen the other guys since."

Rain began falling as the red Ford pickup buzzed across the flint hills, gobbling up concrete.

"Who is George Benton?" she said.

"George Benton was the man who gave me a job at Phillips Petroleum. After I got out of Huntsville, I went looking for work. Every place I went, I told them about the time I served and why I wanted them to know up front, so nobody could come back later and say, hey, you didn't tell me about that.

"George was the only one who cared more about what I could do for him than about my record. Four months after I started work, his plane crashed in a snow storm over the Colorado Rockies. They never found his body."

She took his right hand in both of hers and pressed it to her lips.

At Wichita they pulled into a Wendy's for burgers and coffee. Back on the Interstate heading toward Kansas City, Jodi started singing what she called car songs, like Bill Grogan's Goat, You Are My Sunshine, and This Old Man. Lucas joined in the parts he remembered, which wasn't much.

They sang up all the songs they could think of, including White Christmas and Amazing Grace, then lapsed into a time when Lucas drove and Jodi talked.

CHAPTER TEN

Jodi's story

My daddy was the finest man I ever knew. I thought if I could find a man like him, I'd marry him and be the happiest wife God ever put on his green earth. Daddy grew up on a farm and couldn't wait to have one of his own. After he saved enough money for the down payment, he asked mama to marry him, and she said yes. They scraped and saved and scrounged for years to pay the farm off early. The banker told him there was plenty more money where that came from, and if he ever needed it, the door was always open.

My daddy never liked owing anybody anything. He never needed any more money till I was about six years old. That's when the rains didn't come and the crops didn't grow. The bottom dropped out of the market, and farming wasn't good. Daddy kept trying to make it work, but things got worse. He finally went to the bank for another loan, and before he knew it he was in debt over his head. It was a struggle for him to realize he couldn't pull himself out of the hole the bank helped him dig.

Mama used to tease that he cared more about the farm than he did about us. He scolded us and said we were more important to him than anything else in the world. He finally sold the farm to pay the bank, and we moved to town. Mama got a job as a checker at Safeway, and daddy started looking for work. He never stopped trying to find some way to get his farm back. He was disappointed when he found out the door the banker said would always be open was slammed in his face.

One day I came home from school and found daddy at the kitchen table with his head in his hands. I knew he was hurting. I slipped on upstairs in that old house you saw back there, and I never let him know I saw him cry. When I got to my room, I cried too.

The next day daddy swallowed his pride and went to work at the packing plant. He didn't like working there. He knew it was where people went to work when they couldn't find anything else to do. Now he was one of them, and that hurt him bad.

Daddy liked buying things for mama and me. He worked overtime to afford them. Every pay day he'd bring us something, like Stover's chocolate for mama, and M&M's for me, because he knew I loved them. I still do.

One night about midnight mama got a call from the foreman at the packing plant. He said a hoist got loose and hit daddy in the head, and could she come. I was already in bed upstairs. Mama woke me and took me with her. When we got to the plant, daddy looked awful. His head was bleeding. He was lying there with nobody doing anything for him. He died two days later.

I thought mama was going to die too. She moped around for weeks after the funeral, and didn't have much to say to me. She didn't miss a day of work though, because we needed the money. The job helped keep her mind off what happened to daddy. She said she loved me as much as ever, and please don't blame her if she kept to herself for a while.

She once told me about an old maid aunt of hers whose friend was killed in a car wreck.

Aunt Pearl never got over that. Her friend's name was Carl Clevenger. Every year on the anniversary of his death, Aunt Pearl would climb the stairs to her bedroom and lock the door. She'd see no one, talk to no one. She didn't eat or drink anything all day.

Aunt Pearl and Carl wanted to get married. After her father died, her mother let her know she expected Pearl to take care of her for as long as she lived. All those years, until her mother died of heart failure at the age of ninety-four, Aunt Pearl was grieving for Carl Clevenger. On the day her mother died, Aunt Pearl went to town and bought herself a new gingham dress. When she got back home, she went upstairs to her room, and put on the new dress. She fixed her hair and face–which she hadn't done for years. She took her father's old twelve gauge shotgun out of the closet, where it stood unused forever. She placed the muzzle of the gun in her mouth, pulled the trigger, and splattered her brains all over the walls and ceiling.

I never worried that mama would do that. It was a long time after daddy died before she could sit down at the table and eat a whole meal without breaking down. She ran to her room upstairs, where I heard her sobbing and crying for hours.

When I was ten, mama brought home a man from the Safeway to have supper with us. His name was John Barquist, produce manager at the Safeway where mama worked. John was younger a big guy with dark wavy hair, and a look women went for. It was a couple of years after daddy died. I could see why mama was attracted to John, but little did I know all that would change.

At first it was hard for me to adjust to mama having him around. But John was attentive to her, and after a while it wasn't too bad. John would take her to movies, and sometimes they'd go to dinner

and dancing at the American Legion in Wichita. John was good to mama, and she said he was a good worker.

One Sunday afternoon when we got home from a picnic, mama said to me, "Do you like John?" I said I guessed he was all right. Then she said, "Would you like to have him for a step-daddy?"

I was so shocked I about dropped my drawers. I tried not to show my disappointment that mama would even think about marrying someone besides daddy. But I figured by then it was all cut and dried any way. Two weeks later I sat on the front row of the Baptist Church and watched my mama get married to John Barquist.

Mama and John went to Denver on their honeymoon, and I stayed with Tess at her parents' house. One night I heard Mr. Harmon talking about John to Mrs. Harmon. I didn't understand it all. I didn't like what he was saying, but I couldn't stop listening.

"Barquist is a lush," Mr. Harmon said. I didn't know what a lush was, but the way he said it didn't sound like anything I'd want my mama married to.

"Well, now," Mrs. Harmon said, "we don't know that for sure."

"And besides that," Mr. Harmon said, "Paulie Camper told me Barquist has two other wives some place already, and nobody knows for sure he's not still married to them."

"If I believed everything Paulie Camper said," Mrs. Harmon said, "I'd have a head full of sour potato peelings."

"Well, I know old Paulie's memory is failing on him, but I've heard other people tell stories about John Barquist that didn't sound right," Mr. Harmon said. "Like that time Harry Sharp was in Kansas City and saw Barquist pull over to the curb in a long black chauffeur-driven limousine and proposition some whore right there on the street."

"Roscoe!" Mrs. Harmon said, I guess because Mr. Harmon said whore, but he said that's what the woman was.

"Harry said the woman got in the car, and it drove away." Mr. Harmon was pretty strong about that.

"A chauffeur-driven limousine!" Mrs. Harmon said, like she was having trouble believing it. "And that poor little Jodi. Why, if she weren't Tess's friend—"

Tess called me then, and I couldn't hear any more.

It didn't take long for the honeymoon to be over. John drank heavily and often. Sometimes he'd come home at two or three o'clock in the morning stewed to the gills, and mama was waiting up for him. I'd hear them talking, in muffled voices at first, then after a while their voices weren't muffled any more. It was like they declared war on each other. Mostly it was John doing the screaming. Even when I covered my ears with a pillow I could still hear him yelling at mama, calling her all kinds of dirty names. Mama cried and ran upstairs to her room and slammed the door. I wanted to go to her, but I knew she wouldn't want me to know what happened.

Mama kept working at the Safeway, and John kept boozing it up until he finally got fired from his job. He didn't stop drinking. He just stopped working.

One night mama came home from work, and John was waiting at the door with his hand out. He'd been drinking as usual. He told mama to give him her pay envelope.

After John lost his job at the Safeway, mama gave him money because she thought he was trying to find another one. But he never demanded money before. Mama looked at him like she didn't know what to do. She couldn't believe John would treat her that way. I was standing at the bottom of the stairs. When she looked at me I could tell she was afraid of John.

"Give me the money," John said. Mama said no, and John yelled at her, "Just give me the goddam money!" He grabbed at her, but mama ducked away. John staggered after her and caught her arm and slapped her across the mouth. Mama screamed and cried. I cried too.

I knew something bad was happening but I didn't know how to stop it. I yelled at John not to hit mama any more, but he didn't stop. I ran at him and pounded his back with both my fists as hard as I could. He slapped me away, and grabbed mama's arm and ripped the envelope out of her hand. He knocked her down and stumbled out the door, with mama's crumpled pay envelope in his hand.

That scene was repeated many times. Mama never fought back because she believed a woman should do what her husband said. She'd promised to love him in sickness and in health. She thought John had some kind of sickness that made him do bad things.

John Barquist was not hard to hate. I didn't tell anybody how he abused my mama, except my friend Tess. Tess already knew what a bastard John was. She heard her parents talk when they thought she wasn't listening. Tess told me about riding her bike past our house and saw this long black car stop out front. She said a man got out of the car and went to the front door.

Tess saw John open the door. The man handed him an envelope stuffed with something. They talked for a minute, then the man got back in the car and drove away. I don't know what they talked about, and Tess didn't know what was in that envelope, but John Barquist never hit another lick of work.

He cheated on mama too, I know that much. I'll never forget the night we heard a knock on the door and mama went to see who it was. This woman was standing there, holding a baby in her arms. She said to mama, "I thought John would like see his son on his birthday."

Mama about fell over. She said John wasn't home. The woman said, "You tell him I was here, and he's got hell to pay next time I see him." Of course, John denied he ever heard of the woman, but every year after that, on the baby's birthday, John didn't come home.

When I was fourteen I came in from school one day and John was home. Mama was at work. He said to me, "Come sit on daddy's lap" while he drank beer and watched TV, making out he was my daddy. I thought, if my daddy was here he'd beat the bastard to a pulp.

"You're not my daddy," I said.

"Aw, c'mon," John said. "Don't be that way."

I turned away, but he grabbed me and pulled me onto his lap. I sat there hating him, wishing it wasn't against the law to kill people.

"Go get daddy another beer," he said.

I went to the refrigerator and brought him the bottle, glad for the chance to get away from him, even for a minute. He grabbed my arm and pushed me to the floor and piled on top of me. I fought to get away from him. I used some of the words I heard him say to mama, but he was too strong for me. He ripped off my underpants and didn't let me up till he passed out on the front room floor. I ran to the bathroom and threw up my insides. I never told mama. I was afraid if I did, he'd treat her even worse than before.

One of John's big deals was throwing food against the wall and carrying on like a wild man at mealtime. Supper was always a special time for mama. She loved to cook. On John's birthday she fixed his favorite chicken fried steak with mashed potatoes and cream gravy. Every time we went out to a restaurant that's what he ordered. Chicken fried steak with those gummy potatoes and cream gravy thick as wallpaper paste.

Well, this night mama topped it off with his favorite German chocolate cake. Something happened—who knows what? Like some little kid throwing a tantrum, John picked up the steak and potatoes and splattered them against the wall! He flushed the German chocolate cake down the toilet.

Mama was heartbroken. She said to me later, "He's not a bad man, honey. He's just not thinking straight these days. He hasn't been himself since he lost his job."

If he'd done it just once in a while it wouldn't have been so bad, but it happened two or three times a week. I swore to myself someday I'd pay him back for what he did to my mama.

When she got sick, I waited on her hand and foot, hoping all the time that John wouldn't come home. We never knew what mood he'd bring with him, or what he might do. Sometimes he'd go upstairs to mama's room. He'd hold her hand and talk to her so sweet, like butter wouldn't melt in his mouth. Then, the next time he might not go up to see her at all. Most often he stayed downstairs and screamed at me about something, ranting and raving, calling mama names and carrying on like a madman.

One time when I couldn't take any more of his abuse, I stood up to him when he came reeling in through the front door. He headed upstairs where mama was sick in bed, and I knew he was going to hurt her.

"Where's your mama?" he said, like he didn't know she couldn't even get out of bed.

I screwed up my courage, and said, "John, if you hurt my mama again, I'll kill you."

He got a funny look on his face, like he believed I would. Then he came after me, threw me down, and raped me right there on the front room floor.

After that he left and stayed gone for three days. I prayed he'd never come back. He did though.

For some insane reason, mama still loved John, and kept saying he would straighten himself out once he got another job. I don't know if it had anything to do with that envelope Tess Harmon saw that man give John that day, but he never got another job, and he never straightened himself out.

When mama died, John wasn't home. She made me put my hand on my heart and promise to take care of him after she was gone. Well, I took care of him all right. I cooked and scrubbed and washed his filthy underwear till it made me sick.

We didn't stay in Baker's Bluff long after that. John got a wild hair to go to Arizona, and we took off for Phoenix. That's where he wanted to live. After we got there, he acted like he thought I was willed to him, from sunup to sundown.

Any time a boy came near me, John beat him up and ran him off. He'd smash their car windows with a baseball bat, slash their tires, and punch holes in their gas tanks. One boy—Ollie McCracken was his name—the one I told you about. Ollie stood up to John one time and John about killed him. Ollie never came back.

I prayed that John would die in some horrible accident, causing him to suffer forever before he died. One time I prayed that God would take him. I was afraid if he didn't, I'd find some way to kill him.

One night he was sitting at the kitchen table with his back to me. I was tempted to grab the knife I used for peeling potatoes and carrots. It was right there on that little part that sticks out from the end of the cabinet. The knife had a sharp point. I could have grabbed it, stabbed John in the back, and been rid of him forever. I was trying to work up the nerve to do it when he turned around and looked at me as if he knew what I was about to do. My nerve melted like sugar in coffee.

Sometimes John ran through the house stark raving naked, chasing some whore he brought from a bar. He'd pop her wherever he caught her, including my bedroom. I'd pretend to be asleep, lying there listening to their stupid giggling and moaning and groaning and carrying on, all the time wishing I had a gun to fill them both full of holes.

The last time I saw John was the night he crawled in my bed. I fought him off for as long as I could, but he was too big and strong. When it was over, he passed out and I was able to roll away. I grabbed my baby Jason out of his crib and got out of there, and didn't stop running until I got to my friend Gloria's house.

Many times John told me if I ever left him he'd kill me and my baby. But I couldn't take it anymore. I was more afraid for Jason than for myself.

I know, I told mama I'd stay with him, and I tried to convince myself she'd understand. I couldn't raise my son in the same house with that evil monster. And I promised myself that someday–.*SOMEDAY!*–.I'd make John Barquist pay for all the mean things he did to my mama.

Jodi slumped against the seat, and buried her face in her hands. "It's not a pretty story, is it?

Lucas found no words for a response. He concentrated on the road ahead. For a time they rode without uttering a word.

"You think Barquist might come after you?" Lucas said, then.

"It's like I can feel him out there somewhere. Some evil thing that sees all and knows all. I feel dirty just saying his name."

"What did he think about your wanting to be a singer?"

"Oh, he thought that was really funny. He said he had more talent between his legs than I had in my whole body. He knew I wanted to go to Nashville. I don't know how he'd find out that's where I'm going."

"How about your friend?"

"Gloria? She'd never tell. She hates him as much as I do. She'd die first."

CHAPTER ELEVEN

Barquist meets Bellows

The black Olds Eighty-Eight pulled onto the shoulder and waited for the rain-soaked hitchhiker to catch up. John Barquist slid in beside Henry Bellows, then slammed the door shut.

"How you doing, old buddy?" Bellows said. "Was that your car I saw pulled over back there?"

Barquist didn't answer.

"Bad time for car trouble." Bellows steered back onto the road. "I haven't seen this much rain in a coon's age."

John wiped a hand over his wet face, in no mood for idle chatter.

"Where are you from?" Bellows said, trying to coax some kind of response out of a man who was silent as Mount Rushmore.

"Arizona," John grumbled.

"Well now," Henry said, "we may be neighbors. I'm from Mesa."

Barquist didn't care less where his talkative host was from. His thoughts were of a young lady who ran away from him, and how long it would take to find her. He wasn't sure where he was, but he thought it was some place in

Oklahoma.

Bellows kept trying to engage his passenger in conversation. "Have you lived in Arizona a long time?"

"No." John's mind was on getting to a bus station where he could buy a ticket to Nashville. He didn't know where it was, but the bus would take him there. He wouldn't have to worry about where it was, nor when he'd get there. He had no idea how long it might take to find Jodi–little bitch!–but he would show her if it took forever.

"Where are you bound for?" Bellows said.

"What?" John was irritated. He had more things to think about than listening to some old codger quiz him about where he lived and where he was going,

"Is there some place I can drop you?" Henry said.

"Why don't you just drive, man, and stop asking so damn many questions?"

"Now, wait a minute, mister–."

"No, you wait, old buddy," Barquist snarled. "I didn't ask to ride in your goddam car, and nobody is paying me to listen to your stupid conversation."

"What's that?"

"Pull over," Barquist said, glaring.

"Now, listen, I–"

"Just pull over and stop, dammit!"

"Yes, I will pull over," Bellows said, red faced with anger. "You're getting out of this car right now!"

He skidded the Olds onto the shoulder and stopped. Barquist threw the door open and rumbled around the front end, preventing Henry from driving away without him. He came up on the driver's side and yanked the door open. "Move over!" he yelled.

"Like hell I'll move over."

"Just move it over, man, and don't gimme no shit."

"This is my car and I'll–"

Barquist hit him a stunning blow with a folded fist. Henry slumped unconscious on the seat. Barquist rolled him onto the passenger side floor. He took off one of his army surplus field boots and pounded the older man's head until he didn't move. He pulled the boot on, shifted into Drive. The Olds screeched onto the rain-slick Interstate. Somewhere along the way he'd find a place to dump Henry's body. Because Henry was from Arizona, bound for who knew where, he likely wouldn't be missed for days.

CHAPTER TWELVE

Sunset and Kansas City

They arrived at the same time. Lucas pulled into a Phillips station, moved up to the last pump, and stuck the nozzle in the tank.

Jodi hopped out of the truck. "I'll see if I can get Chase." A cold drizzle quickened her pace to the outside phone booth.

Lucas watched her dial, wait for an answer, and smile when somebody did. He guessed it was Chase Witherspoon. She tossed a glance at Lucas while she listened. He couldn't tell whether she liked what she heard, but he saw her scribble something on a scrap of paper.

Jodi hung up the phone, came back, and handed the note to Lucas. On it was an address some place on Warwick Boulevard. It meant nothing to him, since he was not familiar with Kansas City streets. He replaced the nozzle, twisted om the gas cap, and went inside to pay. He asked the stocky, bearded young man at the cash register how to get to Warwick Boulevard.

"East of the Plaza a couple of blocks," the man said, flashing a tobacco stained grin. "Turn left off 47th. You might want to be kinda careful over there. Some of those streets are pretty weird." He handed Lucas his change. "Some of the people are too."

Lucas took his change, waved thanks, and left. He found Warwick and turned left off 47th Street like the man said. The Phillips cashier was right about the weird streets. Lucas wouldn't have to be a country boy from Borger, Texas to get lost where he finally found the address on Warwick. It was a stately old brownstone house which, like many others in midtown Kansas City, was converted to apartments. He braked to a stop at the curb, and tossed a questioning look at Jodi. He had no notion as to what was about to take place, and he was pretty sure she didn't either.

"Do you want me to wait for you?" he said.

"No." She grabbed his hand. "I want you to come with me."

A crumbling concrete walk led them to three steps up to the front porch. A couple of yellow cats scurried away from the screen door that looked like it was bashed with a baseball bat. Parked in the driveway was a gray four-door Dodge. At the wheel sat a bald man in a gray suit. Lucas nodded to him. All he got in response was a stern scowl.

The man in the Dodge watched with no apparent interest until Lucas knocked on the door of the house. "Who you looking for?" the suit said.

"Chase Witherspoon," Jodi said.

"I don't think he's home," said the gray suit. "If he is, he's in trouble."

The sound of scuffling feet filtered from the other side of the door. A man's harsh voice yelled, "We got him!"

The man in the car got out and rushed to the front door. "You folks need to stand aside," he said to Jodi and Lucas. "Police business."

They did as they were told. The door burst open and four gray-suited men hurtled through it. The three men in front almost collapsed in a heap. In the middle, two men, each clutching one of Chase's arms, struggled with the thin, handcuffed young man with a full beard and shoulder length brown hair. The fourth gray suit was shoving him out the door from behind.

Jodi's eyes were glued to the face of the young man with

the beard. Lucas saw her lips silently form the word "Chase."

The gray suit in the back shot a stern look at Lucas and Jodi. "Who are these people?" he demanded to nobody in particular.

"I don't know,"' said the man from the car. "Friends of his, I guess."

The man in the back looked at Lucas and Jodi as if trying to divine how good friends they were, and whether they might be involved in whatever it was they were hauling Chase away for. He made an off handed gesture as if dismissing the matter. He made a sudden move toward the car, shoved Chase into the back seat, and climbed in beside him. The driver started the motor and shifted into reverse.

With a soft, tranquil voice, Chase Witherspoon from the back seat of the car said, "Can I say something?"

A gruff voice said, "Make it fast."

With searching eyes, Chase looked at Jodi as if trying to transmit a message. He ignored Lucas. "I'm sorry," he said with a wan smile. "I didn't know this was coming down. If you want to wait–"

"He won't be back," snapped the gray suit closest to Jodi. He slammed the car door shut, and yelled, "Let's get him the hell out of here!"

The car screeched out of the driveway and onto the street. As it sped away, Jodi heard Chase yell, "Remember Curtis Blaine?

Jodi nodded yes.

With a broad smile, Witherspoon was whisked away in the gray Dodge.

Lucas took Jodi's hand and led her to the truck. "You're shaking like a leaf," he said. "You want to tell me about it?"

"I can't believe it, Lucas. Chase Witherspoon. Is he a junkie, a robber? Did he kill somebody? Why are they dragging him away?"

Lucas offered her an "I don't know" shake of his head, and stepped on the gas. He spotted a restaurant with a sign that said "Winstead's" and parked in front. Inside, they found a brown leather-bound booth, and Lucas grabbed the plastic-covered menu. Winstead's specialty appeared to be hamburgers. When a young blond waitress wearing a broad smile asked what they wanted, Lucas ordered a burger for himself and another for Jodi.

Jodi sat as if in a trance. When the waitress brought their food, Jodi hardly touched hers.

Lucas decided Jodi was not going to volunteer any information, He took a bite of hamburger, washed it down with a swig from his water glass. "Who is Curtis Blaine?"

Jodi took a moment to answer. "I never knew Curtis." She nibbled at her burger. "Chase used to talk about him." She gave Lucas a quick look, as if she just thought of something he ought to know. "Chase was one of those that bastard Barquist ran off. He and I met one Saturday afternoon, one of the few times John allowed me to drive the car. When he drank up all the booze, he sent me for more because he was too drunk to drive. He sent me to get more.

"Any way, Chase and I were trying for the same parking spot in front of Walgreen's. I yelled at him, and all he did was smile and motion me to go ahead and pull into the parking space. When we got inside the store, I bumped a candy rack and scattered stuff all over. Chase helped me pick it up and put it back.

"He asked if he could buy me a drink, and I said no thanks, I don't drink.

"Well," he said, "how about a cup of coffee or a Coke?" He seemed so nice, I said yes.

"When Ollie didn't come back, Chase and I got to seeing each other. He said he didn't mind about the baby, that he understood things like that. He came to the house a few times till John made life miserable for both of us, and Chase said he couldn't take it anymore. If he hung around, he said, sooner or later there'd be a big blow up between himself and John, and he didn't want that.

"Chase came back to Kansas City and played clubs and shows with different combos. One of them was Curtis Blaine's band. Curtis cut a few records and stayed busy around town, and that's how he and Chase got together. He's a good lead guitar man, and he helped out on the vocals. Curtis took him on. They played some gigs in Las Vegas and some of the better clubs around the country. About a year ago at O'Hare in Chicago, Curtis got buzzed with a big metal belt buckle in his suitcase. When they opened the bag, they found some cocaine and stuff, and it went on from there. Curtis went to jail, and the band broke up."

"And that's why Chase asked if you remembered Curtis Blaine," Lucas said.

Jodi's hand went to her mouth as if struck by a horrible thought. "Oh, lordy!" she gasped. "Dope! Chase wanted me to know why they were busting him. I can't believe it. Chase Witherspoon a dope head?"

"Maybe a peddler," Lucas said.

"Chase wouldn't push that stuff." But, even as she protested Witherspoon's innocence, her words carried the hollow sound of doubt.

"If he used it, he'd sell it to get more," Lucas said.

"Nobody could make me believe Chase was a dope peddler."

"So, what are you thinking now?"

"Well, there goes my job in Kansas City."

She fell silent. Lucas knew her thinking wheels were spinning. After a moment she perked up and looked him squarely in the eye. "Lucas," she said earnestly, "from the day you're born until you ride in a hearse, nothing is so bad that it couldn't be worse."

He didn't have to guess that bit of homespun philosophy was drawn from her mother's well of wisdom. It wasn't easy to put it together with her current situation, but Lucas was relieved that her determination was again showing signs of life.

"You want to tell me what that means?" he said with a grin.

"What that means is somehow, some way, come hell or high water, I'm going to get to Nashville, Tennessee. I sure as hell am not going back to where I came from."

"Tough lady. How come you keep quoting your mama all the time?"

"Because my daddy never said anything."

They found a motel on Broadway, and Lucas parked under

the canopy.

"Make sure it's clean," Jodi said. "I can't sleep on sheets somebody else slept on."

A tall man in a black pin-stripe suit and a red tie greeted Lucas at the desk. He had a vacancy in room 342, and the rate would be $47.89 for the night.

"Could I take a look at it?" Lucas said. "I mean—"

"I know," the man said with a knowing smile. "The women always want to know if it's clean."

He handed Lucas a key with the room number on it, and said, "She's welcome to inspect it."

Lucas took the key to the truck, and invited Jodi to inspect the room.

"Well, this looks like a nice place," she said. "I guess I trust him this time."

Lucas gave a bellboy the okay sign. The boy grabbed their bags and led the way to the elevator. He unlocked the door of room 342 and carried the bags inside.

"My name is Aaron," the boy said. "If you need anything, please call for me."

"Are the beds clean?" Lucas said.

The boy gave him a startled look, as if he'd never been asked that question.

"For forty-seven bucks," Jodi said, "it sure ought to be clean."

Lucas flipped Aaron a bill, and the boy left.

Jodi giggled, and stripped off her clothes as she headed for the bathroom. She showered and shampooed. When she emerged a towel was wrapped around her body and another one bee-hived around her wet head. She sat down in front of the mirror and began fussing with her hair.

"Do you know anything about the stars?" she said.

Lucas thought about that for a minute. "You mean like Emmy Lou Harris, Johnny Cash—folks like that?"

"No, silly, I mean the stars. In the sky. My mama used to say the stars ruled the world."

"Uh-huh. Them and the lawyers."

"Lawyers?"

"And General Motors. I had this friend Frank Stickney

who believed whatever was good for General Motors was good for the country."

"What did he mean by that?"

"Frank never said, but he went to his grave believing it."

"Some kind of guy, huh?"

"Yeah. Frank carried the mail for a while till he wore out all the dogs in the neighborhood being nice to them. He was a philosopher too. One of his favorite sayings was, when the mind is closed, no truth can enter."

"He must have been talking about you."

"How so?"

"Well, you don't believe in the stars, but I think they cause lots of things to happen that we don't know about."

"I wouldn't be surprised."

"I do, Lucas. I believe we were supposed to meet just the way we did."

"And you believe the stars did that?"

"Yes. God knows what we're doing all the time. He controls the stars, and they control what we do." Hair brush at half mast, she peered at his image in the mirror. "It's something you feel, like knowing when you love somebody. You know because it happens inside."

Lucas grunted and nibbled at her ear.

She gave him a good natured elbow in the ribs. He grabbed her and kissed her on the mouth.

"Those stars of yours may know something we don't," he said, "but I think we're in charge of what happens to us. Either way, Jodi, I believe in you. And I believe one of these days you'll be one of the biggest country stars the world ever knew."

"You're putting me on."

"No. And just to prove it, tomorrow morning I'm putting you on a bus to Nashville, and I'll bet in no time at all people will be hearing your records on the radio all over hell and half of Texas."

"Lucas—."

"Why, I bet it won't take longer than the middle of next week before Jodi Parker, superstar, will be in such demand she'll forget all about lil' ole Lucas Malone."

"That's not true."

"Well, now which part is not true?"

"I'll never forget you."

"What about the other part—about your being a big star?"

"Well," she said with a grin, "do you think it'll take that long?"

He gave her a solemn look that said he missed her already. Tomorrow she'd be gone.

Through the gray early morning haze, Lucas and Jodi witnessed the birth of a new day. They peered out their motel room window and watched the Kansas City Sunday come alive. In the distance gleamed the gold dome of a church with a cross topping its tower. Hovering clouds beheaded the gray buildings standing like statues in the heart of the city. Cars darted like lizards along silent Sunday morning streets.

Sometime today, Jodi Parker would realize her dream of arriving in Nashville, where Lucas promised the world would welcome her with open arms, and all things good would come to her. She envisioned swarms of people with open arms awaiting her arrival, eager to blaze for her the trail to inevitable stardom. All a part of the dream, she knew, with no notion how she would be greeted, nor if, indeed, she would be greeted at all.

Lucas observed the uncertainty etched on her face, like she was questioning whether she was ready to face what lay ahead in the mecca of country magic.

"You're mighty quiet," he said. "Are you okay?"

"Okay? Why wouldn't I be okay?"

"Nothing's bothering you?"

"Nothing's bothering me."

She began placing things in her open bag on the bed. When Lucas called the bus station about the schedule to Nashville she was ecstatic. She anticipated the journey like a four-year-old on her first visit to Disneyland. Now she was moping, wishing she could delay her departure, as if closing her packed bag would signify some frightening finality.

"Yesterday," she said, "you told me you were my best friend. Did you mean it?"

"Yes."

"Even though we hardly know each other?"

"Lots of people live together for years without knowing each other as well as we do after two days."

Her hand caressed the spot above his right eye where Leon left a purple bruise. "I don't know what I'd have done without you, Lucas."

"You'd be all right, Jodi. We were lucky to be in the same place at the same time."

She threw her arms around his neck. "You're right, Lucas," she sniffled. "I am afraid."

He couldn't hold her close enough, but he tried. He didn't want to let her go. He didn't want to lose her to a world he knew nothing about, the world where he hoped she'd be happy. The strange new world of music to which Cal Slater opened the door. Jodi questioned whether she was strong enough to walk through it.

"What about Cal Slater?" Lucas said.

"Cal Slater is a name scratched on a piece of paper. I know him as a voice on the phone."

"He said he'd help you, didn't he?"

"He listened to my tapes, and said he liked what he heard. Going to Nashville was my idea. He didn't recommend that I come, but I knew that was where I wanted to be. And it gave me the courage to get away from John Barquist."

"Everybody's afraid of something, Jodi. The day I walked into George Benton's office to talk about a job, I was so shaky I wished I hadn't come. After a couple of minutes I found out he was a man just like me, and everything turned out fine."

"But what if Nashville doesn't turn out fine?"

"Well, you're a believer. Put those stars of yours to work. Even if everything doesn't work out the first time, it's not the end of the world. You'll have other opportunities. You're too tough to give up after the first try."

She turned away and spread her arms in a gesture of frustration. "My little Jason, way off out there without his mama. I don't know, Lucas. There's something about it that doesn't feel right."

"I bet one of these days ole Jase will be telling you how

proud he is of you because you at least gave it a shot. And you know what, Jodi? Most people don't mind losing as much as not having the chance to win. This is your chance. If you don't go through with it, you might regret it for the rest of your life."

"That's easy for you to say. You don't have anything to worry about."

Lucas gave his head a thoughtful scratch. "Now, let me think about that," he said. "Is this the same lady who told me she had more guts than the packing house? Come on, Jodi. You've come too far to turn back now."

Lucas parked the pickup three spaces from the bus station entrance, and gave Jodi a solemn look. She hadn't said a word since they left the motel. He waited for her to break the silence. She didn't.

He lifted her bag and guitar out of the back of the truck and carried them inside. Jodi followed him through the automatic glass doors to the crowded waiting room. He dropped the luggage, steered Jodi into a chair, and went to the counter to check her in.

"The bus is loading," the lady ticket agent said. "Leaving for Nashville in nine minutes."

Lucas told Jodi that. "Oh, Lucas," she cried, "I wish you were coming with me."

"So do I, Jodi, but we've already talked about that. Remember, I'm on your side, no matter how things turn out. I'd only be in the way if I went with you."

"I want to stay with you."

She couldn't know how badly he wanted her with him, but he also knew how important it was that she go without him.

"I don't know anything about the music business, Jodi. Cal Slater sounds like a decent kind of guy who'll do what he can for you. One thing for sure, you know what you want, and Slater may be able to help you get it. You can't give up on that."

From the loud speaker came a man's raspy voice announcing the departure of the bus. "Departing for Nashville in four minutes," he said. "Now loading."

A redcap grabbed Jodi's bags and tossed them into the bowels of the bus. Lucas handed him a couple of dollar bills, and looked into Jodi's misty eyes. "You know how to get in touch with me," he said. "Be sure to let me know where you are."

"I will."

"We can talk any time."

A brief kiss and Jodi was gone. She found a seat by the window. She looked back at Lucas with tears in her eyes. The bus crawled away. Jodi waved at Lucas with a wan smile.

He saw her lips form the words, "I love you."

He waited for a long moment, and caught a final glimpse of Jodi as she threw him a kiss. The bus made a wide turn, as it disappeared around the corner. A minute later, Lucas revved up the Ford and turned its nose toward Chicago.

CHAPTER THIRTEEN

Goodbye, Henry Bellows

John Barquist never heard of Cairo, Illinois. All he knew about it was a roadside sign that told him Highway 24 went there. He followed it through Kentucky on its way to Tennessee.

He looked for a place to dump the dead body of Henry Bellows. He found it on a dirt road that wound off the highway down along the banks of a river, and turned off the highway. He searched right and left for a secluded spot where the body wouldn't be discovered for days—maybe never—giving him time enough to carry out his heinous chore in Nashville and be gone, and nobody would ever know he was there.

At the edge of the river he spotted a small aluminum fishing boat tied to a sapling on an earthen ramp. He eased the Olds that way, careful not to get so close the car might slide into the water. With a nervous eye he glanced around to be sure he wasn't seen by a fisherman. Satisfied he was alone, he popped the trunk lid and hauled the body of Henry Bellows into the boat. He secured it to the bottom with the anchor line. He took the jack handle from the trunk of the Olds and ripped a jagged hole in the bottom of the boat, shoved it into the river, and watched it take on water.

Crickets chirped, bull frogs croaked, and the river gurgled against the sides of the small boat as the current carried it downstream. Barquist watched from the bank until it began to sink. Within a few minutes the boat disappeared into the Tennessee River. He slid under the steering wheel of the Olds, and sniffed irritably at the odor of rotting tree roots. He turned the key, shifted into reverse, and spun back onto Highway 24, headed east, in a raging sweat to get to Nashville.

Chapter Fourteen

Welcome to Nashville

His name was Emil Enlow. He hadn't always been a cab driver, nor was he always seventy-two years old. He quit school after second grade and started shining shoes on the street corners of downtown Nashville to help his widowed mother feed and clothe himself and a younger brother and sister. By the time he was old enough to drive, Emil saved enough money for the down payment on a used Dodge. He put a "Taxi" sign in the window, and started hauling people around.

That was fifty-six years ago. He often entertained his passengers with his harmonica version of "Listen to the Mockingbird." While he unloaded their luggage, he kept his feet busy with a toe dance that brought smiles to their faces. His passengers often tossed him a few coins, encouraging him to go into what he called his "fast dance," and the coins kept coming.

One day a man named George Hayes, known by country music enthusiasts as the Solemn ole Judge, needed a ride from the airport to Ryman Auditorium, the home of the Grand Ole Opry. Emil rendered his dance routine, and Mr. Hayes was so impressed he invited Emil to dance on the stage of the Grand Ole Opry on Saturday night. Emil did. He played his harmonica and did his fast dance, and brought the house down in waves of applause.

Emil drove his taxi seven days a week, but, for twenty-seven years, Saturday night found him on the stage of the Grand Ole Opry. Then, in 1974 the Opry moved from the Ryman to the luxurious new Opryland Theater. Emil didn't go. He said the Opry wasn't the same in that "fancified" new theater. It "lost character" when it moved from the old church, and he didn't want to do it anymore.

He kept dancing, though, driving his cab every day, picking up fares at the bus station. He didn't care much for the airport crowd. Many of the fares were too snippy. He didn't like being snipped at by people who depended on him to "carry" them wherever they wanted to go. But the bus folks were always nice to him. He enjoyed helping people like Jodi Parker.

He scratched his gray beard and puffed at his corncob pipe. "You new in town, missy?"

"Yes," Jodi said, eyes sparkling with wonder. "My first time here."

"Uh-huh," Emil grunted with a knowing nod. How many others had he greeted on their arrival in the music capital of the world who displayed the same wide-eyed eagerness, anticipating the time when the world would bow at their feet? How many had he hauled back to the bus station. He knew their disappointment. They took away with them nothing but a heart full of shattered dreams of fame and fortune? Fame often turned to shame because they failed to accomplish what the folks back home expected of them. What could they say to their friends and family?

"Lots of fine folks come to Nashval," Emil said to Jodi. "I carried most of 'em one time or 'nother. You a musician?"

"I play some and sing some," Jodi said. "Mostly I like to write."

"Uh-huh. It's good you can write. Might give you a little edge against most of 'em. Musicians come cheap 'round here. Must be thousands of 'em lookin' for work. More thumb picks than toothpicks in Nashval."

"I'm supposed to see a publisher named Cal Slater."

Emil cast her a silent glance, as if he knew something she needed to know. With a bewildered shake of his shaggy head, he scolded himself, blaming old age for a lapse of memory.

"Most folks blow in here, don't know nobody, not even a name," he said. "Can't get jobs. Think the world's gonna spin faster 'cause they hit town. Most of 'em can't carry a tune in a gunnysack, but they keep comin' anyhow. Then—when it don't work out for 'em, they go crawlin' back home, hopin' nobody sees 'em comin'." He tamped the bowl of his pipe, and said, "They don't call this Heartbreak City for nothin'. Some people see failure as worse than death."

Jodi smiled uneasily, and stirred in the seat beside him.

"Folks with talent find out talent all on its ownself ain't enough. You don't know nobody, you don't get no place in this town. Them they do know might steal 'em blind. 'Specially some o' them shyster so-called publishers, promoters, and record companies that set up shop on 'bout ever' corner." He turned onto Sixteenth Avenue South and stopped at the address Jodi gave him.

"This is as far as we go, missy," he said.

Emil stuffed Jodi's fare in a shirt pocket and hobbled around to help with her bags. He moved to get back in the car, and came to an abrupt halt. He looked at Jodi with a dead stare, like something she ought to know just came to mind. With a bewildered shake of his shaggy head, he looked at her with sadness in his eyes. "You say you 'sposed to see Cal Slater?"

"Yes, sir. I sent him a tape of some of my songs."

"Oh, little missy," he said. "I—I am so sorry. I don't know why I—.I don't think you— You ain't gon be seein' Mr. Slater."

"Not see him? Why not?"

"Lord hep me, missy, I hate to be tellin' you this. Two days ago in Memphis they was a bad car wreck. Three people died. One of 'em was Cal Slater."

Bitter tears filled her eyes. "Killed? Cal Slater is dead?"

"I'm so sorry, missy."

"I came all the way from Phoenix to see him." Distraught, disappointed, at her wits end, she wept.

Emil opened his arms, and Jodi walked into them. It was not the first time he'd consoled a broken heart. To Jodi, it didn't matter where the kindness came from.

"It's gon be all right," Emil said, as they clung to each other. "We gon work it out."

"What can I do?" she sobbed.

"You want to get in the car?" Emil said. "Maybe if we talked a little we could come up with somethin'." He opened the car door and she slumped dejectedly onto the front seat. "I don't want to see nothin' bad happenin' to you," he said. "It's comin' on dark. You want me to carry you some place where you can think about it, maybe work out in your mind what you want to do?"

Lucas said the same thing back in Baker's Bluff. He'd bought her supper, and gave her time to decide what she wanted to do. How long ago was that? To Jodi it seemed like half of forever, though she kissed him goodbye only that morning at the Kansas City bus station. Where was Lucas now when she needed him so? Why didn't he come with her to help her navigate a world she didn't know?

CHAPTER FIFTEEN

Hello, Chicago

Between swipes of the wiper blades Lucas kept an eye out for signs pointing to Naperville. Hugh Landry sent him directions, but so far he'd seen nothing that told him which road to take. Was his vision blurred by the rain? Or maybe it was his preoccupation with thoughts of Jodi on her way to Nashville, whether she arrived, and what happened to her.

He could have gone with her. The clock wasn't ticking against him. Old Hugh would be tickled to see him no matter when he got there. But he needed time–time to reflect on what took place between himself and Jodi. Time to take a look at whatever he felt was turning his life around. He knew he was in love with her.

"Yeah, I know what you're going to say."

"Love?" sneered the accusing voice he never seemed able to escape. *"You only met her two days ago, for crying out loud! How can you talk about love for a girl you picked up on the highway, and spent a few hours with in a bar and a motel? Are you out of your mind?"*

"Maybe," Lucas conceded. But he wished he hadn't sent a scared little girl off to Nashville by herself.

Emil, Jodi's new friend

"Missy," Emil said, "you want me to carry you back to the bus station?"

Jodi got there because Lucas helped her, and she couldn't let him down. She came all that way to see Cal Slater, but Cal was dead. Even so, taking the bus to some place else wouldn't solve anything. It would only close the curtain on a beautiful dream, and mark her as one of those disappointed failures Emil told her about. She was where she wanted to be. But what was she to do now?

She glanced toward the house that was converted to Cal Slater's office.

"I'd like to go sit on that porch," she said to Emil.

"On the porch," Emil said. It was not a question, but the way he said it, Jodi could tell he was puzzled as to why she'd want to sit on the porch of the old house Cal Slater wasn't in.

"Mr. Slater must have sat there sometimes, thinking things over," she said. "Maybe that'd be a good place for me to do the same."

"Uh-huh." Emil questioned whether that was a good idea.

"Did you tell me your name?"

"Emil. Emil Enlow."

"Emil Enlow? Haven't I heard of you?"

"Not likely," he said. She probably was too young to remember him from his Opry years.

She put out her hand. He hesitated briefly before taking it in his own.

"My name is Jodi Parker," she said. "You're a very kind man, Mr. Enlow, and I appreciate what you've done for me."

She got out of the cab, and started carrying her bag to the porch. Emil grabbed it and her guitar and walked with her.

"I don't like leavin' you here all alone this way, missy," Emil said. He placed the bags on the edge of the porch. "Why don't you let me drop you some place where–."

"I'll be fine, thanks." She knew no one in Nashville, and had no place to go.

He wasn't sure she'd be fine. His look told her so. "All right," he said finally, turning away. "You knock 'em dead now, ye hear?".

Emil was her introduction to Nashville. She was sorry to watch his cab ease away from the curb and disappear down Sixteenth Avenue.

Adding to her dilemma was the hand-written note taped inside the glass front door: Due to the death of Cal Slater, the offices of Slater Publishing will be closed until further notice.

Cal Slater was dead. Slater Publishing was closed until further notice. Maybe forever! To Jodi it was like St. Peter hung a "closed" sign on the Pearly Gates. Closed until Further Notice!

The excitement, enthusiasm, pent up energy, and anticipation of meeting the man she trusted to launch her music career—all melted away. The reality of being denied the blessing of meeting Cal Slater, who could have made her dream come true, trickled painfully into the heels of her size six boots. Distraught, drained of energy, she sank wearily onto the edge of the porch. Eyes misty with bewilderment, she never felt so alone—alone in a world in which she was a total stranger, where she knew nobody, except kindly old Emil Enlow. And she sent him away.

Second thoughts flooded her mind. Maybe coming to Nashville wasn't a good idea. Maybe she should have stayed back there in Phoenix, enduring John's abuse. At least she'd be with her son. Being away from him showered more loneliness upon her. And, back in Phoenix, she'd have a place to sleep tonight, which she didn't have now.

Who did she think she was anyway? How long must she live with a dream before yielding to the reality that it's only a dream? Dreams rarely come true. She silently prayed for a way out of her predicament.

The sun was looking for a place to hide. The voice of reason told her she couldn't sit there on that porch all night. There was no way to know whether the door of Slater Publishing would ever again be open. The one thing she was sure of was that if it did, Cal Slater wouldn't be there. And, more important, the money Lucas gave her wouldn't last forever.

Her thoughts were interrupted by the sound of screeching

tires. She looked up to see in the deepening shadows a car braking to a stop at the curb. Out of a yellow Cadillac convertible crawled a lanky young man who called to her from behind dark glasses.

"Are you okay?" he said. She didn't answer. He walked around the car and up the sidewalk to the porch. "You look lost."

"No, I'm not lost."

"I guess you heard about Slater."

"Yes."

"Well, uh–can I give you a lift some place?" He nodded toward the luggage. "I'm pretty good with bags and guitars. I used to be a bellhop."

Jodi had to do something. Maybe accepting his offer of a lift was what she had to do. She stood up.

He hefted her bags and led the way to his car. "What's your name?".

"Jodi Parker."

"Jody?"

"With an 'i'."

"You just get to town?"

"Yes."

"Where are you from?"

"Phoenix."

"Hmmnn. Phoenix is a long way off."

"I know."

"I'm pleased to make your acquaintance."

"Thank you."

"I'm Josh Campbell."

Josh Campbell! Star of the Grand Ole Opry?

Campbell opened the passenger side door, waited for her to get seated, and tossed her luggage in the back seat. In spite of her uncertain situation, Jodi couldn't deny the thrill of being so close to a genuine country music star who helped her into his yellow Cadillac convertible!

He slid his slender six-foot frame under the wheel and started the motor. "How did you know Slater?"

"I didn't really know him. I sent him a tape of some of my songs, and we talked a couple times on the phone. He didn't know I was coming to Nashville."

"Cal's death is a huge loss to country music. Some drunk ran a red light and crashed into him, then walked away without a scratch."

Jodi felt an emptiness she couldn't describe.

Campbell apparently shared her feelings. "We buried Cal this afternoon." He shifted into gear. "Well, we could sit here and talk all night, or you could tell me if I can drop you off some place."

"No." She still had no place to go.

"No? Meaning—"

"I have no place to go."

"And you don't know anybody?"

"Nobody."

"Uh-huh. Well, now—"

"I did meet a fine old gentleman named Emil."

"Cab driver?"

"Yes."

Campbell grinned. "Emil Enlow. A great talent. Everybody knows Emil."

Jodi's eyes clouded up, and Josh caught sight of a tear trickling down her cheek.

"Here now." He reached into the glove compartment and brought out a box of Kleenex. "Those eyes are way too pretty for such ugly tears."

She took a Kleenex and dabbed at her eyes." I'm sorry," she sobbed.

"No need to be sorry. It happens to all of us one time or another." He guided the car onto the street. "If you don't know anybody, and you don't have any place to go, how about a place to stay tonight?"

She smiled and shook her head.

"You really are in a fix, Jodi. What in the world are we going to do with you?"

He reminded her of Lucas, adding to her loneliness. Between sniffles, she said, "Why did you stop for me?"

"Well, I was driving past and saw this little girl sitting on the porch all by herself. She looked loster than anybody I've seen in a long time. Right away I guessed you came to see

Cal, and I knew you weren't going to."

"Thank you."

"Actually, you can thank that Cadillac of mine. You know how traffic slows for railroad crossings? Well, that Cadillac has a way of slowing down when it sees a pretty girl sitting all alone on someone else's porch at sundown."

That brought a chuckle, and Jodi folded the Kleenex into her palm.

"To tell you the truth," Campbell went on, "I was only spreading my day's supply of Southern hospitality. It's a requirement around here, you know. If they find out you didn't use all of it, they take away your grits. And it's impossible to survive in Nashville for more than two days without grits." As though struck by an earth shattering notion, he said, "Do you like barbecue?"

"I love it."

"Okay then. I'm going to treat you to the best barbecue in the free world at Smoky Joe's downtown. Joe does his own cooking, and he's got that out-of-this-world sauce that hereto has been denied all but kings, presidents, and ladies of the court. If it doesn't absolutely melt in your mouth

I'll buy you a condo in Cancun."

If Josh's intent was to bolster Jodi's spirits, it worked. She tossed the Kleenex aside, and managed a small laugh at this crazy man who claimed to be Josh Campbell.

Campbell pushed open the door to the restaurant with a "Help Wanted" ad in the window. He was greeted by the sweat-shiny face of the smoky one himself.

"Hey, Josh," Joe called from behind the barbecue pit where he was flipping ribs and chops. "How come you stay gone so long, man?"

"I don't stay gone so long, man," Josh mimicked. "I just can't stand your cooking more often than about every nine days."

Joe beamed. "Yeah. You and them other camels, huh?"

Josh ushered Jodi to a booth and sat across from her.

A slender, brown haired waitress brought water, and asked what they would like. Josh ordered ribs for both of them. When the waitress went away, Josh said, "You sent

Slater some tapes?"

"Actually it was only one tape with six songs on it," Jodi said. "The one he liked best was called 'Marty's Place.'"

"What's that about?"

"Marty Robbins."

"Hmmn. You know Marty died a while back."

"Yes, but Mr. Slater thought his fans would appreciate the song as a tribute to Marty."

"Did you keep a copy of the tape?"

"I did. Would you like to hear it?"

"Yes, I would like to hear it. Singers are always looking for good material. But there are vultures in this town who could swoop down and grab a good song right out of Fort Knox. And they could snatch up your tape and copyright every song on it before you knew what was happening."

"Oh, I didn't–"

"What I'm saying is–" He waved to someone Jodi couldn't see. "If Cal Slater thought your tape was that good, you need to be careful who you show it to."

His words echoed the warning of Emil Enlow. If things were that risky, how would she know whom to trust? How could she be sure Josh Campbell wasn't one of those he warned her about? But surely a country star like him would have access to good material without having to steal it from some writer.

She had to trust someone. She couldn't go around with a head full of music that was useless till someone like Josh Campbell thought it was good enough to expose to the Nashville establishment. He was the only performer she knew. He could have left her parked out there on Slater's front porch, but he didn't. He was kind enough to rescue her and haul her to Smoky Joe's for barbecue. That was worth a lot.

"So," she said, "what do I do now?"

"A man just came through the door who might be able to help you. His name is Tom Crocker. He was a close friend of Slater's. Tom was once married to Bobbie Sue Whitworth."

Jodi remembered Bobbie Sue. One of her favorite songs was Bobbie Sue's recording of

The Door is Always Open (If You Want to Come Back Home).

Three years before, Bobbie Sue was killed in a Fourth of July boating accident on Lake Taneycomo in the Missouri Ozarks near Branson.

"Okay," Jodi said. "How do I get to see Tom Crocker?"

Again Josh waved a hand, and a moment later beside their booth appeared a thin, lean-faced man six-feet-three inches tall. His deep set brown eyes seemed to devour Jodi, making her feel like she was the only person in the world he cared about at that moment.

"Jodi Parker," Josh said to Crocker. "Jodi, Tom Crocker."

Crocker clasped her hand in both of his. "I'm pleased to make your acquaintance."

Josh explained Jodi's plight. Crocker showed sincere interest with a nod of his forty-nine-year-old graying head. From a shirt pocket he brought a pale blue business card and held it out to Jodi.

"When you get time," he said to her, "maybe you'd like to stop by for a chat." He smiled and walked away.

Jodi covered her face with both hands, and shook her head. "I can't believe it. Why is this happening to me?"

"What?"

"This." She spread her arms. "All of it. Here I am eating barbecue with one of country music's biggest stars, and some man with the eyes of an angel just happens by, and invites me to stop by for a chat when I have time."

Josh shrugged. "That's Nashville. Part of that old time Southern hospitality I told you about. You never know what's going to happen. We've been expecting Elvis to come back any time." He stuffed a forkful of beef in his mouth. "Now, what's going to happen to you? You said you had no place to stay."

"I saw a motel on the way here. You could drop me there, if it's not out of your way."

He gave that a thoughtful nod. "I don't mean to be pushy, but you're welcome to bunk in at my place if you'd like."

"Thank you. You're very kind, and I appreciate it, but I need some time to think about where I go from here."

Josh dropped her bags inside the door of the Best Western room and flipped on the light. "Are you going to be all right?"

"I'll be fine. Thank you so much."

"Will I see you again?" he asked.

"I hope so."

"I'd like to hear from you after you talk to Crocker." He stepped to the telephone table, found a sheet of paper, scribbled something on it, and handed it to Jodi. "That's my phone number. Will you call me?"

"Yes. I'll call you."

"Goodnight then."

"Goodnight."

She closed the door behind him and leaned against it for a long time. Her eyes were misty, and her heart full of hope. How could she be so lucky—meeting three wonderful people in a town full of people she didn't know? Maybe dreams did come true, after all. She was glad Lucas insisted she come, though she wished he'd come with her. For the little girl from Baker's Bluff, Kansas, she never could have guessed what lay in store for her in the city of her dreams.

CHAPTER SIXTEEN

The monster arrives

Nashville, Tennessee was not a place where John Barquist thought he'd ever find himself. He hadn't lost anything there he needed to go looking for–except Jodi Parker. Nashville was a bigger city than he expected. Finding Jodi turned out to be a greater challenge than he imagined.

Devoid of talent and musical ambition himself, Barquist couldn't believe anyone would want to go there. He'd much rather be back in Phoenix boozing it up and chasing broads. But the humiliation of Jodi's running out on him stuck in his craw. He was spurred to vengeance by a lascivious, maniacal mind.

Standing on the corner of a busy downtown Nashville intersection, Barquist sneaked a nip from the bottle he carried in a brown paper bag. He peered into cars that hurried by, searching for the face belonging to Jodi Parker. He'd already scoured the clubs and honky-tonks, sure she'd be some place where country music was playing. Though he hadn't found her, he promised the devil he would not quit until he did.

CHAPTER SEVENTEEN

So, Lucas, where have you been?

There was no question in the mind of Lucas Malone that his college friend Hugh Landry was smarter than most people he knew. Lucas was Hugh's favorite target on the football field. He found him open for many long gainers during their playing days at Baylor. Tall, dark and athletic, not only was Hugh the Baylor Bears quarterback. He also was the undisputed brain of their graduating class, respected by men and loved by women.

One of those women was Jennifer Coan, known as Miss Campus Personality, Homecoming Queen, Football Queen–Whatever required beauty, charm, and congeniality, Jenny was it during her four years at Baylor. After they married six years ago, Hugh and Jenny settled in her hometown of Naperville, Illinois. Hugh was welcomed aboard as an account executive at Merrill Lynch in Chicago.

Hugh didn't participate in the Seven Eleven episode for which Lucas spent three years in Huntsville prison. Regarding Landry as the team leader, on and off the playing field, Lucas still was nagged by the question of why Hugh was not there when the decision to hit the convenience store was made. Lucas's time in prison denied him the opportunity to discuss the matter with his friend. That wasn't the reason he made the trip to Chicago. But maybe now he could get some answers. He found a phone booth at a Phillips gas station, looked up the number in the book, and dialed.

"Lucas!" Jenny screamed when she heard his voice.

"I hope I'm not interrupting something important," Lucas said.

"For you I'd stop in the middle of having my second kid! We'd about given up on your ever coming north."

"Well, you know how it is with Texas. Once you get in, it's hard to get out. Is Hugh in?"

"No, and I'm not sure he'll be home tonight. He's playing in a golf tournament in Milwaukee. I'll be here though, and I know Hugh would want you to high-tail it on up here whether he shows up or not. You're only an hour or so away. Do you have directions?"

"Well, I can get to Naperville, but–"

She told him how to find their address once he got into the city.

"Why don't you just come on up here, Lucas? And don't worry about Hugh. He's probably off chasing some broad any way."

Lucas knew that was a joke. Hugh had all the woman he could handle at home.

"He thought he might stay overnight to see a client in the morning," Jenny said. "But don't let that slow you down. I'm still better looking than he is."

"Okay then, I'll be there."

Chicago might be a great place to visit, but Lucas already knew he wouldn't want to live there. Herding his red Ford pickup through bustling traffic on a Sunday afternoon was no picnic. He finally turned into the driveway of the handsome ranch style home in the middle of a lush green lawn, surrounded by maple trees. He whistled a breathy sigh, and slumped against the seat. He stepped down onto the gravel driveway. He looked forward to his visit with old friends, but his thoughts were of Nashville and Jodi Parker.

Hardly had his boots touched the ground before Jenny popped out the door and ran to greet him. "Hold this," she said. She deposited her baby daughter in the arms of Lucas Malone, grabbed him around the neck, and planted a kiss squarely on his mouth.

Jenny was always friendly, but her greeting was somewhat warmer than Lucas anticipated.

"Come on in, Lucas," she said. "I just talked to Hugh. He's on his way home."

"And who is this lady I'm holding here?" Lucas said.

"That, Lucas, is Melinda. Melinda, Lucas."

Melinda's reaction was a toothless grin, and an arm-waving squeal Lucas interpreted as a sign of welcome.

"Melinda how much?"

"Melinda Kay Landry. She'll be a year old in a couple of weeks. When she was born she weighed in at seven pounds and two ounces, and she's the answer to her daddy's prayers."

"I bet she is."

"Hugh longed for someone he could boss around," she said, "and Melinda doesn't talk back. At least not yet."

Jenny's face was a work of art, and Lucas loved it. High cheek bones, brilliant blue eyes, soft, inviting lips that set the pulse to pounding. Her glowing smile seemed to say, "How nice of you to think of me."

Lucas followed her into the oak-paneled great room. She waved him into a plush brown leather recliner. Lucas sank into it, still cuddling the wide-eyed Melinda.

"I apologize for not giving you warning," he said.

"Don't worry about it. Hugh would really be upset if you trooped all the way up here from Texas and didn't show your face around here."

She took Melinda from him, placed her in a circular playpen, and shook a rattler in her face to make her smile.

"What can I get you to drink?" Jennifer asked Lucas.

"How about a cold Bud?"

"We can do that."

She went to the wet bar and took up a can. She popped the top, and poured the contents into a frosted mug from the refrigerator. "I bet you didn't know I was the head bartender at the Alpha Chi house." She delivered his beer with a mischievous wink.

Nothing she did surprised him.

She popped a can for herself and folded her bare legs under her on the sofa opposite him.

"So, what brings you so far from your stomping ground?"

"Hugh has been at me to get up this way. I got some time off and figured I'd better be getting it done before you guys forgot who I was."

"You know better than that, Lucas. Hugh has always thought of you as one of his closest friends. And you are still in Borger?"

"Still in Borger, still at Phillips, still–."

"–footloose and fancy free," she added for him. "You haven't found anyone you want to settle down with for the rest of your life?"

"Well, it's more like I haven't run into anybody who'd put up with me."

"You guys!" she chided. "You're all alike–afraid you'll miss out on something running loose out there. Hugh and I wouldn't be married yet if I'd waited for him to ask me."

"Actually, I've been pretty busy, and haven't been looking real hard."

"Ha! You wouldn't have to look if you'd slow down long enough to get caught. I know lots of girls who'd like to get their hands on you, Lucas."

Hmmnn. Hands on, or clutches? he mused, recalling the sneering accusations of the Voice. For a fleeting moment, he felt an urge to tell Jenny about Jodi, how they met, how they loved, and how they parted. Nah. That wouldn't work. Jenny would grill him like an ambitious prosecutor running for governor. She'd ask a lot of questions he didn't want to–or couldn't–answer, and he wasn't ready for that. He thought it best to stick to a safe subject.

"Hugh has been at Merrill Lynch, what–five years now?"

"Six. He's doing really well," Jenny said. "Got a few good breaks along the way. He's up for another promotion."

Lucas sipped at his beer, and pinned her with a silent look.

The chill that rippled down her spine told her the mood in

her great room was about to switch from congenial to serious.

"You know the luckiest thing that ever happened to him?" Lucas said.

"Me," she said with a nervous giggle.

"After you," he conceded with a grin. "The second luckiest thing was he wasn't with us that night after the Texas game."

She didn't have to be told which night he referred to—the Saturday night after the Baylor Bears beat the Texas Longhorns. The night Lucas and two other members of the football team held up the Seven Eleven. She'd wondered when Lucas would get around to talking about it, hoping he wouldn't.

"The night you guys held up that store," she said flatly.

Lucas nodded.

"I can't tell you how sorry I am for what happened," she said, "but I'm glad Hugh wasn't there. He's not as strong as you are, Lucas. He couldn't have survived those years you spent in prison."

Her sympathy was little comfort to the man who survived those three years, but he let it pass.

"He would have died there for sure," Jenny said. "Hugh Landry is the finest man I know, but he also is the biggest pushover. He'll tell you about it."

Lucas didn't know what she meant by that, but he'd soon find out.

The sound of skittering tires kicking up gravel told Jenny Hugh's car was skidding to a stop on the driveway

"There he is now," she said. She swept up Melinda from the playpen and hurried away to greet her husband. A moment later, Hugh burst through the door with his arms full of wife and daughter.

"Hi, guy," he said with a broad smile. "You been messin' with my women?"

"I tried," Lucas said. "They wouldn't have anything to do with me."

After a couple of drinks and an hour of hashing over old times, Jenny put Melinda to bed and announced that dinner was served. In the middle of cherry cobbler topped with vanilla ice cream, she decided the time had come for serious talk. She nodded toward Hugh, and said, "Lucas mentioned how lucky you weren't with the guys the night of the hold up."

Uneasy quiet settled in like a cat on a cloud. Hugh's coffee cup stopped half way to his lips. He stared at Jenny. "I was in Dallas."

Lucas cleared his throat. "No big deal."

"I should've been there," Hugh said. "Good or bad, right or wrong, I should've been there." He waited while Jenny refilled their coffee cups. "I had some serious business to take care of that night."

"Well, you know," Lucas said. "It's just—you were always the one with his head on straight. We sort of looked to you to keep the rest of us in line. After the Texas game, we wondered why you weren't there to join the celebration."

Hugh was having difficulty finding words to describe the situation.

Jenny came to the rescue. "Hugh was attending an abortion."

Lucas kept his head down, hoping he heard wrong.

Hugh said, "Do you remember Annabelle Copeland?"

Lucas nodded. Every man on the football team remembered Annabelle Copeland. They dubbed her Availabelle.

"It was the day we lost to TCU," Hugh said. "I threw three interceptions, fumbled on the eight yard line, and lost the game."

"I booted a couple that day too," Lucas said.

"For an hour or so after you guys left the locker room, I beat myself up. Then I took a shower, got dressed, and started walking. I don't know how far I walked, nor in which direction, when who should happen along but little Miss You-know-who, and offered me a ride. My first mistake was getting in her car. Right away she starts talking about going to her place 'for a little nip.' Hating myself for losing the game, I was pretty much out of it. After a couple of beers things got to moving too fast. The bottom line is, I wound up in bed with Annabelle.

"Jenny and I were planning to get married."

"We had set the date," she said.

"Two days before the Texas game," Hugh went on, "Annabelle greeted me in the hallway and announced that she was pregnant. My reaction was so what?"

"Campus punch board," Jenny put in. "Screw anything in pants."

Hugh said, "Annabelle told me women knew how to tell who the father was, and it was my baby."

Jenny rolled her eyes at Lucas.

Hugh wasn't finished. "I wasn't ready to be a father. I convinced Annabelle to have an abortion. I made the arrangements through a friend of mine in Dallas, and the best time he could get was that Saturday night—after the Texas game." He gave his head a bewildered shake. "And that's where I was when you guys hit the Seven Eleven. If I had it to do over—"

"Forget it, Hugh," Lucas said. "We can't blame you for our stupidity. But we never had a chance to talk about it before. I was locked up, and you were a thousand miles away. Forget it."

It was a long drive for a short visit, but by morning Lucas was ready to head back south. He waited while Jenny belted Melinda into the back seat of the station wagon. He followed her in his pickup to the Illinois Central station where Hugh boarded the train to downtown Chicago.

Lucas and Hugh parted with an amiable handshake.

"Are we still friends?" Hugh said.

"You bet."

Hugh left him with a cuff on the chin and climbed aboard as the train sped away.

Lucas patted Melinda's cheek, and stood still while Jenny kissed his.

"I hope you're not disappointed in Hugh," she said. "He thinks the world of you."

"No way, Jenny. It was a tough time for him." He took her hand and held it between both of his. "It wasn't easy for you either."

She shook her head with a wan smile. "Will you come

again?"

"I will."

He gave Melinda's chubby hand a squeeze, and said goodbye. He climbed into his pickup, and pointed it toward Interstate 55 South. By mid-afternoon he bypassed St. Louis. He overcame the urge to veer southeast to Nashville, and sped west on Interstate 70.

CHAPTER EIGHTEEN

Jodi visits Tom

The door squeaked open and Jodi stepped into Tom Crocker's office on Sixteenth Avenue South. It wasn't much of an office—more like the living room of the home it once was. Leaning into

one corner was a big black guitar with "Martin" inscribed on the neck. Stacks of albums and records of various artists and labels lined the floor along two walls. Framed gold records covered the wall behind a desk. A tape player peeked out from under a mound of tapes and cassettes.

Jodi fantasized that one day she'd see her name on that wall. From the next room she heard a husky man's voice she recognized as Tom Crocker's. "Hell no, I won't split with him," he was saying. "It's my song. I've got the paperwork on it, and there's nothing he can do about it." Silence, and Jodi decided he was on the phone.

"That's all right," Crocker said. "I'm not hard to get along with, but when somebody tries to steal from me, I get a little upset." Jodi thought he didn't sound upset. "Bailey Klamm is famous for that. He throws out material submitted to him, then when someone else picks it up, he wants a finder's fee, and I won't play that game." More silence. "All right. Any time. Call me back when you've got something."

Jodi heard the phone drop into its cradle. A moment later,

in the double door connecting the two rooms appeared a gaunt man with a hawk nose, and graying hair that missed a couple of trips to the barber shop. The smile on his face reflected the tranquility she remembered from their meeting at Smoky Joe's. Was this the man, she pondered briefly, whose feet were covered with white cotton socks and no shoes, in whose hands Josh Campbell recommended she place her future?

"Mr. Crocker," she said, "I'm Jodi Parker. You said I could—"

"Oh, yes, I remember," he said with a smile. "Smoky Joe's, wasn't it?"

Relieved, she stuck out her hand. Crocker gave it a welcoming shake.

"I apologize for making you wait," he said. "One of the girls is having a birthday, and they've all gone to lunch to celebrate." He cleared away some albums off a green sofa and invited her to sit. "I wasn't invited," he said, seating himself in a recliner facing her. "It's a girl thing. I'm sure you know about that."

From a shelf behind him he reached for an audio tape, and held it up between them. "I've listened to your tape, Jodi. I can see why Cal Slater was interested in your work." He paused, his eyes fixed on hers. "I don't know how well you knew Cal, but he was one of the most respected men in Nashville, and he'll be greatly missed." With a quick smile he closed the curtain on Slater, and changed the subject.

"Now then," he said, "I especially liked 'Marty's Place.' It reflects the story as many of his friends remember him. I believe Marty would be pleased with what I heard in your lyrics."

Nobody ever heard Tom Crocker sing a song. He played no instrument, and made no secret of his inability to distinguish one note from another. Yet, by the Nashville establishment, he was recognized as an outstanding creator of lyrics. Other writers often staked their careers on Crocker's appraisal of their work. If he heard something he liked, he'd knock down doors to steer it through proper channels. Such a challenge, even his competitors conceded, was too great for him to resist.

Jodi Parker didn't know that. What she did know was, she was fascinated by Crocker's interest in her work, as she was by Josh Campbell's guileless acceptance, and the concern of Emil Enlow. Emil told her, "I don't want to see nothin' bad happenin' to you."

Jodi's thrill of being in Nashville was enhanced by the kind acceptance of an unknown wannabe from Baker's Bluff, Kansas.

"How long do you plan to stay in town?" Crocker said.

Jodi's impulse was to shout, "Forever!" but she thought that would be a bit presumptuous. What she wasn't ready to confess to Crocker was that her money was in short supply. She'd stay for as long as it lasted. And anyway, she asked herself, where else could she go?

"I hadn't really thought about that," she said.

Crocker responded with a solemn nod. Many times before he'd heard those words from many new arrivals. He suspected, as with most people who hitched their hopes to a trip to Nashville, money was a problem. Crocker saw aspiring writers and performers from all over the country swarm into Nashville to make their marks. They'd invested everything they owned, and whatever they could borrow, to get there. In the face of Jodi Parker, he read signs that she was one of them.

Crocker's dedication, in search of the next song to hit the charts, was to listen to whatever crossed his desk, or flooded his mailbox. He never knew where the next hit was coming from. He spent many hours appraising songs performed by writers and singers whose future he concluded was not in music. At least, not in Nashville.

Jodi's material he found promising. What she needed was someone to guide her through the wilderness to the promised land. He never considered himself the Moses of country music, but neither did he want to see her exceptional talent go to waste. If Fred Rose hadn't taken time to listen to a young man who wandered into his office one day, the world might have been denied forever the music of Hank Williams.

"What we need to do," Crocker said, "is set up a demo

session so we can show your songs to artists and record companies around town." He paused. She was silent. "You seem hesitant," he said. "Is there something I need to know?"

"I promised a friend I'd be doing the demo. Mr. Slater said—"

"Is that your voice on the tape?"

"Yes, sir."

"Well," he said, "I think that would work out all right. Now then— By the way, where are you staying?"

"At a motel a couple of blocks over."

He rummaged through a desk drawer and came out with a card. "We keep a couple of rooms at the Andy Jackson Hotel for some of our out-of-town guests." He handed Jodi the card. "You might want to take this over there. Ask for a man named Wally Sheppard."

She took the card with Crocker's name on it, and a scribbled note on the back.

"Wally is a friend of mine," Crocker said. "He'll help you get settled."

"I have money," she said.

He was not surprised at her show of pride and independence. The I-can-do-it-myself spirit flashed like a neon sign by so many who came with so little. Especially the women. Men readily accepted help.

"One thing you need to remember, Jodi."

"Yes?"

"There are lots of good people in Nashville. Most of the big names got help to get where they are. Some of them will be willing to do what they can for you. Others, though, will expect something in return. It won't take you long to find out who they are."

There it was again—the ominous note sounded by Emil Enlow, Josh Campbell, and now Tom Crocker.

"Nashville is different from any other place," Crocker said. "The faces change every day. The newness never wears off. The word of the day for any newcomer is caution. If someone offers to help, let them, but don't do anything in a hurry. Are you driving?"

"No, sir."

He picked up the phone and dialed. "I'm calling a cab for you. It'll take you to the Andy Jackson. Just ask for Wally. He'll take good care of you. Is that all right with you?"

"Yes, sir. Mr. Crocker, does everybody who comes to Nashville for the first time get treated like this?"

"Like what?"

"Like I'm Tammy Wynette or Loretta Lynn, or—"

He smiled and pressed her hand in both of his. "Only the special ones."

She heard the taxi's horn as he led her to the door.

"There's your ride," he said. "Get yourself a look at our town, and I'll give you a call."

She walked out the door to the cab at the end of the sidewalk. She was surprised to see Emil Enlow holding the door open for her.

"Howdy, missy," he greeted her with a broad smile.

"Emil!" she said, truly glad to see him. She felt like a big star who just walked down the red carpet at a movie premier.

"I see you findin' your way 'round all right," he said.

"Yes, thank you."

"You gon go see Wally?"

"Mr. Crocker thought I should."

"Uh-huh. That's good. I'll carry you over there. Mr. Wally is a good man."

Hello, Wally

Wally Sheppard was a dumpy little guy with a thin fringe of graying red hair that circled a bald pate. With fifty-year-old eyes, he peered at the card Jodi gave him.

"Tom Crocker sent you over here, did he?"

"Yes, sir."

Wally's face lit up with a toothy grin, and he hugged her with what he called "a big Ole Nashval welcome!" He grabbed her bags, and headed for the elevator. He stepped aside to let her enter ahead of him.

Sheppard used to be a country DJ in Yankton, South Dakota. "I went to all the shows," he said, leading the way to her room. "I taped interviews with the stars, and– Well, I got the bug, and I just had to see Nashval. Once I got here, I couldn't leave. Country music was in my blood." He set Jodi's bags inside the door to her room. "I tell you what, dolly. Why don't you do whatever it is you ladies do at times like this, then come on down to the coffee shop and I'll pop for lunch."

She hesitated, then Tom Crocker's words popped into her mind: If someone offers to help, let them.

"You know, dolly," Sheppard said, "Tom Crocker has a good eye for people, and I don' t question his judgment. If he sends somebody over here for me to look out for, I look out for them." As he turned to leave, he said, "See for lunch?"

"See you for lunch."

Settling in Nashville, Sheppard became a promoter of talent. He booked performers for concerts and shows all over the country. Topping his list of clients was Bobbie Sue Whitworth, who was married to Tom Crocker.

Bobbie Sue came out of the hills of east Tennessee with a singing voice of rare quality, raw talent Tom Crocker helped make marketable. He guided her career, selected songs that fit her talent, rejected any he thought were "not good enough."

Bobbie Sue became a major star, got so rich and famous she decided one day she no longer needed Tom Crocker. Wally scolded her. "Without Tom," he said, "you never would have got the breaks that made you a star."

Even so, after four years and one son, Bobbie Sue turned her back on them and walked away.

She claimed they weren't "good enough" for her. She attained a level of success where she believed she was bigger than Tom, bigger than Nashville, and maybe even bigger than country music. Without the guiding hand of Tom Crocker, her career began to decline. She sought solace in alcohol and drugs, missing show dates, costing her the respect of fellow performers, and dragging her into the depths of emotional depression.

Sheppard booked her into the Grand Palace in Branson. Bobbie Sue didn't show up for the afternoon performance. It didn't take long to find out why. He watched the shore patrol pull her body out of a speedboat she crashed into a marina on Lake Taneycomo. The coroner said the cause of death was a drug overdose.

So devastated was Wally by the death of Bobbie Sue he gave up promoting talent and turned to a career in hotel hospitality. That allowed him to stay close to the music and the people he loved without becoming emotionally involved in their lives.

"Nashval's got more genuine music talent than any other city in the world," Wally said to Jodi over lunch. He brushed his mouth with a white cloth napkin. "That's one thing that makes it so cruel. Nothing is sacred, except for the 'hit'. There is no reward for second best. I know singers who'd sacrifice their grandmothers for a hit song. Big stars whose names you'd recognize right of. Some of whom would be singing for food on the street corners if it weren't for the Opry. One big record is all it takes to get famous. If you're lucky enough to get invited to perform on the Grand Ole Opry you get more famous. Bookings start rolling in, and the money starts piling up.

"Where am I going with all this? That's the dark side. The bright side is, there are people who will bend over backwards, forwards, and sideways to help anyone who shows promise. One of them is Tom Crocker. Before you came down I had a call from Tom. He says you have talent he hasn't heard since Patsy Cline set this town on fire before you were born."

Patsy Cline!

"Patsy had fire, in her voice and in her personality," Wally said. His eyes reflected the excitement of his recollection. "Patsy had sincerity and depth, and how she could sell a song!"

Jodi gave her chestnut head a dazzled shake.

"Tom Cocker can make you a star, dolly," Wally said. "He won't tell you that, but you need to know he can. He knows Nashval, he knows the business, and he knows the right people." He fixed Jodi with a steady gaze. "It won't happen overnight, but it can happen. Once you get there, you never want to forget where you came from. That's one thing that makes the great ones great." In a confidential tone, he said, "Tom Crocker believes you have the talent to take you wherever you want to go. You must give yourself time, and don't try to get there too fast."

Jodi was trying to digest Wally's remarks when a pretty blond girl named Margo Buckner dropped by their table with a hug and smile for Wally. Margo was Jodi's age, in white jeans, a pink top, and white western boots. At her side was a slender young man she introduced as Guy Ferguson, a studio guitarist.

Wally explained that Margo was from Crocker's office. Her smile put Jodi at ease.

"Tom told me about you," Margo said. "We're having a little get-together at my place tonight to celebrate a birthday. We'd like to have you come."

Jodi cast Wally a questioning glance. He said, "It would be a good place for you to meet some nice people."

"Tell me where and when," Jodi said.

"I know where it is," Wally said.

Margo and Ferguson moved away. Jodi said, "She seems nice."

"You know, Jodi," Wally said, "in spite of the gloomy picture I've painted about Nashval shattering more dreams than it makes come true, it's still one of the friendliest places in the world."

Jodi was on a high she hoped would last forever, though it was a bit frightening to be treated like royalty. If this was the bright side of Nashville, she wondered what the other side must be like.

Let's party!

The door to Margo's apartment was jammed shut. Jodi thumbed the bell a couple of times, but got no answer. The cacophony of laughter and voices sifted through the door to the hallway. She tried the door knob. It turned, but the door didn't budge. She was about to turn away when a slender young man with shoulder length brown hair stuck his head out the door.

Josh Campbell.

"Hi there!" he said. "I told Margo how we met, and she put me in charge of seeing that you have a good time."

He shouldered the door open and guided her through a maze of western boots, blue jeans, colorful miniskirts, shirts and tops. Jodi never saw such a mass of people in one room, laughing, talking, all at the same time. Around a white baby grand in one corner a quartet of harmonizers huddled, apparently oblivious to what was going on around them. Beer and booze flowed, and on each face was plastered a smile, happy, phony, or noncommittal. Inquiring eyes glanced about the room, assuring that they missed nothing. Some were drawn to the small, chestnut haired young lady rescued by Josh Campbell. They wondered who she was.

A slightly built young man about Jodi's age caught her arm and said, "I'm gonna by you a draink."

"Thank you," she said, "but I don't drink."

"Don't draink?" he said, slurring the words. "Ev'body drainks somethin'. It ain't civilized not to draink."

Again he tugged at her arm, but Campbell drew her away. "Knock it off, Lenny."

"She ain't havin' no kind o' fun," Lenny said, "if she–"

"The lady said she doesn't drink," Josh said. He took the glass from Lenny's hand and dumped its contents onto the little man's head. The booze trickled down Lenny's face, drawing chuckles from around the room. "And neither do I," Campbell said.

Lenny squared off, assuming an aggressive stance with hands poised for combat. Campbell placed a hand on the little guy's forehead and held him at arm's length. Lenny flailed away aimlessly with his fists. Onlookers whooped it up in appreciation of Campbell's chivalry, and of Lenny's effort to defend his honor. With a giant swing that missed, Lenny lost his balance and collapsed on the floor flat on his back. Campbell helped him to his feet, and Lenny stumbled away out of sight. He won the award for best spontaneous performance of the evening.

Jodi said to Campbell, "I never saw so many people."

"Yeah. There probably won't be this many on hand when Hank comes back."

Across the room, Jodi caught a glimpse of Margo waving in her direction. But, it was Campbell who responded. "Don't go away," he said to Jodi. "I'll be right back." He excused himself and elbowed his way across the room.

Jodi squeezed into a spot at the end of a couch, and settled down to await Josh's return. A chunky, bald man with bulging eyes and huge ears moved over to make room for her. "Bailey Klamm," he said, sticking out a beefy hand for her to shake. "Don't I know you?"

"No," Jodi said, ignoring the hand.

"I thought I knew everybody," Klamm said with a tobacco-stained grin. "You must be new in town."

Jodi didn't like this man. She didn't know him, and she didn't want to. A sudden thought struck her. "What did you say your name was?"

"Bailey Klamm. You must have heard of me. I own a record company and a publishing company."

That was the name she heard Crocker mention on the phone.

Out of a pocket, Klamm fished a card with his name on it. "Come see me sometime, and we'll talk about—"

"So, there you are." It was Josh Campbell, peering down at Jodi.

"We ain't missed you," Klamm said.

"Well, well, if it's not sweet old Bailey Klamm," Campbell said, "the scourge of Sixteenth Avenue. The vultures are out early this year." To Jodi, he said, "Do you want to get out of here?"

"Okay."

He took her hand and ran interference for her as they headed for the door.

"Hey, Josh," he heard a man call. "You guys leaving?"

Josh looked around and saw Guy Ferguson waving at him. "We're leaving," Josh said. "We've had about as much fun as we can stand for one night." He nodded toward Jodi, and said to Ferguson, "Do you know Jodi Parker?"

"We met at lunch," Ferguson said.

Jodi waved and Campbell took her by the arm. "We're gonna boogie on out of here, Guy," he said. He steered Jodi toward the door. "Tell Margo we'll talk later."

"Don't let him mess around too much, Jodi," Ferguson chided. "Ole Josh ain't the man he used to be."

Josh settled behind the wheel of his yellow Cadillac. "Any place special you'd like to go for supper?"

"I'm a stranger in town, you know," Jodi said. "The best eating place I know is Smoky Joe's."

"Smoky Joe's it is." He shifted gears and said, "Hang on."

He whizzed along the streets, careening around corners, dodging traffic. At that time of night most of the shows were not yet out, and the streets weren't crowded. Jodi tightened her seatbelt.

"Uh-oh," Josh said when he heard the siren behind him. He glanced into the rear view and saw the flashing lights. "Here comes trouble."

He pulled over and parked at the curb. The patrolman got out of the cruiser and ambled up to the driver's side of the Cadillac. "Could I see your driver's license, please, sir?"

"Driver's license?' Josh said. "I don't have a driver's license."

"You don't have a driver's license?"

Jodi sank lower into her seat.

"No, sir. The judge took it away from me three weeks ago. But you know who I am."

"Yes, I know who you are. My wife used to listen to you on the radio when she was a little girl."

"A little girl? I'm not that old!"

"Why don't you knock it off, Josh, before you kill somebody?"

"Well, to tell the truth, I—"

"I won't write you up this time, but once more and I'll haul you in." He turned away. "You better get that young lady home before she shakes to death."

Josh burst out laughing.

"What's funny?" Jodi wanted to know, relieved that the incident was over.

"It's a little game we play. That officer was Jimmy

Blaylock. We've been friends for years. I make it look a lot more reckless than it is, and he likes chasing me to see what pretty lady I'm hauling around."

"Really? Do you do that often?"'

"Uh—no. No no, I just— And here we are at Smoky Joe's Barbecue Emporium," he announced, like the train engineer at the kiddie zoo. Josh tossed a friendly jab at the smoky one, and got one in return.

"When are you gonna learn how to cook?" Josh said.

"'Bout the same time you learn how to sing."

Josh chose a booth near the front door. A red-haired waitress in a green uniform appeared and asked what they wanted.

"The Smoky Joe express with a little extra sauce," Josh said.

He glanced at Jodi. She said, "Sounds good to me."

"It didn't take Bailey Klamm long to find you," Josh said.

"Who is he anyway?" Jodi said.

"A small time operator with big time ambitions. Did he offer you a contract?"

"He doesn't even know who I am."

"He doesn't have to. Klamm would sign Elsie the cow if he thought she'd go to bed with him."

Jodi chuckled. "You can't be serious."

"Dead serious. Klamm has signed some good artists, then bled them blind. Some of them he accosted almost before they got off the bus, eager to be offered a contract. He can tell who the fish are, and he hangs out the bait. I was once one of them. I signed with Bailey for a year."

The waitress brought their food.

"You couldn't get out of the contract?" Jodi said.

"No way," Josh said. "Klamm tied me up tighter than a trailer hitch. Like most of us country kids," he said around a mouthful of barbecue, "I grew up listening to the Grand Ole Opry, and couldn't wait to get on it. I wrote a few songs I knew were the greatest since Hank Williams. I sang some of them on our local radio station in Indiana. I headed for Nashville when I was twenty one. Bailey nabbed me at the bus station. And the rest, as they say, is history."

Smoky Joe slapped Josh on the shoulder. "Hey, man," he said, "some little guy says he wants to see you out back."

"See me?"

"Says he owes you."

"People who owe me don't usually come looking for me."

"It's that little Lenny shit, Josh."

Campbell groaned.

"He claims you put him down in front of his friends at some party," Joe said.

"Okay," Josh said wearily. "Tell him I'll be out there."

Jodi said, "Do you have to go?"

Josh got to his feet. "It's the code of the West," he said wryly. "If you get called out, you're honor bound to answer the call."

"He brought a couple of guys with him," Joe said.

"Who are they?"

"Them two scrounges, Haskell and Luther."

"Uh-huh." To Jodi, he said, "You wait here. I'll go see what they want."

"If this is about me," she said, "I'm going with you."

Josh shrugged and headed for the back door with Jodi close behind.

In the shadows of the dimly lit alleyway Campbell recognized Haskell Newman standing behind and to the right of Lenny Bateman. Luther Helms glared at him from Lenny's left. Haskell had a scraggly beard, and about a yard and a half of stringy black hair with a yellow headband. Luther was a blimp whose nose was so close to his pea-sized eyes it was difficult to distinguish one from the other.

Lenny was swaying closest to the door. Josh noticed he hadn't grown any since he saw him at Margo's party an hour before. He was still a scrawny, sandy-haired kid with an outstanding talent for playing lead guitar, but a poor judge in his choice of friends. Josh liked Lenny, but the little guy was hell on wheels when he was drunk.

Lenny was drunk. He blinked, surprised to see Jodi following Josh out the back door of Smoky Joe's.

"Yeah, Lenny," Josh said. "What's happening?"

Lenny waved an unsteady hand in Jodi's direction. "All I

wanted," he stammered, "was to–.to–buy her–one li'l ole dr–draink."

"She said she didn't drink."

"If I coulda just–"

"Come on, Lenny," Campbell chided. "I was wrong to dump that drink on your head. But you were pushing her to do something she didn't want to do."

Glassy-eyed, Lenny dragged a sleeve across his mouth. "I'm gonna ski–skin your ass–and nail it–nail–it to the door of–of the Grand Ole–Opry."

"I don't want to fight you, Lenny," Josh said, moving away.

Jodi yelled, "Josh, look out!"

Josh turned in time to sidestep Lenny's headlong dive, and the little guy wound up with his nose in the dirt.

Josh grabbed him by the shoulders and slammed him against the wall. Lenny slid to the ground, rolled his eyes, and lay still.

Haskell and Luther made a move as if to rush Josh with a knife and a tire tool. They pulled up short when Joe waved a meat cleaver at them.

"You don't want to do that," Joe growled. "Now, why don't you boys pick up what's left of your ugly little friend and haul his skinny ass off my property?"

Haskell and Luther grudgingly dropped their weapons and laid hold of the unconscious Lenny and dragged him down the alley out of sight.

Josh called after them, "Tell Lenny to call me when he wakes up." He nodded to Joe, shook his f hand, and turned to Jodi. "Are you all right?"

"I'm all right. I was worried about you."

He pinned her with a steady gaze. "Come on," he said. "We better get you home."

Home for Jodi was the Andrew Jackson Hotel, where a frightening message awaited her.

A call from Jodi

Lucas picked up the phone on the lampstand beside his bed and said hello. He wasn't expecting a call from anyone. If it was Jodi this late at night, he figured something had to be wrong.

"I can't believe it, Lucas," he heard her say. "I had a message from my friend Gloria in Phoenix. She said John Barquist forced her to tell him where I was."

"She told him you were going to Nashville?"

"Yes! I didn't believe she'd do that. What am I going to do, Lucas? What if he's on his way here now? What if he's already here?"

"Well, try to calm down, Jodi, and let's think about this for a minute. Have you called the police?"

"No."

"You need to do that. When did Gloria tell Barquist where you were going?"

"I don't know. A few days ago. I don't know. She didn't tell me when we talked before. She was afraid Barquist would kill her if she didn't tell him where I was."

Lucas did a quick calculation. He concluded that Barquist had time to get to Nashville from

Phoenix, and Jodi had reason to be worried. He was seething inside. This was not some pumped up school kid she was dealing with. She needed to be protected from an addle-brained, alcoholic psycho bent on doing her harm, maybe even killing her.

"Jodi, you know I can't come there because of commitments here. That man Sheppard you were telling me about before—tell him what you've told me. I know the police can't do much without a dead body, but Sheppard may know someone who can." Even if Sheppard couldn't help, Lucas was anxious for somebody in Nashville to know she was in serious danger if Barquist got to her.

"Oh, Lucas, I love you so much!" she cried, her last words before goodbye.

Lucas hung up and slumped wearily into his chair. When she needed him most, he couldn't be there.

Jodi called again the next night. "Lucas, I'm scared," she said. "Gloria called again and asked if I'd seen or heard any more of John Barquist."

"Have you?"

"No." She didn't want Lucas to know she didn't mention Barquist to Wally Sheppard. And she didn't contact the police. She was afraid Sheppard and Crocker wouldn't want anything more to do with her if she became a problem. "I don't know what's going on here," she said. "Tom Crocker said he'd call me about a record session, but I haven't heard anything from him."

"Maybe he doesn't have anything to talk about yet, Jodi. At least, you're where you want to be."

"No, I'm not! Where I want to be is with you. These people have been so nice, but I could never put a price on what you've done for me."

"Speaking of which, how is the money holding out?"

"I'm okay. And, Lucas, Wally got me an interview with Billy Starr. He's a big time booker here in Nashville. I'm supposed to see him about opening for some other acts. Also, one of the girls is leaving Crocker's office, and I may get her job."

"Good for you, Jodi."

"And, Lucas, you know what?"

"What?"

"That girl–Tabby McCloud is her name–she made some demos for Mr. Crocker, and they were so good he got her a contract with Mercury Records. That's why she's leaving–to go on the road promoting her record. Isn't that great?"

"Good things will come your way too, Jodi. Just hang in there, and be patient. How's that boy of yours doing?"

"Jason? I miss him so. I can't wait to get him here. If things work out, I might be able to bring him before long. Gloria has never been to Nashville, so she's looking forward to bringing Jason."

"That's good. I'm glad for you. And, Jodi–"

"Yes?"

"Call me any time. If I'm not here, I'll call you back."

"I will."

CHAPTER NINETEEN

Finally! A call from Crocker

"**I** thought you'd like to know I talked to Les Munson over at SilverStar records about your songs."

Jodi's heart leaped. Was it good news or bad?

"He listened to your tapes," Crocker went on, "and said he'd like to hear you sing some more. I've set a session for you at Bradley's on Monday at noon. Will that work for you?"

Work for me? Jodi was ecstatic, so thrilled she couldn't answer.

"Munson asked me to drop your session tape by his office when it's done." He paused, expecting a response. "Are you there, Jodi?"

"Y–yes, I'm here."

"I might be late getting to the studio Monday, so I'll ask Margo to see that you get there. You know Margo."

"Yes, sir."

"This is a good opportunity for you, Jodi. If Les Munson wants to hear more, that's a good sign."

"Yes, sir." She got goose bumps just thinking about it. "Thank you so much, Mr. Cocker. I'll be ready."

Call Lucas! her heart said. She slipped out of her boots, peeled off her top, flattened out on the bed, and reached for the phone. Her fingers couldn't dial fast enough.

"This is Lucas Malone," she heard his recorded voice say. "If you want to talk to me, leave a number, and tell this damn machine who you are. I'll call you when I can."

Disappointed that she couldn't share her news with him, she left her number. She hoped he'd get the message and call soon.. A half hour went by and she didn't hear from Lucas. She thought a hot bath would be good. She stripped off her jeans and underpants along the way. She immersed herself in a cloud of fleecy pink softness, listening for the phone.

Into the steaming water she sank with the abandonment of the queen of Sheba. She visualized her delicate skin being caressed by clove-scented bubbles, massaged by the gentle hands of pampering maiden slaves. With the promise of Crocker's phone call ringing in her ears, Jodi decided the queen had nothing on her. She pulled the plug and heard the water swirl and swish down the drain.

She toweled herself dry when the phone rang. She flung the towel around her dripping body and dashed to answer. "Lucas, guess what!"

She was disappointed the voice on the other end of the line was not Lucas's.

"I was wondering," Josh Campbell said, "if you'd like to join a hungry-eyed hillbilly singer for supper tonight before the Opry."

"Supper?"

"Food."

"Where?"

"Your choice, my treat."

"I don't know. I'm waiting for a call from a friend."

"Uh-huh. You sound like you're about half way down in the dumps. I wasn't supposed to tell you, but I've been assigned by the gods of sunshine and laughter the pleasant task of cheering you up for the evening."

"You're good at that. Are you asking me out on a date?"

"I'm asking you out to supper. What do you say?"

"All right."

"Why don't I swing by and meet you in the lobby about seven?"

"I'll be there."

Campbell was as good as his word. He said he would be in the lobby at seven, and when Jodi and seven arrived in the hotel lobby, that's where she found him.

"So, where are we going for supper?" he said, taking her arm.

She grinned, and said, "Where else?"

He escorted her to his top-down Cadillac, opened her door, ushered her in, and closed the door. Assured she was seated and comfortable, he climbed under the wheel, and drove through the balmy summer night which Southerners claim to have created. Jodi was still marveling at the wonders of Nashville as Josh squeezed the Cadillac into a parking spot at Smoky Joe's.

Josh asked the nice young lady in the short skirt who asked what they wanted if she would please bring him the barbecue combo and a beer.

The nice lady in the short skirt said yes, and turned to Jodi.

"I'll have the same with a glass of water," Jodi said. The lady in the short skirt left.

"My! but you do look scrumptious this evening!" Josh said.

"What's going on?" Jodi said with a grin.

"I beg your pardon, miss–"

"Who are you trying to impress?"

"Well, I took inventory and decided I didn't get very far being who I was, so I thought I'd try out my new personality."

"I like the other one better."

Smoky Joe's was a favorite hangout for Grand Ole Opry performers not scheduled early in the show. Jodi's eyes lit up at sight of Porter Wagoner, Loretta Lynn and Conway Twitty. Lenny Bateman stopped by to say hello as the waitress delivered their meal. A slender redhead was clinging to his arm.

"Are we still friends?" Lenny said to Josh.

Josh waved him off with good humor and Lenny strolled away with his redhead.

"He's quite the ladies' man," Jodi said around a forkful of barbecue.

"Yeah," Josh said with a humble sigh. "For some reason they all seem to flock around the guitar pickers, and the rest of us have to scramble for the leftovers."

"I know," she said with a wry grin. "I feel so sorry for you. Just some old country boy way off down here away from home, struggling to get by."

He paused in mid-chew and gave her a long steady gaze. "With that kind of talk, "you could get yourself in a heap o' trouble. I'd hate to see anything serious come over you."

Jodi was enjoying the jibe until she felt herself being crowded to the wall of the booth by the bulk of Bailey Klamm.

"I know who you are," Klamm said to Jodi. He exposed his gold fillings with a toothy grin, as if he just discovered a cure for the common cold.

"What do you want, Bailey?" Campbell said.

"Trying to corner the market, Josh?" Bailey said.

"What are you talking about?"

"As if you didn't know," Klamm snorted. "Sitting across the table from the next queen of country music."

Josh looked at Jodi, and saw the red flush of embarrassment sweep her face. "Where did you hear that?" he said to Bailey.

"It's all over town," said Klamm. "Tom Crocker showed her tapes to Les Munson, and Munson is signing her with SilverStar Records. You know Munson don't sign no fish."

Jody wished the floor would open up and swallow her. She wished she had told Campbell about Monday's session, but she wanted to tell Lucas first. On the way to the hotel, she said, "I don't know anything about what Bailey said. All I know is Mr. Crocker booked a demo session for noon Monday at Bradley's."

"I knew about that. I hadn't heard about the other part."

"What is Bradley's?"

"Owen Bradley's studio. It's a quonset hut left over from the war, but it produces the best sound in Nashville."

She took a moment to let that sink in. "I didn't know

anything about signing with SilverStar."

"Well, I hope he's right. Les Munson is a good man to have on your side, but you can't put too much stock in what Klamm says, Jodi. This town lives on rumors. Every other week somebody starts one about the next Reba or Loretta, and they make book on when it'll happen. Anyway," he said with a steady gaze, "I already knew you were that good."

"You devil," she said with a grin. "You never even heard me sing."

"I don't have to. Most people who are not very good can't wait to tell you how good they are." He offered her a serious nod. "Out of you I haven't heard a peep." He parked the convertible near the hotel entrance and said, "Jodi, do you feel anything happening between us?"

She folded her hands in her lap and didn't answer. They'd known each other for a few days only. All she knew about Josh Campbell was that he was JOSH CAMPBELL!—a big country music star, and a very nice man who took her under his wing.

"Most of the girls I meet want something from me," he said, "but you don't want anything."

"Yes, I do," she said. "More than anything in the world, I want to be a good writer and singer."

"Well, apparently there are people who think you are already that."

"Not yet."

"You'll know when it happens."

"You should know, Josh. You've been there."

"Yes, I have, and it's a great feeling just to be mentioned in the same breath with Merle Haggard, Willie Nelson, and Waylon Jennings. That's what I want for you, Jodi, and I want to help you get there."

"I can't do that," she said with the warning words of Tom Crocker rolling around in her head. "You've done too much for me already. I can't take advantage of you that way."

"Take advantage? Let me be the one to decide when—"

"Josh—"

He drew her to him and kissed her soundly on the mouth.

"Let me go," she murmured. "Please."

She slid away from him, and out the car door, heading for the hotel entrance.

"Are you coming to the Opry?" he said.

"I don't think so."

"Will I see you later?"

She paused and faced him. "Really, Josh, I've got some things I need to do."

"Lucas?" he said.

"What!" She was shocked and irritated that he read her thoughts.

"The way you answered the phone earlier, I knew he must be somebody special."

"I don't think that's any of your business."

"Yes, it is. We've known each other only a short time, but you're very important to me."

"Goodnight, Josh," she said, and walked quickly away. "Thanks for dinner."

Stuck under her door she found a yellow Western Union envelope. It was a message from Lucas. "Sorry I missed your call. Working early and late. Chat later." Folded inside the message was a money order. Her eyes filled with tears. The money was enough to help her move into that small apartment she located, anticipating Jason's arrival.

"Damn you, Lucas," she cried. "I love you!"

CHAPTER TWENTY

Let's go to Bradley's

At eleven o'clock Monday morning Jodi's phone rang. She said hello and heard Wally Sheppard's voice. "There's a young lady down here in the lobby named Margo who says she's supposed to pick you up and take you some place."

Jodi was so excited she didn't even say goodbye. She slammed the phone down, grabbed her guitar, and took off for the elevator like she might not make it downstairs before time ran out. Margo and Wally were waiting when she got there.

"My my!" Wally said to Jodi. "Don't you look like somebody come!" He glanced at Margo. "You two would make a beautiful set of bookends."

Margo took charge of Jodi's guitar and led the way out front where she placed it in the back seat of her Buick station wagon.

"I'm supposed to deposit you at Bradley's," Margo said, shifting into gear. As she drove, she said, "You'll meet a man named Earl Bartle. He's the producer on your session. There'll be other people there, including Lee Rice and his band. Have you been in a recording studio before, Jodi?"

"No, never."

"One thing you need to remember is that all those people are as anxious as you are to get a good cut. Tom has taken care of everything. He said to tell you he won't be there at the beginning, but he will be there before the session is over." She paused a moment, and smiled, "He thinks you're pretty good. I think so too. I listened to some of your stuff."

"Thanks, Margo."

Earl Bartle was forty, slight of build, with a pencil line mustache, and a mole on his left cheek. He was a veteran of more recording sessions than he could remember. He worked with major country music stars, as well as with some pop and rock luminaries who headed south to record with the

Nashville sound.

Bartle dismissed rap as non-music. "A bunch of no-talent people who talk dirty and get paid for it." He introduced Jodi to Lee Rice. Rice was short and stubby with lamb chop sideburns, and a beer belly that hid his belt buckle. He was a poor physical specimen, but he put together a group of six musicians voted the leading country band four years running.

Jodi had trouble believing all those people were there because she was.

"Is everybody ready out there?"

The voice of Earl Bartle on the studio speaker gave Jodi a start. Through the plate glass window separating the studio from the control room, she saw three men wearing headphones, flipping switches, turning knobs, and pressing buttons.

"Jodi, can you hear me?" It was Bartle's voice again. She nodded.

"You'll have to say something out loud," Rice said. "He can't hear you when you nod your head."

"Yes," she said, louder than she needed to. That brought chuckles all around, including from the control room.

"Okay," Bartle said. "We're gonna run through 'Marty's Place' a couple of times to make some level adjustments, check mikes and all that good stuff, then we'll– Are you okay, Jodi?"

"Yes, I'm fine," she said, trying to control her shaking knees.

"Good. It's been a while since we lost a singer, but one does get away from us now and again."

The band had heard that before, but they laughed anyway.

"Now," Earl said, "we're gonna go ahead and run through it with the band, Jodi, then

we'll lay one down. When I holler 'rollin' that means we're ready to record. And, Jodi, if you have any questions, or if you'd like to stop and start over, don't hesitate to say so. We're here to do a good job for you."

"I won't."

She felt more relaxed when she heard the band move into the melody of 'Marty's Place.' All she'd heard before were her voice and the strum of her guitar. Now, the sound of six professional musicians playing her song sent chills down her spine.

"Rollin'!" Bartle said, and after the third take, he had what he called a "pretty good scald."

Through the control room window Jodi saw Tom Crocker. He was saying something to Bartle. Bartle was nodding his head at what he heard. Good or bad, she wished she could hear what they were saying.

Bartle said something to the other people in the control room, then got on the studio speaker. "Jodi," he said, "Tom wants to hear you do the first four lines acappella. For those of you pickers who may not know, that means without the band." That brought a time worn, good natured scoff from the band. "Just the first four lines, Jodi," Bartle said, "then we'll sneak the band in under you. Lee, are you and Jodi together on this?"

"We done worked it out," Rice said.

"We're rolling." Bartle counted down from four. Jodi took a deep breath and sang: "I rode with him in the hills outside El Paso, I watched him place gardenias in pretty Carmen's hair, I sailed with him to that far away isle of golden dreams, when he walked the streets of Laredo I was there—"

Bartle gave Rice a hand cue, and the band began a subdued accompaniment as Jodi sang.

"Sounds like you've done it again, Tom," Bartle said with an appreciative nod. "That little lady has a great set of pipes."

Crocker concentrated on the voice coming from the control room speaker.

"A little bit of Patsy Cline," Bartle said, "a little bit of Connie Smith, and a whole hell of a lot of Jodi Parker!"

Crocker settled into his chair and listened. One day, he predicted, that voice would belong to the queen of country music.

CHAPTER TWENTY-ONE

The monster seeks its prey

Nashville, Tennessee, was not a place John Barquist thought he'd ever find himself. He hadn't lost anything there that he should go looking for–except for Jodi Parker. Nashville was a much bigger city than he imagined, and finding Jodi turned out to be a greater challenge than he thought. Devoid of talent and musical ambition, Barquist couldn't understand why anyone would want to go there. He'd rather be back in Phoenix guzzling booze and chasing broads, instead of tramping around a city he knew nothing about, looking for somebody he wasn't sure he'd find.

Jodi's running out on him stuck in his craw, spurring him to the vengeance of a lascivious, maniacal mind. On the corner of a busy downtown intersection, he sneaked a nip from the bottle in a brown paper bag, watching the cars go by, peering at faces, hoping to see one that looked like Jodi Parker. Without success he'd searched night clubs and honky-tonks, certain she'd be where country music was played. He didn't know where she was, nor where else to look, but, his addled brain wouldn't rest until he found her.

Am I any good?

The record session behind her, Jodi grew anxious about its outcome. She felt good about her performance, especially the Marty song. But she'd heard nothing about it, except for the band members' encouraging words after the session.

Rice told her, "It come off good," but from Crocker, she heard nothing, and wondered why. Was she not good enough to risk his bucking the establishment with what he heard, even though Les Munson asked him to "bring it around?"

And what about Bailey Klamm? Did he really know something, or was he just starting another one of those rumors Josh warned her about?

One thing she knew for sure was she needed a job, since she could hardly wait to bring Jason to Nashville. Even if Crocker got her signed with SilverStar, royalties from record sales would be months down the road. She talked to Crocker about the opening in his office left by Tabby McCloud's departure. He said, "We need to talk about that," but so far, no talk and no job.

"What about Billy Starr?" she asked.

"Absolutely," Crocker said. "He's one of the best. Go ahead and meet with Starr."

"Maybe I could work here in the office in the day and do some singing jobs around town for

Mr. Starr at night."

Crocker thought that was a good idea, "But first, you need to get with Starr, and find out what he might be able to do for you."

CHAPTER TWENTY-TWO

Meet Billy Starr

Jodi bolstered her courage and eased open the door with a sign on it that said "Starr Talent." Greeted by a blond young woman with a broad smile, Jodi told her who she was, and why she was there.

"I'm Kathy Mason," the woman said. "Mr. Starr is expecting you. Didn't Wally Sheppard call about you?"

"Yes."

"Excuse me a moment," Kathy said, "and I'll see if Mr. Starr can see you now." She disappeared into a cavern of highly polished panel.

Jodi waited. She glanced around the office at three young people sitting at desks—two women and a man, staring at her with pleasant looks on their faces. Did they know something she didn't? Did they look that way at everybody who came in? Why were they looking at her like that?

Kathy Mason reappeared from the cavern and said, "Jodi, you want to come with me?" She escorted her to the office of Billy Starr. "Mr. Starr," she said through his open door, "Jodi Parker is here to see you."

Jodi stepped inside, and Kathy went away.

At sight of the biggest mahogany desk she ever saw, Jodi

was awe struck by its wide expanse, marred only by a white telephone sitting on the upper left corner. Behind the desk sat a huge, middle aged man with a fringe of graying brown hair encircling his bald pate. Heavy brows hovered above black eyes round as billiard balls. Thick lips and a puffy face rendered Billy Starr's perfect white teeth almost eerie.

Starr said not a word. He stood up, his pallid face expressionless as a sheet of blank paper. He held out his ham-like right hand toward Jodi, not to greet her with a friendly gesture, but to receive what she brought with her.

Jodi, intimidated by this wordless, imposing monument to arrogance, silently relinquished the tape dub of her recording session. Almost, s he wished she hadn't come.

In his dark blue, double breasted suit, Starr appeared even larger when he stood up. He glared at her with eyes she half expected to pop out at any moment and burn holes in her face, as though he questioned her right to be there.

Jodi stood because she was not invited to sit. Starr inserted her tape in a stereo player mounted in the wall behind his desk. He pressed the play button on the stereo, and resumed his seat in the rich brown, leather-upholstered chair from which he'd risen. He leaned back in the chair, hid his face with both hands, and listened, wordless and unmoving.

When no more sound issued from the stereo player, Billy Starr uncovered his face. He stared into space for a silent minute, eyes unblinking, as if contemplating the beginning of World War Three.

Jodi felt an urge to ask whether he was all right, but dared not break the spell.

When he finally broke the silence, she read nothing in his expression that told her whether he was impressed with what he heard.

"Please, sit, Miss Parker," he said.

Jodi was startled by the cultured British accent that glided off his tongue. For a moment she stood transfixed, stunned by his gentle voice. Fascinated by his hail-sized diamond-studded French cuffs, and the brilliant diamond stickpin adorning his red silk tie, she eased onto the plush wingback chair facing the mahogany desk.

Once again Starr got to his feet, paced back and forth behind the desk, gesturing with fingers glittering with diamonds.

"Have you any notion, Miss Parker–" Billy Starr's soft, soothing words caressed her hearing organ. "–how good you are?"

Taken aback, she searched for an answer, and realized he was still talking.

"If you don't know, you certainly need to be aware that you are blessed with extraordinary ability. There is no greater tragedy than spending a lifetime not knowing of what one is capable." With a casual wave of his bejeweled hand, he segued deftly into a different line of thought. "Suffice to say," said he, "had I not been impressed by the first note I heard, I would not have bothered listening to the last one.

"You are quite good, Miss Parker. Most people in my position would not want you to hear that, fearing your demands for compensation would increase with their appraisal of your worth. The basic talent is unmistakable. A rough edge here and there, but then– I understand you are working with Tom Crocker."

"Yes, sir."

"Sly devil," he said with the trace of a smile. "No one in the business is a better judge of talent than Crocker." The smile disappeared. He grabbed the white phone and said into it, "Miss Mason, put Miss Parker down for the Cactus Club tonight at eight-thirty. I want to see how she comes across with a live audience." He hung up and said to Jodi, "I'm looking at a couple of other people at the club tonight. I trust you will be able to make it."

"Oh, yes," she said quickly, as if afraid he might change his mind. She had no idea where the Cactus Club was, but she'd find it. "I'll be there."

"Are you familiar with Nashville?"

"No, sir. This is my first time here."

"Miss Mason will help you with directions. Goodbye, Miss Parker."

Jodi left Billy Starr's office somewhat bewildered, but

pleased that he seemed impressed by what he heard on her tape. And he thought enough of it to invite her to the Cactus Club. She didn't know what the Cactus Club was, but she was pleased by Starr's invitation to be there. Her thoughts were interrupted by the sharp blare of a car horn. A moment later Tom Crocker braked to a stop at the curb.

He greeted her with a warm smile. "How about a ride?"

"Hello!" She slid in beside him.

"Sheppard said I probably would find you here. You met with Starr?"

"Yes, I just did. And, as a matter of fact, he spoke very highly of you."

Crocker gave his head a slight nod as though he deserved the praise. "Billy's that way. He looks for nice things to say about people."

Jodi wondered if the accolades Starr passed out to her were no more than "nice things" he'd

Say to anyone.

"How did you and he get a long?"

"Very well," she said with a smile, "after a few awkward minutes. He asked me to come to some club–" She glanced at the card in her hand. "The Cactus Club. I'm supposed to be there at eight-thirty tonight. He said he wanted to see how I did with an audience."

"Does that bother you?"

"The audience? Not really. I guess that's what he wants to find out."

"He often does that. He owns the Cactus Club. He likes to use it as a sounding board for new talent before he commits himself. Billy is a bit odd, but he's a good businessman. If he likes you, there's nothing he won't do to help you succeed. If he doesn't like you, you'll never hear from him again."

He shifted the car into motion. "I hear you've made friends with Josh Campbell."

Jodi guessed there really weren't many secrets in Nashville. How would Crocker know, or care, who she was hanging out with?

"That's good," Crocker said. "Josh is a fine young man, and a good talent. He'll be one of the big ones before he's through."

Jody absorbed that, but had a notion Crocker hadn't said what he came to say.

"I heard something else too, Jodi." He gave her an inquisitive look. "Do you know a man named John Barquist?"

Her heart almost stopped, but there was no use tip-toeing around it. "Yes, sir, I do."

"Sheppard says Mr. Barquist has been around town asking questions about you. I don't mean to pry—and you can tell me it's none of my business if you wish—but Wally described him as scaly."

That was John all right. Trance like, Jodi nodded, fearing everything she dreamed of and longed for since she was little was about to disappear like a puff of smoke.

"You realize you and I have some mutual interests now," Crocker said, "and I'm concerned about you."

"Mr. Crocker—"

"More people than you know want you to succeed. You may have heard Les Munson is considering adding you to his talent staff."

She didn't tell him Bailey Klamm shocked her with that news.

"I don't want anything to happen that would jeopardize this opportunity for you, Jodi. You may not be aware that many people work for years, sacrificing huge pieces of their lives, separating themselves from family and friends, to achieve what has come to you in a very short time."

For a long moment, she rolled it around in her mind, wishing she'd told him about Barquist as Lucas suggested. Now, Crocker had found out about Barquist from someone else, and she felt like she'd betrayed him.

"Mr. Crocker," she said with all the courage she could muster, "John Barquist is my stepfather. I took care of him for nine years because my dying mother asked me, and every minute of those nine years I wished he would die."

Crocker showed little surprise at her statement, and waited for her to go on.

"Barquist threatened to kill me and my son if I ever left

him."

"You have a son?"

"Yes. Jason will soon be a year old."

"Is Jason with you here?"

"Not yet. He will be as soon as I can afford to bring him from Phoenix. I've moved into a small place where I can take care of him." She gave him her new address.

"Yes, Wally mentioned you'd moved out of the hotel." He found her address and braked to a stop near the front entrance." Tabby is starting her promotion tour on Friday. I thought you might want to start in the office on Monday. Will that work out for you?"

"Yes, sir. Thank you so much."

"The job doesn't pay a lot, but it'll give you a chance to meet some people, and learn about how we do things."

Again, she said, "Thank you."

"Now, about this Barquist fellow–"

"Mr. Crocker, John Barquist is an alcoholic maniac who beat my mother, and abused me for nine years. If you wonder whether I'm afraid of him–yes, I am. When he's drunk the lord only knows what he might do.

"I don't know where he is. I haven't seen him nor heard from since I left Phoenix, and I hope I never see him again. But I want you to know, sir, I am so grateful for what you've done for me. I want nothing more than to be the success you seem to believe I could be. What you've done is a dream come true. Please believe me, I'd give it all up, if it's a problem for you."

She said her piece, and wiped away tears she couldn't hold back.

"Please be careful, Jodi." He covered her hand with his. "If there's something I can do, will you

let me know?" He reached across and opened the door for her.

"I appreciate your concern, and I will let you know." She slid out of the car. "Do you still want me to start work on Monday?"

"Absolutely!"

She offered an appreciative smile. "Mr. Crocker, Bailey

Klamm offered me a contract with Mask Records. I told him I'd think about it. And I'd like to know what you think."

For a moment Crocker sat with his head bowed, as though seeking wisdom from a higher power. "Jodi, you know we're still working with Les Munson."

"Yes, sir."

"You know, you can read all the books, talk to all the experts, listen to all your friends, but in the end, the only one who can say what is best for you is you. You asked my opinion, and that is, don't get involved with Bailey Klamm. He's a barnacle on the backside of the music industry, and the world has much more to offer you than Bailey Klamm."

Jodi smiled. "Thank you, sir. That's what I thought."

Crocker smiled his approval. Jodi turned on a heel and strode away.

The apartment manager hailed her as she passed the office door. "There was someone to see you," the buxom elderly woman said, peering over the tops of her eyeglasses. "A–gentleman–was asking about you."

"A gentleman? Did he leave a number?"

"No. Only his name. A Mr. Barquist."

CHAPTER TWENTY-THREE

The Cactus Club

"**I**'m gonna get you, Jodi!"

The Cactus Club was alive with tinkling glasses, the air heavy with cigarette smoke. Couples' elbows and butts collided on the small dance floor. Jodi was in the middle of the second chorus of "When Will I Be Loved?" when she heard the drunken voice cut through the din.

"I'm gonna get you, Jodi!"

At first she tried not to believe it was him.

Billy Starr had asked her to do one more number. The crowd liked the way she sang it, and said so with their applause. Then, once again she heard the harsh, blaring voice, louder and closer. Shot through with fear of the man whose brutality she thought she'd escaped, cold chills gripped her body. John Barquist! Drunk and raging.

Her knees trembled out of control. She glanced around the room in search of the horrid face that went with the threatening voice. Jodi never missed a beat of her song. There he was! In the back of the room! Stumbling drunkenly toward the bandstand, crazily waving his flabby arms.

"I'm gonna get you, Jodi!" He lunged at her with the jagged neck of a broken beer bottle.

Jodi screamed and ducked away. Two members of the band leaped on Barquist and wrestled him to the floor. A third man twisted the broken bottle from his hand.

"Somebody call the cops!" a voice shouted.

Fiery eyed, bull headed, and wounded bear strong, Barquist shook himself free and made a wobbly getaway out the exit.

Jody was frightened out of her wits, and collapsed onto a chair.

Billy Starr came lumbering toward her. "What the hell was that all about?" he demanded in a rage. "Was that guy after you?"

"Mr. Starr, I—"

"I can't have stuff like that coming down, Miss Parker. It's bad for business."

Stunned, she responded with a bewildered nod, terrified by the dread that Barquist would be back, or that he might find a way to get to her later.

"Keep that bloody baggage away from here," Starr shouted as he moved away, "or you'll never work for me!"

From somewhere, Josh Campbell appeared. To Jodi, he said, "Are you all right?"

"Oh, Josh," she cried. "I'm so glad to see you!"

"What's chewing on the fat boy?"

"That man who was trying to get to me—"

"The one I just saw tearing out of here?"

"Oh, Josh, Josh!"

He reached for her, and held her close.

"Would you please drive me home?" she said.

"Whenever you're ready."

Josh Campbell needed to know about John Barquist. While he drove, Jodi talked. By the time he parked his Cadillac near the entrance to her apartment building, she was through talking.

Josh said nothing for a long, silent moment. His respect for Jodi mounted as she told the story of how Barquist abused her, how she wanted him dead, but couldn't kill him when she had the chance.

How he threatened to kill her and her baby if she ever left

him. The courage she showed by staying with Barquist for nine years because her mother asked her to.

"It looks to me like your friend Lucas was right," Josh said. "This Barquist is a wild man who means to hurt you if he gets to you, and there's nothing you can do to stop him. Until they find a dead body, the police are sleeping in a hotbed of apathy. I hope the body they find will not be yours." He took her hand. "Do you want me to stay with you overnight—just in case?"

She gave him a look that told him she wasn't sure it was a good idea.

"I'll sleep in the bathtub," he drawled.

Caraaash! The windshield of the Cadillac was shattered. It sprayed the front seat with shards of glass. The raging Barquist swung a baseball bat, smashing windows around the car.

Josh and Jodi threw up their arms to protect their faces from flying glass.

"Get inside!" Josh shouted to Jodi.

She scrambled across his lap and made a dash toward the building's entrance.

Blind with rage, Barquist didn't see Jodi escape. He kept pounding aimlessly, polluting the air with obscenities.

Campbell's instinct was to challenge the rampaging Barquist, then thought it better to outrun him to the apartment and make a stand there to keep him from getting to Jodi. He leaped from the car and made a headlong dash into the building, and up the stairway to where Jodi was waiting in her doorway. Josh ducked inside. Jodi followed, slammed the door behind her, and threw the deadbolt.

"Are you okay?" Josh said.

"I'm scared to death."

"Okay, now, Jodi, listen to me—"

They heard a loud crunch, and saw the hole bashed in the wooden door. Barquist's hairy arm reached through the jagged hole, fumbling for the lock.

Campbell grabbed Barquist's arm, but Barquist tore it loose and threw off the deadbolt. The door flew open and he charged through it. He made a beeline for Jodi, wielding the bat in a windmill motion, screaming like a wild man, "I'm gonna get you, Jodi!"

Terrified, Jodi tried to elude the enraged bull, but bumped into a coffee table and fell to the floor between it and the sofa. Ignoring Campbell, Barquist threw his bulk on top of her.

"I told you I'd get you!" he bellowed. With a beefy left hand he grabbed at her throat, ripping at her blouse with the other.

Jodi screamed and fought, but couldn't free herself.

"You didn't believe old John, eh? You didn't believe I'd do what I said I'd do, eh?"

Campbell clamped both hands around Barquist's neck and yanked him backward, but the hulking madman broke free, and shoved Josh aside. Josh grabbed a chair and shattered it with a blow to the big man's back. Even dazed by the blow, Barquist staggered to his feet. He lunged at Campbell, and bull-headed him to the floor, piled on top of him, and went for Josh's throat with both hands.

Jodi bounced to her feet. Spotting the abandoned baseball bat, she grabbed it and cracked it over Barquist's head. He stopped pounding Campbell, and looked at Jodi through glazed eyes. He struggled to his knees, spread his massive arms and, with a final roar of rage, collapsed in a senseless heap at Jodi's feet.

She swung the bat back to strike again. Campbell, realizing Barquist was out cold, yelled, "Don't do it, Jodi!"

For a long moment she held the bat above her head, weeping, terrified, bordering on hysteria. She fought the urge to split the head of the monster she t knocked unconscious. Payback for his abuse of her mother, for her son, for the years of hatred and torment, and for the dammed-up anger at the animal who for so long she prayed to see dead. Her body trembled, her hands shook, and her face was streaked with tears. She tossed the bat onto the ugly, unmoving body of John Barquist.

"Josh!" she cried. "Oh, Josh—"

He gathered her in his arms. "It's all right," he whispered. "It's all over. Now we can call the police."

CHAPTER TWENTY-FOUR

Caged animal

John Barquist was in jail, locked away where he could no longer terrorize Jodi Parker. With him behind bars, she felt safe to concentrate on her new job, reviewing music tapes submitted to Crocker's publishing company. Reports of her tape session were encouraging, though she hadn't signed with Munson's SilverStar Records. She didn't know why. The last time she mentioned it to Crocker, he said, "Patience, Miss Parker," in a light hearted mood. She took that to mean nothing happened in a hurry in the music industry. Though some decisions were made on the spur of the moment, others often "took a while."

Munson wanted to "hear more", indicating he at least was interested. Crocker didn't appear anxious about it. She hoped that meant things were developing in her favor. As soon as he learned something positive, she was sure Crocker would let her know. Meanwhile, all she could do was wait.

A Captain Schmidt of the Nashville police department called one day with an update on the Barquist case.

"A fisherman ran across a sunken boat in the river," the captain told her. "A body was found in the boat." Schmidt paused to give her a moment to absorb that, to ask a question or make some comment. She did neither. Schmidt continued with his written report. "We were able to identify the body as that of an individual who was reported missing in Arizona. Two days ago we found an abandoned 1979 Oldsmobile Eighty Eight with Arizona license plates. It was registered to the individual whose body we found in the boat. Upon a thorough examination, we discovered a number of fingerprints on the steering wheel, most of which belonged to an individual named John Barquist. Barquist is now in the custody of the Nashville police."

Again the captain paused, and Jodi thought he must have heard her heart pounding with relief that John Barquist was behind bars. Even so, the captain heard nothing but silence on the other end of the line.

"Miss Parker?" he said.

"Yes, I'm here."

"Personally, I have an idea this bastard will be locked up for a long time. He won't be bothering you anymore."

"Thank you so much, captain."

"Have a nice day."

She'd heard it said that "all things come to those who wait." Lucas said as much, and

sure enough they came. Two days after Captain Schmidt's report, she received a call from Billy Starr.

Starr said without preliminary, "I have arranged for you to open for the Statlers in Memphis on the seventeenth. Miss Mason will contact you with the details." He didn't wait for a response.

Never again did she hear Billy Starr refer to the Cactus Club incident.

A talk with Tom

With a sense of apprehension she eased open the door to Tom Crocker's office. He'd left a note on her desk while she was out to lunch. All it said was, "We need to talk."

All manner of possibilities raced through her head, most of them bad. Had she not been doing her job well? How about the record session? Had it not turned out as well as she hoped? Maybe Les Munson decided he didn't need her on his talent staff. Did Billy Starr change his mind about her opening for the Statlers? If so, why didn't Starr call her himself?

John Barquist! Did Crocker's note have something to do with that?

Not knowing what was going on, she was gripped with the fear of failure she expressed to Lucas on the phone two nights ago. Her whole life revolved around her making good in Nashville. If she failed, what would become of her and Jason? A thousand times she asked herself that question, struggling with answers that offered little promise

Still, she had to believe people were trying to do for her what she couldn't do for herself. She glanced around, suspecting everybody else in the office saw the note before she did. The three other girls were looking at her. Two of them quickly turned their eyes away. The third one, Margo, kept looking at her. She smiled. Jodi wondered why. It was not the kind of smile that told her anything. Was Margo sharing the joy, or feeling her sadness?

Jodi stewed for a while, anticipating the worst. She suddenly felt foolish. Make a move and find out what it was about, she told herself. If it's bad it's bad, if it's good it's good. Either way she wouldn't know whether to mope or jump for joy till she found out. She pushed a strand of hair back off her face and pressed her palms along her thighs to smooth the wrinkles in her skirt, then struck a beeline to Crocker's door.

"You wanted to see me, Mr. Crocker?"

"Come in."

He didn't call her by name. He always called her by name when he spoke to her. Why didn't he call her by name?

"Have a seat."

Jodi moved into a straight back chair facing him. She didn't like the way he looked at her. The way the vet looked when he said her cat died. The little smile on Crocker's lips was different than usual. Was he trying, gently as possible, to break the bad news?

Calmly as always, Crocker slid a paper toward her across the desk. "I need you to sign this," he said. "It's a recording contract."

Jodi took a moment to catch her breath. "A contract?"

"Yes. They're pressing your record over at SilverStar. Les Munson sent the contract over while you were at lunch."

She tried to accept the news as casually as Crocker delivered it. It didn't work. Her heart leaped. Tears of gratitude flooded her eyes, and she buried her face in her hands, happy, unbelieving. Relieved. Unable to speak.

"It'll take a few weeks for your record to hit the market," Crocker said. "But DJ's all over the country will have advance copies of it when it's released."

Jodi struggled to contain her excitement. A real live singer with a record about to be released! And DJ's will be playing it on the radio for people everywhere to hear!

"I can't tell you what this means to me, Mr. Crocker."

"I know."

"There's no way I could ever repay you and Mr. Sheppard, and all the others."

"Yes, there is."

She cast him a startled look.

"I haven't mentioned this before because things can happen pretty suddenly around here. Heartbreak and disappointment are hard to get used to. The fact is, people who heard you sing are excited about your future, and they—we—are eager to see you succeed.

"What's happening to you is what thousands of people all over America dream of—making it in Nashville. Many of them work at it for years, playing beer joints, honky-tonks, and county fairs, hoping for the big break, but they never see their names on a marquee. Others become what some call overnight sensations after struggling for half a lifetime." He swiveled around to a file behind him and brought out a stack of tapes, cassettes, and CD's, and tossed them on the desk. "We get bucketfuls of these every week from aspiring writers and singers. Some are good, some not so good, but very few are good enough. If you don't know already, one day you'll realize how fortunate you are. Yours is a rare talent, Jodi. We had nothing to do with creating it, but you brought it to us, and we provided the outlet for it."

"I–I don't know what to say."

"Let your music say it for you. You can do that best by being whoever you are. That's what got you here. Many of the people who come with stars in their eyes and hope in their hearts try to get too big too fast. They forget where they came from. Never think of yourself as bigger than those who helped you get here."

An echo of Wally Sheppard's words. What happened to Bobbie Sue flashed across her mind. She wondered if much of what Crocker was telling her he learned from his experience with his late wife.

"Making a record is easy, Jodi," Crocker said. "Anybody can do it. There are people all over the country, Nashville included, who'd be happy to take your money for putting your voice on a piece of tape and telling you how great you are. The hard part is getting a record played on the radio, getting out there where the people are, hoping DJ's will like you, and what they hear, enough to schedule it for air play. It's a tough hill to climb for new artists, and many of them give up before they're half way up the hill."

He came around from behind his desk and placed an arm across her shoulders. "I don't want that to happen to you, Jodi. It would be a terrible waste." He walked her to the door, and closed it behind her as she left.

Thrilled as she was, Jodi suddenly felt lonely. And Lucas Malone, with whom she most wanted to share her good news, was many miles away.

Music in the Panhandle

"At a quarter past supper time, it's seventy-four degrees in the Big Country."

The voice belonged to Ted Michaels. He was a disc jockey on the radio station whose signal blanketed the Texas Panhandle.

"We'll have a few clouds, and maybe a sprinkle or two

overnight and into tomorrow morning. The weatherman is trying real hard to be good to us. And right now I'm going to be as good to you as anybody has been all day. There's a bright new voice on the country music horizon I want you to hear. It belongs to a young lady named Jodi Parker, a name and a voice you never heard before. But I'll bet you my half interest in Dallas County you'll be hearing a lot of it for a long time to come. Listen up now, Texas, as she shares with you her tribute to the late great Marty Robbins. Ladies and gentlemen, Miss Jodi Parker."

"I rode with him on the hills outside El Paso—"

Lucas swerved his pickup, slid onto the shoulder, almost lost control. Jodi on the radio! He turned up the volume to get the full benefit of the soft, resonant voice, as if she were singing to him.

"His friends all wondered how he kept the pace," she sang. "But he became a legend in the country in his time, no one could ever take old Marty's place."

Yeeeow! Lucas whooped and hollered all the way home. Chill bumps raced up and down his spine. Jodi told him the record was coming out, but she didn't know when. Now there it was, all over hell and half of Texas. She did it! That kid really did it! He stepped on the gas, anxious to get to a phone. People stopped to stare when they heard a wild man ripping through the streets of Borger shouting out his rolled-down window, "I love Jodi Parker!"

That day now seemed ages ago. Billy Starr kept Jodi busy with show dates, the crowds loved her music as well as her down-to-earth, outgoing personality. Her career was whipping along at a breathtaking pace. She worked hard and long promoting her records, visiting radio stations large and small, chatting on-air with DJ's, convincing her that her stuff was what Tom Crocker called "good enough." Awed that people "paid good money" to hear her sing on Starr's personal appearances, she ate it up, and went back for seconds. Other artists, Josh Campbell among them; were recording her songs and, with misty eyes and a joyful heart, she welcomed her son Jason to Nashville.

Jodi and Lucas spent late night hours on the phone when

she described, with a voice filled with excitement, the cities she played, and Opry stars with whom she shared the stage. Every conversation ended with, "Lucas, can you come?"

Thrilled by the sound of her voice on the radio, and glad for her success, Lucas wanted to go wherever she was to watch her perform. He wanted to share the joy of her success, but conflicts prevented his doing so.

Until now.

CHAPTER TWENTY-FIVE

Miss Jodi Parker!

Starr booked Jodi for an appearance in Dallas with Josh Campbell. Lucas promised her, and himself, he wasn't going to miss this opportunity to see her perform. He arrived at DFW an hour before they told him her flight was scheduled to arrive. He must have drunk a gallon of coffee before she got there, wearing out the people at the Continental desk, checking on whether her flight was on time.

"Jodi Parker, please." Finally! He had trouble curbing his excitement at the sound of the woman's sing-song voice on the PA system.

"Miss Jodi Parker, please come to Continental Airlines. Jodi Parker to Continental Airlines, please."

Lucas popped up off the crapper, and zipped up his pants. Half way out the men's room door, it occurred to him that he had not flushed the stool. He'd later ask himself why he bothered to go back and flush it, but at the time it seemed like the thing to do.

He took off running past snack bars, gift shops, restaurants and bars. He was suddenly struck by the thought that Jodi might not recognize him. They hadn't seen each other for—how long? Maybe he wouldn't remember what she looked like. Was she the same girl he put on that bus in Kansas City? He flipped the thought into the air. No way would he not know Jodi Parker. He'd never forget her.

She'd probably changed some, he conceded. And she was circulating in a different world now, with different people– people he knew nothing about, except for what she told him in their late night calls. But he'd know her. He stepped up his pace to Continental. He could pick Jodi Parker out of a crowd of a thousand people. All he needed was to hear her voice, and lay eyes on the little girl he found parked beside the highway on a rainy Friday afternoon ten miles from Baker's Bluff, Kansas.

He pulled up at the Continental desk. Jodi was nowhere in sight. He asked the slender lady behind the counter whether Jodi answered the page, and was told she did not. He waited. Why was he pacing back and forth, nervous as a teenager on his first date? Like when he heard Jodi on the radio the first time. He made the rounds of all the bars and restaurants, feeding the juke boxes with quarters by the handful. He couldn't hear enough of "Happy go lucky, happy go Marty....his friends all wondered how he kept the pace..."

Next to Lucas at the counter, he heard a man say, "You had a call for Jodi Parker?"

Chubby, bald, middle-aged, and impatient, the man said to the lady behind the Continental counter, "She's on her way. Miss Parker will be here in a moment."

Lucas wondered who the man was, and how he knew so much about Jodi Parker. Then, like a sudden flash of a bright light in his eyes, there she was, surrounded by half a dozen people who seemed anxious to please her!

Lucas thought she looked different in black, soft leather boots almost to her knees, white pants, ankle length, and a pale blue silk top that fit a bit too snugly. Her lips and nails glistened bright red. Maybe this was not the same girl he knew, after all.

The bald man guided her to the desk, and the Continental lady handed her a piece of paper. Jody glanced at it, then handed it to the bald man.

"Here, Alex," she said, "you know more about this than I

do."

Lucas couldn't get near Jodi. People were calling out to her, waving their arms, shouting instructions. By now other people who heard her name called, pushed and shoved to get her autograph on scraps of paper, magazines, and record labels. Lucas felt as out of place as a lemon in a bag of oranges.

Jodi was turning away, wading through the crowd. She never saw him!

"Jodi," he said. His voice caught in his throat.

She followed Alex through the crowd, looking around as though expecting someone.

Lucas couldn't let her go! He found his voice, and yelled, "Jodi!"

She saw him then. "Lucas!" She ran to him.

Lucas grabbed her and swung her off her feet.

A gruff voice behind him said, "Who is this guy?"

Jodi nodded toward a group of people. To Lucas, she said, "We have to go with them."

She hustled out of the terminal and into a waiting taxi. Lucas watched as the man she called Alex crawled in beside her.

Squeezed into the back seat of a different cab with three strangers, Lucas couldn't remember being so lonely. After all the emotion and anxiety of looking forward to being with Jodi again, he saw her for less than a minute.

Deposited in a downtown hotel, he was ushered into a suite of rooms full of milling, jabbering, laughing people, none of whom Lucas knew, and nobody told him who they were. Jodi was not one of them. Lucas staked out a spot near a window overlooking a busy Dallas street, wondering if he'd ever see her again.

That's what he was thinking when she popped into the room decked out in a blue denim outfit like the one she wore the first time he saw her. With no makeup, her face was shiny clean. Her nails no longer glistened with red polish, and her chestnut hair hung loose on her shoulders.

Now here, he thought with a smile—here is the Jodi Parker he remembered.

"Alex," she said to the chubby one who materialized at her side, "could you arrange for me to have some time alone with my friend Lucas?"

Alex herded the others out of the room, and Jodi sat on a mauve colored sofa. "Come sit by me," she said to Lucas. He did as he was told.

"Who are these people?" he said with a puzzled expression.

"Alex is my manager. He takes care of accommodations, and makes sure I get paid when I work. The tall blond girl you saw is my friend Gloria. You remember her." Lucas nodded. "She's the one who took care of Jason for me when I left Phoenix, and brought him to Nashville after I got settled.

She's my hairdresser." She continued down the list of other people, and their responsibilities. "They keep me going." She touched his cheek with her fingertips. "I've missed you so, Lucas. It seems like forever since I saw you last."

"I know." He took her hand and pressed it against his face. "You've come a long way since then, Jodi."

"So have you. I'm so pleased about the promotion you told me about."

"But my biggest kick is knowing you got what you came after. Fame and fortune are a long haul from Baker's Bluff, Kansas."

She grinned, remembering. "It's a long haul from any place I ever was before. From horseshit to baked ham." They laughed at that. I'm so lucky to have people like Tom Crocker and Wally Sheppard and Billy Starr on my side. But it never would have happened without you."

"I don't think I contributed much."

"Yes, you did. You were there when I needed you, and that means a lot more than money. Josh Campbell gave me a lot of encouragement along the way, but–"

"Josh–uh–"

"Josh Campbell. He has two records in Billboard's Top 25 this week. I wrote one of them," she said with pride.

Lucas knew who Josh Campbell was. He also became familiar with Billboard Magazine since Jodi's singing career was taking off.

"I bought one of those," he said.

"You bought Billboard?"

"Yep. The DJ's kept screaming about how great you were," he said with a grin, "with your records climbing the charts and all, I figured I'd better be finding out what they meant by the charts."

"God bless the DJ's!" she said. "They're the ones who make the world go around." After a thoughtful pause, she cocked her chestnut head to one side. "But you are the one who opened the door to that world for me."

"Well, I knew you could do whatever you put your mind to, Jodi. And of course, you've got all those guts."

She threw her head back and shrieked with laughter. "More guts than the packing house!"

"It looks to me like you've got the world by the tail," Lucas said, "and I couldn't be happier for you. Your career is skyrocketing, you've got Jason with you, other people are recording your songs, and—" With a sweep of his hand, he said, "All these people are falling over themselves to please you. What more could a kid from Baker's Bluff, Kansas ask for?"

She cast him a questioning look, disturbed by a coolness, something strangely distant, that she never heard in his voice before. She got to her feet, strode to the window, and peered out over the city below. Pensive, deliberate, yet seeing nothing. When she faced him again, she said, "I've been trying to find a way to repay you for all you've done for me."

"You don't need to pay me, and I don't want you to. The money was a gift, not a loan. It was just lying around doing nothing. I thought it was time I put it to work. It was something I could do, and I'd do it again."

"I'm not talking about the money, Lucas, though I never would have made it without your help. You've given me so much more than money. Confidence, reassurance, encouragement. Just being there when I needed to unload on you. That meant so much to me. You didn't know it then, but you were my guardian angel, and the world's greatest friend. I love you for that, and for so much more." She sat beside him again, and covered his hand with hers. "I think I've loved you ever since you almost drove away and left me parked out there on that highway in the rain. But you rescued me, looking droopier than a baby chick that just popped out of the shell."

Lucas grinned at that, recalling.

"Do you know what I really want, Lucas?"

"Well, what could you want that you don't already have?"

"I want you on my side."

"On your side?"

"I get the idea you don't like what I'm doing. You don't like the people I work with, and—" She took a deep breath. "I wonder if maybe you don't like me any more."

He gave her a startled look. His throat went dry, drained of feeling, robbed of the one thing he wanted—the girl for whom his arms ached, and couldn't wait to hold again.

"That's not true, Jodi."

Who was afraid now? Back in Kansas City—how many lifetimes ago?—he tried to mitigate the fear Jodi felt. Her fear of failure, fear that Nashville wouldn't work out for her. "What if I can't make it?" she'd cried.

Even as he tried to bolster her courage and reassure her all would be well, could it be that he was the one who was afraid? Was it fear that kept him from arranging to come when she asked him to? Fear of what? Of getting too close? Is that what he would have told Jenny had he broached the subject? If he'd shown up when Jodi asked him to come see her perform, would it have been a step toward a commitment he was not ready to make? Or— Tell the truth, Lucas. Could it be you were jealous of her success? That you lost her to another life? Was their brief encounter in Baker's Bluff sufficient grounds on which to build a forever life?

He wrestled now with the fear that he was losing her, blaming her new life, her new friends, her success, for keeping them apart. All these people scurrying around, strangers, smothering her with attention, even as they strived to keep her alive. Squeezing him out of her life.

"Jodi," he said quietly, churning inside. "There's no way I could tell you how I've looked forward to this day. Wanting to be with the frightened little girl who needed help but was too proud to accept it from a stranger. Some guy who wasn't sure where she was going, wanted to go with her wherever it was." He gave his head a bewildered shake. "This is a totally different world for me."

"It's different for me too, Lucas. The only thing that isn't different is how I feel about you." With misty eyes, she said, "I wish you could take me the way I am. I'm still the same girl I was back then."

"Not quite, Jodi. Maybe I've changed some. I never thought so, but it may be. And so have you."

"Like hell I have!" she flared. Hurt and angry, she bounced to her feet and strode away from him. Why couldn't he understand, now more than ever, how she needed him? She needed him to keep her connected to what she was before, reminding her of something she never wanted to be again. The person she'd always been, the one who, Crocker said, was the one who got her where she was. She needed him to balance the bad she suffered then with the good things that were happening to her now. Why couldn't he see that she missed him and wanted him as much as he wanted her?

"It don't make a shit," he said defensively. No sooner were the words off his tongue than he wished he could call them back. Were they uttered out of pride, or stupidity? Or maybe it was his country boy insecurity. Nothing this good ever happened to him before, and he had difficulty handling it. He didn't know the answer, but he didn't want it to get away. One thing was sure: He couldn't bear the thought of losing Jodi Parker.

"It does to me," she shot back. "Who's afraid now, Lucas?"

"What the hell, Jodi? It's no big deal."

She knew it *was* a big deal. Not to her only, but to him also. What was it somebody said about pride going before a fall?

"I've got no claim on you, Jodi. You don't owe me a damn thing."

"Yes, I do! I owe you everything. I wouldn't even be here if it hadn't been for you."

Lucas fought the urge to scream out how lost he felt

without her. Mad at himself for his stupid remarks in a careless moment, he strode to the window and looked out at the bustling streets of Dallas. Why did he wait so long to come to her? All those months he longed to see her, to hold her, to crush her to him, and let her know how much she meant to him. Where was all that desire and longing now? He hadn't even kissed her.

Jodi took up a small handbag from the coffee table in front of the sofa. She started walking away.

"Jodi," Lucas said. Desperation pushed itself out the top of his head.

"Don't make a shit," she said, flinging his words back at him.

"Jodi, I–"

She paused, and faced him with a wan smile. "Lucas, for as long as I can remember I've hoped for someone to want me because of who I am, not what I am. I believed you were the one. We didn't have a lot of time to get acquainted, but what I saw, and what I felt made up for a lifetime of hoping something good would come my way. You were that something. Whatever happened to me for the rest of my life, I wanted to share with you. It hasn't been easy being away from you, and it's not easy telling you this now.

"When I was fourteen I was raped by that idiot my mama was married to. I've got a son whose father has never seen him. Since you and I parted in Kansas City, I've fought off more men than it would take to bury a wet mule, and not a one of them knows I go to bed with my underpants on. The one time I might have got serious about someone else– Yes, it was Josh Campbell, but I couldn't do it, because you were always there, between him and me. Watching over me, caring for me, keeping me out of trouble. My guardian angel.

"Some of those people gave me the chance to earn respect for myself, to blot out some of the dreadful past, giving me something to hope for. My mama used to say you're as good as the people you run with. The people I ran with soon learned no meant no, that I didn't hop into a different bed every night to get where I wanted to go. I'm almost there, but not quite. And thanks to you, I can hold my head up, and bow down to no one.

"Long ago I promised myself if I had to sell my body to support my son, that's what I'd do. But you saved me from that. I make a good living for him and me, doing what I love, and nobody is going to take that away from me. Nobody.

"You once told me I was a tough lady. There are times when I'd like not having to be so tough. You've looked forward to this day, Lucas? So have I. I could hardly wait for it to get here. But, so far it has been a disappointment. You haven't touched me, and you haven't even looked at me like you want to. And right now I don't give much of a damn about anybody. If you want to come with me under those circumstances, you're welcome as hell. Maybe we can find our way back to where we started." She took a step toward the door. "Everybody needs a friend sometime."

"Jodi."

She paused, but didn't look at him.

"The first time I heard you sing on the radio, I whooped and hollered all the way home."

She cast him a sideways look.

"You told me you'd be some place in Ohio that night, but I couldn't find you. I called the record company in Nashville, Tom Crocker too, but got no answer. I must have stuffed a week's pay into juke boxes all over town. I couldn't get enough of 'Marty's Place.' "

She crinkled the corners of her mouth into the tantalizing little smile he'd dreamed about.

"My friends deserted me," he went on. "They thought I'd lost my mind. And by around midnight I started wondering about it myself. Every time I heard you sing, it was like the first time we were together. The more I thought about it, and all that has happened for you since—

"When I watched you ride away from Kansas City on that bus, I probably was more scared than you were. Yes, you pegged me right. I was afraid you'd go off down there and get yourself famous and forget all about me. But, I wanted you to go. I knew that was what you wanted. Then, when I saw you at the airport I was scared all over again. What scared me most was that I might do something dumb to botch things up for you, and I couldn't stand to lose you."

For a moment she hesitated, then smiled, and held out her hand. Lucas grasped it and drew her to him, with a kiss on her mouth.

"You're not going to lose me, Lucas," she whispered. "I need you in my life."

CHAPTER TWENTY-SIX

Heeere's Jodi!

Lucas watched from the wings, excited as if he he'd won the Power Ball. Marveling, as Jodi came alive on stage. Dancing, prancing, teasing with her body and her voice, captivating the audience with the talents she was born with, charisma and personality that couldn't be taught.

Behind him, Lucas heard a man's voice say, "Howdy." He looked around and saw the slender man with long brown hair and a bushy mustache.

"You must be Malone," the man said.

"I wouldn't want to be anybody else."

"I'm Josh Campbell."

Lucas nodded. "I know."

"I'd rather be you," Campbell said, putting out his hand.

Lucas gave it a shake. "How's that?"

Campbell nodded toward the stage. "She's headed for the big time, you know."

"You think so?"

"I hope you know what you've got there."

"I know."

"Well," Campbell said, "I've got a gig to do. You must be some kind of guy, Malone. Good luck to you."

Josh strode briskly past him onto the stage where he joined Jodi in a chorus of Rocky Top.

They finished the number. Josh waved the audience into a rousing applause, a standing ovation for "Miss Jodi Parker!"

Shivers of delight rocketed down the backbone of Lucas Malone.

Jodi acknowledged the audience's response with bows and blown kisses. In the front row she waved to Tom Crocker, Wally Sheppard, and Billy Starr. They stood up and applauded with broad smiles. The audience followed with a standing ovation. Jodi responded with bows, and tossed kisses.

They couldn't see her tears of joy as she raced offstage. She leaped into the waiting arms of Lucas Malone.

Jodi Parker found a home.

THE END

ONE MORE MAN TO KILL

a short story

CHAPTER

"Give it up, Hacker, you've got one more man to kill."

Three months ago Clete Hacker was released from Leavenworth Prison. He served six years for bank robbery. The day he was released, Hacker went on a vengeful rampage– hunting down the jurors who said he was guilty. He'd found eleven of them, and shot them dead. He was now looking for juror number twelve.

Hacker's search was for a black man, named Elijah Bridgewater. Bridgewater was a former slave. After the Civil War, he headed west from the Mississippi plantation where he was born thirty-two years before. From age seven– sunup till dark drove him in– he worked rice paddies, cornfields and cotton fields. Lured to Kansas by land agents' touting of a "New Promised Land," Bridgewater found his way to Nicodemus, a settlement of former slaves on the banks of the Solomon River.

In 1876 Kansas, a black man was not highly regarded as a public citizen. Even so, Bridgewater's name was drawn from a hatful of potential jurors, and was selected to sit on a Graham County jury. The other jurors gave him a quizzical eye. They wondered what he was doing there– one black man on a jury of twelve. Whoever put his name in the pot didn't know he was black, a former slave.

There was a public uprising about a black man serving on a white man's jury. During the war, Kansas was a free state, where slavery was against the law. Even so, some white citizens demanded that Bridgewater be removed from the jury. Others protested that he was a citizen of the state of Kansas, and had the right to serve. The matter was resolved when the Court assumed a position of neutrality, which allowed Bridgewater to decide whether he'd go or stay.

Bridgewater stayed.

The man on trial was Clete Hacker. The jurors found him guilty and he was sentenced to six years in Leavenworth. The day he was released, Hacker swore he'd kill them all.

Will Savage was looking for the same man Hacker was after. Savage earned the reputation of being able to find people the law gave up on. A former range detective, he was persuaded by the law to leave his ranch near Junction City long enough to track down Bridgewater.

Savage got word that Bridgewater hired on as a blacksmith for a rancher somewhere west of Nicodemus. Will's job was to find Bridgewater, and use him as a lure for nabbing the elusive Hacker.

Savage's first stop was a visit with Graham County sheriff, Bert Twiller. Twiller had an encounter with Bridgewater one night when the black man got into a tussle with a couple of ranch hands with a wild hair about nudging elbows with him at the Bad Ass Saloon.

"What happened?" Savage asked.

"I locked him up."

"You locked who up?"

"Bridgewater," Twiller said.

"Did he start the ruckus?"

"Bridgewater? Well, no, but I–"

"Why'd you lock him up if it wasn't his fault?" Savage wanted to know.

Twiller searched for an answer that didn't come easy. He was a skinny man with shoulder length gray hair and a whine for a voice.

"Well," Twiller whined, "them two punchers fell flat-assed on the barroom floor. The black man put 'em there. You know, him bein' black and all—"

"So, you locked him up because he was black."

"I let him go the next morning, and posted him outa town. I'd had enough trouble. I figured if he stayed around he'd cause more."

"Did he leave?"

"He didn't want to. Said it wasn't his fault. I said to him, I ain't askin', I'm tellin' you," Twiller said. "They'll be back, I told him, and they'll bring some guns with 'em. I said, you leave town, or I'll throw you back in my jail."

"You know where he was going?"

Twiller shook his head. "I heard him say something about a job. All I know is he took off ridin' west."

"How long ago was that?" Savage asked.

"What day is this?"

"Tuesday."

"Last I seen of him was Sattidy. I'm damn glad he's gone."

Savage reined his bay west. There was a lot of Kansas out there. It would be a long hard ride across the High Plains looking for a man he didn't know and never saw, even a black man. Somewhere this side of Colorado a man named Bridgewater, was looking for a job. Savage went looking for him.

The signs of life Savage encountered along the trail included prairie dogs skittering from one sagebrush to the next; rattlesnakes daring him to get close, an occasional deer that wouldn't let him, and a band of yipping coyotes.

A two-day ride brought Savage to a rickety log cabinon the prairie. He was greeted by an old man with a gray beard, and a patch over his left eye. Puffing on a corncob pipe, the man aimed a twelve gauge shotgun at Savage's belt buckle.

Savage said, "Howdy."

"Howdy yourself," the man replied. "Who are you?"

"My name's Savage."

"What the hell you doin' out here anyhow?"

"I'm looking for a man named Bridgewater."

"Ain't nobody around here by that name. Why don't you just keep on movin'?"

"You know, mister," Savage said, "I had you pegged right away as a man who'd help a stranger locate this man."

"Well." The old man's mood softened. "Can't be too careful any more. What kind o' man is he? What's he look like?"

"Black man. Used to be a slave."

"You sayin' he's a nigger?"

"I'm saying he's a black man, who used to be a slave," Savage said with an edge to it.

The old man squirmed a bit at Savage's challenging voice. "Aw, I never meant no— My name's Wesley Haggard—"

"In your place, Wesley, I wouldn't want to get caught calling that man anything but black."

"I just—you know–You say his name's Bridgewater?"

"That's right. Elijah Bridgewater. You won't need that shotgun. You can put it away."

"Well, you know– " Haggard looked as though he'd rather hang onto the gun, but he leaned it against a fence post. He pushed his straw hat back off his forehead, and scratched his head with the same hand. "By gar, thinkin' back on it," he said, "I think I did hear somethin' 'bout a black man back a spell.

Stopped for water out around the Barton place. They wondered where he come from. I never seen 'im, but I heard somebody make mention – "

Savage got interested. "How long ago was that, Mr. Haggard?"

"Well, out here it's hard to keep track o' time—I—I can't tell you when it was for certain. Well, now maybe it was—"

"Thanks anyway," Savage said, restless to be gone. "How do I get to the Barton place?"

"Oh, it ain't too far west o' here. You're headed in the right direction. I tell you, If you—if you—uh—well if you ride hard, you'd oughta be there by this time tomorrow."

Savage offered him a thoughtful nod, reined his mare around, and pointed her head west.

"You a lawman?" Haggard asked.

"Nope. Cowman."

Savage pulled his hat down against the lowering sun, and wondered how far he'd have to ride to get to where he was going. The sun was sneaking down behind the lumpy western hills, and he decided he'd do well to camp for the night. He stripped the saddle off the mare and tethered her to a sycamore limb beside a thirsty stream. He set a fire of dried limbs, dumped a double handful of coffee into a coffee can of water, and listened for the gurgle while it perked.

He never heard the gurgle.

How far he'd traveled, Savage didn't know. But he knew his body was saddle weary, and needed to bed it down. He used his saddle for a pillow, and stretched out beside the fire. Before the coffee stopped gurgling, he was dead to the world.

Half way through the next morning Savage met a young rider on a black horse. Savage guessed he was maybe fourteen. The boy pulled up beside him, shaded his eyes from the already blazing sun, and said, "Where you headed?"

"The Barton place," Savage said. "Am I pointed in the right direction?"

"You're going the right way, but you've got some riding to do yet. Why are you going to Barton's? You looking for somebody?"

"A black man named Bridgewater."

"A black man. Hmmnn. I don't know if it's the one you're looking for, but there was something going on back there where I come from. Something about a black man."

"Where was that?"

"Mile or so back. There's a hook in the trail that takes you back to the right about half

a quarter. I got out of there as fast as I could."

"Where are you going?" Savage asked.

"My uncle has a couple of sections up north. Runs some cattle on it," the boy said. "I'm gonna go see if he needs a hand." He spurred his black into action. "Good luck to you. I wouldn't get too close to what's going on back there."

Savage found the clearing in the middle of a stand of scrub oaks. From one of the trees, a black man dangled with a noose around his neck. Savage cut him down, and laid him on the ground. The man coughed and gasped for breath. Savage helped him with a drink from his canteen. Stuffed inside the man's shirt pocket he found a scrawled note on a piece of crumpled paper. "If you lookin for that black bastard Bridgewater you found him."

"You Bridgewater?" Savage said.

The man on the ground nodded with effort, gasped for breath, and rubbed the red marks on his neck.

"Can you tell me who did this?" Savage asked.

Bridgewater shook his head wildly. "Hack–Ha—that man– Hacker—he–" he wheezed. His head rolled to one side. He quit breathing.

Savage buried the body of Elijah Bridgewater in a shallow grave.

Hacker was out there some place. He probably wouldn't be easy to find, but Savage had to go see. He knew of a place over east a way called Cross Creek. He'd been by there a time or two in the past, looking for somebody the law couldn't find. He took a chance that Hacker, having completed his bloody mission with Bridgewater's hanging, headed that way to celebrate with his friends.

On the high ridge to his left, Savage spotted a lone rider. The rider kept pace for a while, then spurred his mount, and disappeared. He wondered if the rider was the same boy he talked to before.

Cross Creek didn't amount to much. A couple of saloons, a mercantile, and a small café. Half a dozen horses were tethered at the rail in front of the Dead Beat Saloon. If Hacker was there, he shouldn't be hard to find. Savage pulled up in front of the Dead Beat. He dropped rein over the hitch rack, and took a look around.

On his way inside, he heard laughter and loud talk. At the doorway he paused briefly. The laughter and loud talk stopped. Savage moved to the bar. At a nearby table he heard a loud whisper, "That's him."

Behind the bar stood a short, chunky man of fifty-two. Cal

Winthrop was his name. "What can I do for you?" he asked Savage.

Savage took the crumpled note from his shirt pocket, and laid it on the bar. "I thought you might be able to tell me who wrote this note."

Winthrop was no friend of Clete Hacker's. He knew about Hacker's bloody killing spree. Three of the jurors Hacker murdered sometimes stopped by the Dead Beat for a drink on their way to someplace else. Cal, without moving his head, shifted his eyes to Will's left. "The one in black," he whispered.

"You got a cold beer to dampen a weary traveler's throat?" Savage asked the bartender.

Winthrop said nothing. He turned away, then set a bottle on the bar.

"How much?" Savage said

Winthrop shook his head. "No charge. Be careful."

Savage took the bottle with him to the table. Two men and a boy were already there. He recognized the boy– seated at Hacker's right– as the one he met on the trail. A middle-aged man wearing a coonskin cap, sat to Hacker's left. The man in the middle was dressed in black, ruddy complexioned, six feet tall. He had to be Clete Hacker.

H was. Savage thought he wavered as though he'd already drunk too much.

"Mind if I join you?" Savage said. He didn't wait for an answer. He pulled out a chair and sat down.

"If I were a betting man," Savage said with a strong look at the man in black, "I'd bet you are Mr. Hacker. Is that right?"

The man in black said, "I'm Hacker. What the hell is that to you?"

"I'll tell you what that is to me. You knew who I was before I got here. That young man on your right lied to me, but I have no quarrel with him. The gentleman on your left, I don't know, but I didn't come here to see him either. My name's Will Savage. I came to see you, Mr. Hacker.

"I promised a man I'd do my best to round up a black man named Elijah Bridgewater. He used to be a slave. I found him. He had a rope around his neck. He was about a breath and a half short of breathing his last. With most of it, he told me you hung him on that tree. Is there anything to that?"

"Damn right." Hacker took a moment to think about that. "I hung the black bastard, and I'd do it again."

"I don't think you'll be around for that."

Hacker fell silent, then made a token move toward his gun.

"I wouldn't do that, Mr. Hacker," Savage said. "The way I see it, you killed twelve men out of pure damn meanness. You've got one more man to kill. You're looking at him."

Hacker sneered, turned to his friend and chuckled. He reached for a bottle and poured himself a glass of whiskey.

"You got a lot o'guts—"

"So I've been told."

"—bustin' in here— What the hell do you think you're doin'?"

"I've got a deal for you, Hacker," Savage said. "I promised a man I'd find you and bring you back. I'm not leaving here without you. You can ride your horse, with your hands and feet tied. Or you can ride with your dead body across your saddle, tied hand and foot under that horse's belly. It's up to you." Savage stood up. "Let me know what you decide."

Hacker jumped to his feet and went for his gun. It never cleared leather. The bullet he hoped would kill Will Savage was still in the chamber. Savage holstered his Colt .44.

Hacker's body slumped onto the table. The boy beside him screamed, and hugged the dead man's shoulders.

To Savage, the man in the coonskin cap said, "He was the boy's daddy."

Savage gave his head a sorrowful shake, and squeezed his eyes till they hurt. He wished he could do something for the boy. What could he do?

"I'll take care of him," said the man at the table.

Savage gave him a thank you nod. He unbuckled his gun belt, laid it on the bar, and walked away.

Cal Winthrop knew what that meant. Will Savage fired his gun for the last time.

THE END

REUNION AT KENNEDY HIGH

a novelette

CHAPTER ONE

Jennifer's Johnny is dead

It wasn't her fault she wasn't dead. She couldn't even take credit for being alive.

The face staring back at her from the dressing table mirror wasn't hers. It belonged to some gray haired old lady whose youth long since faded, leaving an expanse of pale skin and puffy eyes. Her body, lumpy as a bag of turnips, was once the slim, graceful curves of Jennifer Coan, Homecoming Queen. A painful reflection of aging years. The wrinkled face was like her mother's looked the day she died of cancer twelve years before. The deep lines in her face left room for no more. The face looking back at her was all she had. What happened to the Jennifer once adored by all?

It was not always so. After she and Johnny married–he was the math teacher at Kennedy High–they topped everyone's social list. Johnny thought it was because of his respected status on staff. Jennifer knew better. She was the spark that breathed life into any social gathering. Beautiful, bright, and outgoing, she fluttered about with a provocative smile, flattered everyone, called them by name with a peck on the cheek.

No longer was she the belle of the ball. Not since Johnny

retired.

When she was nineteen, Johnny Beason, six years older, squired her around to parties, greeted with hugs and smiles. They often danced the night away because Johnny loved to dance, and Jennifer loved Johnny. She and Johnny dated for six months before he kissed her. She was happy then. Why was she not happy now?

Thursday morning Johnny came home after walking nine holes of golf, and announced, "I can't do it anymore."

For years after he retired, at eight o'clock every morning Johnny headed for the golf course. By himself. Back home, he relaxed in the rec room downstairs. He fiddled with the television that displayed three screens at once. He could watch a recorded baseball game, a football game, and Wheel of Fortune at the same time. At one o'clock in the afternoon the television went off, and stayed off till the Five O'clock News. He watched until six when the TV was done for the night.

Almost overnight, Johnny's legs began to fail, his pace reduced to a shuffle. In his refuge below, he settled into his Lazy Boy recliner, content with his television, his books and his bathroom.

Jennifer couldn't erase the horrifying image of Johnny sitting on the bathroom stool where she found him this morning. Bent double, head in his hands, red and white plaid pajama bottoms ruffled around his ankles. Voiceless. Motionless. Dead.

That was Johnny. For years he lived within himself. He died the same way.

Jennifer was fraught with anxiety on the edge of hysteria. She couldn't think beyond that terrifying moment. Overwhelmed by challenges she never had to face—left with the unthinkable responsibility of facing them now. Alone.

Closing in on her were threats of what her life would be like without Johnny.

She was suddenly struck by the image of the little white pills in the brown bottle tucked away in the bathroom medicine chest. She took them to help her sleep nights when Johnny didn't come up from his den. She often found him there the next morning, asleep in the recliner.

Frightened by the thought of surviving without him, Jennifer threw open the door of the medicine chest, seeking relief from the agony of not knowing how to cope with a world without Johnny in it.

There! She took the bottle down, twisted the lid off, and dumped a handful of pills into her palm. Her hand was half way to her mouth. She stopped. The phone! Who'd be calling now?

She grabbed the phone off the table outside the bathroom door, and said hello.

"Hi, Jennifer," came the cheerful voice. "This is Pam."

"Yes, Pam?" Should she tell Pam she found Johnny dead? Could she tell her? Could she tell anyone? She didn't even have the presence of mind to call 9-1-1.

"Tom and I are going to the Kennedy High reunion," Pam said. "Are you and Johnny planning to go?"

"I–I don't think so. Could we talk another time, Pam? I'm–"

"Oh, sure, Jennifer, if you– Are you all right, Jen?"

Jennifer plopped the phone down. Still holding the little white pills, she looked at them as if they were tiny pieces of evil she never saw before. On the table beside the phone lay the blue envelope addressed to Dr. and Mrs. John H. Coan. Their invitation to the reunion. Emblazoned across the front of the envelope was KENNEDY HIGH FOREVER!

Miss Lorena

With a happy heart, Lorena Clark anticipated her one hundredth birthday celebration. For fifty-five years–even before Crestview High became Kennedy High after the president was assassinated in Dallas–she dedicated her life to teaching the kids she loved. Revered alike by students and peers, she retired and moved to the family's country estate.

Though no longer teaching, Lorena maintained contact with some of her former charges. She was proud of their accomplishments as doctors, lawyers, broadcasters, a priest in New Orleans, a space scientist in California, farmers, a pharmacist, a plumber and a state governor.

Times when she was away from home, Lorena's door was never locked–"in case somebody needs a place to spend the night." Somebody–usually a male former student–often stayed at her house when he came to town, encouraged by the plaque mounted on her front door: Come on in. Food's in the fridge, bed's in the back. If you make a mess, clean it up. Tell your mama I love you.

Lorena never married. Her students were her family, teaching them was her life. Even now, after years of retirement, some called from Germany, London, the Philippines, with birthday wishes. They loved Lorena because she loved them. She taught them things they didn't learn at home: self-confidence, morality, human dignity, respect for each other. They loved her for her compassion, even for scolding them when they needed scolding.

"Your dream is out there some place," Miss Lorena stressed in the classroom. "Find it and hang on. Never give up on it. And never ever give up on yourself."

Asked how she wanted to be remembered when she died, Lorena said she didn't want to hear any moaning and groaning. "Throw a big-ass party," she said, "and celebrate what we have together."

One of her invitations made its way into the hands of Toddy Malone.

Toddy was not the sharpest tack in the box. In second grade he was sent home for exploring with his forefinger the secret places of six-year-old Peggy Whipple's anatomy in the cloak room. At fourteen, Toddy was invited by his twenty-nine-year old Social Studies teacher to attend the unveiling of her bosom in the back seat of her car. Asked by authorities what happened, Toddy said he probably would never do it again. He didn't. The teacher was sent away for child molestation.

With the compassionate aid of Miss Lorena, Toddy finally made it down the aisle to the tune of "Land of Hope and Glory" to collect his high school diploma.

After graduation he was offered a job as dog walker at the

local animal shelter. That sounded like fun. He took the job. Toddy loved animals. He loved them so much he was charged with animal abuse for raping his favorite canine. The case was thrown out of court because the victim's testimony was unreliable.

When he was nineteen, Toddy ran naked through the shopping mall. He holed up in a cardboard box behind the mall until it was safe to come out.

Toddy didn't marry till he was forty-three. Her name was Candy Stickle. He met Candy in the Walmart pet food department. He followed her to a dogfight where she cheered a couple of pit bulls trying killing each other.

Toddy fell in love with Candy. She had three kids and cancer. Toddy speculated that Candy viewed him as a sympathetic soul who would provide food and shelter for her kids after she was gone. That was all right, Toddy said.

It was not the cancer, that did Candy in.

One of Toddy's pearls of wisdom was: "You never know what's going on in the back room till you push the door open."

One day Toddy did.

On top of his brown leather sofa, Toddy spotted Candy flat on her back with her legs spread apart, shoeless feet in the air. On top of Candy was a puffing, breathless Vinny Dewar, Toddy's best friend.

Toddy had to make a decision. He could close the door behind him as he left without making his presence known, or he could resort to drastic action.

He chose the second option. Toddy reached to the gun rack on the wall. He lifted the twelve gauge shotgun his daddy warned him never to touch. With the twelve gauge, utilized heretofore for scaring the hell out of sparrows trying to occupy the bluebird house in the back yard, Toddy Malone splattered the family room walls with the brains of his wife Candy and his best friend Vinny.

Convicted of double homicide, the future for Toddy was bleak. It promised only a stroll down the hallway to the execution chamber. His death row cell was lonely. He missed Vinny.

Candy's kids became wards of the state.

At one minute past midnight, after six years of unsuccessful appeals, Toddy sniffed a nose full of lethal gas and died. Only the warden, the prison chaplain—saddled with the responsibility of saving Toddy's soul—and a cub reporter from the local paper, watched him do it.

CHAPTER TWO

Ellen's foggy memory

So forgettable was Toddy Malone as a member of the class of '87, even threatened with of extinction in a bed of red hot coals, Ellen Glover couldn't have recalled what Toddy looked like. She also wasn't aware that Toddy's soul floated away to its final resting place last midnight.

At the moment Ellen was watching the tall man behind the cash register at the neighborhood grocery. He counted into her palm the change from her two twenty-dollar bills.

She dropped the three bills and twenty-seven cents into her shoulder bag. A nice man. She had a feeling she'd seen him before. But where and when she couldn't recall. Mid-fifties, graying hair, clipped mustache hovering over thin lips. One of those "golden agers" working part time to stay busy, Ellen guessed. Probably retired from a cushy job at some bank.

"Thank you so much," the cashier said with a twinkle in his soft blue eyes. "I hope you'll come again."

How refreshing. Most cashiers uttered something insipid like "have a nice day," caring little what kind of day she had, or whether she ever came again. This one didn't even ask the asinine "paper or plastic?"

Ellen became aware of a coffee stain on the front of her pink blouse. She just came from a book club luncheon at the Methodist Church where someone bumped her elbow, causing the coffee stain. She wondered whether the man behind the counter noticed it.

At forty-eight, married to the same man for twenty-six years, why did she care what this strange man thought? Still, she drew together the lapels of her navy blue jacket to cover the stain.

Ellen shopped at this store since she and Howard moved into the neighborhood twenty-four years ago. This man was different from the others who checked her purchases. She assured him she would be back.

With a parting smile, she took up the bag of groceries and headed for the exit. She placed it on the back seat, and settled behind the wheel of her silver-colored Chevy Lumina parked at the curb. She fastened her seatbelt and adjusted the rearview and side-view mirrors before she turned the key in the ignition. The motor whirred, and she eased the car out of the parking space.

Howard often reminded her that women could neither park nor back properly, and held school on how to do it. A technical engineer, Howard believed for any project the first move was "getting all your ducks in a row," cautious as a cat surveying the safety factor before venturing forth. After thirty years with the phone company, Howard accepted a buy-out. He struggled since with the boredom of having nothing to keep him busy. Neither fishing nor hunting excited him, and golf he reserved for when he got old.

Ellen was relieved and pleased when Howard accepted the offer of "ambassadorial representative" for that Veterans organization four months ago. She didn't know what that meant, but Howard was happy doing it, and it got him out from underfoot from time to time. Out-of-town meetings, conventions, and seminars were good for him. While he was away, Ellen found plenty to keep her busy with book club, bridge, church, and volunteer turns at three different charity organizations.

She turned into her driveway. A green VW bug was parked

there. Ashley was home.

Her daughter bounced out the front door. "Mom, you won't believe it!"

Ashley grabbed up the bag of groceries from the back seat of the car, carried it into the kitchen, and parked it on the cabinet beside the refrigerator.

In faded jeans, white gym shoes and floppy green tank top, Ashley looked more like a teenager than a twenty-three-year-old PE instructor at Kennedy High.

Ellen brushed Ashley's cheek with her lips. "What won't I believe?"

"We have a new basketball coach!"

Ellen blinked. Okay, she thought vaguely, as she removed items from the brown paper bag.

To Ashley, anything new and different was a major development. Ellen admired her daughter's enthusiasm for the arrival of a new basketball coach at Kennedy High.

Thirty years before, in her senior year, Ellen was a cheerleader, played clarinet in the school band, and was voted Football Queen at Kennedy High. She recalled no time, however, when she was as excited about any of those accomplishments as Ashley was about the new basketball coach.

"Why wouldn't I believe it?" she said.

"It's Hayden McCoy!"

From the bag Ellen retrieved the package of ground chuck she'd mold into hamburger patties for Howard to charcoal on the patio grill. Next came the gallon of two-percent milk, a glass of which would accompany two sour cream donuts for his breakfast after he consumed three cups of black coffee. She placed the milk and ground chuck in the refrigerator. She waited for Ashley to say something about Hayden McCoy that would help her identify this latest phenom to enter the life of her daughter—and whose name she obviously was expected to recognize.

"Taylor McCoy's son," Ashley said.

There it was.

Around the plastic container of white stuff, Ellen placed on the second shelf of the white refrigerator a jar of white mayonnaise. Her fingers froze. Her eyes were drawn as if by a magnet to the little white bulb flooding the white fridge walls with glaring white light. Her mouth was dry. Her heart was racing.

She wished Ashley would go away.

Mindy gets a ride

Trudging along Interstate 70, Mindy Carson breathed a sigh of relief when a man in a Ford Taurus pulled over and stopped beside her.

"Where you goin'?" said the fat-faced man behind the wheel through the rolled-down passenger side window.

His name was Charlie Gann, fifty-five, wearing an open-collared blue shirt and a Texas Rangers baseball cap.

Weary from walking in the mid-June heat, Mindy took a deep breath. "That sign back there said there was a truck stop up ahead."

"That where you wanta go?" Gann said with a gap-toothed grin.

That wasn't where Mindy wanted to go. She was on her way to Crestview for her old teacher's one-hundredth birthday celebration when her car ran out of gas a couple of miles back. She hoped to get help at the truck stop. Slender, blond, and forty-seven, Mindy left Kansas City that Friday morning, assuring her teen-aged son and daughter she'd be back Sunday night.

She nodded yes in answer to Gann's question.

"Well, come on then," he said. "Hop in. I'm headed that way. You might as well ride along."

He pushed open the door. Mindy climbed in, grateful for the lift.

Gann shifted the Taurus into gear. "That your car I seen off the road back there?"

"Yes. I ran out of gas. My husband always filled the tank for me. I don't always remember to do it."

"Your husband?"

"Jerry Carson. He took care of things like that."

Took care? Gann thought. "Where's he at now?"

"He was killed in Afghanistan."

"Afghan, huh?"

"He was a Marine infantry captain."

Gann leered at her, suddenly aware his fortunes might be changing for the better.

Nothing good happened to Charlie lately. Six days ago he was released from Texas State prison after serving seven years for bank robbery. While he was behind bars, his three kids scattered, his wife sold the house. She was now living with a deputy sheriff somewhere in Illinois. Gann was on his way there to settle that score.

"Pretty little thing like you hadn't oughta be runnin' around way off out here by herself," Gann said. "All kinds of bad things could happen to you. Never know when some crazy might—

What's that?" He braked to a stop on the shoulder, and went to investigate the noise in the back of the car. "Open the glove box for me, hon," he said, "and press that yellow button."

Startled by his familiarity, Mindy thumbed open the glove compartment. Inside the box, her eyes went wide at sight of a snub-nosed pistol. She hesitated.

"The yellow button, hon. Just push it for me, will you?"

She pushed the yellow button and the trunk lid popped up. In the rear view mirror she saw Gann had his head in the trunk. Yielding to her woman's instinct, she grabbed the pistol and dropped it in her shoulder bag.

She heard the trunk lid bang shut.

Gann came back and settled behind the steering wheel. "Wasn't nothin'." He moved the car back onto the highway. "Empty beer bottle rattlin' around back there."

Mindy noticed a change in his attitude. He was sullen now, and inquisitive. She shivered at the thought he might know she took the gun. She felt threatened by it before, but now, not knowing what he might do, she wished she hadn't taken it.

"Where you goin' after the truck stop?" he said.

"The first thing I have to do is get some gas for my car."

He cast her a steady, slit-eyed look. "I mean after that."

"St. Louis." She didn't want him to know her true destination. "I'm going to visit a friend."

"What kind of friend? Man, woman, boy, girl? I mean, what kind of friend are we talkin' here?"

Frightened by his aggressive manner, she was not eager to reveal to this total stranger her personal plans. Since she was in his car, however, with no easy way to get out, she decided she'd better appear cordial.

"A friend from college," she said. "He and I are working on a project together."

Gann emitted a dubious chuckle. "I bet you are. I got a bird's eye view of what kind of project you two are workin' on."

Shaken by his derisive attitude, Mindy knew she needed to find a way to get out of the car. What about the gun? Could she—would she—have the courage to use it to defend herself if it came to that?

"Coupla old college chums," Gann went on. "Plannin' a big ol' happy reunion, eh?"

Her heartbeat quickened. Could he know about the reunion at Kennedy High?

"Is that it?" he said. "Since you got no man no more, you got nothin' to slow you down, so you're gonna live it up with your old college playmate."

Mindy breathed easier when the truck stop came into view.

Gann pulled into the bay and stopped.

She said a hurried thanks and reached for the car door handle.

"Just a minute," Gann said.

Mindy froze.

"We got some business to 'tend to," he said.

Mindy, confused and frightened, couldn't let go of the door handle.

"You wanta gimme the gun?" Gann said, voice cold, eyes icy slits.

A quick glance told her she didn't close the glove box. He knew she had the gun!

She tried to open the door, but he clamped a rough hand around her wrist. With a sudden jerk she twisted free, pushed the door open, and leaped out.

Gann ran after her. He grabbed at her shoulder bag. She yanked the bag away, the gun went flying, and landed ten feet away. They both ran for it. Mindy got there first and snatched it up.

The diving bully knocked her down. She struggled to hold onto the pistol. There was a deafening explosion. Gann's eyes went wide, his mouth flew open, and his heavy body plopped on top of her.

Stunned with by the thought that the shot might have killed him, Mindy wriggled out from under his flabby body. For a moment she stared at his contorted mouth that looked propped open, but no sound came. She had to do something. Trance-like, she moved toward the truck stop entrance.

She held the gun as though it was a part of her hand. She gripped it as if she couldn't let go. Slowly, she pushed open the door to the truck stop.

Inside, she was greeted by Elvis Presley shouting from the jukebox, flooding the place with "You ain't nothin' but a hound dog." People at the half dozen tables downing burgers and Bud paid her no mind. A dark-haired waitress in a tight-fitting western outfit scurried about, taking orders and delivering food.

If anyone heard the shot, they must have thought it was a backfire, rousing no curiosity.

At sight of the gun, though, waving in the trembling hand of Mindy Carson, what a moment before was bustling activity, now was dead silence. Elvis stopped singing. All eyes stared in disbelief at Mindy. Nobody moved.

Unsteadily, she moved toward the counter by the door.

Behind the counter, seventy-three-year-old Hazel Gillespie gasped wide-eyed, eying the gun, wondering whether she should raise her hands.

In twenty-nine years of operating the truck stop, never had anyone pointed a gun at Hazel. After she lost her husband in that hunting accident in '94, she grew gray and frail. Her primary concern was avoiding cholesterol. She scrutinized every label before she bought anything at the grocery store to be sure it was fat-free.

Business was good at the truck stop. As long as she took the pills her doctor prescribed, life was bearable. Never did Hazel dream one day she'd be staring into the muzzle of a gun in the hands of a strange blond woman.

Suddenly the image of her daughter Eunice, and Eunice's five kids, flashed across Hazel's mind. Would she ever see them again?

Hazel watched the woman with the gun, uncomfortably aware that everybody else was watching her. She owned the place, and "in charge" was her responsibility. The gun was pointed at her. Customers waited to see what Hazel was going to do. Hazel didn't know what she was going to do. She didn't want to do anything about it. She shivered at sight of the gun in the woman's shaking hand.

Mindy wasn't sure what she was doing was what she wanted to be doing.

Hazel couldn't believe what happened next. She heard the woman whisper, "I think I just killed somebody."

Mindy slumped in front of the cash register. The gun dropped from her hand and skidded across the concrete floor. It came to rest at the booted feet of a tall man in a white Stetson. The boots and Stetson belonged to Wade Lambert.

Growing up on a Missouri farm, Wade's ambition was to be a highway patrolman. Right out of M.U., he got a job in law enforcement, married the lady dispatcher in the Sheriff's office, and was the father of her four kids. After thirty-three years of service, Wade could retire, but chose not to.

Slender as a scrub oak, durable as the boots he wore, Wade loved his job, including the bad stuff. He often asked himself what he'd do if he retired—fade away, rock his life away on the front porch of the old folks' home? He was still a young man with lots of good years ahead. He wasn't ready to turn in his badge.

Lambert watched Mindy, as did everybody else in the place. He was about to move over to coax the gun from her when she collapsed. Lambert knelt beside her, checked her pulse, and helped her to her feet.

Lambert patted the body of Charlie Gann. He confessed to himself this was a part of the job he never got used to. Touching dead bodies, feeling the pain of someone like Mindy Carson, agonizing over taking a life, though Lambert assured her it was not her fault. While the legal determination was not up to him, Lambert's opinion was that Mindy feared for her life, and the weapon accidentally fired when she tried to defend herself against a convicted felon.

"Charlie Gann," Lambert announced to his partner, Lynn Whitman. He handed Whitman the gun he retrieved from the floor, along with some papers from Gann's body.

To Mindy, Lambert said, "You're a mighty lucky lady, ma'am. This man served time for bank robbery and child molestation. We got a report that he killed a man in Joplin yesterday and stole the car he was driving. We don't know yet where he got the gun."

Mindy thumbed a tear from her eye. "I'm so sorry."

"Be glad you're alive," Lambert said.

"Thank you so much."

"We know where to find you if we need you. You're free to go." With a smile, he said, "Have fun at the reunion. I graduated from Kennedy a few years ahead of you. Wish Miss Lorena happy birthday from a skinny kid named Lambert."

"I will."

Hello, Taylor McCoy

He poured himself a cup of hot tea and set it on the table beside his recliner. Pretty good tea, he thought. Not as good though as Lou used to serve him. But not many things other people made were as good as Lou's. Strange and frightening how rapidly his life changed since Lou's stroke. He had to learn to do all the things she did for him.

Time was when being Taylor McCoy–star shooting guard of the NBA–meant a life of fun and fame. Now, all that was gone. All but the memories. And the pain. The pain of blowing many thousands of dollars on fancy cars and homes. An airplane he never learned to fly. Walking the streets— looking for people to take the money he handed out.

In those days money wasn't the primary incentive for athletes. The money was good, but McCoy's motivation was the desire to play the game he loved. Arriving at the professional level fulfilled a dream the country boy never thought would come true. The fun and opportunity were worth more to Taylor than what he was paid to play. Pro basketball was still a game then, "not a billionaire's toy" as it is today.

Players played because they weren't happy doing anything else.

No regrets, though. Tylor did it all. He was glad he still had money to pay for the little neighborhood grocery. The hours weren't bad. The apartment upstairs was adequate for what he needed. And he was close to the health care facility where he could visit Lou. He was grateful Hayden would be the Kennedy High basketball coach in the fall.

Lou was better off where she was. She got professional care he couldn't give her while he took care of her at home the first year after she was stricken.

He set a match to his briar pipe, and exhaled a fog of gray smoke. He flipped on the lamp beside his chair, and settled back with his library copy of "The Bridges of Madison County". Midway through the third page his thoughts began to wander. He laid the book aside and relit his pipe. Wonder why Ellen didn't know who I was.

He knew her right off. Yeah, it was a long time ago. Time dims the images of things you'd rather forget. But if you think about them long enough the memories come alive. He watched the way she walked. The casual, provocative way she cocked her head when she looked at him. Her auburn hair showed a hint of gray at the temples. Those eyes. Gray with flecks of blue. They sent all kinds of messages.

Maybe she really didn't know who I was. After all, it was twenty-four years ago.

He refilled his pipe, put a match to it, and returned to

"The Bridges of Madison County".

Ellen Glover wasn't easy to forget. Even after twenty-four years.

CHAPTER THREE

Jennifer's dilemma

For a long moment Jennifer stared at the blue envelope on the table beside the phone. She knew it was coming. She and Johnny talked about whether they'd attend the reunion. She was so shocked from finding Johnny she didn't even break the seal. Now, with a trembling hand she gently stroked the envelope. She tried to decide if it was safe to open it. In her right hand she still held the little white pills from the brown bottle. Three times the hand with the pills went to her mouth, and three times she turned her head away. Which was worse, living without Johnny, or dying with the pills?

What if it didn't work? What if there weren't enough pills to make her die? What then? Would she be disfigured and ugly for the rest of her life, or only so sick she'd wish she were dead? Her fear of death abruptly became less ominous than the fear of living alone. She snatched up the phone, punched in the numbers, and heard the voice of her friend Pam.

"This is the widow Coan," Jennifer said with a nervous chuckle.

"Widow what?" Pam said, laughing.

"Widow Coan."

"Jennifer? What are you talking about?"

"My husband is dead, and that makes me Widow Coan."

"Are you all right, Jen? Have you been drinking?"

"Johnny is dead," Jennifer said with body wracking sobs. "I found him on the stool in the downstairs bathroom an hour ago. Johnny's gone!"

"Oh my! Have you called anybody?"

"No. I thought you might do that for me."

"I'm calling 9-1-1 right now, then I'm coming over there. You sit down and try to relax. I'm on my way."

Daddy calls home

Ashley Glover didn't know yet about the death of Johnny Beason, nor was she aware of what happened to Jennifer.

By morning the news spread that Jennifer's friend Pam Perkins found her on the bathroom floor. The brown bottle with the little white pills was empty. Jennifer swallowed them. All of them. She didn't respond when Pam tried to rouse her.

Jennifer was dead.

Pam also found Johnny still slumped on the stool of the downstairs bath room. She called 9-1-1. The Meds came and gurneyed both bodies away.

Pam threw up on the kitchen floor.

Ashley kept chattering away about how wonderful it was that the son of Taylor McCoy, former all-pro guard of the NBA, was persuaded to coach basketball at little known Kennedy High in Crestview.

Ellen wished she could stay forever with her head stuck inside the refrigerator. She didn't want Ashley to see the shock on her face at the mention of Taylor McCoy.

She kept rearranging the items in the refrigerator, shifting the pork chops, milk, and ground chuck she just placed there. There seemed to be too little room for everything. She tried the items in different positions as if fluffing a flower arrangement, mindless of her fumbling hands.

Like a deep sea diver with an empty oxygen tank, she must

come up for air.

"Oh, yes," Ellen said finally. "I remember McCoy." Trying to appear casual, she wasn't ready to reveal even a hint of the one indiscretion she committed years before–the time she strayed for a brief interlude from her promise to "honor and obey."

That's when she remembered Taylor McCoy. Chicago. The Hilton Hotel!

Ellen was rescued by the buzz of the phone on the kitchen wall. Ashley grabbed it. "Glovers," she said, the way her dad always answered.

"Well, now, I sure hope so," a man's voice said on the other end. "That's exactly who I called."

"Daddy!" Ashley squealed.

"What are you doing at my house, young lady?"

"Guess who's the new basketball coach at Kennedy High."

"Umm. Let me think. Dustin Hoffman?"

"No, daddy. It's Hayden McCoy!"

"Taylor's kid?"

"You remembered!"

"Why sure. Hayden coached his team up north to State the last two years. I hoped they'd be able to land him. He'll be good for dear old Kennedy High. Is your mom handy?"

"She's right here." She handed the phone to Ellen. "It's Dad."

"I never would have guessed." Into the phone, Ellen said a cheerful "hello."

Ashley listened. She watched her mother's expression change from sunny to cloudy. The conversation was brief. Ellen uttered only "uh-huh," "yes," or "I see." With a wan smile, she handed the phone to Ashley to hang up.

Ashley sensed her mother heard something she didn't want to hear.

"Mom?"

"It's nothing," Ellen said. "He's in Chicago. Your father won't be home till Sunday evening."

"That's not nothing, Mom. The reunion is Saturday."

"I know. Something more important came up."

"Dad said that?"

"No. I said that."

"But it's the reunion, Mom! Miss Lorena's birthday. She'll be so disappointed not to see Dad. He was one of her favorite students. You said so yourself."

Ellen cast her daughter an oblique look. "Your father was one of everybody's favorites, but they'll have to get along without him this weekend."

"What could be more important than his old teacher's hundredth birthday?"

"He didn't say that either."

"Wouldn't you think Dad would want to be there for the big celebration?"

"You know your father."

"Well, I think this is one big royal crock of—"

"Ashley."

"What!"

"Let it go."

With a soft palm, Ellen caressed her daughter's cheek. "Don't be too hard on your father. Things that are important to us women are not always as important to our men."

"I still think it's a big unholy crock of—"

"Ashley, let it go."

CHAPTER FOUR

What happened to Marcy?

Last night she had no idea she'd be dead today. Her name was Marcy DeBaugh. She was forty-seven years old. Two years ago she divorced her husband. Her kids were up and gone. She loved being a cop.

The only sound in the room was a telephone receiver off the hook. Its piercing beep-beep-beep filled the room with an eerie constancy.

"Uh-oh." Sergeant Walter Hook gave his head a sad shake. "No wonder she didn't answer her mother's calls."

The body was sprawled on the carpet between the couch and the coffee table. Her head lay in a pool of blood. Hook breathed a deep sigh. "Oh, great God." He picked up the receiver, and placed it in its cradle.

He knelt beside the body. Her chest and head were covered with blood. The left side of her face was blown away, her hair matted with blood. Terror filled her wide open eyes that could no longer see. Hook gently closed the eyelids.

"Marcy DeBaugh," Hook whispered to himself, "is dead."

"I know."

Hook heard the voice behind him. "I killed her"

Chicago Night

"You slimy bastard!" the blond young woman screamed as she slipped into a blue dress, covering her naked body. "Why didn't you tell me you were married?"

"Married?" Howard Glover said.

"The ring on your finger!"

"The ring? It was there when you crawled in bed with me." He laughed, deepening the wrinkles at the corners of his mouth. "Would it have made a difference?"

"Hell, yes it would have made a difference," the woman stormed. "I don't date married men." Her name was Delsie Whitmore, a senior at Northwestern University.

"I'm not only married," Glover said, unabashed. "I've got a daughter older than you."

"You have a daughter?" Her manner softened.

"Yes. She's a PE instructor."

"A PE instructor. Where?"

"Crestview. You wouldn't know—"

"Kennedy High?"

"Kennedy— How would you know that?"

"My mother graduated from there."

"Your mother?"

"Olivia Whitmore. Her name was Stone then. Olivia Stone."

"Must have been before my time," he said, "Does that mean you went to Kennedy too?"

"No. My parents divorced when I was little. I came here with my father."

She took her purse from a nearby table and dug out a lipstick. She applied the crimson tip to her lips, and cast him a quizzical look. "In bed with me," she said, "did you ever wonder what it would be like with your daughter?"

Howard was ready for the conversation to be over. "That's not something I care to discuss with you."

"I mean, you old guys—" Delsie said. "You make all the conventions. Your ass hasn't warmed the seat on the plane before you start sniffing out some ball of fuzz to take to bed. I don't know if you don't get enough at home, or if you just need to stretch your balls to see if they still work, but let me tell you something, buster–"

"Buster?"

"–I may be cheap, I may be easy, but I had a daddy like you. I swore I'd never go to bed with a married man because of what he did to my mother. Yes, I live with him because he's where the money is. What he did to my mother and me, you're doing to your daughter and your wife. And you should be ashamed of yourself."

"A sanctimonious whore."

"I'm not a whore."

"Like hell you're not."

"Like hell I am!" she protested. "Just because you picked me up at a convention bar doesn't mean I take money for what I do. I go to bed with men because I like it." With a hand on the doorknob, she said, "I hope your daughter never finds out her father chases anything with boobs." She slammed the door, and was gone.

Howard took a long look at the door, betting it would open. The girl would be standing in it. In tears, begging him to accept her apology.

The door stayed closed. There was no girl, and no apology.

Howard shrugged with an indifferent smirk.

CHAPTER FIVE

I want to meet your brother.

Carol Everett's elbow nudged the man in bed beside her. "Did you hear what I said, Robert?"

"I heard you. You want to meet my brother? Why?"

"I need to. I can't explain why."

"You don't even know my brother."

"I know you." She sat up and pinned him with a serious look. "We've been married long enough for me to know, if he's your brother, he's a good man. He needs someone to take care of him now."

"Come on, Carol. Martin doesn't want to be taken care of. He's the most independent, self-centered man I ever knew. He always had to be in charge. He never needed anybody."

"He does now. Blind, in a wheelchair because of that accident, he needs somebody."

"You think it's you he needs?" Robert said.

"I know about those things. I took care of my parents for years before they died. I know what he's going through."

"What about your job at the paper?"

"I can work around that. Robert, I know you don't understand, but, I need to do this. I need to help your brother."

"He won't go for it."

"At least, I'll have tried."

"You're the best wife a man could have, Carol. Martin is the worst brother."

Carol meets Martin

"Stop treating me like an invalid!"

"Martin, you are an invalid. The sooner you admit it, the better your chances for recovery."

"There is no chance for recovery and you know it. I'm condemned to this damn chair for the rest of my life. You're waiting on me hand and foot. Don't stand there staring at me!"

"I'm not staring at you."

"Yes, you are. I can feel your eyes on me," Martin said.

"Do you want me to leave?"

"No, I don't want you to leave. I want you to stop treating me like a two-year-old."

"Would you like me to call Robert?" she said.

"Why would I want you to call Robert?"

"The Kennedy High reunion is coming up. I thought you might want to go—just the two of you. You don't get together often enough."

"There you go—preaching again."

"I'm not preaching. I just think you need to spend more time with your brother. The reunion would be a good time for that. I know Miss Lorena would be glad to see you there."

"A blind man? Nah. I couldn't see her. I don't like having to be pushed around all over the place."

"I bet Robert would like to go with you."

"If my brother wants to spend time with me, he knows where I am. All he has to do is follow the flight of the buzzards. They hover over dead bodies."

"You're not dead, Martin."

"I may as well be."

"There's a lot of life left in you yet," Carol said.

"That's easy for you to say. You've got two good legs, and

two good eyes. You're not being coddled all the time, twenty-four hours a day."

"How would you know what I've got?" she asked. "I've been married to your brother for four years and you've never seen me. For all you know I could be crawling around on the floor with no legs and one eye."

"No. You're a lovely lady."

"You don't know that. You haven't even touched my face. All you know about me is what you hear me say. Most blind people want to find out what other people's faces feel like so they can form some kind of image of what they look like. You've never bothered. For all you know I could be old and ugly as homemade soap."

"No. Your voice. It's so gentle and soothing. It couldn't come from a homely face."

"Give me your hand."

"No, I—"

"It's all right."

"I don't—"

"You're afraid, aren't you? You don't want to shatter the image of what you think I am. Touch my face. There."

"Scars?"

"Yes."

"On your face."

"When I was little, I got into a can of lye my mother kept in the bathroom for cleaning. I didn't swallow any of it. But, like any two-year-old, I spread it on my face. My mother heard me scream. She found me in time to keep it from eating my face away.

"Now you know. I'm not the lovely woman you thought I was."

"Oh, Carol!"

"Do you know in the seven weeks I've been coming here, that's the first time you've called my name?"

"Why, no—I—"

"Your brother says you're the most independent human being he ever knew."

"Robert said that?"

"He says you never needed anybody in your life. He says

you're selfish, and always have to be in charge."

"Robert wasn't much of a brother to me."

"How about you? Were you a good brother to him?"

"I practically raised him. Our father left when we were kids. Our mother died a few years later. I spent my life trying to get ahead. I worked nights, weekends and holidays to outlive the nobody label my father pinned on me. I was almost there when that damn fool ran that light and turned my life upside down. But, I made sure Robert was taken care of."

"Except for–"

He took a moment to think about that. "Pretty sneaky, aren't you?" he said. "And you're right. I gave him everything, except what my kid brother most needed. Myself."

"You want to call Robert now?"

"You dial."

CHAPTER SIX

Barn lot: Morning

His lungs were about to burst. His legs ached. His eyes burned like fire. Andy ran as fast and as far as his thirteen-year-old legs would carry him. He couldn't outrun the image of his daddy, wild-eyed, in a blue-veined rage, hunkered over Cletus Box.

No way could he outrun the sight of Cletus, lying there in the hay-and-manure-saturated barn lot. The horror of seeing the pitchfork sticking out of Cletus's belly, pools of blood forming in the dirt, Cletus pleading, "Please, don't let me die!"

Blood soaked Cletus's blue cotton shirt, oozing down into the waist of his blue-and-white striped Big Smiths.

Andy saw his daddy glare at Cletus with more contempt than compassion.

Cletus was sixty-seven years old, thin as a toothpick. "That's my dog," he yelled when Efton brought the setter into the barn from his truck.

Efton Wooten was a big man, broad shouldered and round as a barrel. His graying eyebrows twitched when he was mad. They twitched when he yelled, "No, it ain't your dog!"

"You stole my dog," Cletus insisted. "And now you want

me to pay you to get him back?"

That's when it happened. Andy saw it all. Powerless to stop it. Once Efton set his mind on doing something, right or wrong he got it done.

Andy saw Efton plunge that pitchfork into Cletus's stomach. He saw Cletus grab his belly, hands red with blood as he fell to the ground. Wriggling like a worm on a hook, Cletus wheezed for breath. He begged Efton. "Don't let me die!"

That morning Andy and his father loaded four dogs into the cage on the bed of the Chevy Silverado. He fed them bones and meat scraps from the packing plant down the road from the farm. His father bred, bought, sold and traded dogs for years. But, one of the dogs Andy hadn't seen before–the sleek, liver-spotted setter with alert eyes and the stub of a tail in constant motion. That was the dog Cletus Box died for. Andy's dad killed him.

"Ain't nobody needs to know about this, boy," Efton said. "Now, go on, git!"

Andy took off at a dead run toward home. Somewhere along the way he collapsed in the shade of an elm tree. He crawled to where he could rest his back against the trunk. He gave his head a bewildered shake, cheeks wet with tears. Andy couldn't run any more.

Like a dream, the whole thing played over and over as if in slow motion.

Andy couldn't run fast enough to leave the killing behind. Back there where it happened. Back where the nightmare he couldn't outrun took place. Andy tried to block it out of his mind. Like Mrs. Crews wiping the blackboard clean with a foot-long eraser. But it didn't go away, and he knew what he saw was not a dream.

At the hearing this morning, the prosecutor asked Efton what took place. Efton was calm as frozen molasses.

Andy wiped his eyes when he heard his father lie.

"Cletus and me was havin' some words," Efton said on the witness stand "He said I stole his dog. I told him I never."

"Why were you holding the pitchfork?"

"I just picked it up to get it out of the way so's I could

bring more dogs in. Old Cletus, he stumbled into it."

"And you didn't have in mind using the pitchfork on Cletus because he accused you of stealing his dog?"

"No, sir. Never at no time would I of done such a thing."

For thirty-five years Andy carried the burden of guilt, watching his father kill Cletus Box over a dog. The incident burned itself into his brain like a red hot branding iron.

Even after he and Lessie were married and had kids, he couldn't bring himself to tell her about what he saw his father do to Cletus. Even so, at times he saw in her eyes a strange, silent look. He wondered if she knew.

Never did he utter a word to anyone about it. Until now.

Efton Wooten was seventy-four years old. His white hair hung long and unkempt around the edges of his bald pate. His dark, piercing eyes stared across the courtroom at Andy. Stewing over what the boy must have thought when he went to the prosecutor and told what he saw at Cletus Box's barn thirty-five years before. Calling the law on his own daddy! Saying he killed Cletus Box.

Andy wasn't proud of it. Turning his father in to the law was the last thing he wanted to do. But the guilt of saying nothing, as his father warned him, was a load he could no longer carry. Long and hard Andy mulled it over, time after countless time, before easing open the door to the prosecutor's office. By the time he closed the door behind him on the way out, he knew his father was finally going to pay for the murder of Cletus Box.

The jury filed out. Andy swept tears from his eyes. Testifying against his father was the hardest thing he'd ever do.

When the jurors returned, the judge pounded his gavel, and told the foreman to read the verdict. He did. Guilty as charged.

Efton glared at Andy as they led him away in handcuffs. "I hope you burn in hell!" he shouted.

Andy offered a silent nod.

The prosecutor assured Andy he did the right thing. Justice was done.

Andy wouldn't live long enough to forget it. He pondered

the truth of the prosecutor's statement on his way to the reunion at Kennedy High.

CHAPTER SEVEN

Olivia: Morning

"**I**'m calling about your ad," the gravelly voice said when Olivia Whitmore answered the phone.

"Yes?" she said.

"The one in the paper about the ten grand."

With the aid of Estee Lauder, at fifty-four Olivia preserved much of the beauty for which she was envied in her younger years. Time altered but little her slender figure, maintained through compulsive gym workouts three times a week. Dark, gray-streaked hair framed her face.

Her normally vibrant features grew pale in anticipation of the plot launched by the newspaper ad. Her perfectly manicured, long-fingered hands began to tremble. The ad said only, "If you could use $10,000, call 555-7890 before noon Friday."

For two days Olivia's tranquil existence was disrupted by a steady stream of calls from old men, young men, and three women. They were lured by the possibility of landing a ten-thousand-dollar windfall. Impressed by none of them was Olivia. She judged from what she heard in their telephone voices, mostly the sound of greed. So frustrating the experience became that she was sorry she placed the ad, and for hatching in the first place the plot from which it sprang.

Olivia's daughter Delsie called from Chicago the night before with the news. She met a man whose daughter was the PE instructor at Kennedy High.

"Don't you think that's weird, mom?"

"Why, yes it is rather strange," Olivia agreed. "How did it come about?"

"Some friends and I were helping out at a convention, and I ran into this man. We got to talking, and I thought it was quite a coincidence."

"Helping out how, Delsie?"

"Well, you know. Serving, a little dancing. He asked me out later."

"Did you go out with him?"

"Well, not really out, you know. Just—I thought, since you went to Kennedy High,

you'd be—"

Olivia didn't like what she heard in the voice of her daughter. To her, it sounded like something wasn't right. "Delsie, who was the man?"

"Well, I'm not sure. I remember he told me his first name was Howard. I'm not sure about the last name. Drover. Grover maybe."

"Could it be Glover?"

"That sounds about right. Yeah, Howard Glover."

Visions of ominous goings on began taking shape in the mind of Olivia Whitmore. Her daughter and Howard Glover? 'Not really out,' Delsie said. Whatever that meant, to Olivia it didn't sound right.

She'd heard whisperings of Howard's escapades, but kept them to herself. Every time she saw Ellen she fought the urge to tell her what she heard. Olivia wasn't one to spread gossip about other people's indiscretions. But this was her daughter. This was Delsie. No telling what else happened besides what she told her mother on the phone. What if whatever it was came about against Delsie's will? What if she was forced into— Did Delsie's father know about this? Did he and his wife even care?

Now, here was this man on the phone with a raspy voice

with whom Olivia had no desire to speak.

"I think I made a mistake," she said into the phone, hoping he'd be turned away.

"I changed my mind. I don't need you now. I'm sorry."

"Look, lady, you put the ad in the paper," the man said. "You must've had a reason for doing that. Whatever it is, that's what I'm calling about. Now, do we talk about the ten grand, or what?"

His threatening approach put her on guard. This was not someone with whom she wanted to do business. But then, he knew her phone number. He could find out where she lived if he wanted. Would seeing him create a more serious problem than not seeing him?

What am I thinking? she chastised herself. She condemned the man without even seeing him. He's probably a very nice man, down on his luck, who needs help. She could invite him out for a brief interview, explain that she didn't need his services after all. Maybe it would be all right if she offered him a small check for his trouble, and that would be the end of it. In any case, he'd be the last person she talked to about the ad. She'd shut off her phone for a day or two, satisfied that there would be no more calls.

"Do you have a car?" Olivia said to the phone.

"Yes. An old one."

She didn't care if it was old or new, but the admission told her something about the man. At least he was being honest, a no-frills man who got to the point and rode it out.

"I'm at 5543 Morning Glory Drive," she said. "Do you know where that is?"

"I'll find it."

"At three o'clock this afternoon, park your car across the street and walk up the driveway to my house."

"What time is it now?"

Olivia checked her watch. "Ten-forty-five."

She heard the click on the line. She frowned at the receiver, half expecting the voice to return. It didn't. She pondered whether he'd appear at three o'clock.

He did. His name was Peter Gatewood.

CHAPTER EIGHT

Mark rebuffs Elaine

She placed her hands behind his head and pulled his mouth toward hers. He moved away. "What?" Elaine said.

"What what?" Mark said.

"Why won't you let me kiss you?"

"Because I love, and you belong to Richard. It's been three years since Evelyn died, and the kids are up and gone. I'm tired of living alone. There are times when I need to be with somebody. To hear a voice in this house that's not mine. The only somebody I want is you. Go tell that to Richard and see how long it takes him to show up here with his shotgun."

"Richard doesn't own a shotgun. It's a thirty-ought-six. Anyway, I wouldn't tell him."

"Like hell you wouldn't tell him. You tell him everything. What is it with you women that you cannot not tell everything?"

"I won't tell him," Elaine insisted.

"You don't have to. He's not deaf and blind. How can he watch us when we're all together, playing off each other, and not know? He knows.

"The one time I find a gorgeous lady I'd like to spend the rest of my life with, she's my best friend's wife. I'm sixty-four years old, for God's sake. And you're what—forty-three?"

"Forty-seven."

"How many more chances will I have to fall in love?"

"When did you start loving me?"

He ran his slender fingers through thinning gray hair. "You won't believe it."

"When? How long ago?"

He pinned her with a steady gaze. "I've loved you all my life. I started looking for you when I learned what love was about. I didn't know it was you. I didn't know it would be you when it happened, but you're the answer to my dream."

Elaine made a move toward the door.

"Where are you going?" Mark said.

"Home."

"Tell Richard I love you."

"Yeah." Her hand was on the doorknob. "You've got a funny way of showing it."

"What does that mean?"

"You won't even let me kiss you," she said.

"You think I don't want to kiss you?"

"You want to go to bed with me?"

"Yes, dammit! I want to go to bed with you. I want to smother you with kisses, and roll you around all over the place till you scream for mercy."

"Well then?"

"Well then hell! We both love Richard. I couldn't do that to him."

"What about me? You say you love me."

For a long moment he stared into her eyes. "I would love you, if you were bow-legged, cross-eyed and had horns. If I never see you again, I'll see you in the sunrise, in the twinkle of a star. I'll see you in the dewdrop on every rose in the garden. I don't have to see you every night, every week, or every whatever. You're the dream I've lived with half my life, believing it would never come true."

"Are you going to the reunion?" she asked.

"I'm too damned old. I graduated way ahead of the class of '87."

"That's okay, Mark. Miss Lorena would be happy to see

you."

"If I could see you there—"

"That might be arranged."

"Oh, yeah, yeah, yeah. How?"

"Richard will be hunting antelope in Wyoming that weekend."

"How do you know that?"

"I told him."

"You told him?"

"It's an annual event. He and George Blessing have done it for years. Richard didn't go to Kennedy High. He doesn't care about the reunion."

All Mark could muster was a silent nod.

Who is Ross Kemper?

Walter Hook made a slow turn. He looked into the face of a man whose graying brown hair covered his ears. His green eyes reflected relief of one who decided not to jump off the cliff after all. When he spoke his voice was calm and cold. "I know. I killed her."

"You killed a cop," Hook said.

"Had to. She was going to take me in."

"Why would she take you in?"

"Until tonight, I didn't know she was a cop."

Hook was a cop. Twenty-two years. He debated with himself whether he should take this guy in. It wouldn't be wise, though, to make a move for the gun in its shoulder holster.

"Yeah?" Hook said.

"She knew I killed Silas Pugh."

"How would she know that?"

"I told her."

"You told a cop you killed Silas Pugh?"

"Like I said, I didn't know she was a cop. Strange things happen in bed."

Hook rolled that around for a moment. "You called me. Why?"

"She said you knew about Pugh."

"You want to tell me why you killed him?"

'He killed my father," the man said.

"Who are you?"

"Ross Kemper."

"Kemper. I remember your father Joseph as an honorable man. I went to his funeral. He died of a heart attack."

"Because Pugh stole his business. He also stole his money—and his wife. Everything but me."

"Did you have to kill Marcy DeBaugh?"

Kemper brought a hand gun from a pocket, and pointed the gun at Hook.

"Now I have to kill you."

"You know you won't get away with this. You can't kill us all."

Kemper smiled. "I can try."

Police Headquarters was a flurry.

"They found Hook," somebody yelled. "Two shots in the head."

Lt. Jack Carpenter couldn't believe it. "Who did it?"

"Damned if I know." Inspector Lance McGee grabbed his hat. "I'm on my way out there."

"Where to?"

"Marcy DeBaugh's."

"Hook and Marcy?"

"She's dead too. Hook was there on a call."

The dispatcher screamed, "Some stupid bastard is holed up in the court house tower. He's picking off cops one at a time!"

"How about the SWAT guys?"

"They're on their way."

Four uniformed officers lay dead on the street.

Inspector McGee took charge. "Three men get in the building, work your way up to the tower and get in behind him."

"How do we get up there?"

"He found a way. Go look!" McGee said. "Alive if you can, dead if you have to. The rest of you spread out, and don't let him forget you're here."

A barrage of SWAT shots peppered the tower. Five minutes later, gunshots from inside the tower told McGee his men made it. He nodded, shook his head, and turned away.

Kemper was dead. On his body they found a crumpled blue envelope.

KENNEDY HIGH FOREVER!

CHAPTER NINE

The Peter Gatewood

Olivia was startled by the sound of the doorbell playing the first line of "Over the Rainbow." It reminded her of fun times when the three of them traveled in the car. Galen and Delsie rendered their version of his favorite song from "The Wizard of Oz."

She wished Galen were here now to greet the man waiting for her to answer the door bell. She wouldn't have to face him, explaining she didn't need him after all. She pressed her sweaty palms against her thighs and eased the door open.

He was taller than he appeared, walking up the driveway. His brown leather jacket covered a beige shirt open at the collar. His khaki pants were neatly pressed. His ruddy face was clean shaven, except for a thin mustache.

Peter Gatewood was fifty-eight years old.

Olivia stood aside as he entered her living room. She invited him to an overstuffed chair beside the walnut coffee table. He sat.

"Would you like something to drink, Mr. Gatewood?"

"Coffee, please."

"Cream or sugar?"

"Just coffee, thanks."

Olivia stepped to the kitchen and brought a cup and saucer, and placed them on a small table beside his chair.

She went away again, and returned with a Silex coffee pot. She poured his cup full. She sat opposite him, and watched him sip at his cup.

"Your name is Gatewood?" she said.

"Gatewood, yes," he said. "Peter Gatewood. Most people call me Pete."

"Where are you from, Mr. Gatewood?"

"Here and there."

"What kind of work do you do?"

"Not much of anything lately. Jobs have been hard to come by. That's why I called about the ad."

"Hmmn. About the ad—I'm not sure—"

"Look, lady," he said calmly, "I'm not here to tell you the story of my life, and I have no interest in hearing yours, aside from what you can do for me."

Shocked by his abruptness, Olivia was eager to end the interview. She wasn't sure how to go about it without arousing his anger.

He sipped at his coffee and stared at her with dark eyes. "I don't mean to frighten you, but I haven't worked for seventeen years."

"Seven—"

"That's how long I served for killing the man who raped my wife."

"Oh!"

"That's how I got this voice—surgery for throat cancer while I was in prison."

Olivia didn't know how to react. She went for the coffee pot and refilled his cup.

"You—killed a man?" she said.

"I'm not a criminal. I had a good job as a lab specialist. When I tell people about the killing, nobody wants to hire me. They probably think I killed once and I'd do it again.

I guess they're afraid it would be them."

She cleared her throat with a nervous glance at the man who confessed to being a murderer. Though respecting his candor, she too pondered whether he might kill again. For money? For ten thousand dollars?

CHAPTER TEN

Jail cell

"**I** don't know what you're looking for," Homer said. "You say you're from the paper?"

"Yes." The young lady looked at him through the bars of his cell. "I'm Susan Welch from the Chronicle."

"All I can tell you is what I know."

"That's why I'm here. I want to hear your side of the story."

"M'name's Homer Bee. One day me and my wife Glory popped in to see our friends Luther and Sally at their new double-wide in Mobile City. The last time we saw 'em was at the County Fair hog callin' contest. Luther was good at that. Won first prize three years in a row.

"I knew Sally from Kennedy High when she got pregnant. I didn't do it. Billy Haworth did. Billy's daddy took it pretty hard. When he heard about it, he hauled Billy into the woods behind their place one day and come back without him. They found Billy hangin' from a sycamore tree. The sheriff, Jimmy Piper, he said it was suicide. Jimmy figgered Billy was so upset about gettin' Sally pregnant he hung himself. Jimmy lied. Billy's daddy never said no different.

"Sally kept the baby after Billy was found hangin' from

that tree. She said she owed him that much. Luther was in love with Sally from the time he seen her the first day of school. He said Sally's baby boy didn't make any difference. He said it was all right with him. Him and Sally got married the year we all graduated. They named the baby Clive. Last we heard, Clive was some kind o' lawyer over there at Shadrock."

Homer took a deep breath, lit up a Lucky with his back against the wall.

"Luther took me and Glory to supper at the Blue Bell Café that day. Glory had a taco salad. Sally had beef stew. I had a pork loin sandwich and a bottle o' Bud. Luther had a prime rib dinner, and four or five beers. By the time we got back to their place, he was weavin' and glassy-eyed.

"Glory said we better go.

"Luther said, 'You cuttin' out so soon?'

"I said we had some things to do.

"Well dammit to hell, Homer,' Luther said, 'if I done somethin' to hurt your feelin's—'

"I said no."

"'Ole Luther took a coupla steps toward me like he wanted to fight. I knew it was the beer doin' the talkin'. I didn't want to fight him, so I stepped aside. Luther fell flat on his face. I started to help him up. Sally said, 'No, he's all right. I'll take care of him.'

"She didn't though. Lucky Duckworth, the undertaker, did. Ol' Luther never got up off the floor. Heart attack, they said.

"Me and Glory didn't go to the funeral.

"The next thing I knew, Jimmy Piper was out to my place askin' me all kinds of questions about what happened to Luther. He wanted to know if I had anything to do with it, and I told him no. I don't know what Sally told him. I don't think he was satisfied with what he heard from me.

"Me and Glory, we talked about it. She was standin' right there when Luther fell. Sally might've thought I shoved Luther or somethin' when he come at me. Glory says I didn't. Luther was so drunk he couldn't stand up.

"I played on the basketball team with Jimmy, and there

was some things we didn't see eye-to-eye on, but it didn't amount to much. I didn't know what kind o' sheriff Jimmy'd make but I voted for him. Had no reason not to. He kept comin' back out home to talk about Luther, like he thought I didn't already tell him everything I knew. Like he was gonna hear somethin' different every time he come. He didn't. There wasn't nothin else to tell.

"I liked Luther. Glory and me, we used to go fishin' and campin' with him and Sally. Luther was a bully in school, and stubborn as a corner post, but he was a good ol' boy. I liked him. He never meant to hurt nobody. Luther hurt himself more'n anybody else. Jimmy Piper knew that, but I guess what I told him wasn't good enough. Last time he come to my place, he said, 'I got to take you in, Homer. You're all I got to go on.'

"I said, "The hell!" but he took me anyway.

"Now here I am, coolin' my heels in Jimmy's jail, waitin' to find out what happens next. I guess I won't be goin' to the Kennedy High reunion. Glory says she won't go without me.

"That's all I know."

CHAPTER ELEVEN

Janet Whitton

A tall woman, thin and pale from lack of outdoor exposure, Janet Whitton was forty-eight years old. Dark hair swept her shoulders. Thick, colorless lips found no reason to smile.

Her dead mother was a fastidious housekeeper. It was hard to imagine this house belonged to her daughter. The kitchen table was littered with empty cereal bowls. Toppled Wheaties and Kellogg's corn flakes boxes jumbled together with loaves of dry bread, and cold greasy bacon. The kitchen countertop was covered with dirty pots and pans, empty pop bottles and Campbell soup cans.

Her father was Logan Beach, a tall, balding man with large ears. He greeted his daughter with a smile and a hug.

"How you doing, baby?"

"Oh, Dad, I'm so glad you're here. I apologize for the mess. Mom would turn over in her grave if she saw this. The kids were here over the weekend. They never clean up after themselves."

"That's okay. You've been through a lot lately."

"You have no idea what it was like. And I hate to unload on you."

"It's all right. That's what dads are for."

"I'm exhausted," Janet said. "I haven't slept for more than an hour at a time for weeks.

I had to be with Clayton. I watched his body dwindle from a hundred-eighty to ninety-seven pounds. That's when he breathed his last.

"They told me what killed him. Some disease that ate his insides, and destroyed his vital organs. It was impossible for him to cope. I lived with it for three months.

"He had no appetite. He lost his eyesight, the right one first. He was alert to the end though, and the last word he uttered was my name. Oh, Dad," she cried. "Oh, Dad!"

He wrapped her in his arms. "I know, sweetie. It's hard. It's so hard. We went through it with your mom after her stroke. We have to try to stay strong—walk through the valley, and pray we'll come out safely on the other side."

She moved away and wiped her eyes. "The medical people came and wheeled him out. With him went twenty-six years of my life. Thank God we had that time together." She offered her father a tearful smile. "You want to hear something funny?"

"What's that?"

"We talked about going to the reunion at Kennedy High. It was Clayton's idea. He wanted to be there." She broke down. "What do I do now?"

He held her close and brushed her hair with a gentle touch. Her tears flowed from a broken heart. So did his.

"The kids don't know yet," she said.

"You want me to call them?"

"No, Dad. That's my job. I'll call them."

CHAPTER TWELVE

Here it comes

One time Ellen strayed from her vows to Howard Glover. In a way, it was his fault. He took her with him to that Telephone Company convention at the Chicago Hilton.

Taylor McCoy was one of the professional athletes invited as an attraction to spark attendance.

He was several years ahead of her at Kennedy High. She knew of him only as a star athlete. Everybody did. His picture was posted in the hallway as a member of the Hall of Fame.

"Howdy," Taylor said when Howard introduced them.

Howard knew she and Taylor both attended Kennedy High. "You know Taylor McCoy," he said to Ellen. To Taylor, he said, "Take care of my little girl."

Taylor took his seat beside her at the dinner table. "I hope you don't mind that I've been watching you," he said when Howard left. "I'm glad we got together."

"I know who you are, but we never met before," she said.

"Too bad we weren't at Kennedy at the same time."

The waiter brought the wine and glasses. "Anything more I can do for you?" he asked.

"Not just yet, thank you," Taylor said. "But don't forget us. We'll have more wine."

Maybe it was the wine that clouded Ellen's thought processes. Or maybe it was because Howard didn't come back when she thought he would. Recollections of Kennedy High didn't take much time because Taylor was there seven years before her. As the evening wore on, the wine kept coming, and Howard didn't. He was off some place in meetings, or gabbing with friends.

"It looks like you're going to be alone for a while," Taylor said. "We could go up to my room and relax if you'd like."

"Oh. I don't know—" Her head was spinning a bit. She never had so much wine before.

"It's okay. I understand," he said. "I don't want you to feel uncomfortable. I just thought—"

"Well, if we weren't gone long. I thought Howard would be back before now, but—"

Drowsy, she thought about it for a moment. Howard did tell him to take care of her.

"Okay," she decided. "Maybe it would be all right."

He flipped on the television to a movie. She sat beside him on the sofa. He slipped an arm across her shoulders. Her head rested on his. She slept.

CHAPTER THIRTEEN

Saturday night—live!

Hundreds of former students of Miss Lorena's at Kennedy High awaited the appearance of the lady of honor. From seven states and three foreign countries they swarmed in to celebrate her hundredth birthday.

There was a breathless moment when the curtain parted— and there she was! Wheeling herself onstage to a standing ovation. Whistles, applause, and loud cheers. And—Surprise of surprises! At her side was Howard Glover. The ovation continued to the tune of "He's a jolly good fellow."

Howard responded to their warm reception with big smiles. He waved. And bowed. He helped Miss Lorena to her feet, and to the podium.

Howard spread his hands for quiet. "Ladies, and gentleman," he said. "What a joy it is to be here, to be a part of this momentous occasion—the one hundredth birthday of a wonderful lady, whom we love, and who put up with us for over fifty years—"

Ashley whispered to her mother, "Mom, it's Daddy!"

No, Ellen thought. It was not a pleasant thought. The haunting memory of one fateful night in Chicago occupied space in her conscience for twenty-four years. And now she faced it. He is your daddy. The thought pushed its way to the front of her mind. Your father is sitting two rows in front of us beside his son—the new basketball coach at Kennedy High.

Should she tell Ashley? Could she tell Ashley?

Peter Gatewood hid himself in the shadows in the back of the auditorium. He placed his hand on the bulge inside his coat pocket. His mission was to earn the ten thousand dollars Olivia promised if he killed Howard Glover.

Elaine Weaver sat across the aisle from Mark Whitlow. He cast her a questioning glance. With a slight shrug and lifted ye brows, she offered an almost imperceptible move of her head. It told Mark she didn't know why Richard, seated beside her, decided to come after all.

Gatewood removed the pistol from his pocket. He took a long look at it, turned it over a time or two. He put it back in his pocket. Seventeen years in prison he paid for a killing. Ten thousand dollars weren't enough to pay for seventeen more. He turned and walked away.

Onstage, Howard was still talking. "And now, ladies and gentlemen, it is my great pleasure and honor to present to you the eternal queen of Kennedy High—Miss Lorena Clark."

Again the audience rose for a building shattering ovation.

Miss Lorena pleaded for quiet. "This is the highlight of my career," she said into the microphone. "I'm so happy to see you. It has been such a long time. This night, this moment, is the crowning glory of my entire life I've been looking forward to." With a sneaky smile, she said, "I know that's not grammatically correct." A chuckle made its way around the gathering. "But when you're a hundred years old, who the hell gives a damn?"

The crowd roared with laughter and applause.

"The best years of my life I spent with you," she went on. "I asked you here to recall the good times, and help celebrate my final birthday."

There was a stir in the room, a shuffling of feet, and questioning glances. What does she mean—her final birthday?

"You were my family. I loved you then, and I love you now. There's something you need to know."

Her audience leaned forward to catch every word. What was she going to tell them? Was Miss Lorena going to reveal some deep dark secret from her past? Had there been a romance she never mentioned to anyone?

"You have never seen me weep," Miss Lorena said with a strong voice. "And you will not see me weep now. It's no time for tears."

Breathless silence greeted her words.

"I've been informed that I had six months to live."

"Oh, no!" swept the gathering. Hands covered trembling lips.

"I've told you I had no plans for dying. Woody Allen once said, he had no fear of dying. He just didn't want to be there when it happened."

Nervous laughter trickled around the room.

"I never knew of anyone who arranged his death on his birthday. I got as close as I could, I wanted see you one more time. Tomorrow is the day."

The audience responded with outcries of shock, tears of sorrow, and comfort-seeking hugs.

"Shed no tears for me," Lorena said. "Where I'm going there'll be no time for weeping." With a wave of her hand, she shouted, "Let the party begin!"

In the back of the auditorium the doors flew open. In marched the Kennedy High School band, filling the hall with a rousing rendition of "When the Saints Go Marching in."

Miss Lorena's parting words were, "Tell your mama I love you."

THE END

CHURCH IN THE WILDWOOD

a short story

CHAPTER ONE

Chet Pinkerton plopped his saddle onto the front porch of the Mercantile.

Harley Farnsworth watched him do it. Harley's cane-bottom chair leaned on its hind legs against the mercantile wall.

"Howdy," Chet said. "Pinkerton's my name."

He didn't know Harley. He didn't care about Harley, or much of anything else, except his horse tripped in a gopher hole. He shot him, and lugged his saddle on his back two miles in scorching July heat into Wildwood. He didn't know Wildwood either, but that's where he was.

Farnsworth spat a stream of tobacco juice. "Howdy. Whatchy doin' here?"

Chet raked the sweat from his brow. "My horse broke a leg."

"Had to shoot im, dijy?"

"I shot him."

"Reckon you'll be lookin' for n'other 'un, huh?"

Chet nodded. "You know where I can find one?"

"I heard tell a while back, some feller had a horse for sale. He died." Farnsworth splattered another stream of juice. "Horse died too."

Pinkerton took a look around. Nothing unusual about the punchers going into and out of the saloon on a sweltering afternoon.. Nor about their horses tethered on both sides of the dusty street. He doubted any of them would be for sale.

"You might try over yonder at the livery," Harley said. "Hanky Pank'd prob'ly know if they's a horse for sale 'round here."

"Hanky--"

"Pank. Hanky Pank. His daddy Lanky used to run the livery till he got caught stealin' horses. They hung 'im."

"Well, I've got to have a horse," Chet said.

"You ain't one 'em railroad Pinkertons, are you?"

"No, sir. I'm a preacher."

"Preacher, huh? Gonna preach in Wildwood, are ye?"

"Yes, sir, I am."

"Some folks 'round here ain't never seen a preacher."

"That's why I'm here."

"You don't look like no preacher to me. Never seen one totin' a side arm."

"Yeah, well, things are different these days. I don't use it much. Mostly for rattlesnakes and coyotes."

"We got plenty of ' em 'round here." Harley chuckled. "Some of 'em's two-legged. Them's the worst kind."

"I guess I'll just--"

"You know what I think, mister?" Harley said.

Pinkerton looked at him as if he didn't care what he thought, but he'd listen.

"I think you ain't no damn preacher."

"Well, I'm sorry you feel that way about it. God will forgive you for that."

"I think you're that son-of-a-bitch that raped that little girl and th'owed her in the river."

"No, that's not me."

"Never figgered you'd own up to it."

"I've never been here before. I'm sorry about that. It's a tragic thing, but I'm not the one who did it."

"Like hell you ain't. I seen your picture in the sheriff's office."

"Now, wait a minute," Chet said. "We need to talk about

this. What's your name?"

"Don't make a damn what m' name is. But, you ask anybody in this town, and they'll tell you Harley Farnsworth don't lie."

"I didn't say you lied, but you're talking to the wrong man."

Harley's chair bounced off the wall and landed on all fours. He hailed a man crossing the street. "Hey, Pete, I think we got 'im."

"Got who?"

"The one that th'owed that little girl in the river."

Pete hot-footed it over there. People along the street wondered why he was in such a hurry to cross the street. Within minutes half the town's people gathered around to see what was happening.

"What's going on, Harley?" a gravelly voice shouted.

"This here's the one that raped that little girl, and th'owed her in the river,"

"He don't look like no raper to me."

"Rapers don't always look like rapers," Harley said.

"I bet that's him though," another voice piped up.

"How do we know it's him?"

"Yeah, that's him all right," Pete jeered.

Lucy Poe was twelve years old when it happened. She was now thirteen, standing on the edge of the mob.

"Where's Lucy?"

"Ask Lucy if that's him."

The crowd made way, and the freckle-faced teenager stepped forward.

"He done it, didn't he, Lucy?" Harley coaxed.

She squinted at Chet as if she wasn't sure. She hesitated.

"Lucy?" Harley said.

Lucy nodded, and heard an angry voice shout, "Get a rope!"

Somebody got a rope. Three men grabbed Chet and held him while another man threw the noose around his neck.

The crowd screamed and jeered and shoved Chet to the ground. They kicked him, spat on him, and dragged him toward the cottonwood tree at the end of the street.

"Th'ow the rope over that limb," Harley yelled. "Let's get this raper hung!"

Two gunshots silenced the mob. All eyes turned to where stood a tall man with a Colt.44 in each hand. He spoke one time. "How many of you sons-of-bitches am I gonna have to kill to get my brother out of there?"

One careless cowhand couldn't resist the temptation to make a name for himself. He went for his gun, and died in the dust of Main Street with a .44 caliber slug in his chest. The rope went limp, and the noose fell away from Chet's neck. With his head, the stranger motioned him to move away from the mob.

Chet did. He turned away with a long look at the crowd, the hardest at Harley. He took the reins the stranger offered him, and climbed aboard a bay mare. To Harley, Chet said, "I'll pray for you."

He put a spur to the mare's flank and followed the stranger at a dead run to the end of the street and out of sight.

"Where's the sheriff?"

From around the corner of the Dealer's Choice Saloon, Sheriff Whit Spradling skidded his horse to a stop, slid out of the saddle, and demanded to know what was going on. "Who fired those shots?" he said.

Harley told him. "We was gonna hang the one that raped Lucy. Already had a noose 'round his neck. This stranger showed up, fired 'em shots. One of 'em hit Lester. He's dead."

"Lester's dead?"

"Yeah. He never had a chance."

"Sounds like murder."

"The stranger claimed to be the brother of the man we was gettin' ready to hang"

"Harley," Spradling said, "you can't go around hanging people unless the judge says so." He raised his voice so all could hear. "You people go on about your business. I'll take care of this." To Harley, he said, "You're about a foot and a half shy of a hangman's noose yourself right now. Clear out and take these people with you." He climbed back into the saddle. "I think I know who that man is. I'm going after him."

Harley said, "Need some help?"

"Not from you." The sheriff spurred his mount west. "I need four men on horses. Saddle up. Let's move out!" He called for four men and got six.

ABOUT THE AUTHOR

David Estes is an accomplished author with seven books to his credit. He draws on his wide experience, from the cotton fields of Oklahoma and Texas where he grew up; to the islands of the South Pacific where he served as a United States Marine; to the marketplace in America where he pursued a career in radio and television advertising. Now retired, David writes westerns and mystery novels from his family farm in West Central Missouri.

OTHER PUBLICATIONS BY DAVID A. ESTES

Available at Amazon.com, Barnes&Noble.com,
Booksamillion.com and more online retailers.

Big Boy
Bag of Gold
Blood on the Wall
Bye Bye, Sweet Susie
Angel on My Back
Wet Dogs Don't Ride
Ajax & Elbow Grease

www.ingramcontent.com/pod-product-compliance
Lightning Source LLC
Chambersburg PA
CBHW070646180626
46817CB00006B/2260